BURN TO SHINE

ALSO BY
JONATHAN MABERRY

JONATHAN MABERRY

BURN TO SHINE

A JOE LEDGER AND ROGUE TEAM INTERNATIONAL NOVEL

 ST. MARTIN'S GRIFFIN
NEW YORK

BURN TO SHINE. Copyright © 2025 by Jonathan Maberry. All rights reserved. Printed in the United States of America. For information, address St. Martin's Publishing Group, 120 Broadway, New York, NY 10271.

www.stmartins.com

The Library of Congress Cataloging-in-Publication Data is available upon request.

ISBN 978-1-250-89266-9 (trade paperback)
ISBN 978-1-250-89267-6 (ebook)

Our books may be purchased in bulk for promotional, educational, or business use. Please contact your local bookseller or the Macmillan Corporate and Premium Sales Department at 1-800-221-7945, extension 5442, or by email at MacmillanSpecialMarkets@macmillan.com.

First Edition: 2025

10 9 8 7 6 5 4 3 2 1

This is for Spencer Mulligan, Lloyd Pitts,
  Eric Linden, and Nik Pelekai.
World-class stuntmen for some of my favorite
  action flicks and fans of Joe Ledger.
Friends in the industry . . .

And, as always, for Sara Jo.

TENTH LEGION
PART 1

For what is it to die but to stand naked in the
   wind and to melt into the sun?
And when the earth shall claim your limbs,
   then shall you truly dance.

—KAHLIL GIBRAN

The most beautiful thing we can experience is
   the mysterious. It is the source of all true
   art and science. He to whom this emotion
   is a stranger, who can no longer pause to
   wonder and stand rapt in awe, is as good as
   dead; his eyes are closed.

—ALBERT EINSTEIN

CHAPTER 1

"You're going to want to take that call," I said.

The guy with the gun frowned at me. "Call? What call?"

His cell phone rang. A burner phone. The kind criminals and terrorists use because no one is supposed to be able to track them.

"That one," I said.

CHAPTER 2

HIDEAWAY MOBILE HOME PARK
TUCKERTON, NEW JERSEY

He kept his gun pointed at me as he dug the cell out of his jacket pocket, thumbed it open, and hit the green phone icon.

"Yes . . . ?"

"Put this call on speaker, Mr. Norris," said a voice. Male, authoritative, with a bit of a New England Kennedy accent.

I wasn't close enough to hear him from Norris's phone. But I could also hear it clearly through the earbud I wore. The bud looks like a freckle, and his guys hadn't found it when they patted me down. And by a pat-down, I mean something as intimate as a Swedish massage in a good spa. No happy ending, because they took all my other goodies. Keys, fake ID, box of minty Tic Tacs, pack of Kleenex, and my gun.

"Who the fuck are you?" demanded Norris.

The voice said, "I am the person who, for the moment, has your best interests at heart. That consideration ends if you refuse to put this call on speaker."

Norris looked at the other three men in the room. They were all big, all wearing windbreakers over polo shirts and khakis. A kind of uniform. Paramilitary contractor chic. All the rage these days.

"What the hell is this shit?" he asked his friends.

"Ticktock, Mr. Norris," said the voice.

"Maybe do it, Rick," said one of the thugs.

Norris looked dubious, but the situation was already strange. So, he muttered something wonderfully obscene under his breath. I was impressed. Goats and strap-ons factored into it. Then he hit Speaker.

"Now tell me who you are and what the *fuck* is going on," he demanded.

"My name is unimportant," said the voice. "What is important is that you and your three colleagues have made a critical error. There is a narrow doorway of opportunity still open in which you can walk back your mistake. If you release your prisoner and let him leave, then that door stays open. If you do not, it will shut with a bang."

"What the hell are you talking about?"

"I do not think I need to repeat myself."

Norris tried to bluff. "What prisoner?"

Norris and his goons all grinned at that. Big joke. I smiled, too.

The voice on the phone said, "I am talking about the person seated on your twelve o'clock, forty-three inches from you. He is more valuable alive and unharmed to me than are you and your colleagues. It is in your best interest to release him. All you need to do is nothing. He gets up and walks out."

"Nice try, asshole, but I have guns on him right now and—"

There were four shots. They came all at once, overlapping, muffled by distance, smothered by glass, aluminum siding, and insulation.

Norris and his buddies went down hard and . . . messy.

I had blood, brains, and—god help me—teeth and part of a nose all over me.

I would say that I love what I do for a living. And it's true most of the time. Sometimes, though, I really hate my job.

INTERLUDE 1
THE MANSION
UNDISCLOSED LOCATION
TWO YEARS AGO

"I . . . dreamed that I was dying," she said.

The room was dark, and all she could see were shadows. Some were fixed and unmoving and over time resolved themselves into things she knew she should recognize. When she did, it took a little longer to assign them names. Wall. Closet door. Bureau. Drapes. Ceiling.

Other shadows moved. What were they?

Blades that cut the shadows that clung to the ceiling.

What was that called?

She fished and fished and finally reeled in the words.

Ceiling fan? Was that right? Was "ceiling fan" a real thing?

Yes, she decided. It was. So were the other things. The walls and doors and heavy drapes that blocked out the . . . the thing. The bright thing. Sun? Yes, that was it. She could not see it, but she knew the drapes blocked out the sun.

There was another thing. Closer than all the others. Right there. Right next to her. What was it?

Was it a person . . . ?

Or, maybe . . . a man?

His face was awash in shadows, and she wasn't able to pick out details. For a while, she accepted that it was a faceless face. A shape with no definition. No . . . parts.

And yet it spoke. Even without a mouth.

"Did the dream frighten you?" he asked. A soft voice. Accented—she knew that much but could not put a name to which *kind* of accent. Not foreign, though.

"Yes."

"Were you very afraid?"

"Yes."

"Are you still afraid?"

She paused before answering that question.

Then, finally, she murmured, "Yes."

It was very soft, the way a self-aware child might say it, and all the more heartbreaking for that.

"What are you afraid of?" asked the shadow man.

"I'm afraid that I'm dying."

"No," he said. "You are not dying. Is that really what you were afraid of?"

She thought about that as she watched the blades of the ceiling fan slice and slice. The breeze they made stirred the man's hair, and that made her realize he *had* hair. And a brow. Cheekbones. A nose and a chin.

But she still could not see his eyes. Or his mouth.

"I thought I was dead."

"Ah," he said.

"Am I dead?" she asked, and the asking of it terrified her so deeply that she began to cry.

"Shhhhh," he soothed. "Shhhh, now."

"Please," she begged. "Am I dead?"

"No, sweet pumpkin," he said softly. "You're not dead."

"Then . . . am I . . . alive?"

There was a pause, and though she could not see any mouth, she somehow knew he was smiling.

"No," he said. "You're not alive, either."

That's when she started to scream.

And she screamed for a very long time.

CHAPTER 3
HIDEAWAY MOBILE HOME PARK
TUCKERTON, NEW JERSEY

There are two doors in most double-wide trailers—living room and utility. Sometimes kitchen. The shooters came in through both, weapons up. Two in the front, two in back, with a shaggy white combat dog in close company.

None of them were in full combat rig, though I knew they had very thin and very tough spider-silk and Kevlar X9 body armor under their street clothes. The two who came in the back were as mismatched a pair as you could find. The guy was a Cajun with coal-black hair, ice-blue eyes, a face that was youthful and charming. The woman had intensely dark skin and intensely fierce eyes, and she had scars that spoke to a horrific past.

The pair who came in the front weren't any closer to being a matched set. There was a black man with a shaved head and graying goatee, and the kind of wiry build that explained why someone of his age was still running with the fast dogs. His partner was six and a half feet of overly muscled white guy with blue eyes, blond hair, and a don't-fuck-with-me grin on his face.

They cleared every room of the trailer home while I sat, zip-tied to the chair.

When they were done, the older black man sent the young white kid and the black woman outside.

"Mother Mercy," he said, "get up top here. Gator Bait, you take a stroll. See who else is awake. Both of you keep it on the DL. No muss, no fuss."

They melted away.

Then he and the giant stood in front of me. The dog came and sat between them, eyes fierce but tail thumping like a puppy's.

"Any reason you're still tied up, Outlaw?" asked Bradley "Top" Sims. "Or you getting lazy in your old age?"

I grinned, then did that trick with sharp twists and leverage that snaps the zip ties at the connector. *Pop!* Looks like a great feat of physical strength, but it's really just physics.

Wrists freed, I half stood, then lifted the chair, the legs of which slipped easily out of the plastic cuffs.

Harvey "Bunny" Rabbit, the ex–volleyball jock from Orange County, snorted. "They legit cuffed you below the chair's cross brace?"

"If Norris and his goons were clever, farm boy," said Top, "they'd still be alive."

He tapped his comms.

"Pappy to Merlin. Package secure. All hostiles down."

That's when Ghost, the vicious man-killing, titanium-toothed fur monster, jumped at me and tried to lick me to death. Yup, dead men, blood, and brains all over the place, and the highly trained combat dog goes all six-week-old puppy on me.

I told him to sit his furry ass down, and he did. Though he still looked happy. He loves this sort of stuff.

Top came close and used his thumb and index finger to turn my face one way and then the other, studying the damage.

"You'll live," he said.

"But he won't be pretty," said Bunny.

"Wasn't to begin with," replied Top.

"Thanks for rescuing me," I said, "and—I mean this with my whole heart—fuck you both."

Bunny laughed. Top smiled. A bit. His brown eyes studied more than my bruises. He looked deep into my eyes and read what was there to be read. What I let him read. Which, given this was Top, was a lot.

"You good, Outlaw?" he asked gently as he handed me an armored vest.

I knew what he was asking. Ever since the Darkness thing a year or so back, he did these spot checks on me after anytime I get shoved into a bad place. The reason I let him is because I went a little crazy back then. Okay, full disclosure—crazi-*er*. While searching for the group of killers who murdered my entire family, I went pretty far off the psychological reservation. As the personification of the darkness that had been born within me at that mass funeral, I did more than merely hunt for criminals. I ruined them. Destroyed them. And nearly destroyed myself in the process.

As far as I'm concerned, that aspect of me is gone. One hundred percent.

Not everyone agrees with me. Or, maybe it's that I went so far off the reservation that reasonable doubt is . . . well . . . reasonable. And Top, being more than my strong right hand in Havoc Team, is also wise, kind, and insightful. He knew that if I strayed out of the light, then I was more than a danger to myself—I could easily endanger my team. And the mission.

Do I fault him for that caution? No, I damn well do not.

"I'm good," I said, meaning it. "This was nothing."

He nodded and stepped back.

I'd been in civvies for the meet at the bar, so the vest made me feel a lot more comfortable and confident. And before you call me silly and weak, even scorpions have armor. So there.

I finished attaching the vest with Velcro and plastic clips, strapped my gun belt on, and checked my sidearm. I was carrying a Colt M1911 .45 ACP that used to belong to my father. Norris had examined it but, except for ejecting the round in the chamber, hadn't messed with it. I worked the action, swapped in a new magazine, chambered a round, made sure the thumb and grip safeties were on, and holstered it. A comforting weight.

On my other hip was a Snellig 22A-Max gas dart gun with a full magazine of Sandman that shoots high-velocity collagen-shell darts filled with a cocktail of chemicals designed around the veterinary drug ketamine, but with BZ—3-Quinuclidinyl benzilate—to cause intense and immediate confusion and DMHP—Dimethylheptylpyran, a derivative of THC—for muscle failure. We call it Sandman because when you get hit, you go down and go to sleep. Not a nice sleep, mind you, but into a version of the Twilight Zone that Rod Serling would have done if he were both high and mad at you.

That gun was also, in its way, comforting.

Top said, "No one else at home here, but the clock's ticking."

"Yes, it is." I nodded to Bunny. "Toss the place. Anything electronic goes in a bag. Same for weapons, IDs, papers, travel docs, the works. Norris and his goons are Tenth Legion, and those assholes are paranoid as hell, so look for trips and traps."

"On it," he said and began his search.

To Top, I said, "Nice circus trick with the four shots."

"Yeah, well, that was Gator Bait's idea. He had drones feeding us thermal scans with in-room mapping. We took up our spots and waited for Merlin to give the word."

Merlin was the combat call sign for Mr. Church. Our boss, the spooky bastard who always sounds cool and calm but is never to be messed with. What just happened was a clear example of why.

Top unslung his pack and handed me some other items—a pair of Scout glasses, my lock knife, and some useful electronic stuff that went into various pockets.

I turned to my dog. "Ghost, bang-bang, boom-boom." He immediately went into search mode, looking for anything with an explosive scent signature or the smell of gun oil. More than once, he found what we couldn't, and this was one of those times. First thing he found was a hidden compartment in the living room that, when opened, revealed enough guns and ammunition to lay siege to a moderate-size country.

Top picked up a few boxes of 9mm ammunition, grunted, and showed it to me. They were all from the most popular manufacturers— Federal Premium, Remington, Winchester, Fiocchi, CCI Blazer,

Hornady, PMC, Magtech, Underwood, Wolf, and Tula—but when I looked closer, I could see that these were not standard rounds.

"Reloads," I said.

"Uh-huh. Packaged to look like off-the-shelf." He removed a few bullets at random. "Well now, look at this."

The rounds were 9mm but definitely not something you could buy at Walmart. The tapered tips were a flat gray and so dense it was hard to scratch one with a thumbnail. These were 9×19mm armor-piercing cartridges, which boasted a considerably greater stopping power and penetration than standard rounds and were designed to penetrate military-grade body armor. Sadly, none of this was illegal.

"Makes me wonder what other modifications they've done," I mused.

"Wouldn't surprise me to find some explosive rounds for long guns somewhere around here."

We found plenty of high-capacity magazines, bump stocks, and other items that were protected under the sixth circuit court's interpretation of the Second Amendment.

Understand, I'm not anti-gun. I mean, clearly—standing there with a gun on my hip, and one that was passed down in my family. I'm a former cop and currently a SpecOps shooter. I used to hunt with my dad, uncle, and brother. I have no issue at all with sensible gun ownership. But this . . .

No, this was an army preparing for war.

I was about to tell Top to start bagging samples when Ghost gave a single sharp bark. We turned to see that he had stopped his search in the middle of the small kitchen, scratched twice at the linoleum floor, then retreated a pace and sat down.

We froze. One bark and one scratch was guns.

One bark and *two* scratches was for something a lot scarier.

We left the guns, crept very carefully past Ghost, and knelt on opposite sides of the scratched place, studying the faux wood grain pattern of the durable polymer flooring. I took a penlight and held it so the light swept along the surface at an angle that would show us the faint line of a hidden panel. Which it did.

"They were hiding it from civilians," sniffed Top in disapproval. "Even local cops would have tripped it."

As soon as he said it, his expression changed to one of mild alarm.

"Outlaw," he said, "if it's all the same to you, I think I'd like to get the hell out of this box and retreat to minimum safe distance. Maybe call some bomb squad guys down to take a look."

"I'll meet you outside," I said, getting very carefully to my feet and waving Ghost back.

"Donnie Darko," called Top. "Kitchen floor's rigged hot. Clear the decks. Do it now."

We left the trailer as quickly as safety allowed. We could have taken our time getting out of there.

The trailer didn't explode for nearly thirty seconds.

INTERLUDE 2
THE MANSION
UNDISCLOSED LOCATION
TWO YEARS AGO

She stood naked in front of the mirror.

It was a large mirror, and she could see all of herself, from hair to toenails.

Every inch.

The lines. The curves. The planes.

And the scars. The wounds. The marks of violence.

It was all there to see. And as the hours passed, it became clear that it was a story to be read.

"What happened to me?" she asked.

The man sat on the edge of the bed. He was dressed in lightweight slacks and a polo shirt. Her nakedness had not elicited so much as a raised eyebrow. Nor had she expected it to. Since the first time she woke, he had not reacted to her as a woman. There was nothing even remotely sexual about his touch, his voice, or even the movement of his eyes. That was a comfort to her, and there were few comforts on offer.

"What am I?" she asked.

Her fingers glided along the ridges of a long Y-shaped incision that ran from beneath each collarbone and then joined mid-chest to plunge all the way down her torso to her groin. The lips of the incision were a very pale grayish pink, the stitch marks dark purple. The flesh around it was the color of mushrooms grown in a dark forest. In the center of her chest were two black holes. One above the joining of the Y and the other below it. She touched them. Inserted a finger into one. It did not go far, but it was far enough to send a shiver through every nerve ending.

"What *am* I?" she asked again. Begging this time.

"What you are," he said, "is beautiful."

She turned and looked into his eyes. They had been a soft golden color, like amber. Now, though, they were different. There were many shades of gray and green and yellow. Unhealthy colors that swirled like ink poured into a glass of water.

She took a single stumbling backward step. He made no move at all. Only his eyes moved. The color moved. And his lips formed a smile that was every bit as strange and alien and unnatural as those colors.

"You are exceptionally beautiful, my dear," he said in a voice that was not the one she was used to. This new voice was darker somehow. Gravelly. Strange. And . . . old.

"What *are* you?" she gasped.

"I am magic," he said. "I am chaos."

"What does that mean?"

"You will understand in time, my dear. I am what I am."

"Then what am I?"

"You are my daughter. You are my angel. You are my queen." He paused for a delicate moment. "Together we will set this world to burn."

CHAPTER 4
HIDEAWAY MOBILE HOME PARK
TUCKERTON, NEW JERSEY

It was a big goddamn explosion.

The C-4 beneath the kitchen floor blew out every window, tore the doors from their hinges, and punched upward hard enough to send the roof soaring into the night sky. The force bent the walls out, and the heat set fire to everything that could burn.

The shock wave picked us all up and flung us like rag dolls in every direction. I somehow managed to grab Ghost, and we smashed through strings of colored lights and various shrubberies, across patios, picking up part of a Coleman grill, a yellow lawn chair, and an American flag along the way.

My back slammed into the passenger door of a parked Chevy pickup, and if it wasn't for the body armor I wore, I'd have broken my ribs and maybe my spine. Even so, it felt like the Hulk and Thor punched me simultaneously front and back. The impact tore a sharp yelp of pain from Ghost.

And as we hit the ground, his 115 pounds of body-armored shepherd landed on my crotch.

I pushed him off and rolled onto hands and knees, fighting to ignore the Fourth of July fireworks going on inside my head and the screaming pain in my balls. A hand helped me up. Belle.

"They're coming," she said, though her voice was muffled and distant.

I was half out of it. "What . . . ?"

She clapped her hands in front of my face—very fast and very loud.

"They. Are. Coming," she repeated, spacing the words.

And then I understood. Realization brought clarity.

The trailer park was sparsely populated, with none of the occupied homes closer than fifty yards from the one that went boom. But Norris's double-wide had gone boom really loud.

Suddenly, everyone was pouring out of their mobile homes.

All of them were armed.

I'm not talking a baseball bat set by the door to deal with intruders. I'm talking locked and loaded. Handguns, combat shotguns, and automatic weapons. The kind of stuff Norris had hidden in his home.

All of the people coming out of those motor homes were male, early twenties to midthirties, fit, and pissed off. And not one of them had a cell phone in hand to call 9-1-1.

"Ohhhhhh shit," said Remy.

"This is a whole goddamn community of them," growled Top as he backed away toward our vehicle.

Remy was right.

Oh shit.

CHAPTER 5
THE TOC
TACTICAL OPERATIONS CENTER
PHOENIX HOUSE
OMFORI ISLAND, GREECE

On the huge screen at the front of the room was a drone-fed image of the gunmen swarming out of their homes even as flaming debris continued to rain down on Havoc Team.

"Merlin, Grendel," yelled Ledger. "This is Havoc Actual. These are civilians. Rules of engagement?"

Gunfire blasted from the speakers, filling the TOC.

Scott Wilson—a thin, reedy man, turned to the bigger, blockier Mr. Church.

"They have no jurisdiction there."

Church bent over a console and punched a button.

"Merlin to Havoc Actual," he snapped. "Fall back. Engage only if absolutely necessary. Try to avoid casualties, but get your team out of there safely."

CHAPTER 6
HIDEAWAY MOBILE HOME PARK
TUCKERTON, NEW JERSEY

There are all kinds of ways a mission like this can go sideways because there are so many factors and so many variables in play.

These were almost certainly all Tenth Legion PMCs, or they were in training for that job. That meant they were employed by a company legally registered to operate—within certain guidelines—all over the world. They were not, however, allowed to pull triggers on American soil in situations like this. Not in New Jersey, at least.

That said, they could make a very good argument that we were the bad guys. We just blew up a trailer home belonging to the guy who recruited them. And—as any forensic team could later prove—just murdered four of their friends. In strictly legal terms, they were on solid ground while we were on damned thin ice.

Anyone we killed would count as another felony against us. We were already way over the line here—running an op and killing people without official approval from the US government. This wasn't the old DMS days. We were a PMC army ourselves, and one based in Greece. Every action we were taking was technically criminal.

The short version of that was that we were in very deep shit.

"Sandman, Sandman, *Sandman*," I bellowed as I pulled Ghost behind Norris's truck, which was now lying on its side, the tires melting as they burned. I crouched there, drew my Snellig, and began firing darts in the direction of any muzzle flash. There were a *lot* of muzzle flashes. What we call a *target-rich environment*.

Bullets tore into the truck, some of them punching through a lot of metal and whining off behind me. Armor-piercing rounds. Swell.

I could not see the rest of Havoc Team, but I saw a few of the Tenth Legion trainees suddenly stagger and go down. Then one—a big son of a bitch with a military-issue HK416 carbine with the selector switched to rock and roll—suddenly dropped to his knees. There was a big red hole in the center of his chest.

Into the comms, I snarled, "Mother Mercy, switch to Sandman rounds right now."

"Copy that, Outlaw," said Belle in a tone heavily laced with reluctance and disappointment. Her next shot was with Sandman, though it caught one of the legionnaires in the throat. Not a kill shot but one that would offer challenges for the EMTs.

Norris's double-wide had been in a corner of the trailer park, with the others set in clusters moving east and north of it. We had a copse of trees behind us, and the gravel drive that led out to a feeder road that was a two-mile run to the highway. Our vehicle was still on its wheels, though the doors were pitted and the glass spiderwebbed with cracks. There was a lean figure hunkered down behind it, and as I looked, a couple of bats abruptly flapped into the flashing lights of the sustained gunfire. They swooped down among a knot of guys who were turning a pair of dumpsters into a shooting blind. One of the men glanced up, and though I could not see his face, I could read the surprise and confusion in his body language.

Then one bat exploded, and everyone fell down and lay still. Five shooters all at once, victims of one of Remy's toys. The bat was loaded with microdoses of Sandman. He only had two of them, though. We'd used them only once before in South Africa three weeks before, and in that situation, he'd sent them in through the open window of a Hummer filled with Tenth Legionnaires.

There was a ripple of reaction across the trailer park as heads turned toward the sudden cessation of fire from those five. The second bat flew toward a cluster of three shooters and burst apart, dropping them.

The bad guys scattered to new points of cover. Belle began firing as fast as she could pull the trigger, each shot hitting a target. All of us are very good shots—Belle is better by an order of magnitude. Top and Bunny were firing, too, though I couldn't see either of them. My head was still ringing, and my groin felt like it was covered in fire ants. But sitting in a comfy chair with ice packs on my brain and balls wasn't really an option.

"Ghost, stay," I ordered, then I broke from cover and ran like hell for the corner of another trailer. The pause lasted about half the time it took me to get there, but then it erupted again and I felt like the air all around me was filled with murder hornets. I skidded to a stop behind the house, then scuttled backward as the armor-piercing rounds chewed the aluminum siding to mulch. I kept moving until I reached the front door, which stood ajar, then ducked inside and duckwalked to the window. There was a flat-screen TV on which two men were double-teaming a girl who looked like she was *maybe* fifteen. I hoped like hell the asshole who was watching this was the one Belle shot in the chest.

At the window, I peered out and saw several shooters firing at the front of the trailer I was in, but from a quarter angle. Nice. I stayed low and laid the barrel of the Snellig on the windowsill and fired four quick shots through the screen.

One-two-three-four and they were down.

A split second later, a shotgun blast obliterated the other window on the opposite side of the sink. I dropped and crawled to the back door, eased it open, saw that it was clear, and ran.

The shotgun guy fired again and again as he walked toward the trailer I'd just left. He was roaring like a bear and taking big steps with the kind of confidence that made it clear he thought firing a weapon gave him some kind of force field against incoming rounds. So, I shot him in the nuts with the Snellig.

The overall confusion of gunfire was slowing.

I knelt beside a parked three-wheeled camouflage-patterned ATV, using the wheels as cover, and scanned the field of battle. There were bodies everywhere, and in the distance, I saw figures running away. Some went into their trailers—maybe for more ammunition or maybe to hide; the others ran out of the park and across the road before vanishing into a tangle of pine trees.

"Outlaw to Havoc, sound off."

They did. Top, Remy, Bunny, and Belle.

"I have Ghost with me," said Bunny.

"Does anyone see a hostile?"

"Negative, Outlaw," said Top. "They're on the run."

"Then we need to get the hell out of Dodge."

We ran for the SUV, all of us making maximum use of cover. Remy was already behind the wheel and Belle walked backward, turning right and left, her eagle eye looking for threats and finding nothing but slumped bodies. The fire from Norris's trailer was burning fiercely and two small pines beside it were now torches.

"Outlaw," called Top, "lookee here."

I turned and saw that there were two slumbering legionnaires not six feet from the front wheel of the truck, both twitching inside the cloud of their Sandman dreams. Bunny began dragging them away, but I stopped him.

"Load them in the back," I said. "Might as well add kidnapping to the list of things that will keep us off Santa's *nice* list."

"Ho, ho, ho," chortled Bunny. He picked them up and tossed them—not joking, actually tossed them—into the back of the camper body. They landed with the kinds of thuds and thumps that promised unpleasantness when they woke. Though, to be 100 percent accurate, bruises were going to be the least of what they had to worry about. Bunny climbed in with them as Remy started the engine.

In the distance, I could hear the banshee wail of emergency sirens.

We got out of there right damn quick.

INTERLUDE 3
THE MANSION
UNDISCLOSED LOCATION
TWO YEARS AGO

She asked, "What's your name? What do I call you?"

The man stood in front of a pair of french doors that looked out onto a broad lawn. There was a faint dusting of snow on the withered brown leaves.

"My name," he said, "is October."

"Is that a real name or a made-up one?"

"All names are made up, my girl."

"Is it your first name or last name?"

"People call me Mr. October," he said, touching the glass of one door. A cardinal, red as all the sin in the world, stood on the lawn, digging for sleeping spiders with its sharp beak.

"Was that always your name?" asked the woman.

"Of course not. Nor was the name you had when you died."

That sent a shudder through her, and her fingers went reflexively to the autopsy scar beneath her clothes.

"I had other names," she said.

"I know."

Minutes passed before he spoke again.

"What do you want to be called? Are you still Mother Night? Or Artemisia—"

"No," she said, cutting him off. "I'm not either of those people. Not now and never again."

"Fair enough. Give me a new name. Pick one out of the air, if you want. Give me something to call you."

"Mary," she said at once.

"Oh? Why that name?"

But she did not answer.

"Mary it is, then," said Mr. October. "I am pleased to know you, Miss Mary."

CHAPTER 7
THE MANSION
UNDISCLOSED LOCATION
NOW

Mr. October answered the call on the third ring.

"Hello," he said, drawing the two syllables out with a soft Southern drawl.

"Are you watching the news?" asked the caller.

"At the moment I am soaking in a very hot tub and listening to the Orchestra dell'Accademia Nazionale di Santa Cecilia play Alexander Scriabin. His *Poem of Ecstasy*, opus fifty-four."

"Yeah, I'm not into Russian violin music," said the caller.

"Nor am I. But I do have a soft spot for nineteenth-century Russian mystics. I could tell you stories about Rasputin that would turn your hair white. Oh . . . wait . . . your hair already *is* white."

"Boss . . ." said the caller with faltering patience.

"The news. Right," said October. "My mind tends to wander while I soak. What *about* the news? Is it *good* news?"

"Depends on what your long game is. Go look."

"Which station?"

"Pretty much all the local ones in Pennsylvania and Jersey."

The line went dead.

Mr. October reached a soapy hand toward the remote on the marble pedestal beside the tub. He switched on the big flat-screen on the far wall. When it was on, he channel surfed over to the local ABC affiliate and watched firefighters battling a wild blaze at a trailer park. The reporter was ranting as if it were the end of the world. There was a data crawl at the bottom of the screen that read DOMESTIC TERRORISM . . . ?

October tossed the remote onto the table, picked up his glass of Saint-Estèphe, and took a long sip of the rich red wine.

As the trailer park burned, his eyes seemed to flicker with matching heat and fury, though his lips were curled into a predatory feline smile.

CHAPTER 8
ROUTE 9
SOUTH JERSEY

About a million cops, EMTs, and firefighters descended on the trailer park, and on their heels was an army of reporters from every print, cable, and web service.

We were long gone by then.

The images of what happened after the explosion were fed to us by the owl drone Remy left on a tree branch. The four of us saw it all on monitors inside the Ford F-250 with a camper body that rolled along Route 9.

We drove to a Comfort Suites north of Atlantic City and went to our rooms. We had several in a row on the second floor, all with adjoining doors. Bunny and Remy swiped a wheeled laundry cart and used it to bring the two sleeping legionnaires up. They searched them, bound them, and laid the pair side by side on the unused twin bed in my room.

I gave everyone ten minutes to drop their gear, hit the head, and then convene on me in the end unit. By the time they were gathered, I'd changed to jeans and a Hawaiian shirt with pastel-colored octopuses all over it. I lingered for a moment in the bathroom, staring at my face in the mirror. Once upon a time, I looked like a rangy, loose-limbed third baseman from one of the minor-league teams. Blue eyes, scuffle of blond hair, regular features. Now I had a shiner, several bruises on my cheek and jaw, and yet another dent to a nose that already looked like it had been hit at least once from every conceivable angle.

"Well," I told my reflection, "ain't you a peach?"

My reflection told me to kiss his ass. I reminded him that it was physically impossible. Then I washed my face and went out to do the incident debrief.

CHAPTER 9
TRANSCRIPT OF SESSION NOTES
DR. RUDY SANCHEZ AND MR. CHURCH

SANCHEZ: Are you still having the nightmares?

CHURCH: I am.

SANCHEZ: And this is particularly difficult for you?

CHURCH: As we have discussed in previous sessions, Doctor, I am not prone to nightmares.

SANCHEZ: But you dream . . .

CHURCH: Everyone dreams, Doctor.

SANCHEZ: Are you telling me that your dreams are never unpleasant?

CHURCH: That is not what I'm saying.

SANCHEZ: Then please explain.

CHURCH: I dream of all manner of things. People who are in or who have passed out of my life. I dream of friends long gone. I dream of the events related to the work I do. To the war I have been fighting for a very long time.

SANCHEZ: Let's pause there and talk about this last point. You say that you have dreams related to events related to your work. To your war. Given the nature of these events, are these not nightmares?

CHURCH: They are not.

SANCHEZ: Please explain how they are different.

CHURCH: Most of the dreams related to the war are either playbacks of events that have happened, or my subconscious orchestrating worst-case scenarios. I have always had such dreams.

SANCHEZ: I understand, but explain to me how those dreams are not nightmares.

CHURCH: Because in those dreams, even the ones that show things going very badly, I am in control.

SANCHEZ: Of the situation?

CHURCH: No. Of myself.

SANCHEZ: And in the nightmares about what happened in Jerusalem, you are not in control? Is that the difference?

CHURCH: Yes.

SANCHEZ: So, the thing you fear most is that loss of control?

CHURCH: Very much so, yes.

SANCHEZ: Everyone loses control now and then. It is part of the human condition.

CHURCH: I think we can agree that I am somewhat different than the average person.

SANCHEZ: Even so, you are human.

CHURCH: Yes.

SANCHEZ: Moreover, the events in Jerusalem were beyond **anyone's** control. Everyone in that building was exposed to the bioweapons code-named Shiva and God's Arrow. You were heavily exposed to both. It is my understanding, having spoken with Doc Holliday and her team, that it is completely impossible for anyone to resist the effects of those weapons.

CHURCH: I'm aware of the biochemistry, Doctor.

SANCHEZ: And yet you castigate yourself for reacting as any other human would?

(Seven-second pause)

CHURCH: Doctor, you know more about me than anyone else who works for Rogue Team. You know more about me than Aunt Sallie did. You know some of the things I have done in the past. Things that do not bear close moral scrutiny but which at the time I felt were right. Things

JONATHAN MABERRY

that I did not excuse to myself but justified based on the needs in the moment.

SANCHEZ: I do. Where are you going with this?

CHURCH: You also know what I am capable of.

SANCHEZ: Somewhat.

CHURCH: More than most.

SANCHEZ: Fair enough.

CHURCH: There are very good reasons why I abhor and even fear a loss of control.

SANCHEZ: I understand this, but the effects of Shiva and God's Arrow were both of limited duration. Your blood work has been clean since the event. You are free of the bioweapons.

CHURCH: But not of their effect.

SANCHEZ: Which effect?

CHURCH: The nightmares, Doctor. They persist.

SANCHEZ: Are you able to understand and accept that these are echoes only? That, however gruesome or intense they may be, they are only dreams?

CHURCH: And if they are not?

SANCHEZ: How could they not be?

CHURCH: Doctor, you are famous for telling people that violence always leaves a mark.

SANCHEZ: It does.

CHURCH: I have been marked by the violence of Shiva and God's Arrow. I have been marked——scarred——by what I did while under their influence. I killed Brick Anderson. I beat him to death. He was far more than my bodyguard and assistant. He was my good and trusted friend.

SANCHEZ: Is it the loss of someone——a good person who you trusted——that frightens you?

CHURCH: No.

SANCHEZ: Then tell me what about the nightmares causes such unrest in you.

CHURCH: Doctor, in my dreams, I am still under the control of those weapons. When I wake, I cannot be sure that the loss of control has not followed me into consciousness.

SANCHEZ: Have you said or done anything since Jerusalem that makes you question your level of personal control?

(Another pause of significant length)

CHURCH: That is the challenge I face, Doctor. I simply do not know.

INTERLUDE 4
THE MANSION
UNDISCLOSED LOCATION
TWO YEARS AGO

"What is this place?" asked Miss Mary. "Is this *your* house?"

"It's mine," said Mr. October. "And I like to call it the Mansion."

"It's not really big enough to be a mansion."

"No, but I never denied being a bit pretentious." He gestured to the forest visible through the french doors. "I own a vulgar amount of land around here. It used to be a beef farm once upon a time. Owned by an old friend of mine, but he's gone now. I bought it for back taxes and built this house."

"Why didn't you build an *actual* mansion?"

"Oh, that would have raised eyebrows. There was enough scrutiny and local interest when I bid on this particular patch of land. Had I built a mansion, we would have drawn too much attention. A modest house is more practical. And I have been excavating the basement. If I can't build *up*, then I'll build *down*."

Mary grunted, losing interest in the conversation. "I'm hungry," she said.

Mr. October smiled at her. A kindly smile. Friendly, compassionate, caring. Almost a fatherly smile. His eyes had stopped doing that swirly thing. Or, if he still did it, he didn't let her see.

She thought she knew who he was, though. Those eyes . . . she remembered reading about that. Hearing about it. The eyes and a name. Nick something? Nicholas? No, but that was almost it.

"What would you like to eat?" asked October. They were in the drawing room, which had become her favorite place. The crackling flames in the oversize fireplace, the french doors leading out to a stone patio and a big lawn. She sat cross-legged on the hearth, wearing only a T-shirt and socks. Nothing else. The socks did not match, and there were gravy stains on the shirt. She'd worn it for four days now.

Outside, she could see a formal garden that had gone wild. The grass was unmowed, and here and there, clusters of taller grasses waved above the rest. A few slender maple saplings stood alone, growing where they should not. The hedges were huge and furry, humped like grazing bison. Vines coiled like snakes around a twisted elm. In the midst of all of this were wildflowers of uncountable kinds, creating a static firework display of colors to balance the rampant greenery. And all of it wild.

No, she thought, correcting herself. All of it free.

He asked his question again, and it coaxed her from her reverie. She turned to him and gave him a shy look. "Can I have . . . steak? Is it too early for that?"

"You may have whatever you want, my dear," said the man. "How do you like your meat?"

She hesitated because there was something odd about that question. Her reflexes made her flinch from something that at first sounded perverse. But then she replayed it in her head while looking into his eyes. There *was* a deeper meaning, that much was certain, but she did not think it was sex. Something else. Something oddly similar that spoke to a different kind of experience. A different kind of hunger.

"I don't know," she replied, her tone guarded.

He stood up. "That's fine, my girl. I will ask the cook to prepare some choices. That way, you'll be able to make a decision that suits your *appetites*."

She cut him a sharp look because he'd leaned ever so slightly on that last word.

Appetites.

As October walked away, she tried to understand what he implied. Alone, she spoke the word aloud. "Appetite."

The word seemed to linger on her tongue like the memory of something particularly yet unusually delicious.

She thought about steak. The idea of hot meat made her stomach growl and churn, a strange mixture of hunger and repulsion in nearly equal measures. Nearly.

Outside of the drawing room, there was movement, and she turned to see a doe step delicately out of the shadows of the woods and into the sunlight that slanted down through holes in the clouds. So pretty. Young but healthy-looking.

Two smaller shapes followed tentatively. Babies. Fawns who could not have been more than a month or two old. Frail, fragile.

"Beautiful," she said. Then froze and listened to the mental echo of the word. She had wanted to say *beautiful*, but that wasn't the word that passed her lips.

What she actually said was, "Delicious."

CHAPTER 10
COMFORT SUITES ATLANTIC CITY NORTH
ABSECON, NEW JERSEY

Here's how me and mine got to Tuckerton in the first place.

Havoc Team had been doing some months of training following the horror show that was the Jason Aydelotte case in the Holy Land. Or, maybe let's call it *occupational therapy*. Whatever. All of us came out of that mess and logged serious hospital time. And time on Rudy Sanchez's couch. The hits we took in Israel were hard ones. The deaths of Brick Anderson and Andrea Bianchi hit us low and deep.

It's weird how that works. There are some deaths that seem to be written into the script, and although we grieve, we can somehow accept their plausibility. If, say, I had taken the bullets that killed Andrea, I think everyone would be "Yeah, saw that coming," and they'd maybe weep a bit, and they'd get drunk, tell tall tales, and then get back to work.

But Brick and Andrea weren't those kinds of people.

Brick, for all his massive size—and he'd been close in bulk to Bunny—was a gentle guy. Kindhearted, easygoing, fun to be around, smart as fuck, and he deserved to retire off the job and maybe go live someplace down South, where the fishing is good, the beer is cold, and there are plenty of bookstores. Instead, he's buried in Mississippi soil with a cold stone marker to serve as a grossly inadequate statement about who and what he was.

As for Andrea . . . well, he was the heart of Havoc Team, and no one would argue the point. Funny, generous, devious in combat, but able to hang his soldier aspect on a peg when he was off the clock. He left behind a husband and adopted daughter, and at his funeral in Italy, I don't know how any of us were able to look at the kid without feeling that we had, personally and collectively, failed. Her grief was so palpable, I could feel it burned onto my skin. And that's the thing. He died a hero, but we all feel like we deserved those bullets more than he did. Or maybe it's that we felt that he and Brick deserved some kind of hall pass. A Get Out of Death card.

I know it shook a lot of people at the RTI. If this were a movie, you could bet good money that both Brick and Andrea would make it to the end credits. The fact that they didn't made each of us take a closer look at the fine print on our personal mortality.

In the main entrance hall of Phoenix House—which is the official name for the RTI headquarters on Omfori Island—there is a wall of finely carved and engraved gold stars. Each bears the name, rank, and dates of birth and death of those people who have fallen in Church's war. Our war. There are hundreds of them, some dating back to the Cold War, predating both RTI and the DMS. There were two new stars there now. One for Brick and another for Andrea. There was also a lot of wall space left, and every time I passed by, I feared for whose name would be next to join that community of heroes.

The war is the war. That's what Church says. We all echo it. The *war* is not specific. It's not right versus left, or tied to any nation, flag, political worldview, or religious ideology. It is, to put it in the most basic terms, the good guys fighting the bad guys. Brick and Andrea are among the few who have risked all and given all to stand between the innocent and those who would bring great harm to them. That's the war. And it is worth fighting even though every one of us who passes that wall of stars understands the cost.

The war is the war.

Now . . . the other thing that rocked us was the fact that Church had been the one who killed Brick. Sure, we all knew he was under the effects of Aydelotte's ergot-and-LSD-based mind-altering bio-weapon, but I don't think any of us really thought a guy like Church *could* be affected by something like that. His control is evident from near-Earth orbit. He is the calm, fixed point in our shared realities, and suddenly, he was as mortal as anyone, as vulnerable as any normal person.

That is scary.

That is very damned scary. Even though we all *knew* that we should never have held such exaggerated views of him.

This mission in New Jersey was us going back to work with training wheels.

Church was thousands of miles away, in the TOC on Omfori Island in Greece, probably with Scott Wilson and Doc Holliday watching his every move. Havoc was back in the field, but on a gig that was supposed to be a soft-soap look-and-see thing. Information gathering as we built our case against a new group of PMCs—private military contractors—working for a South African company called Tenth Legion. Named after a brutal group of Roman soldiers sent to Israel a couple of thousand years ago to put down a Jewish rebellion. Their excesses are legendary, and the new group is trying to prove they're just as badass.

The rest of Rogue Team International was scattered. Because groups like ours are necessarily *reactive* rather than proactive, we had to wait until something went wrong. The Tenth Legion thing was us reacting to the fact that—seemingly unprovoked—they hit a safe house in Israel where Havoc had been holed up. We weren't there looking for them but had instead come to Israel as part of an investigation of suspicious deaths that were so bizarre we all felt like we were witnessing actual magic. In one instance, two esteemed biblical scholars had gone crazy while examining new fragments of Dead Sea Scrolls and did a murder-suicide thing while apparently believing they were being attacked by bats. Although there were no bats visible, a morgue video showed bat bites on their skin.

It gets weirder.

Then we received video footage of the interrogation of a Boko Haram terrorist conducted by a pair of CIA agents at Camp Lemonnier, a United States Naval Expeditionary Base, situated next to Djibouti. In the video, the prisoner and both agents were attacked by Egyptian cobras. The terrorist and one agent died there, and the other agent lingered in a hospital for two weeks before succumbing to the venom. Those cobras—which are not of a kind found in Djibouti—appeared out of nowhere and vanished into thin air. So . . . yeah, we were all a little freaked.

Did I say a *little*? Poor word choice. All of us were stunned, dumbfounded, shocked, appalled, and at a loss to explain either case. Havoc was assigned the case and we started with the Israeli incident first, but before we could make any headway, the Jason Aydelotte case smashed through our lives like a tsunami.

Confusing, yes. Tell me about it.

We handled the Aydelotte thing—case file code name: Cave 13— and that left us all battered, half out of our minds, and attending funerals of friends.

In the months since, we've been trying to make sense of things. The Tenth Legion attack was, we theorized, a mistake. Someone who knew Top, Bunny, and me by sight and who was involved in whatever the legionnaires were into must have thought we were on *their* trail, and so they did a preemptive hit on us. That didn't go as well as they hoped, but the collateral damage left us with one to interrogate. The trail dried up at the time, but we decided to go looking. So I guess that's both reactive *and* proactive.

As for the it-seems-like-magic-and-I-hope-to-fuck-it's-not bats and snakes thing . . . Nikki Bloom—head of pattern recognition for RTI—found a couple of other incidents of what witnesses believed were new and genuine miracles. Scott Wilson sent Chaos Team to run that down. Their boots hit the ground right around the time Hamas invaded Israel and started that bloodbath. Understandably, the local situation has slowed Chaos Team's investigation to a crawl.

Bedlam Team was off doing something in Ukraine. Following reports of Russians using bioweapons against local forces.

Our newest—and oddest—team, the Wild Hunt, led by former

bad guy Toys, had been rebuilt after suffering losses in the Cave 13 thing and was in Canada following a different line of investigation. Because the Tenth Legion was composed of a lot of PMCs who used to work, directly or indirectly, for Sebastian Gault, Hugo Vox, the Seven Kings, and other groups both DMS and RTI has collided with, Toys thought that he might be able to resurrect some of his old contacts. People who knew the illegal arms trade. Those folks didn't know that Toys now worked for us, and so he was a useful double agent.

Which left Havoc Team in the US hunting recruiters looking for criminals, sociopaths, and politically disenfranchised guys who like to play with guns. A lot of them were clods and lowlifes, but sadly competent when it came to pulling triggers.

Even so, the Tuckerton connection should have been a walk in the park.

Would have been nice.

INTERLUDE 5
THE MANSION
UNDISCLOSED LOCATION
TWO YEARS AGO

Her memories returned.

At first, it was only dribs and drabs—a snatch of conversation, random images, even a few whole memories about some specific incident. But days and days passed with no real gains. Those things she remembered lacked context and therefore felt unreal, like things recalled from old TV shows and movies. Like they were someone else's memories.

And then, one afternoon, after hours spent with Haruspex, digging through files to finger traces of herself, something changed. Tumblers in her head lined up for reasons impossible for even an organic chemist or neuroscientist to explain—the memories were there.

All of them.

Every single one.

From childhood all the way up to the moment on the balcony rail-

JONATHAN MABERRY

ing at the Marriott Marquis in Atlanta. From her adoptive parents reaching for her to Joe Ledger pointing his pistol at her.

Then the fall.

She remembered the fall.

All

    the

        way

           down.

With that tidal surge of returning memories came every bit of context. Who she was. Why she did what she did. The awareness of occasional fugue states where everything was painted black and no details were visible. The knowledge of her own progression from brilliant and comprehensively misunderstood girl to a sly teen who learned quickly to use her looks and some obligatory sex to get exactly what she needed. The version of herself who applied for what she thought was a job with the CIA but was really a talent search for the Department of Military Sciences. Her years at the Hangar in Brooklyn. The trips to incident sites in the hours after Samson Riggs or Joe Ledger tore down the bad guys. The theft of samples and files. And then the rest. Cultivating the disenfranchised teens—the nobodies and throwaways and lost ones living on the fringes—and turning them into her army. The bidding wars she initiated with buyers from every terrorist state and group in the world, and how she screwed them all. The hunt for her. The orders to the mad assassin Ludo Monk to kill Junie Flynn. And then the big reveal at Dragon Con.

She remembered it all.

It appalled her.

It terrified her that she had been that woman. That *thing*.

And the cruelties she had imposed on her own flesh, her own brain chemistry. On her life.

She sat there for hours with all the things she had hidden away in the cabinets and attic spaces in her mind. There was no happy picture. It was not a tale of someone gone wrong. It wasn't another weary example of power corrupting.

No.

She had become a monster through sheer will.

And they had killed her for it.

Finally, in the quiet of late afternoon, the house was empty and the opening movements of the symphony of twilight began with a stilling of the breeze so that there was no sound at all. She rose, then, and walked outside, going barefoot across the lawn. Bringing with her a folding chair and a length of rope.

CHAPTER 11
UNIT 819
BLACK SITE PRISON
UNDISCLOSED LOCATION
SEVEN MONTHS AGO

His name was Toombs and he was in a tomb.

Of sorts.

The prison was—he was positive—one of those that could best be described as a black site. Not quite the hellhole that was Guantanamo, but not too many rungs up the ladder.

He was allowed no contact of any kind with other prisoners. In fact, he never saw any of them. All he knew of the other inmates was some vague yelling once in a while and the occasional terrible scream.

Of the guards, they wore riot helmets with smoked visors, so he never saw a face. They seldom spoke to him, and when they did, it was to give terse orders that he was warned on day one were in his best interests to obey without question.

He had not been read any rights and was brought to the facility while unconscious, having been shot by an RTI agent. The dart fired by the agent's gun was filled with some kind of knockout formula that took him right down and then shoved him into a unique kind of hell. He had the worst dreams—or perhaps hallucinations were closer to the mark—than he had ever had. Terrible dreams filled with bizarre images pulled from the deepest and blackest part of his subconscious. He'd awakened from those nightmares in the cell in which he sat, with no way to know where it was. When he checked his body, he found three separate marks from dart strikes. They were in various stages of healing, suggesting he was dosed repeatedly during a long trip.

The cell had no windows and the lights went out in regular intervals that he had no choice but to accept as the end of full days. His body clock had a very hard time adjusting to the pattern, though, and Toombs speculated that the rhythm was, in fact, not as orderly as it seemed. He reckoned that there were subtle variations on the pattern that he could not verify without a clock of his own. He was given a stack of paperback books on his third day there and tried to make a rough calculation based on pages and chapters read, but that seemed to only confuse things more, and so he stopped trying and just let himself roll with whatever patterns they wanted to use on him.

Time lost much of its meaning.

The only interruptions in the pattern were four visits. Two by a waspish and acid-tongued British man—slim, medium height, white, with pitiless eyes. That man, who never offered a name, asked him hundreds of questions about the Jason Aydelotte organization, particularly its development of the ergot-based Shiva and God's Arrow bioweapons. He was also asked about his role as a field sales manager for Aydelotte's arms sales.

Toombs answered every single question with complete honesty. He did not, however, offer information beyond the scope of those questions. But the answers he did give were bulked up with minute technical information. Toombs knew that knowledge was currency, and his plan was to demonstrate the value of what he knew and then wait for an opening to enter into a negotiation phase for information on things they did not know enough to even ask.

It was a long game, and he used all of his mental discipline and the skills learned in decades of meditation and yoga to manage his emotional reactions to his imprisonment.

The other two visits were from a different man. A Mexican man in his late thirties or early forties. Cultured, urbane, polite, and very smart. His questions had been of the kind used by professionals in the mental health field. Toombs assumed this man was a psychiatrist who understood trauma and also had insights into criminality.

Toombs did not know the names of either of those two men.

And then he had a fifth visit, but from a third person. A stranger, but one who lived up to the adjective at the root of that word. Strange.

Toombs woke up from a nap to find the man sitting on the small chair that, along with a two-drawer bureau, a table, and the bed, comprised the entirety of the cell's furniture. The man was small, slim, and seemed greatly amused by everything. He was smiling when Toombs first spotted him, and although the nature and wattage of that smile varied, he never once stopped smiling.

Keeping any reactions off his face, Toombs sat up, tugged his gray institutional shirt down, crossed his legs, and waited for the pitch. He would not ask first or make any comments at all, because that would convey some kind of need and that would weaken his hand.

After what felt like four or five minutes, the stranger said, "As I see it, my friend, you have three choices."

His voice had a vaguely Southern flavor to it, though Toombs couldn't quite place its origins.

"And they are . . . ?" His own voice sounded hoarse to him. Dusty from disuse.

"Choice one," said the stranger, "is you can remain in custody and bargain knowledge for a chance at seeing sunlight again. There will be some jail time, of course. But if you sing loud enough and in the right tune, that might be counted in years rather than decades."

"Okay. Next option?"

"You remain in custody and keep your mouth shut and do the whole bit. And we are talking about fifty to life."

"You're a lousy salesman, or you're saving the best for last."

The man raised his eyebrows. "Are you in a hurry? Car double-parked?"

"No, I just want to get to the actual reason you're here. Mind you, I appreciate the theatrics. It's just that I have some important not-a-goddamn-thing to get back to."

The stranger chuckled. "Fair enough, fair enough. You're a man who appreciates a straight shooter. That will work for me as well. So here's option three, and I think you'll find it quite intriguing."

"All ears," said Toombs.

"You walk out of here with me. Right here and now. And you go to work for my organization."

"Ah. And does your organization have one of those three-letter names? Maybe starting with an F or a C?"

"Neither. I'm not a fed or a spy, Mr. Toombs. I'm not looking to recruit you as a mole or inside man. And turning states' evidence could not matter less to me."

"Really, now? Who else has the juice to offer me a deal with no jail time?"

"I do."

"Is that right? And who exactly are you?"

"Currently? I am going by the name 'Mr. October.'"

"*Currently* is an interesting word," mused Toombs. "Who are you the rest of the time?"

"You are far more likely to know me by my company name."

Toombs leaned back against the cold wall of his cell. "Which is?"

"Kuga."

"Nice try, but Kuga is Harcourt Bolton Sr., and last time I heard, he was dead."

"Yesss . . . I heard that, too."

"Which makes you what, then?"

"The man who took Kuga away from the late and only minimally lamented Harcourt Bolton."

Toombs considered that. "So, tell me something, Mr. October."

"Yes."

"Why on earth should I trust you? The people who put me in here are the type to try all sorts of tricks."

"You are a prisoner of St. Germaine."

"Who?"

"You know him as Church."

Toombs said nothing, but listened inside his head as pieces tumbled into place. Church ran Rogue Team International, and if the agents who arrested him were part of that group, then it was a likely guess the big black guy with the dart gun was Bradley Sims, who everyone called Top. And the other clown, the muscle freak, was Harvey "Bunny" Rabbit. Toombs didn't know who the British guy was, but the Mexican might be Dr. Rudy Sanchez.

He'd never seen a picture of Church, but scary people he knew were all scared of him. Church and his pet psychopath, Joe Ledger.

This Mr. October did not look like anyone described in a field briefing on RTI, though. So who was he?

"And you are Isaac Calvin Tomberland," said October. "Known as Mr. Toombs or just Toombs."

"Not exactly a news flash."

"No. On the whole, I prefer Toombs. No prefix."

"Most people do." Toombs studied the man. "So, what gives you the juice to spring me from this place?"

"Oh, high intelligence, a useful sense of mischief, and men with guns."

"I didn't hear any gunfire."

"Very quiet guns," said October. "Of a kind I believe you have encountered. Granted, they are not the latest model, but even the old Snellig A31s will get the job done."

He opened his jacket to show a dart gun snugged into a shoulder holster.

"And I'm supposed to believe that the entire staff of this place is sleeping it off and we're just going to stroll out of here?"

October got up from the table and walked to the cell door. It opened with the lightest touch. He paused and said, "I'll be in the black car outside. I'll be there for exactly one minute after I leave the building. You will either join me or stay here and rot."

Then he left.

Toombs got up and looked out into the hall.

There was no one there.

No one awake. At the far end of the hall, sprawled in a heap, was one of the guards. The door at the end of the hall stood open.

"Well . . . kiss my fat dog's ass," Toombs said.

Then he ran down the hall.

CHAPTER 12
PHOENIX HOUSE
OMFORI ISLAND, GREECE
SEVEN MONTHS AGO

Scott Wilson came rushing into the cafeteria without pausing to get a cup of tea from Mustapha. He spotted Church sitting alone in his usual corner and angled that way.

Church set down his coffee cup and leaned back, waiting for whatever bad news brought his chief of operations there on the run.

"Sit," he said before Wilson could blurt out whatever troubled him. The COO did, but immediately leaned forward.

"Sir, there's been an incident."

"Where and what?"

"Unit 819."

"Security cameras?"

"The hard drive was stolen and a virus uploaded to the facility's main computers. Everything is wiped. But only one prisoner is missing."

"Which one?" asked Church.

"The weapons broker," said Wilson. "Toombs."

"Now isn't that interesting," murmured Church.

"I've initiated a search, and Bug has a team on it. They're pulling feeds from CCTV throughout the region. We'll find him."

Church nodded, but he had a feeling Toombs was not going to be found anytime soon.

"Scott," he said as Wilson rose.

"Sir?"

"Make sure this gets tagged in the Tenth Legion and Mr. October files."

"You think . . ." began Wilson, then he paused and nodded. "Of course, sir."

He left, and Church sat there for several minutes, finishing that cup of coffee and two refills. Thinking it through.

INTERLUDE 6
THE MANSION
UNDISCLOSED LOCATION
TWO YEARS AGO

Mr. October stood on the grass and looked up at the corpse swaying gently in the midnight breeze. A quarter moon had cut the flesh of the sky above, and the darkness bled sparkling stars like tears.

He had his hands in his pockets, and when the wind blew hardest, he leaned with it, let it have its way with him. His heart was filled with sadness, though.

"I expected more from you, my girl," he said.

The tree limb creaked as her body swung with the passing breeze. Her bare toe tips brushed the reaching fingers of the grass. He took note of that, musing that it was as if the ground were aching to embrace her, to hold and keep her, to invite her into the purification of rot.

That deepened his sadness but also amused him.

"You cannot have her," he told the ground. "She is not yours to own."

After a long time there in the dark, he bent and set the fallen folding chair upright, shifting it slightly away from where it had been. Then he stepped up onto it. The moonlight caressed the edge of his knife when he removed it from a pocket and snapped the blade into place with a deft flick of his wrist. It was a lovely knife. A Wilson Rapid Response folder that he had recovered from one of the many places where Joe Ledger used—and often lost—versions of that same blade. The one he had remembered Ledger's grip, and it shared that with October. He was amused by that, too, though he had held many thousands of blades of all manner and make over the years. He reached up and sliced the rope. The tension and the wicked sharpness of the steel made that easy, and she fell.

He let her fall, making no attempt to catch her.

She landed in an artless heap, her nightgown riding up high on her thighs. When he stepped down onto the grass, he bent and pulled the hem down. He disliked accidental vulgarity and took no pleasure in glimpses taken without being offered.

October knelt and slowly pushed her limbs into different angles so that she looked like she was merely asleep. Her head lay over to one side, though, and when he ran his fingers over the bulge, he could feel the jutted edge of dislocated vertebra.

He sighed.

As he rose, he removed a cell phone from another pocket, considered for a moment, and then called a doctor. One of many that he owned, heart and soul.

"I need you to set a bone or two," he told the doctor and gave him

JONATHAN MABERRY

the address. "And, I think, plant an RFID chip beneath the patient's skin. Somewhere she won't notice."

Then he pocketed the cell again.

In the trees, an owl was making inquiries.

"Who yourself, old sister," he told the bird. Then he sat down on the chair, picked up one of her cold hands, and held it while he waited.

CHAPTER 13
COMFORT SUITES ATLANTIC CITY NORTH
ABSECON, NEW JERSEY

This is what happened in Tuckerton.

I met Norris at a truckers' bar, using a mutual connection as a calling card. I was supposed to have done twenty-two months of a five-year bit in New Jersey State Prison with a guy who worked with Norris when they were both running with Blue Diamond Security. His friend was dead, chopped down during a joint FBI-ATF raid on a compound in the Pine Barrens, and Bug had fudged the prison records to place my false identity solidly in place. Norris seemed to take the bait because ex-cons have their own network, their own covert lingo, their own networks for communication, and I had done my homework.

Norris left me at the bar to take a piss, and it didn't take a psychic to know he was making some calls to check me out. Bug's cover story for me was unbreakable and therefore deeply plausible. The things he does with MindReader Q1 are spooky as hell.

When Norris came back, he was in a chummy mood, and we had a good chat over a lot of beers. Like all of the members of the Tenth Legion, he peppered the conversation with a lot of cherry-picked quotes from the Bible. Church fed me some useful replies, switching back and forth between the Old and New Testaments. Chapter and verse. Mostly Old, come to think of it. Jesus wasn't nearly as vindictive as his dad. Point is, I could talk the talk, both in biblical and paramilitary terms.

Tenth Legion was officially based in South Africa, run by someone known only as Mr. October. So far, Bug hadn't been able to peek behind his curtain of obscurity. They were hiring a lot of guys from the better-known but less ethical PMC companies. Between the old DMS and the new RTI, we'd put Blue Diamond out of business. Their officers went to jail, and the troops scattered, showing up as trainers in extremist camps of all kinds or joining other teams. The Tenth Legion had very deep pockets, and that was the flame that drew the well-armed moths.

Recruiters were sent to the States because of the proliferation of guns and the dramatic rise in small militia groups. Many of those groups were either harmless or well intentioned, preparing for the Big Crash, which could be variously interpreted as the rise of the New World Order, an invasion by China, cartel armies coming over the border disguised as immigrants, or about a dozen other doom-and-gloom scenarios. I even know of a few militia groups that do some good, helping with order and rescue in places like Tornado Alley and along the path of Southern hurricanes. Good people of the type I admire. The kind who make sure all of their members have been through the full gun safety training and weren't using open carry to prove they had dicks.

But there are a bunch of jokers out there who arm up because they *want* a fight. It's not about preparing to defend the innocent but to provoke conflict so they had a legal—or, in their view, *moral*—right to pull triggers and end lives. Those guys I count among the bad guys because there is no actual moral compass in play. With the current political shitstorm that was the United States, where no two people on either side of the argument seemed able to engage in reasonable discourse, militia groups like that spring up like flies on shit. They wave the flag but neither respect the country it flies above nor understand its symbolism.

Am I preaching? Sure. A bit. But I'm not wrong.

I am fiercely apolitical. I understand politics, but I have an intense dislike of both political parties because most of the people who get voted in do so in order to support whatever lobby writes the biggest check. That's not news, either. Hell, go watch *Mr. Smith Goes to Washington.*

Anyway . . . wandering back to my point.

Tenth Legion wasn't hiring the well intentioned, genuinely patriotic, morally centered, or psychologically balanced. They were hiring well-armed clowns like Norris and his friends back there at the trailer park. The kind who give trailer parks an unfairly bad name.

I thought it was all going to go smooth with me and Norris, because we started having the kind of conversations that don't happen with outsiders. I was "one of us," and when I said I was looking to get back in the game, he suggested we take that conversation back to his double-wide, where there was privacy and—to quote him—"better tequila than they have in this shithole."

I started getting suspicious when he said that we'd go in his truck and leave mine in the bar's lot, promising to drop me off later. So, I wasn't entirely surprised when it turned out his trailer was filled with three other Tenth Legion goons. They pointed guns at my favorite head, zip-tied me to the chair, and entertained themselves by taking turns punching me.

And you know the rest.

Haven't yet decided if Church was just being Church with how he played it or if he was showing off a little bit to *sell* that he was okay. Being the all-powerful voice on high. Not sure. Sure as hell won't ask.

CHAPTER 14
THE MANSION
UNDISCLOSED LOCATION
SEVEN MONTHS AGO

"God," said Mary, "you look like Lurch from *The Addams Family*. Anyone ever tell you that?"

Toombs smiled faintly. "It comes up in conversation now and then."

The room was big, sparsely furnished, and lit on one end by fading sunlight and at the other by a roaring fire. The woman sat cross-legged on the hearth, roasting what looked like a bratwurst on a stick. She pulled it from the flames, blew on it, then took a delicate bite, wrinkled her nose, and stuck the sausage back into the fire.

"I like the skin crisp," she said.

Toombs wandered across the room, being casual about it. He paused to look at a few framed paintings. One was a floral art piece that took notes from Japanese manga. Takashi Murakami, he thought. It looked like one of his.

Another was a neo-Dadaist work with bold colors in dramatic

shades that made up an image of Roman numerals, each in a unique small square. Definitely Jasper Johns, though Toombs was unfamiliar with this specific piece. It wasn't a print—the brushstrokes were genuine, and when he leaned close, he could smell the dried paint.

"Nice pieces," he remarked.

"Oh, those? Yeah. They're okay," said Mary.

He walked over and stood on the far end of the hearth from where she sat. "What's the play, Miss Mary?" he asked.

She grinned. "You like hot dogs?"

"It's a bratwurst, and no. Not much."

Mary took another bite and this time launched into vigorous chewing. Grease escaped from the corners of her mouth and ran down over her chin. Drops fell onto her chest. She wore a sleeveless gray satin shift with spaghetti straps and evidently nothing under it. Her erect nipples pushed out against the fabric. Toombs knew that no woman wore an outfit like that to a business meeting unless her intention was to provoke a reaction. Though he liked her curves and the woman's inarguably beautiful face, he was too seasoned in the game to let his cock do any critical thinking. And he'd seen a lot of sexy women in his time, despite—and even because of—his looks.

"So what are you supposed to be?" he asked. "Eye candy? A distraction? A test?"

"No, honey," she said as she swallowed a chunk of meat. "I'm your boss."

"It's my understanding that I work for Mr. October."

"Oh, that's true. But he and I have an arrangement. We both run this organization."

"And by *organization*, should I assume you mean Kuga?"

She considered the bratwurst, sighed, and tossed it onto the burning logs, stick and all. Then, ankles crossed, she rose to her feet in a single movement that was without effort. He could not call it graceful, because there was something just not right about the woman. Then he got it. If October was rocking a Joker vibe with that shit-eating grin of his, then what was the woman? His Harley Quinn? Decorative and deranged?

"Miss," he said, "I'm all about corporate image and games playing.

I appreciate it. But the vaudeville is for the tourists. I'm sales and management, so the whole thing with the Get Out of Jail Free card October played and whatever this is you're doing is you two burning up calories without needing to. So, can we cut to it, and you tell me why I was sprung and what you want from me?"

He never saw it coming.

Never saw her move.

One moment he was speaking and the next he was on the floor, and the woman was crouched over him, her knees and shins pinning his thighs, one hand clamped like icy steel around his throat and the other hand raised, two fingers and a thumb curled into a kung fu eagle's claw less than an inch from his left eye.

He had no memory at all of being tackled, borne down, and pinned. Toombs had been in far more than his fair share of fights, but he had never seen anyone move with that kind of speed. It was incredible.

No.

It was *impossible*.

Completely impossible.

No human being could move that fast.

She leaned over him, looking down with dark eyes in which absolutely nothing sane lived. Eyes in which there was no real spark of life. Dead eyes. Like a shark's. Very much like that. Then she leaned forward and licked his face from the point of his chin, over his lips and teeth, over his nose, across one eye and all the way to his hairline. It was a sexless, invasive, disgusting act, and despite his control, Toombs shuddered with revulsion.

The woman laughed like a naughty child and got up, turned away from him, and went to look at one of the paintings. The Jasper Johns one. With no warning or comment, she tore it down with such shocking force that the wire snapped and the hook ripped free of the wall with a puff of outraged plaster. She dropped it on the floor, squatted down, and urinated over it.

Then she straightened and walked over to a couch, sank down into it, picked up a copy of *Forbes*, and began reading. The painting— easily forty or fifty thousand dollars' worth—lay there.

Toombs got up very slowly and very cautiously. He had no idea what rules were in play here. October was weird, but this woman was absolutely out of her mind. She was also freakishly fast and strong, and wildly unpredictable.

All of which did more than unnerve Toombs.

It terrified him.

CHAPTER 15
TRANSCRIPT OF SESSION NOTES
DR. RUDY SANCHEZ AND BRADLEY "TOP" SIMS
SESSION #4

SANCHEZ: In our last conversation, we were talking about your feelings of unease.

TOP: **Unease** is one way to put it.

SANCHEZ: Is there another term you'd prefer to use?

TOP: No. That says it.

SANCHEZ: You said that the nightmares had stopped and——

TOP: Let me interrupt you right there, doc. If we're going to use the right terms, then let's not call what I had "nightmares."

SANCHEZ: What word do you feel is more appropriate?

TOP: Bad dreams.

SANCHEZ: As you see it, what is the difference between a bad dream and a nightmare?

TOP: Control.

SANCHEZ: Please explain.

TOP: In nightmares, there's not much control. You get caught up in things, and no matter how you try, nothing seems to work right. You run, but you can never run fast enough. You fight, but your punches and kicks don't do much damage. Bullets, too. The things you fight can't be hurt. No . . . let me fix that. It's not that they can't be hurt, it's that you can't hurt them. You're too weak, or the things you learned don't work against it.

SANCHEZ: Thank you. That's useful. And a bad dream differs how . . . ?

TOP: You can fight, you can do damage, you can even kill.

SANCHEZ: But . . . ?

TOP: But the timing is off. Even when you kill the bad guy, you turn around and find that his bullet slipped past you and killed whoever you were trying to protect.

SANCHEZ: And that's not a nightmare?

TOP: No. Look, doc, I get the subtleties. It **sounds** like another kind of nightmare, swapping out lack of power for lack of timing. Swapping helplessness for failure. But it's not as cut-and-dried as that.

SANCHEZ: I'd like to explore that.

TOP: Why I'm here, doc. Let's take a run at it.

SANCHEZ: We reached an understanding where we were able to accept that the nightmares you had in the weeks following the Cave 13 case were likely due to lingering effects of the Shiva and God's Arrow bioweapons.

TOP: Sure. And they went away. They sucked. They scared the hell out of me, but once I started getting a handle on why I was having them, they faded out. Haven't had one of those in nearly three months.

SANCHEZ: When did the bad dreams begin?

TOP: 'Bout three, four weeks later. So, a little shy of two months.

SANCHEZ: The scenario you use as an example, was that based on a specific dream?

TOP: Kind of. I've had a bunch of dreams where I can't protect those I care about.

SANCHEZ: Who in particular?

TOP: You know most of them.

SANCHEZ: Tell me anyway.

TOP: I was doing a training gig at Fort Merrill. While I was there my son, Henry, was killed in Iraq. Six days before his nineteenth birthday. Then my daughter, Monique, lost both her legs when her Bradley rolled over an IED near Baghdad.

SANCHEZ: As I recall, that was why you agreed to go back into active service and why you accepted Mr. Church's offer to join the DMS.

TOP: It was Major Grace Courtland who scouted me, but yeah. That's why.

SANCHEZ: And a long time ago, we talked about this. To clarify what you hoped to accomplish by making what could easily be mistaken for a sentimental decision to honor them or a decision born of rage. As I recall, you explained that it was neither of those things.

TOP: It wasn't. If I'd gone active for those reasons, the psych screeners would have kicked me back to my training gig. Or suggested I not re-up. No, doc, it wasn't that. I knew I couldn't save them by pulling triggers on the bad guys. I was never that far up my own ass. I just thought I could help by keeping some other parent from getting dealt the kind of cards I got. And maybe keep some bright young lights burning.

SANCHEZ: That's admirable, as I believe I told you at the time.

TOP: Thanks, but the last thing I need or want is a pat on the back for doing what I feel is right.

SANCHEZ: Noted.

JONATHAN MABERRY

TOP: Besides, I'm not dreaming about them lately. Not those kinds of dreams, at least. And it's not like I'm having these ego dreams—what d'you call them? Hubris? It's not that. I'm not kicking my own ass because I couldn't save Andrea or Brick. Nothing like that.

SANCHEZ: Then who or what is the subject of these dreams of frustrated action?

TOP: It's the colonel.

SANCHEZ: Joe Ledger?

TOP: Sure.

SANCHEZ: Tell me about those dreams.

TOP: It's not what you probably think. It's not me trying to keep him from getting shot. Not that at all.

SANCHEZ: Can you tell me what it is?

TOP: It's exactly what you think it is, doc.

SANCHEZ: Tell me.

TOP: It's the Darkness.

SANCHEZ: What, specifically, about it?

TOP: That I didn't do anything when I saw it coming on. That I couldn't help him while he was caught up in it.

SANCHEZ: If there was legitimately anything that anyone could have done to prevent that, Top, then I am as guilty—or perhaps significantly more so—than anyone else.

TOP: This ain't about what anyone else saw or did, or saw and didn't do.

SANCHEZ: Then what is it about?

TOP: It's me seeing—or thinking I'm seeing—shadows of it still.

SANCHEZ: If that were the case, I believe you would report it to me or to Mr. Church.

TOP: Sure. Maybe. Probably. But I can't trust whether
I'm right or wrong about it. And that's what I dream
about. That Colonel Ledger goes into the Darkness
again. No, that's wrong. That's not it. It's that he
never **left** the Darkness and it's still there, still
running him, and I can't see clearly enough to know for
sure.

INTERLUDE 7
THE MANSION
UNDISCLOSED LOCATION
TWO YEARS AGO

Mr. October watched Mary sleep.

It was something he did. There was nothing sexual about it. He was not that kind of person. The emotions he felt were older, stranger, more complex, less open to natural interpretation or categorization—even to himself.

He watched.

And he learned.

When she had been brought to him from Site 44, she was completely inert, her body frozen, utterly still.

Her mind, though . . .

That was what had called to him from far away. It was not a feeling, per se. Not a voice calling out of the darkness, not a ghost haunting him. Nothing so mundane.

No, what drew him was the fire.

Her flame.

Faint at first, barely a spark. Even then, though, that spark was more like molten steel than burning wood. Stronger, denser, angrier.

He had been in California the first time he saw it. Not yet using the name *October*. Sitting by a pool around midnight. No lights on anywhere. Even the moon and stars were absent, obscured by heavy clouds. For a brief moment, he thought he was seeing a firefly out there among the hedges around the pool.

Then October realized that it was all in *his* mind.

That light.

The heat it gave, however small.

It was the birth of his awareness of her.

He had, of course, been aware of her movements before—in Atlanta and elsewhere—when she wore the name of a master manipulator who took the cartoon name of Mother Night. Everyone knew of her because she'd forced that awareness onto the world by hacking into the twenty-four-hour news feeds and across the internet. The black bob haircut, the bee-stung red lips, the manga-styled clothes, and the smoky voice that was both coaxing and condescending. Even though she used proxies—women of a variety of Asian ethnic backgrounds for her posts—the essence of her came through. He even recalled that first message she broadcast . . .

"Okay, monkeys, pay attention 'cause there are three things you need to know, and Mother Night is here to tell you," she said. *"First, if we do not all rise up against globalization, then we do not deserve to be free of the shackles welded around our necks by groups like the World Trade Organization, the Group of Eight, the World Economic Forum, and others like them. We are slaves only if we allow ourselves to be slaves. We are free if we take to the streets and take the streets back. Occupy Wall Street failed because there were too many do-nothing pussies. That wasn't anarchy. The pigs in the system haven't seen anarchy. Not yet. But it's coming. The only action is direct action."*

A bold opening statement. Then . . .

"Second, because complacency is not only a symptom of a corrupt society, it's also a cry for help, I am going to shake things up. Will it take the sacrifice of one in three hundred to force the pigs in power to let true freedom ring?"

October remembered how Mother Night paused to smile. She had perfect white teeth, but smiling transformed her from a pretty girl to something else, something unlovely. The effect was transformative in a chilling way. It was a sardonic, skeletal, mocking grin, a leer that was hungry and ugly. But he loved it.

She closed with . . .

"Third, Mother Night wants to tell all of her children, everyone within the sound of my voice, all of the sleeping dragons waiting to rise—now is the time. Step out of the shadows. Be seen, be heard. Let your glow cast enough light even for the blind to see. 'Cause remember, kids, sometimes you have to burn to shine."

"Burn to shine," October said to the velvet darkness.

He knew then, with perfect clarity, that the light he saw was her light—struggling to stay alight in the vastness of eternal darkness.

Yet the light had faded, and he thought she was gone.

Then, in Canada, at the close of his takeover of the Kuga organization, when he was shucking his identity of John the Revelator, he had seen that light again. Stronger. Somehow insistent. Burning with an aching need to be seen.

And October saw.

Yes, he saw.

It was because of that second, more urgent light that he began to investigate Mother Night and the woman behind the costume and rhetoric. Discovering by slow degrees the brilliance of Artemisia Bliss. Revered then reviled, arrested for stealing technology and secrets from cases worked by the Department of Military Sciences. Rejected by St. Germaine and his people for her betrayal. Locked away . . . and then murdered in prison.

Except she wasn't. That turned out to be an enormously subtle yet elaborate ruse to fake her death.

Since then, he had used the resources of the Kuga organization—*his* organization now—to find her. To free her, even if that was merely to steal a corpse from cryonic storage in an off-book biohazard R & D facility.

Now she was alive again. If "alive" was the right word. Even October wasn't sure what label to use. Undead? Living dead? Living ghost? Revenant?

There were a lot of possible labels, but none really seemed to fit. She wasn't something out of a horror movie. She wasn't like anything that had ever been, and October found that endlessly fascinating.

Now she wanted to be called Mary. *Typhoid* Mary, really, leaning into her love of drama and obfuscation. Miss Mary at home.

Her attempt at suicide was heartbreaking and interesting in equal measures. He had learned so much about her from that incident. The doctor he'd brought was an old ally whom he had already briefed on her unusual metabolism. The doctor was still shocked and frightened, but he did good work. Every bone was where it should be. Muscles and nerves had been stitched. And the RFID chip had been implanted in the thin layer of fat on the underside of her upper arm. The skin was already healing over the tiny insertion point.

October had been able to gaze into the fire inside her mind. It was not true telepathy—even he could not do that. It was his knack for an imposed empathy of a kind that ran very deep and told much.

After a few hours, that flame, and all the insight it offered, had guttered.

When he cut her down and brought her back once more, he was dismayed—even horrified—that the fire was there, but the empathic connection was not. It was like viewing fire through soundproof glass. Shatterproof. Silent. Secret.

October watched her sleep and tried to read any part of her thoughts. He tried to sense her emotions.

It was like trying to read the mood of a burning house. It told him nothing.

Not a single thing.

It was like trying to read Joe Ledger's mind. Or, worse, St. Germaine's. Each of them had furnaces for minds.

Somehow, Mary's was worse.

Far, far worse.

As he watched and the hours passed, he tried to determine if that was a good thing or not. He wanted to let her set fires, because fire was the loving hand of chaos. It burned and in burning imposed change on whatever it touched. Change was the heart of chaos.

Yet he was afraid that he might be underestimating Miss Mary. There was no way to tell if she could control her fires.

Or if she wanted to.

"What have you become, little girl?" he murmured. "What do you want out of this new life you've been given?"

In her sleep, Typhoid Mary moaned softly.

And why am I drawn to your flame? wondered Mr. October.

CHAPTER 16
THE MANSION
UNDISCLOSED LOCATION
SEVEN MONTHS AGO

"Okay," said Mr. Toombs, "you sprang me from prison, took me to the ass end of nowhere, and now I'm living in a haunted house. Or an asylum. Jury's out on which. Is there a point to all of this?"

He sat in an armchair whose cushions were far too soft. To keep from sinking into it—a position guaranteed to cancel out any rapid physical actions—he perched on the edge. Not a dignified posture, but at least he could make a break for the door or the big french windows.

The insane Asian woman sat cross-legged on the center cushion of a long leather couch. She wore a soiled pale pink slip and apparently nothing else. She had positioned herself so he could have an unrestricted view under the slip, but Toombs was neither aroused nor fooled. It was a trick, and there had been nothing but tricks since October brought him to the house.

As for the patron himself, October stood behind the couch, leaning on the back with both hands. Toombs wondered if that position was intended to suggest that the woman, Mary, was in charge and not he. Or maybe he was as repelled by the deliberate and aggressive sexual display as Toombs.

"Of course there's a point," said October mildly.

"He's boring," said Mary. "He's a stiff."

"He has restraint and composure, my dear," soothed October, though he gave Toombs a covert wink. It was not a small one, but a large, deliberately comical one.

Toombs wished he had a gun.

He nearly wished he was back in Mr. Church's prison.

"He isn't very grateful," grumped Mary.

"Oh, don't get me wrong, miss," Toombs said. "I'm happy as hell to be out of jail. Happy to be breathing free air. No, what I am is confused. Deeply and profoundly. *Why* did you break me out? Let alone, how. Why am I here? What is it you want me to do?"

"Right to the point," said October. "Fair enough. And I apologize for the games, my friend. Funny, though, that you called this a haunted house."

"Funny how?"

"Oh," said October airily, "we're in an area known for its spooks and specters. This house, for example, is widely regarded as haunted by the people who lived near here. They even burned it down once, but I had it rebuilt."

Toombs said nothing.

"And, who knows, maybe there are some spirits lingering here."

"There are," said Mary emphatically. "They talk to me at night, sometimes."

Unseen by Mary, October twirled his finger by his temple and rolled his eyes.

"And . . . ?" prompted Toombs. His patience was as thin as tissue paper and his nerves completely raw.

"And no one will ever look for any of us here," said October. "Why would they?"

"Given that I don't know who either of you are, how can I answer that?"

October chuckled. "Okay, no more games. Here's the bottom line, Mr. Toombs. You worked for Dzhabrail Mitrishev's outfit in Chechnya, and then for the Turkish arms dealer Tugay Şükür. After that, you went to work for Jason Aydelotte."

Toombs merely shrugged.

"All three of those men are dead," said October.

Toombs shrugged again. "Fair to say that's the *risk* part of the risk/reward thing. We're bad guys and criminals. Life expectancy isn't typically high."

"Without a doubt. And please don't assume my observation comes with criticism."

"Okay."

"We are *also* criminals. Big shock to you, I know." October laughed. "Let's face it, the Kuga organization isn't an institution devoted to good works."

Toombs offered a small smile. "True enough. Let me ask, though, does that mean I can assume Bolton is really dead like people say? And you're the one who killed him? Or maybe had it done?"

"He's quick," said Mary, and for a moment, her little-girl-insane aspect flickered. Toombs caught a hardness and clarity in her eyes. There and gone, leaving him with the question as to whether the non-sense aspect was only a façade intended to keep men off-balance or if she was shuttling back and forth between sanity and madness. Discovering the answer to that would matter, and he knew it.

"His reputation precedes him," agreed October. To Toombs, he said, "Dear old Harcourt had many uses, among them an extensive list of contacts within certain global communities. Those contacts allowed him to purchase items in bulk and resell them at a considerable profit."

Toombs nodded.

"His unfortunate demise, though necessary at the time, left some gaps in communication with some key players. I could, of course, rebuild them, but not in a way that supports the timeline of certain projects currently in motion."

"Okay."

"It is my understanding that you have long-standing connections with many of these individuals. You are known and respected in the trade."

"And you heard about me from whom . . . ?"

October's eyes seemed to blur for a moment, shifting in a swirl of colors. Toombs glanced at the window to see if it was a trick of the sunlight that slanted through the glass, but the angle was wrong, and when he looked back, the man's eyes were entirely normal.

"Hugo Vox," said Mr. October.

"You knew Vox?"

"Oh, we were very good friends. We played some delicious games together."

"Let me guess . . . the *Sea of Hope* thing? The Red Order in Iran?"

"Those and others."

"And you know I was involved in both of those," said Toombs.

The *Sea of Hope* was a celebrity cruise some years ago. The children of the current president at that time were nearly killed, as were many chart-topping performers and other important people in politics and entertainment.

The Red Order was an ancient group that had splintered off from the Knights Hospitaller back in the era of the Crusades. They were involved in thousands of political and religious murders and were rumored to work with the Red Knights, a cult of genetically altered killers who claimed to be vampires. Those Knights had taken to living in shadows and drinking blood and were widely believed to be the basis for belief in vampires, though Toombs had it on good authority there was nothing at all supernatural about the cult. Scary, though.

Vox had been involved with both groups and with dozens of others, either as a founding member of the Seven Kings terrorist organization or on solo ventures. No one had been more powerful, influential, well connected, or trusted than Hugo Vox. Whole governments had leaned on him as the safest bet to vet candidates for top secret positions. "Vetted by Vox" was a phrase that meant something. Until, of course, it came out that he was a master criminal. *The New York Times* had labeled him "the Modern Moriarty."

Vox, like the other traitor, Harcourt Bolton, was believed to be dead.

"I never worked directly for Hugo Vox," said Toombs. "Where are you going with this?"

October cocked his head to one side and gave Toombs an appraising look. "What would your guess be?"

"There's only one thing of Vox's that still has a significant dollar value attached to it," Toombs said. "Something that could help any Vox wannabe to throw some very heavy punches."

"Say it."

"The Passkey."

October's smile was radiant. So, too, was Mary's.

"The Passkey is very important, my friend," said October. "It exists. It's how Vox kept track of his money, his numbered accounts, the movements of currencies. All that. And it has information on all the people he kept on leashes. The ones he had blackmail info on, the people he could turn dials on. The Passkey is the golden fleece."

"And you want that?"

"I do," said October, but his tone was diffident. "Not only the money, though I am unabashedly greedy. The clink-clink of gold coins, the rustle of crisp bills, the ones and zeroes of cryptocurrency. All quite yummy. And very useful because—let's face it, my friend—

there's a war coming. Not between nation-states but between ideologies. We have been recruiting and training hundreds of soldiers, and although they are armed with top-quality handguns, rifles, and other weapons, these items are conventional. They aren't enough to give, say, a small militia the firepower to take on an entire National Guard unit."

"That's hardly news. That kettle's been on a high burner since the 2010s."

"We have weapons stockpiled. The Passkey also has information on the buyers Vox trusted most. People with whom the Kuga organization doesn't *yet* have a connection. We want them to purchase our toys and then *use* them to create a little chaos here in the States and elsewhere. Nothing does the economy better than ongoing wars. When Harcourt Bolton ran Kuga, he built it up, but he never seemed able to break through the glass ceiling. I want you to be my hammer to do just that. Obtaining the Passkey would make it all the more fun and profitable."

"As entertaining as that is, sir," said Toombs, "I have no idea where the Passkey is. If I had, I'd never have taken the gig with Aydelotte and would have gone solo and made a couple of billion dollars, then retired to Aruba."

October leaned forward. "But you know people who *might* know. Or people who can find out."

Toombs gave that a three-count. "Maybe."

Mary spoke up, her eyes clear and sharp again. "Where would you start?"

Toombs didn't answer her.

October said, "She asks a serious question."

"It becomes more interesting when there is a deal in place between us. Right now, I owe you a solid for breaking me out. I'll repay that debt, but the Passkey isn't how I'll do it. You have more faith in my old contacts than I do. I'm looking for a new start, a safe home, and a clear plan. Offer me a deal or take me back to the clink."

Mr. October clapped his hands in delight. "God, how I love a man who understands the importance of things and wants to keep his quacking ducks in a neat little row. You want an offer, then here it is."

He reached into an inner pocket and removed a thick sheaf of documents, then spread them out onto the table. They were bearer bonds.

"If you look close," he said, "you'll see that these bonds were issued in the late 1970s, before the US government ceased their issuance. These are absolutely clean, and as you'll see, there is an appropriate amount of zeros on each."

Toombs leaned forward and tapped the bonds apart so he could see the values and dates. His calculator brain did the arithmetic. Two-point-five million.

He leaned back and crossed his legs. "It's light," he said. "I made more than that from Aydelotte, and he fucked me over. He screwed everyone he worked for. My trust is going to come at a higher dollar amount."

"It's a signing bonus," said October. "Call it an incentive program. Together, we can find who has the Passkey, and you will devise a way to get said person to unlock it and pour money into our coffers. To that end, I will provide you with the very best weapons and equipment to sell. Some of which, by the way, were once in Jason Aydelotte's catalog. The Gorgon comes to mind."

"I'm listening," said Toombs.

October gestured to the bearer bonds. "If you can help me find whoever has Vox's Passkey and arrange the sale, delivery, and the training for the buyers, then you will earn ten times that amount. In bonds or via money transferred to the numbered account of your choosing. I have a project in the works under the code name Firefall. Gaudy, I know, but Mary likes it. When all of the necessary sales are handled and the buyers trained in how to use Gorgon and other toys, then you retire, fly to Aruba, and forget everything about everything. Buy a nice house, watch the iguanas, live the quiet life. Twenty-five million will buy a lot of anonymity."

Toombs considered for a full minute, aware of Mary and October studying him.

Finally, he said, "I know of a guy who—if he's still alive—might know something useful. I could start with him, but it might take a few months to find him and set up a meet. If he's even still alive."

"Which guy would that be?" asked October.

"Alexander Chismer," said Toombs. "Most people call him Toys."

CHAPTER 17
ST. REGIS HOTEL
325 BAY STREET
TORONTO, ONTARIO
TWO MONTHS AGO

"I thought you were dead," said the little woman.

"Yeah," said the young Brit, "I get that a lot."

"Is that a Snake Plissken line?"

"Who?"

"*Escape from New York*? Kurt Russell . . . ?"

The young man smiled as he took a sip from a martini glass. "Sorry, pet, but I'm not much into American cinema."

The woman, who was not quite four foot ten, took a micro sip from her Bloody Mary. She was dressed in a tweed suit that was appropriate to the brisk autumn breeze outside but looked thirty years out of style. Her hair was a confection of frosted curls intended to give her height.

"No," she said. "It wasn't a line cribbed from a movie. *Everyone* thinks you're dead."

"Perhaps I'm a ghost," he replied.

He wore a medium-weight Canali solid wool two-piece in a muted steel gray and knew he looked damn good in it. He had the narrow waist and broad shoulders to sell the suit and long legs to make it walk well.

They sat at the bar in the St. Regis, each pretending to drink their drinks, but each nursing them to maintain clarity of mind. Outside, the business types were hurrying back to work after drinking their lunch. Inside, the bar was warm, and there was low-key jazz playing from discreet speakers of good fidelity. It was some old Brubeck stuff that was ambitious and entertaining, and loud enough to allow for moderate privacy but not so loud anyone had to raise their voice.

"Where have you been, Toys?" asked the woman. Then she touched her fingers to her lips in a fair bit of theatrics intended to show she was immediately contrite. "Oh god," she said in a more confidential whisper, "I suppose I shouldn't have said your name aloud."

He chuckled. "Oh, no one cares, Maudie. Unlike a fair few of our friends, I'm not wanted for anything. Never been arrested, never charged, and my computer monkeys tell me I'm on no one's watch list."

"I'm so glad to hear that."

Liar, he thought.

Maudie McPherson was in her late forties but fighting it well enough with massage, excellent makeup skillfully applied, and a few Los Angeles facelifts of the kind that did not leave her looking like a mildly astonished duck. Her jewelry bordered on ostentatious, with a drop pendant that had to be at least three full carats and high-end gemstones in the various rings she wore. She placed a hand on his forearm.

Aloud, Toys said, "As to where I've been . . . with all that happened with my former employers, I felt it best to go off the radar for a bit. Let things cool down. But when I found out that no one was looking for me, I came out of my cave, and here I am."

"And by 'cave,' you mean . . . ?"

"Island life has its charms," he said with a vague flick of a few fingers.

When it was clear he was not going to elaborate, Maudie said, "I was equal parts surprised and delighted when you reached out."

"How lovely," he said. "And here I thought I'd been forgotten."

"Forgotten? Toys? God, no. The authorities might not be looking for you, but a lot of the people we both know have been wondering. We thought you might be either in some American black site getting waterboarded or buried under the rubble of what had been Hugo Vox's old fortress in Singer Castle on that island in the Saint Lawrence River."

"Heaven forfend," he said, faking a laugh. "I was busy with a few, shall we say, *errands* for Hugo. I was in Chechnya when he died."

Maudie studied his face. "Then Hugo is actually dead? His body was never recovered. Most of the people I know think he's in hiding."

Nice try, you cow, he thought. "He's dead as far as I know. If he were alive, I daresay I *would* know."

"But you're not sure?" she pushed. "Did you see the body?"

"Oh yes, he had me on FaceTime when they killed him. He hoped his grand demise would trend on social media."

There was a beat.

"You're joking, of course."

Toys only raised one cynical eyebrow.

"Sorry," said Maudie.

Toys took the opportunity to shift the direction. "Just between you, me, and my therapist, I often wonder if I could have helped him get out of there, had I not been so far away. It guts me that I couldn't help after all he did for me."

Maudie used her celery to stir her drink. "There were rumors that he was in Iran, working with the Red Order after all that."

Toys snorted. "So I've been told."

"But you don't believe it?"

"I *want* to," he said. "But I've followed five or six different leads, and they were all shite. He's like bloody Elvis. Everyone sees him everywhere."

"Except you."

"Except me. And I tell you again, Maudie, if Hugo were alive, I'd know."

She studied him, and he allowed it. This was all moving nicely toward the right moment.

"Excuse me for being so nosy on this point," said Maudie, "but there were a lot of people who worked with Hugo. People as close to him as you were. Given that, why would Hugo single *you* out as the one he would have contacted?"

Toys leaned closer and constructed an expression of mingled pain, love, and anger. "Because we were like family."

"He was family with Zephyr Bain and a few others . . ."

"If they were as close, then why didn't Hugo give them the Passkey?"

Maudie went dead still, and her face drained of color behind the layers of foundation. Her lips formed the word *Passkey*.

"Are you saying . . . I mean, he really gave you the . . ."

"Yes," said Toys. "Me. And only me."

"Everyone's been looking for the Passkey for years."

"No doubt," said Toys. "The greedy bastards."

"And you're saying you actually *have* it?"

Toys leaned back and sipped his martini. "Yes," he said. "And that's why I reached out to you, my pet. Because I think it's time to use it."

The Passkey was a computer program that allowed the owner to access hundreds of numbered accounts that, collectively, equaled close to a hundred billion dollars. Vox set it up with two access points—one was a computer-controlled payment system to provide funds for the thousands of people who worked for him. Most of them were not aware that they were part of Vox's empire, and many of those had never heard the name *Hugo Vox*. But the companies that owned the companies that issued their paychecks were set up by Vox.

Very efficient, and it allowed a lot of projects to remain in idle mode, ready for the person who controlled the second access point to call the shots. Vox's genius had been in the long game. He established networks and created infrastructure so that when he put a plan into operation, it rang no bells and proceeded with the same quiet and even mundane regularity as it had for years.

The same was true for those key players over whom Vox had control, either because of the possession of critical blackmail material or through extortion and coercion, with paid teams keeping tabs on the marks and every now and then reminding those people that they were always on call. Had Vox lived, many of those idle operations would have been moved to active status.

Naturally, in the years since Vox's death, some of the people controlled through pressure died, were voted out of office, or became of no use because key circumstances changed. In those cases, teams on standby were given automatic cleanup orders.

Very neat, very tidy.

Once more, Maudie rested a hand on his forearm. "If you have the Passkey and are reaching out to old friends," she said, "does this mean *you* will be taking over for Hugo?"

Toys gave her his most disarming smile. "What do you think?"

"I think you are," she said, giving his arm a squeeze and then letting her hand linger there, soft and warm. "And I'm glad you came to me."

"We're friends, Maudie," said Toys, laying one hand over hers. "You always played straight with me. And you always had the best toys for sale."

Friends was a key word, and Toys watched the way she dealt with it. He wanted her to think that he'd come to her first and maybe even offered favored-nation status, while at the same time playing hard to get. Maudie, he knew, had always been a tough negotiator, but she was insecure and therefore vulnerable. Not to flattery, per se, but to a suggestion of trust, intimacy, or personal connection. He had used that against her before, back when she was selling short-duration chemical weapons to the Seven Kings. Now, with more years carved into her flesh—even if the facelifts hid it—Toys knew that her Achilles' heel was still as vulnerable as ever.

For her part, Maudie was clearly balancing her emotional reaction to the word *friends*—a word overused in their trade but treasured when truly meant—with her desire to make a deal that would benefit her employer, but also create a new vendor-client relationship. There was so much money in the Passkey that she could construct big enough deals to finance an early retirement.

"Can you tell me what you're shopping for?" she asked in the best business tone she could manage. "And then I can tell you how I can put an even brighter smile on your face."

"Man-portable rocket launchers," said Toys.

"Only that?" said Maudie, affecting to look disappointed.

"I'm not talking about off-the-rack dreck like standard RPGs or even LAW rockets, sweetie." He leaned closer. "Rumor control has it that a certain former friend of Hugo's had developed something special. The Gorgon. A missile that can be fired from an ordinary RPG. Something with a guidance chip and a warhead capable of delivering a liquid payload. Delivering it in such a way as to keep the contents viable without the airburst frying the goods."

Maudie's face became wooden, but her eyes were filled with new light. "Oh? And where did you hear about that?"

"Oh," said Toys with a casual flick of his hand, "here and there."

"No," she said with a bit more force, "*where.*"

Toys shrugged. "I suppose I can tell *you*, sweetie. I had been looking to buy some earlier this year. A friend of a friend was about to set up a meeting between me and a chap named Toombs. Tall, pale, zombie-looking bloke. He was working for Jason Aydelotte, and rumor control has it that it was Aydelotte's pet software genius, Marco Russo, who'd developed the Gorgon system. When things came crashing down and those RTI goons smashed Aydelotte's operation, my contacts melted away. I *still* need those rockets, and new rumors have been whispering the name of someone calling himself Mr. October."

She sipped and said nothing.

"This October person runs a PMC group called Tenth Legion—again, according to rumors—and they are buying some items that were not scooped up by either RTI or Mossad."

"Who is spreading these rumors?"

"Oh, honey, you ask that as if I'm likely to actually answer. Be your age."

Maudie sipped to hide a smile.

Toys said, "One additional rumor is that October is either in bed with whomever has taken over the Kuga organization or actually *is* Kuga."

"As for that," said Maudie, "I honestly don't know."

Toys nodded, believing her on that point. "And the rest . . . ?"

"Some rumors are based on truth," she said.

"Does that mean you have the Gorgons for sale? And can we waltz into the haggling phase of tonight's dance card?"

"Well," said Maudie, "before we discuss whether such items are available, we need to clear one hurdle."

"Which is?"

"The payloads are already prefilled. The contents cannot be changed because of a fail-safe built into the warhead. A master chip, in fact, that will detonate it if the warhead is tampered with in any way."

"And would that payload make anyone in its blast radius go bonkers?" said Toys. "What's the American expression—tripping balls?"

Maudie brightened. "You *have* done your homework."

"Hugo and Sebastian didn't hire me *just* for my looks."

"I think we might have exactly what you're looking for," she said.

And in Toys's ear, the voice of Scott Wilson said, "Perfect."

CHAPTER 18
COMFORT SUITES ATLANTIC CITY NORTH
ABSECON, NEW JERSEY

The five of us—plus two slumbering prisoners and one big, shaggy combat dog—were in my hotel room near Atlantic City.

Belle sat cross-legged on the floor, with Ghost's head in her lap. She had become even more taciturn since Andrea died, and somehow that made Ghost want to comfort her. And likely take comfort *from* her. Belle and Andrea had been unlikely friends, but true ones, and she was taking his loss hard. You'd have to know her to see it, though. She mastered the poker face she habitually wore while a prisoner in a genital mutilation and "behavior training" camp in her native Mauritania. Violin and an Arklight team had liberated her, recruited her, trained her, and recommended her to me for Havoc.

She stroked Ghost's thick pelt with long, slow movements that sent my dog into some canine paradise. Frankly, the rhythm and pace were luring me to the edge of hypnosis, too.

Remy sat at the foot of the bed, studying the two legionnaires with unreadable eyes. He was the youngest active field team member in RTI, and there was still a lot to learn about him. He had that smooth Cajun accent and boyish good looks, but to those of us whose ability to read people was a survival skill, I could tell there were layers and layers to him. Much to learn, and every day—every moment of necessary drama—taught me something.

Bunny sat on the floor with his back to a bureau, hands dangling loose over the ends of his knees and a plastic bottle of vending machine cola by one ankle. He was young, too, but far older than Remy in experience. He had a lot of scars that were mostly hidden beneath his beach volleyball tan. He caught my eye and gave me a single, small nod.

Top stood, leaning a shoulder against the frame of the interconnecting door, a kitchen match slowly bobbing between his strong white teeth. There was a bland and meaningless smile on his mouth, and his eyes were half-closed as if in deep thought.

"So, what's the plan, boss?" asked Bunny. "Go to a casino and spend our retirement money on rigged slots? Go canoeing in one of the cedar-water streams near Batsto? Maybe hit the beach in AC and see if we can get a bocce ball game going with retired mobsters?"

"Wouldn't that all be nice," said Top sourly.

"Worth asking," Bunny said.

"Truth is that right now this is all on Bug," I said. "Even he needs time to go through whatever he pulled from the cell phones. Wilson is probably scrambling, too. With the mess we left behind, he's probably on the phone to one of Church's friends in—"

"—the industry," they all said, finishing it for me.

It is a remarkable and inexplicable fact of life that Church seems to have key friends in the most useful places. I've even tried to hoodwink him on this, requesting a trained bear, a retired ballerina, and a hundred pounds of red M&M's for a mission. He provided all three within twenty-four hours. I later found out that the M&M's came out of my pay. Oddly, not the bear or ballerina.

As if waiting for his cue, Bug pinged us.

"Go for Outlaw," I said. "Team's all here, and we have two hostiles, both dosed with Sandman."

"Looks like you guys had some fun," he said. "Half the first responders in South Jersey are at the trailer park."

"Yeah, well, things got weird."

"Weird? With you and Havoc?" said Bug dryly. "That *never* happens."

"Bug . . ."

"Yeah, okay," he said. "So, we're wired into all the calls from police, fire, and EMTs," said Bug. "They found seventeen unconscious men and four KIAs at the trailer park."

I glanced at Belle, who offered me the blandest of *Who me?* smiles.

"Sounds right," said Top. "We know anything about these assholes?"

"We picked images from your body cams, Top, and are running them through facial recognition. So far, they're all exactly what we expected to find. Six from Blue Diamond; the rest are a mixed bag of ex-military and low-level thugs. Some felony counts in their backstory, and for others, there are arrests but no convictions. So far, though, all of them are in the system."

I asked, "What about the ones who ran off?"

"That's going to take longer. All of the trailers in that park belong to a shell company that's owned by another shell company that's owned by Tenth Legion."

Top chewed his matchstick from one corner of his mouth to the other. "Color me shocked."

"However," said Bug, "Gator Bait's owl drones have been taking some good shots of license plates of the vehicles in the area, and I have someone running those. Nikki's running facial recognition on everyone."

"Let me give you two more," I said and sent them pics of the sleeping beauties.

It took Bug maybe thirty seconds, and half of that was probably him opening a new can of Red Bull.

"Guy on the left is Andrew Kemmer, twenty-nine. Did three years in the army and was dishonorably discharged for theft of military property. Because it was minor stuff—communications gear, not weapons—they just kicked him to the curb instead of prosecuting him. He went to work for Blue Diamond a couple of months before we took it down and has been off the radar since."

There was a pause, then he came back on the call.

"Guy on the right is Stuart Huberman, thirty-three. No military background, but get this. He was a youth pastor for a group in Lancaster County, Pennsylvania, and was convicted of aggravated indecent assault of a person younger than sixteen, corruption of minors, possession of kiddie porn, and unlawful contact with a minor. Those crimes involved seven girls ranging in age from twelve to fifteen. He was sentenced to seventeen years but served three and a half before getting cut loose for—and I pause here to gag—*good behavior*. Been working for an HVAC company since."

"Couple of real upstanding citizens," murmured Top. His default setting was that of a kind, compassionate, empathetic guy looking at middle age. He was someone else entirely when it came to harm being done to the innocent, particularly the young.

Bunny was a new father of a little girl, so you can guess where his sympathies lay. Belle had been in that Mauritanian female genital mutilation camp. And when I was a teenager, my girlfriend Helen and I were attacked—I was beaten half to death, and she was gangraped and brutalized, resulting in her eventual suicide.

It was fair to say that Huberman would realize, upon wakening, that he had no friends in that room.

As for Remy, I don't know his full backstory, but he wouldn't have passed Top's screening if he wasn't standing on the same ground as the rest of us. Not everyone needs to experience trauma in order to understand the extent of the damage that continually comes to the innocent. The cold, reptilian look in his eyes assured me of that.

"Bug, did you warn the first responders about the booby trap?"

"The boss did. He made some calls to some friends and made sure that no one went into any of the motor homes. Bomb squad is on scene now, and get this—four other double-wides were rigged the same way. That counts as domestic terrorism—apart from all of the ATF violations—so there's a crew from Homeland inbound. ATF and DEA are sending agents, too."

"Good. Maybe they can figure out what triggered that bomb. Couldn't have been a pressure trigger; otherwise, Norris would have blown his dick off first time he went to the fridge for a beer."

"I'll make sure to pass that along. Oh, wait, hold on, here's the boss now."

The next voice we heard was that of Mr. Church.

"Is everyone on comms?" he asked. When I assured him they were, he said, "Today was an exceptionally challenging one, and I would like to commend you all for the way you deported yourselves. Training takes a soldier only so far, and then there is a need for natural intelligence, insight, and decisive reactions. This could have been a disaster, but it was not. That says a lot for the distance traveled since Jerusalem."

No one looked at one another because we were all, I think, looking inside ourselves. This was the first real comment Church had made about the psychological effects of what we'd all been through. His saying it spoke as much to his own healing as to ours, and it mattered that he said it.

"While Grendel, Bug, and the rest of the team here work through the information we have obtained," he continued, "I would like you to proceed with reviving and interrogating the prisoners."

"What do we do with them when we're done?" asked Bunny.

There was a beat. "A team will be sent to retrieve them."

This time, we all *did* exchange a look. There were only two teams based in this general neck of the woods. One was the Boy Scouts in Baltimore, run by former DMS sniper Sam Imura, but they were currently on an op in North Dakota. The other team was Medusa Team, one of Arklight's most notorious groups. It was run by Empusa, an interrogator who would give the torturers of the Spanish Inquisition nightmares.

Bunny gave a low whistle. "Sucks to be these guys."

"Empusa can have what's left," I said and ended the call. "Prep the bed."

I dug a pair of syrettes of what Doc Holliday lovingly calls *Wakey-Wakey*. It's a wild concoction of atipamezole, physostigmine, rimonabant, and flumazenil to counteract Sandman, then a little amphetamine and a drug for narcolepsy called *modafinil* to wake them up. There's other stuff in there that I don't understand. God only knows what else. Eye of newt, blood of the innocent—who the hell knows *what* Doc and her chief henchman, Dr. Ronald Coleman, put into it. They are actual mad scientists, make no mistake.

The stuff counteracts the effects of Sandman, but don't be fooled. It's not like a puppy nuzzling you to wake up on a lazy Sunday morning. It's not even as nice as being slapped awake. Wakey-Wakey basically pours gasoline into your central nervous system and tosses in a match. You wake up right now, and you absolutely hate it.

Bunny, Belle, and Remy worked together. Bunny lifted the sleepers off the bed so the others could spread black plastic sheeting under them. They wrapped more of the plastic around both men so that they looked like they were wearing a particularly ugly set of Depends. Then they fetched two wire trash cans from the other room and lined them with heavy plastic bags. Wakey-Wakey has some unpleasant side effects.

As soon as they were done, I jabbed the first guy. Kemmer.

It takes about ten seconds for the drug to kick in. Then his body arched upward like he was getting an electric shock. His bladder and bowels cut loose, and he also threw up. Remy was right there to catch it in one of the cans. Top, totally nonchalant, stood next to me smearing peppermint gel under his nose to kill the smell. When he was done, he nudged me with an elbow and offered it to me. I took some. We all did.

Ghost, however, thought it all smelled wonderful.

Kemmer came awake, rising from nightmare into waking hell.

Our smiles did absolutely nothing to calm his terrors.

INTERLUDE 8
THE MANSION
UNDISCLOSED LOCATION
TWENTY-TWO MONTHS AGO

Miss Mary healed.

It took three weeks, but her neck healed.

By the fifth day, she could even bathe herself and use the toilet without making a mess. He made sure Alejandra was with her; the Ecuadorian maid was skilled at more than cooking food and doing laundry. Back when she ran with the charmingly named Grupos de Combatientes Populares in her home country, Alejandra had slit throats and participated in torture sessions of men, women, and children. She was a horror of a person, absolutely without conscience or regret. October found her delightful.

Alejandra made sure that the patient did herself no further harm. But even she had a day off now and then.

Mary was patient, and she waited for her moment, then took it.

The baggie of fentanyl was in Alejandra's closet, way in the back, nicely hidden. But the young woman was so very smart. She understood how people thought and followed a chain of logic until she found something. She had been looking for a gun but discovered 611 tablets of the synthetic opioid. Two milligrams was considered a lethal dose for most people. She took every single pill, washing them down with tap water.

Mr. October came home from a meeting to find her curled in a ball on her bathroom floor, surrounded by a small lake of vomit, her body twitching.

He sighed, called Alejandra, and, when the woman arrived, told her to clean the patient and dress Mary in fresh clothes.

That was the last suicide attempt.

October sat with her all through the night, waiting as the residual effects wore off and her mind cleared. Her awareness of having failed again to take her own life made her cry. He waited out the tears. Then, at around three in the morning, when the house was utterly quiet and the wind had gone to sleep, he said, "You must accept that you cannot die. It will be easier and less embarrassing for us both if you do."

"Why can't I die?" she demanded.

"Oh, you know the answer to that. You told me that you had your memories back now. All of them. You know that you took generation 12 of the pathogen."

But she shook her head.

"Surely you did," he insisted.

"No. I gave that to some minions. Some Berserkers. But I never took Gen-12."

October crossed his legs and studied her. "I am rarely surprised, so please explain."

"When I worked for . . . *them* . . ." she said. She seldom mentioned the DMS in any explicit manner. "I collected samples from the various labs the teams took down. I was part of the team sent to the Middle East after Ledger hunted Amirah down."

"And . . . ?"

"And not everything was destroyed when Gault set off the geothermal meltdown."

"Now that is very interesting. Tell me, what did you find?"

Her eyes flicked toward his, then darted away. "Samples of untested generations of *seif al din*. Gen-12 lets you keep your memories, but your body still shuts down. Partly, I mean. The metabolism pulls back to protect the core functions, but you rot. It's like having Hansen's disease, advanced diabetes, and frostbite all at once. Fingers and toes. Other parts. I didn't want that. I found part of Amirah's notes. Not much. Just enough to understand where she was going. Her goal was to completely refine the pathogen so that it kept the body in peak physical condition while amping up the wound repair systems so that it was hard to . . . hard to . . ."

Her voice trailed off.

"Hard to kill," he supplied. "And you took one of these later generations?"

She was silent for a moment, then nodded. In a nearly silent whisper, she said, "The version I took was Gen-16."

Mr. October leaned back in his chair and considered her. "And now we both know why the fractured neck and severed spinal cord did not kill you. It *should* have. The fentanyl, too."

"I want to die."

He laughed. "Clearly, and yet . . . you can't. You can't even be seriously hurt. I wonder if your broken neck and spinal cord would have simply healed themselves without my doctor resetting your spine and stitching the cord. He labored over you for seventeen hours and is so proud of his work. Such a shame that it wasn't his doing at all."

She stared at him with haunted eyes. In a small, fragile voice, she begged, "Let me die."

"Even if I wanted to, I think we've crossed that bar. You *can't* die." He chuckled and shook his head. "You are your own Frankenstein, my dear."

She turned away to hide her tears.

"When you said that you regained your memories," he said after a pause, "do you remember when Ledger shot you?"

"*Yes.*" The word sounded as if it had been torn from her with pliers.

"Do you remember falling?"

"Yes."

"You fell a very long way, my dear," said October. "Half the height of the hotel. You shattered your skull, broke your back in four places, broke both legs, one arm, eleven ribs, your sternum, your scapula, and one collarbone. All of your organs were lacerated by bone shards. And yet . . ."

She kicked at him, but he evaded the blow.

"*What does that make me if not a monster?*" she shrieked.

"You are immortal."

"I'm not human."

"Well, my sweet little flower, neither am I."

CHAPTER 19
THE TOC
ONE MONTH AGO

Couple of things.

First, I don't like Toys.

I used to actually hate him. Now it's more like I tolerate his existence on this big blue spinning marble of a world. That tolerance is predicated on the knowledge that he is useful, that he's no longer actively evil, and that he is trying to do some good in the world. It's also ameliorated by the fact that he has saved the lives of Junie Flynn—the woman I love—and me. So, there's that in the plus category.

The con in this equation is that he used to be the reptilian right hand of world-class terrorists like Sebastian Gault and Hugo Vox. He has ended the lives of a lot of innocent people, either directly or indirectly. The balance sheet still has the red set against him.

I know he is aware of his sins and, in fact, regards them *as* sins. He holds himself to be irredeemable in both the ethical and religious senses of the word. He's a Catholic—no longer lapsed—who believes he is going to hell and deserves it.

My religious beliefs are mostly in the rearview mirror, but if he wants to burn, then fine. Let him burn.

Or not. It's not my call. If he keeps doing what Church wants, then yay team.

Mind you, if he came down with a case of scrotum lobsters, I wouldn't break down in tears.

Does that make me heartless, intractable, judgmental, officious, and unkind?

A case can be made.

Mr. Church is the one who decided—God knows why—that Toys was worth trying to save. Church has done this with a number of people, turning them away from the Dark Side of the Force and all that. I'm aware that the damage I suffered when I was a teen, and other damage since, has greatly colored my judgment. And, yes, I'm working some of that out in therapy with Rudy Sanchez.

All of that said, over the last year, Toys's usefulness has increased. Church allowed him to form a kind of Dirty Dozen: RTI Edition. The Wild Hunt, they're called. All choirboys like Toys, fighting on the side of the angels. Blah blah.

During the Cave 13 fiasco, I saved Toys's life. Later in that same case, he saved mine. What's interesting is that neither of us hesitated in the moment. We saved allies in this war. Allies do not have to be friends. They don't have to like each other.

A month ago, Toys dove into the international illegal arms community, ostensibly looking to return to his criminal ways. In reality, he and the Wild Hunt were undercover, with Toys using his old criminal connections to help us infiltrate the bad guys and gather intelligence.

His team had been chopped down to nearly nothing in Israel, and Toys was in the process of rebuilding it and training the newbies. Church—following his own schedule—kept pulling Toys away from that and sending him into the field. The meet with Maudie was the most successful of those.

Toys managed to acquire six Gorgons and in the process verify that Toombs was working with October. He also came away from that meeting with a stronger conviction that October and Kuga were the same person. Not a certainty, though. Call it a 51 percent likelihood, which is more than we had.

I was in the TOC with Scott Wilson during the negotiations.

We sat and listened to a series of discussions over three days, with the third day being the wire transfer of funds and then taking delivery of the Gorgons.

When it was all done, I got onto the comms channel and spoke to Toys.

"That was pretty good fieldwork," I said. "You earned your duplicity merit badge."

His response showed the depth of understanding and feeling that has grown between us. "Oh, sod off, you pillock."

You can feel the love.

CHAPTER 20

ANDERSON/CONLEY MEDIA
83 WALTON STREET NW
ATLANTA, GEORGIA
TWO WEEKS AGO

The woman did not look right.

Not at all.

Shawnette Harrison looked up from her terminal and saw her come in. It was ten minutes until the end of her shift, when Shawnette would magically transform from receptionist/scheduler to maid of honor with a plan. The girls were all planning on meeting at Tongue and Groove, a rap club where the bachelorette festivities were set to begin in less than an hour. All six of the bridesmaids would be there as well as fourteen other women in their circle. The headliner act tonight was L'il Drip, a bizarre goth-rap act who pretended to be a vampire and was sexy as hell. From there, the plans became sketchy, and if Miranda wasn't blackout drunk by midnight, then the girls weren't trying.

But this woman who walked in looked like she'd *already* been through a week's worth of such nights in a row. She was dressed in a business suit—a gorgeous Dolce & Gabbana double-breasted pin-stripe in charcoal with a pink camisole beneath. However, the suit was rumpled, and there were suspicious stains on it, and the right hip pocket was torn. Her hair was in a messy bun that wasn't styled to look that way but which had fallen apart. Her makeup was sloppy and smeared, with lipstick that was too intense a blood red and a concealer in a pasty shade of off-white.

The woman stopped just inside the main door and stood there, swaying a little, looking around as if uncertain where she was or why she was there.

Shawnette's immediate reaction of distaste faltered as she wondered if this woman had been in an accident. Or worse, had been assaulted.

"Ma'am . . . may I help you?"

The woman's head jerked around at the sound of her voice, and it seemed as if she just realized there was someone else in the otherwise empty lobby. She took a hesitating step forward. Her lips moved, but she said no actual words. Instead, her mouth moved as if she were chewing something. It was odd and unpleasant, and Shawnette's hand strayed in the direction of the security buzzer.

Then she seemed to recollect herself and walked unsteadily up to the desk.

"Is . . . Mrs. Anderson available?"

"Um . . . do you have an appointment?"

It was a simple question, but the woman looked troubled as if trying to calculate its meaning.

"Is she available?"

"Ma'am, do you have an appointment?" Shawnette glanced down

at the schedule for the last hour of business. There was nothing on it except a courier who was on his way with a contract for the company's in-house counsel.

The woman reached into her jacket and fumbled around for several seconds before finally producing a letter. Unlike her clothes, the envelope was crisp and official-looking, with the logo of one of the bigger Atlanta-based film companies on it. That changed the complexion of the moment. She held it out until Shawnette took it.

"If she's not available," said the woman, her voice oddly shaky, "then see she gets this."

Shawnette took it. "Mrs. Anderson only sees people by appointment, ma'am, but I'll make sure she gets this. Can I give her a name . . . ?"

The woman smiled. "Mary," she said.

The smile was strange. Bad strange. Crooked and flickering and even a little nasty.

Then she turned and shambled out.

Shawnette got up and walked to the door and watched the woman get into a black SUV that was parked directly outside. The car pulled away and vanished into the early rush hour traffic.

"Weird," she said aloud.

As she walked back to her desk, she studied the envelope she still held. It was slender, probably only a single page. When she got to her desk, she buzzed Mrs. Anderson's assistant and told her there was a delivery. Two minutes later, the elevator opened, and the assistant, a stick-thin blonde named Carly, took the envelope.

Carly and Shawnette were, at best, civil to each other. Never chatty, and so Shawnette didn't tell her much about the woman who called herself Mary.

There was nothing else of note that afternoon, and Shawnette closed down the lobby, tidied her desk, went to the ladies' room to freshen her makeup, and then headed out for an epic night with the girls.

The symptoms did not kick in for nearly an hour.

By nine forty that evening, she was in the hospital with nurses and doctors working over her as the machines went *ping* and *beep* in a symphony of failing organs.

CHAPTER 21

BARAKA SHAWARMA MEDITERRANEAN GRILL
68 WALTON STREET SW
ATLANTA, GEORGIA
TWO WEEKS AGO

"Mary . . ." said the man who stepped into her path.

The woman was about to pass the restaurant, and she twitched and yelped in surprise. When she turned toward the man, who was dressed in a tropical shirt with a pattern of turtles swimming in stylized waves, Mary regarded him with eyes that were glassy and vague.

"Y-yes . . . ?"

"How did it go?"

The young woman stood there, fidgeting, trying to straighten the torn pocket flap. Her lips twitched every few seconds.

"Go . . . ?" she asked.

"Did you deliver the envelope?"

"What? Oh. Yeah. I guess."

"You *guess*?"

Mary looked at him for a moment. "Who are you again?"

"David," he said. "David White. I brought you here."

"Oh. Yeah."

"Did you deliver the envelope?"

She looked down at her hands as if expecting to see something. After a moment, she nodded and looked up at him. "I gave it to her."

"To who? To Mrs. Anderson?"

"What? Um . . . no. To the receptionist."

White thought about that for a bit, then nodded. "That'll probably work."

"Oh? Will it? Good. . . ."

"Time to go, honey. Van's right there." He gestured to a white panel van idling at the curb.

"Go where?" she asked in her dream voice.

"Somewhere you can rest," said White. "You did good. Come on now."

He did not touch her and instead walked around her to the back of the van. He opened the doors and stood back as she climbed in.

The interior of the vehicle was covered with thick blue Tyvek sheeting over floor, walls, and roof. There was a folded furniture pad against one wall.

Then David White looked up and down the street to make sure no one could see what was going on.

"Where are we going again?" asked Mary.

"It's okay," he said. "Sit down on the floor. Make yourself comfortable."

After a slight hesitation, she did. White closed one of the rear doors and positioned himself so that the other door hid him from passing cars. He reached up under the front of his shirt and removed a small handgun with an almost delicate sound suppressor.

Mary said, "What . . . ?"

David White shot her twice in the chest and twice more in the head. The .22 rounds punched through breastbone and skull but lacked the force to exit. The rounds bounced inside her head, ripping through brain tissue. Mary—whose real name was Diane Wilson—slumped over onto the floor.

He tossed the gun inside, closed the other door, and went around to the passenger side, got in, and nodded to the driver. The man was a brute with distinctly simian features.

"I'd have done that," the driver said.

"It's done," said White. He pulled his cell, hit a saved number, engaged the scrambler, and when the call was answered, he said, "Typhoid Mary number one is done and done."

"Excellent," said Mr. October. Behind him, Miss Mary laughed aloud. "Thank you, Mr. White."

David put his phone away, rubbed his eyes, blew out his cheeks, then nodded to the driver. "Let's go dig a grave."

CHAPTER 22
COMFORT SUITES ATLANTIC CITY NORTH
ABSECON, NEW JERSEY

Kemmer stared at us with huge, red-rimmed, absolutely terrified eyes.

Imagine what he saw. Four men, one woman, and a huge dog. All of us smiling down at him in ways no one ever wants to see. He could probably smell himself, too, and it's difficult to be a hard-ass when you're wearing a plastic diaper filled with your own filth. Hardly a macho moment.

The fact that he didn't ask who we were spoke volumes. No way to know if he recognized anyone, but he understood how deep in the shit he was. Pun intended.

"I . . . I have rights," he sputtered.

Top gave him the warmest smile in North America. "Not in this room, you don't."

"None that I can see," agreed Bunny.

Belle merely smiled in silence. Tenth Legion was a white religious extremist group, and here was a black woman—extremely dark-skinned—wearing a shoulder holster and giving him a look that would have scared the hairs off of Hitler's balls. I bet he was more afraid of her than of Ghost. Certainly more so than the rest of us, even Top.

I said, "We know you're with Tenth Legion, so we don't need to do that dance. You were kicked out of the army, and you worked with Blue Diamond. We know that and a lot more. I can tell you your Social Security number, cell phone PIN, and shoe size."

His eyes clicked over toward me.

"Fuck you."

"Interesting point," I said. "Or, how about *you're* fucked, and you have exactly one chance of getting out of this alive and with a whole skin, and that's to answer every question we want to ask. How's that sound?"

"Suck my dick."

I sighed, a bit dramatically. Selling the world-weary don't-make-me-do-this-the-hard-way attitude.

"We're all very impressed with how tough you are," I said. "Applause, applause. Now let's get back to the real world, where you are between a rock and a hard place. If you have a civil conversation with us, then we hand you over to the feds with a nicely worded request to give you easy time in some puppies-and-foot-massage country club prison. How's that sound?"

His reply was, "*Judge not, that you be not judged. For with the judgment you pronounce you will be judged, and with the measure you use it will be measured to you.*"

Top grunted. "Matthew chapter seven, verse one."

Kemmer glared at him. "Fuck you, nigger."

Bunny grinned. "Uh-oh. He called you the N-word."

Top touched his chest. "I'm wounded, Farm Boy. I may die. Catch me as I fall."

"And that nigger cunt, too," snarled Kemmer.

Belle said nothing. Her alligator smile never flickered.

"You're not making a lot of friends here, son," I said. "And trust me when I say that you need friends. You need our goodwill."

Kemmer fired back with another biblical quote, and he gave us all a mocking sneer as he spoke. "*Many are the afflictions of the righteous, but the Lord delivers him out of them all.*"

Once again, Top provided context. "Psalm thirty-four, verse nineteen."

Kemmer, still smiling, clenched his teeth, and we all heard the faint crack of something in his mouth. Instantly, his body began to thrash as wildly as it had when we'd dosed him with Wakey-Wakey. A white foam bubbled from between his lips, his eyes rolled high and white, and then he settled back with a terminal slackness.

We stood there, staring at him.

"Suicide pill in a tooth," said Bunny. "Fuck me sideways."

"Call me crazy," said Remy, "but I half-ass feel bad for him."

Belle gave him a withering look.

"On the other hand," Remy said, "I hope he rots in hell."

That earned him a single curt nod. When Belle went into the bathroom, Top leaned close to Remy. "Do you actually enjoy waving your dick over the woodchipper? Saying shit like that?"

"It was meant as a joke," protested the young Cajun. "Sarcasm, y'know? Or is it irony? Either way, I didn't mean anything by it."

But Top just shook his head. "You were dropped on your head as a baby, weren't you? I mean multiple times. And from considerable elevation."

Remy colored and said nothing.

I walked around to the other side of the bed and bent down over his buddy, Huberman. I stuck fingers into his slack mouth and pried his jaws wide. Very wide.

"Somebody get me a pair of pliers," I said.

INTERLUDE 9
THE MANSION
UNDISCLOSED LOCATION
NINETEEN MONTHS AGO

"What's all the noise?" Mary asked as she came into the drawing room. She wore pajamas that needed washing, and her hair was matted with something red and sticky.

Mr. October looked up from a large and very old Bible that lay open on the mission table near the french windows. There were hundreds of colored Post-it notes sprouting from between the pages. He wore a smoky-blue cardigan over a darker blue dress shirt and had incense burning in a bowl next to his coffee cup. The incense smelled of roses and gardenias.

Beneath them, the floor vibrated with the sound and force of heavy construction work being done in the cellar. October leaned back in his chair and offered her a fatherly smile.

"I'm building you a playhouse," he said.

Mary frowned with suspicion. "Playhouse? You think I'm a child and want to play with dolls and dishes?"

"Ha! No, hardly that, my dear," he said mildly. "You said you want to play with that trove of information we received."

Her face brightened. "You mean the Jakoby stuff?"

"Of course."

She stared down at the floor as if able to see through it. "You're building a lab?"

"Oh, it's more than a lab. It's a *dream* lab. Once everything is installed, you'll find that it is more than state of the art. It's *bleeding edge*. I can get you brand names on any of the stuff you want more details on. And also surgical tables, breeding tanks, and all the rest. Sequencers, refrigerators, and freezers. Incubators. Biosafety cabinets. Centrifuges.

A water bath. Analytical scales. Pipettes. Frankly, some of it is a complete mystery to me, and maybe even to you. Science has marched on at quite a lively pace since you've been gone."

"Gone . . ." she echoed. "That's a polite word for it."

October merely smiled. He took a sip of coffee and held the cup between his palms, rolling it gently back and forth so that the brown liquid eddied but did not spill.

Mary knelt and placed her palms on the floor. "Why are they doing so much drilling? The basement was finished."

"No, the basement was small. While you've been out on your little trips to the various camps and training centers, the construction team has been quite busy. They've greatly increased the square footage. They built a corridor so there is a rear exit in case anything happens up here. There are generators on concrete pads out back, and the cables and whatnot have already been installed. More power than you'll ever need, and it's off the grid. Even if the local power goes down, the generators will keep running. Plenty of fuel, too."

Mary straightened.

"Why?" she asked. "I'm a computer software engineer. If you're building a genetics lab and surgical suite, I wouldn't know what to do with them."

"I doubt that is true."

"I'm not that kind of doctor, and you know it."

"*You*, my dear girl, do not need to know which end of a scalpel to hold or how to sequence DNA. Your role is that of project administrator. I have people out recruiting some of the very best minds to come and work for you. People who *do* know how to cut and splice, augment and all of that. You have the Jakoby records. You know what those beautiful twins, Hecate and Paris, accomplished. And what they *planned* on doing and would have done if St. Germaine and his thugs had not killed them. That's why you—shall we say—*appropriated* their records when you worked for the DMS. You hired that molecular biologist—can't recall his name at the moment—to do the gene therapy on those brutes. You had Berserkers with you when you played your games at Dragon Con in Atlanta."

"Where I *fucking died.*"

"*Died* is such an imprecise word for what happened to you, Mary.

You used *borrowed* science from Amirah to evolve into something extraordinary. If not for Ledger and his team, this would be a vastly different world. Perhaps not as much fun, but it would have become a reflection of your own personality. Your flaw was trying to destroy the world rather than throw it into chaos."

She said nothing, but her gaze was intense.

"With the equipment being installed downstairs, you can build on what Amirah and the Jakobys began. Not to end the world but to throw it into turmoil."

"Into chaos," she said, the words dripping with venom. "That's what you want. That's why you brought me back."

"I have never pretended otherwise, my girl. Wanting to end it, to have it consume itself, was shortsighted."

"It would have made me a god," she snapped.

"A god? Of what? A barren world? What's the win there? No, no, Mary my sweet, you were what can best be described as *damaged goods*. Your life had been stolen from you by the DMS and the courts. That process and those policies destroyed Artemisia Bliss. You reinvented yourself as Mother Night, which had its moments of pure brilliance. You had everyone convinced you were a mad anarchist who wanted to see the world burn. But you wanted that world to burn *down*, to become your tomb because you thought—no, *knew*—that life as you knew it was over. You knew that Church and Ledger would eventually find you and do exactly what they did. But you wanted your death to be glorious. Historic. It was there in your catchphrase—*Sometimes you have to burn to shine*. You wanted doomsday."

"You've tried to burn things down, too," she countered acidly.

October sighed, sipped his coffee, and set the cup down. "It is my curse, I think, to always be misunderstood. Of *course* I want the world to burn, but not to burn *down*. Fire is transformative. War is transformative. Diseases are transformative. I want change to happen, and to keep happening, because that is what feeds me. It's what I *am*. If I am anything, Mary, it is chaos. Chaos is not Armageddon. Chaos is not the end of all things. It is the bloody and painful process of giving birth to something new."

He got up and walked over to her and looked into her eyes.

"I do not want this vast, complex, beautiful world to die. I have, in fact, gone to great lengths to prevent apocalyptic moments." He laughed. "If the world were to die, *I* would die. I love life, my dear. I will not let anyone end this world."

She began to speak, but he held up a finger.

"What we are doing with the Tenth Legion isn't to end the world . . . it's to end complacency, to prevent stagnation, to light *controlled* fires. If you know anything about the chemistry of forest fires, you know that once the ash cools and soaks into the soil, it turns that soil more fertile, and from it springs new life in wild abundance. Destroy a city and people will build back with delicious energy and vigor. Start a war and all of the sciences speed up and offer new gifts of technology, medicine, architecture, artwork, literature, music. Make guns available to as many people as possible and they will create chaos with them."

He touched her cheek with incredible gentleness.

"Do you understand me, my dear child?"

Mary had small tears, as delicate as jewels, in the corners of her eyes. She nodded.

"The Jakoby twins and their father—the man who had been Josef Mengele and who reinvented himself as Cyrus Jakoby—were agents of chaos. Amirah was not. She went mad and wanted to destroy what she believed was an impure world. She was eliminated to prevent her excesses. I *steered* Joe Ledger to her and watched from the shadows of a cave as he killed her. But her pathogen, *seif al din*, endures. You are the most beautiful proof of that. I will acquire samples of all known strains of the disease. You will have access to it, and the scientists who will bend it to your will. Yours and mine. I know how I will use it, and that will be sparingly. Sebastian Gault had it, and he did not allow it to be released without checks and controls. He released it in isolated places, demonstrating its potential. Those demonstrations sparked chaos and action."

Mary said nothing.

"You are the most advanced mutation of that pathogen. But you are *not* contagious. For reasons we do not yet understand, though I expect your new team of scientists will eventually suss it out. But . . . tell me, Mary, if you had the most contagious variants of it, would you really want to destroy the world? Would you end it all so that you can live in the silence of your global tomb? Or . . . would you use that excellent and incomparable brain of yours to play with it, to throw kindling on the fires of chaos, and share with me all of the miraculous changes that would come of that?"

He withdrew his hand from her cheek.

"I don't need an answer now, my dear," he said. "But we will return to this conversation soon."

Mary nodded.

October smiled. "Now . . . go and take a shower. Wash your hair. Clean yourself and dress in fresh clothes. You are a queen, you are the Lady of Chaos. *Be* that."

He turned away, walked to the french doors, opened them, and stepped out into a swirl of snowflakes of the most exceptional purity.

Mary watched him for a very long time while below her the construction crew worked tirelessly to build her laboratory.

CHAPTER 23

THE ATLANTA JOURNAL-CONSTITUTION

Health officials in Atlanta are monitoring a possible outbreak of typhus on Tuesday.

Several employees of Anderson/Conley Media on Walton Street have been hospitalized with a rare form of typhus fever. Rare disease experts at the Centers for Disease Control and Prevention (CDC) have been consulted, and results of their investigation are pending.

Typhus is a group of highly infectious diseases spread by mites, lice, and fleas, and has had a long history of causing illness and deaths. In the Middle Ages up through World Wars I and II, typhus outbreaks were common in areas where poverty, cultural disruption, and reduction of basic hygiene were common. It is less common in modern times but by no means unknown. There was a serious outbreak in Los Angeles County in 2018/19, mostly among the homeless. A similar outbreak struck Pasadena at the same time.

Of the three major types of disease—epidemic typhus, scrub typhus, and murine typhus, the latter has been on the rise, with 171 cases reported in 2022 and close to 300 cases in 2023.

Dr. Kim Rehyun, spokeswoman for the IDSGA (Infectious Disease Services of Georgia), said, "This is an unusual case. The onset was notably rapid, and the environment of that office building is not one where you would expect to find this kind of infection."

When asked if the citizens of Atlanta need to be alarmed, Dr. Kim advised everyone to "be alert, be cautious, maintain personal and household cleanliness, and report any unusual incidents of fleas or flea bites to their health care provider."

Health officials are coordinating an effort to identify all persons who might have been exposed.

Details are still emerging on this outbreak. For updates and additional information, go to our website and click on the TYPHUS UPDATE link.

CHAPTER 24
INTEGRATED SCIENCES DIVISION
PHOENIX HOUSE
OMFORI ISLAND, GREECE
TWO WEEKS AGO

Dr. Ronald Coleman was in the mess hall drinking coffee and eating a honey-dripping Greek pastry. His tablet was open on the table and he was scanning science news compiled by one of MindReader's algorithms.

When the reports about a typhus outbreak popped onto the screen, he loaded the full story and read it through. His pulse jumped a little when one of the experts quoted in the report, a doctor at the CDC whom Coleman knew well, speculated that it was a "novel strain."

Coleman immediately toggled over to his email app and sent a quick note to his colleague. By the time he finished his coffee, there was a reply. His friend, Dr. Nancy Rickert, wrote to say that they believed they were looking at a modified form of "scrub typhus," a deadly form of the disease believed to be present only in the Asia Pacific region, though there was an outbreak in Chile in 2020. Unlike the Asia Pacific version, in Atlanta, the vectors were not chiggers but an unusual version of the dog flea local to Georgia.

"Huh," he grunted, and wrote back, "Any chance of obtaining samples of the fleas and the novel typhus strain?"

When his friend said yes, Coleman contacted RTI logistics to have them picked up at the CDC lab and flown to Greece.

Dr. Rickert wrote, "Looks isolated. No cases outside of that one office building. We're looking into deliveries of any kind to offices there for shipments from Chile or Asia. So far, we're calling this an 'isolated incident.'"

"Keep me posted," requested Coleman.

And that was that.

Other matters concerning RTI pulled on him, drawing his energy and his attention away from the typhus incident.

CHAPTER 25
COMFORT SUITES ATLANTIC CITY NORTH
ABSECON, NEW JERSEY

The *other* guy, Stuart Huberman, woke, went through the anticipated scatological mishaps, but settled down into a bug-eyed staring contest with me that lasted five whole seconds. Then he turned his face away, refusing all contact.

"Pretending that if he can't see you, you can't see him," said Remy. "Had me a bluetick hound once that used to do that."

"Yup," I said. "He looks to be just about that stupid."

"I had a smarter guinea pig once," mused Bunny. "Dumb as a box of lint, but at least *he* was cute."

I sat down on the other bed, which was four feet away. "So, here's the bad news, Stuart. May I call you Stuart?"

"Fuck you," he mumbled.

"Stewie, then. Here's the situation, Stewie . . . that pain you're feeling in your lower jaw? Yeah, that's where I pulled the tooth with the cyanide cap. So . . . you're not going to opt out of our conversation. And, Stewie? Just so you know, I still have the pliers."

I saw him begin to tremble.

I'm not actually as cruel a bastard as I sometimes seem. Part of it is the theatrics of interrogation when there's a clock ticking. Part of it is the pretense of retaliation that could encourage a useful response without having to do anything really nasty. The tooth doesn't count, because of what it was used for. I'm not the kind of cat who goes in for the slow-motion body horror of mutilation. Actually, I hate the whole enhanced interrogation dance.

That said, Mr. Huberman here had sexually assaulted seven girls, the youngest of whom was twelve, using his job as a youth pastor to gain and then obliterate their trust. He did short-change time for it and was out joining cretins like the Tenth Legion. His designation as someone deserving of kindness, compassion, and mercy was pretty damned low.

Without turning and in a weak, frightened voice, Huberman asked, "You took my salvation pill? Why would you do that?"

I saw Top mouth the words *salvation pill* as he slowly shook his head.

"Because I want to have a conversation," I replied, "and that becomes significantly more difficult if you're dead. I forgot to pack my Ouija board. As for your buddy—he crunched his pill, and now he's cooling meat."

He shook his head. "That's bullshit. The pills just knock us out until an extraction team can come get us."

"Really? That's what you believe? Why don't you take a good look at your boy Kemmer. He's right next to you. That bitter almondy smell is cyanide."

I gave him as much time as he needed to work up the courage to turn and look. His eyes went wide, then his brows knitted in confusion.

"If he's dead," protested the prisoner, "it's 'cause you assholes killed him."

"Stewie," I said, "take a look at us. Consider the situation. Do you really think we need to lie about something like that?"

"It's just a knockout thing . . ." he insisted weakly.

"Apparently not, Stewie. It should bother you that your bosses *did* lie to you. They don't give a cold pile of monkey shit about you. They lied and fooled you all into letting them put suicide pills—not *salvation*, mind—in your mouths. Hell, it's a good thing none of you idiots had any peanut brittle. You'd all be toes up by now."

His eyes, big and blue and full of dread, turned to me. "Wh—who are you people?"

Top said, "He's Bob Barker back from the grave and I'm Wayne Brady, and this is *Let's Make a Deal: Terrorist Home Edition*."

Huberman blinked a dozen times in rapid succession. "Are you with Homeland?"

I showed him the pliers. "If you ask one more stupid question, you're going to lose another tooth. Maybe two."

He went pale as bad milk. "Don't hurt me."

And I could see Top stiffen at that, and as if I could read his mind, I knew what he was thinking. *Don't hurt me.* How many little girls had said that to him? And how often had it ever worked?

I stood, snapping the pliers. "Your call. Front teeth or another molar?"

"No!" he wailed. And pissed himself again. The stink of it was intense. Ghost rose and put his front paws on the end of the bed, looked into Huberman's eyes, and growled, showing his titanium teeth.

That did it. Everyone has a pressure point. I guess for my pal Stewie, it was a big dog with a lot of wolf looking out of his eyes. Hell, if Ghost wasn't my dog, I'd be scared of him, too.

"I want—" he began, but I cut him off.

"If the rest of that sentence includes 'immunity' or 'a lawyer,' this is going to get loud and messy."

"No! Please . . . Don't. Tell me what you want, man. Just ask. Anything . . . For God's sake, anything."

I placed the pliers on the nightstand between the beds and sat back down.

"Then let's get started."

CHAPTER 26

THE TOC
PHOENIX HOUSE
OMFORI ISLAND, GREECE

Scott Wilson stood next to Church as they watched the interrogation play out on the screen. A lot of work had stopped in the TOC because of the more dramatic moments, and a few people looked deeply troubled. Even knowing that most of what Ledger said and threatened was emotional blackmail rather than actual intention did little to ameliorate the feelings of disgust.

"Well," said Wilson dryly, "your boy loves his work."

He often referred to Ledger as "your boy" when speaking with Church. It was his deliberately passive-aggressive way of disowning Outlaw's excesses, particularly since the Darkness situation.

"Would you prefer he soft-soap a serial child molester who is our only viable link to a terrorist organization hiding behind a warped interpretation of Christianity, Scott?" asked Church. "If Huberman had not been dosed with Sandman, he would have continued to try to kill every member of Havoc Team. And we know for certain that Tenth Legion is planning something very big, but we are woefully unaware of what that plan is. So, tell me how you would conduct this same interview?"

Not to be browbeaten, Wilson replied, "I'm not criticizing *what* Ledger is doing. My point was that he seems to enjoy it."

Church turned very slowly to face him and in a quiet voice said, "It sometimes astounds me that a man as experienced and perceptive as you can so comprehensively misunderstand Joe Ledger."

Wilson gave a waspish sniff. "Not everyone in RTI believes that Colonel Ledger is entirely free of the Darkness."

"I can accept your caution, Scott," said Church. "But I strongly caution *you* about letting it prejudice your insights or cloud your judgment."

The conversation stalled right there, and in a chilly silence, they watched the rest of the interrogation.

CHAPTER 27
HENRIETTA PURE DOG BREEDING
POCAHONTAS, ILLINOIS
TWO WEEKS AGO

David White sat on a rock and smoked a joint while his driver, CJ, dug the grave.

The Latina who had called herself Mary—not Maria—was wrapped in the Tyvek. The bundle had been sterilized with a solution of vinegar and bleach, then wrapped in another shroud of blue industrial plastic.

CJ, who had the ape face, had the chest and shoulders to go with it. He dug with machinelike precision, his skin glistening faintly with sweat. He was stripped to the waist, and White was distractedly interested in the way the overdeveloped muscles bunched and flexed. There was nothing sexual about his interest . . . it was like watching an organic machine. Like watching a CGI character in a superhero movie.

"That's deep enough," said White when his joint was down to a smoldering roach. He flicked it into the grave and began building another spliff, packing it until the papers barely closed around it. The type he had was Brownie Scout, an indica strain known to pack a punch. He needed it.

So far, he had committed eleven murders for Mr. October. The three false Marys and the others at Site 44. Before that, he had only ever killed one person. He could feel the weight of it pressing down on his chest every time he took a deep hit.

Eleven people.

Fuck.

He watched as CJ lifted the latest Mary as easily as White raised the joint to his lips. This was the last one. That's what Mr. October said. It's what Mary said.

The last one.

Number eleven. White realized that he did not even know the woman's real name.

She was Mary. *A* Mary.

Now she was cooling meat in a plastic wrapper being buried in a copse of trees near a closed-down puppy mill. Once the grave was filled in and the sod replaced, no one would ever even think to look for her. From what little he knew of Miss Mary's operation, it was likely this latest false Mary had been recruited from some other part of the country. October was careful like that.

The brute of a driver climbed out of the grave and began shoveling dirt over the corpse.

White took a very long hit, held it until his lungs felt ready to burst, feeling the pot do its alchemy inside of him. Then he exhaled long and slow.

He wondered what hell would be like when he got there.

INTERLUDE 10
THE MANSION
UNDISCLOSED LOCATION
TWENTY MONTHS AGO

"I have a present for you, Miss Mary," said Mr. October. He stood in her bedroom doorway with a paper shopping bag looped over one arm.

The young woman looked up from the book she was reading, her eyes darting to the bag. "A present? Give it to me," she said brightly.

"Patience, patience, my dear one," he soothed. "But before I give you your gift, tell me what you think of that book."

She closed the cover and regarded the title. *Competing Theories for Integration of Digital and Quantum Computer Systems.*

"It's okay."

"Only okay . . . ?"

"It's pretty basic."

October smiled. "It's the most advanced textbook used at MIT."

"So?"

"And you think it's too basic?"

Mary shrugged, then swept a strand of hair out of her face, tucking it behind an ear. "I read it once and thought it couldn't be that thin, so I've been going through the chapters on integrative algorithms thinking maybe I missed something new, but it's . . . I don't know, it's just too simple."

That made October's smile brighten.

"Then maybe this will give you more pleasure."

He let the straps of the bag slide down his wrist and onto one extended finger, then held it out to her. The woman plucked the bag greedily, set it down, and tore the paper to get to the prize.

It was a small device in a leather cover not much bigger than the textbook she'd been reading, though very slim. She glanced up at him in mild confusion. "What is it?"

"Open it and tell me," he suggested.

Mary pulled the Velcro fastenings apart and opened the cover to reveal a monitor screen and a compact keyboard. It was not a standard keyboard for a laptop, though. This had panels that extended out on either side—one covered with numeral keys and related symbols, and the other completely filled with specialty keys. The woman frowned, and for a moment, all she did was sit and stare at it.

"Do you know what it is?" he asked softly.

"It's a . . . computer . . . but . . ." Her words drifted off, and there was a dreamlike quality to them.

"It is. And do you know what *kind*?"

"I . . ."

She seemed unable to find the right words and chewed her lip, her fingers poised above the keys but not yet touching them.

"Do you recognize it?" asked Mr. October.

"Yes." Her voice was small as a timid child's.

"Do you know its name?"

She did not answer. However, tears formed in the corners of her eyes.

"Shall I tell you its name?" he asked.

Mary almost pushed the computer away. Sweat beaded her brow and upper lids as if her struggle to remember something was draining her as much as heavy physical activity.

"My girl," said October, "let me tell you a truth. When you were injured—"

"You mean when I *died*?" she snarled.

"Yes. When you died," he conceded gently. "You knew this machine. Or, at least, one very much like it. This is yours. Your creation. It was the sum total of your genius at the point when you died. But so much of that knowledge is locked away behind scar tissue and damage. It is my own desire, dear one, that this little gift of mine will help you unlock those memories. It is my greatest hope that—instead of me telling you your name—this will trigger your own memory of who and, more importantly, *what* you are. What you are for real. The majesty of you. The exquisite magnificence of you."

The tears fell down her cheeks.

"I . . . I'm afraid . . ."

"Of course you are," he said and stroked her long black hair, his fingers gliding along the edge of streaks of pure white that had become threaded through it. "But fear is good. It makes us wise. It makes us careful. It refines our hate and sets our ambition alight. Do not fear *fear*, my girl. Embrace it. Enjoy it. Revel in it. And *use* it. Because I can say without the slightest exaggeration that the people who matter in this world, the people who have real power . . . they fear you more. They feared you greatly before, but they will crumble beneath the hammer blows of their fear once they behold what you have become."

"You talk in circles." She sniffed, then pawed away her tears.

"Everything I say to you is the truth. Forgive me if I tend toward poetic phrasing." He bent down and whispered in her ear, "Touch the keys. They know you and will open its secrets for you."

Even then, it took many long seconds before she allowed her fingers to make featherlight contact with the plastic keys. Then she immediately jerked her hands back as if the contact had generated electric shocks.

Mr. October said nothing. Now was the time to let her make the next step.

Mary's breaths were coming faster, and he could almost hear her heartbeat.

Then she placed her fingers once more on the keys. She touched one special key. A capital letter *A* that was not part of the normal arrangement of keys, for there was a smaller *A* there. This one was in the upper-left corner, and as soon as her index finger touched it, the screen went from empty blackness to a bright screen of welcome.

A word scrawled quickly across the screen to spell out a single word. A name.

Haruspex.

After nearly a full minute of simply staring at the word, she began typing in commands. Special, complex codes that opened window after window. October shifted so he could see her eyes. The screen was reflected there, but he saw past it and read the eyes themselves, watching for the moment when the triggers of familiarity opened the vault doors of true memory.

He was a patient man.

And that patience was rewarded.

CHAPTER 28
TRANSCRIPT OF SESSION NOTES
DR. RUDY SANCHEZ AND AÏCHETOU "BELLE" AHMED

SANCHEZ: How have you been feeling?

BELLE: Fine.

SANCHEZ: Since the exposure to Shiva and God's Arrow, I mean.

BELLE: Fine.

SANCHEZ: Are you having any nightmares?

BELLE: No.

SANCHEZ: None at all?

BELLE: No.

SANCHEZ: I don't mean only associated with the hallucinogenic weapons.

Are you having any nightmares at all?

BELLE: No.

SANCHEZ: Any bad dreams associated with your earlier life in Mauritania?

BELLE: No.

SANCHEZ: Belle, it's more useful for both of us if you give me something more than one-word answers to my questions.

BELLE: Okay.

SANCHEZ: Tell me about the dreams that you do have.

(Long pause)

BELLE: Everyone dreams.

SANCHEZ: Agreed. But what are your dreams?

BELLE: Just dreams.

SANCHEZ: What do you dream about?

BELLE: Stuff.

SANCHEZ: Can you please be more specific?

BELLE: Ordinary stuff.

(Another pause)

SANCHEZ: Do you enjoy working with Colonel Ledger?

BELLE: Yes.

SANCHEZ: Do you have any issues or complaints about working with Joe Ledger?

BELLE: No.

SANCHEZ: Are you unhappy about anything?

BELLE: No.

SANCHEZ: Is there any topic you would prefer us to discuss?

BELLE: No.

SANCHEZ: Are there any questions you would like to ask me?

BELLE: Yes.

SANCHEZ: Please, feel free to ask anything?

BELLE: May I go now?

CHAPTER 29
COMFORT SUITES ATLANTIC CITY NORTH
ABSECON, NEW JERSEY

The sad truth is that Stuart Huberman was a very small fish in a very large pond. He talked for a couple of hours. He did his best to answer all of our questions, and although he tried his best, he did not know enough.

The upside is that those small details helped us verify some intel we already had. It spills out like this . . .

The Tenth Legion were in what Stewie called "recruitment over-drive." He said, "They're bringing people from all over. Jersey, Pennsylvania, Ohio, down south, all over."

"And they're all here?" I asked.

"In training camps."

"How many camps are there?"

"I don't know. Twenty, twenty-five."

That was not comforting news.

"Where is the closest camp?"

"I don't know. I was only at one," said Stewie. "Camp #9. It was in White Haven, up in the Poconos. But it's not there anymore."

He explained that there was a security leak of some kind, and they issued what he called a "cut-and-run" order. That meant that the entire camp was shut down fast. Everything was stripped and packed into one semi. He did not know where they took the stuff. He said that from the time the camp commandant got the cut-and-run until the truck rolled was under an hour.

"Bullshit," said Bunny.

"Hand to God, man," swore Stewie. "We practice it all the time. At least once a day. Best time at Camp #9 was forty-seven minutes. That's all the tents, all the gear, those collapsible Quonset hut things. Everything. Anyone leaves something behind, they get two in the head."

"Hell of an incentive program," said Remy.

Stewie stuck his chin out. "The Tenth Legion is the army of God. We have to be ready at all times."

"How's that working out for you?" asked Top. Stewie declined to answer.

He told us that he'd heard that the Tenth Legion was formed by a man known as Mr. October. That rang a serious bell in my head. While we were running with the Cave 13 case, October's name had come up a couple of times.

Lilith, the woman who runs Arklight, told Church that her spies had been hearing the name *October* and that serious people in the terrorist community were afraid of him. He was emerging as a player, but a player in what exact game was unknown. One theory that Church had was that this October was an arms dealer who was in direct competition with Harcourt Bolton—a.k.a. Kuga. When Bolton was killed at the end of the Relentless case, a power vacuum had been created, and Church and Lilith both believed October was trying to fill it. Another theory was that October was attached in some way to the Tenth Legion, but that was just that . . . a theory.

Until now.

Stewie had actually *seen* October via Zoom during an orientation session with thirty other recruits on his first day at Camp #9.

When I asked him to describe the guy, he said, "He's pretty average, I guess. He was standing next to Dick Rollins, who's at least six feet tall, and Mr. October was shorter. Five nine, maybe. He has black hair kind of greased back and with a little gray in it. Bushy eyebrows. Clean-shaved. Big lips, almost like a nig—"

Here he paused, realizing that both Top and Belle were listening. Top was smiling in a way that would make stronger men than Stewie reconsider their life choices. Belle's eyes were unreadable, and yet somehow they conveyed menace.

"Almost like a girl's," Stewie amended clumsily. "Real pale skin. Big front teeth with one of those gaps between them. Like David Letterman has. Dresses in nice suits. Wears a cross on a silver chain so it hangs down over his heart."

"Accent?" I asked.

"Huh? Oh, I don't know. Maybe Tennessee. Could be Alabama. I don't know. Speaks slow, smiles a lot. Always seems happy."

"Happy about what?" I asked.

"I dunno. Life. God. Doing God's work. Happy because we're going to cleanse this country of all the . . ." His eyes flicked to Belle again. "Anyone who's not one of us."

I let that go and asked, "If there was an actor from TV or movies he looked most like, who might that be?"

Stewie gave that real thought. "Not from TV or anything, but he kind of looks like Jimmy Joe Beacon."

"Who?"

"You know, from the *He Will Rise* megachurch. Guy with all that frosted blond hair. Always on cable."

In my ear, I heard Bug say, "Got it."

"What did this Mr. October say during that Zoom?"

Stewie paused for a long time, and I could see him trying to decide what to say. I gave Ghost a silent signal with my little finger. He came and sat by my leg, looking at Huberman, growling very softly.

"Now's not the time to start playing games, Stewie. I haven't fed my dog in hours, and I bet he thinks you look tasty."

Then it all spilled out.

Mr. October welcomed the recruits and gave what amounted to a pep talk, all full of vague truisms culled from the extremist anti-government, anti-anyone-who-isn't-white-enough playbook. All about how both Republicans and Democrats were drifting away from Jesus and falling into sin and dragging the rest of the country down with them. He talked about sins both political and biblical, and promised God's retribution. He talked about adhering to the more forceful vengeance practices of the Old Testament God, the one who outranked the more passive Jesus. He said that this plague was spreading out across the world, polluting whole nations, and threatening the right and natural supremacy of the white race. He praised Hitler and Mussolini and Stalin. Had a lot of nice things to say about Vladimir Putin. Interestingly, none of Stewie's heroes were part of either the radical Right or Left in America. When I pressed him on that, he said that it wasn't about politics. He didn't give a shit about who was in the White House or Congress.

"It's about God looking out for his people. His *real* people. Christian Americans."

He went on, talking about the inherent godliness of Jim Jones and David Koresh, saying they had *parts* of the answer, but they failed because they did not commit completely and without reservation to the true will of God. And then closed with a promise of holy retribution to be levied by men like those gathered in front of the bar's big flat-screen.

None of that part was new. Every law enforcement agency and intelligence group involved in counterterrorism had heard it before. If it wasn't a warped take on Christianity, then it was Muslim extremists, Jewish extremists, and a whole bunch of others. At this point, I would not be unduly surprised if the Last Thursdayists or the devotees of the Flying Spaghetti Monster became radicalized. After all, everyone else seems to be doing it lately.

And even though I'm a lapsed Methodist, I have read a lot of sacred texts from other religions and, as I recall, a lot of them talk about peace, love, tolerance, and acceptance. But the extremists don't give a damn about those parts of the holy books or the lessons of history's great teachers. They cherry-pick scripture in order to justify their actions. That offends even agnostics like me, and I know it had to be turning dials on people of more substantial faith—like Top, Remy, and Belle.

"Your friend Norris was recruiting for Tenth Legion," I said. "He indicated that there was a training camp within driving distance. Tell me exactly where that one is."

Stewie did not want to tell me that, probably because it was too specific and he likely had friends there. I didn't have to turn any dials on him, though. He swallowed and nodded.

"There's a couple you can drive to from here," he said.

"Where are they?"

"I . . . don't know."

"Stewie . . ."

"No, God's honest truth, man. My camp was in the Poconos, and they don't tell us where the others are. Keeps people like you from trying to shut us down."

"Are you lying to me?" I asked.

"I swear to God. When my camp was shut down, I was told to come here to Jersey and hang out at the trailer park until me and the other Camp #9 guys were reassigned. The only thing I heard was maybe we'd be going to a camp somewhere over the river, north of Philly. That's where we were going to learn where our targets are and get all kinds of tactical info."

"Targets . . . ? What does that mean?" I asked. "Be precise."

"The targets," he repeated. "We're not training just to jerk off. There's a war coming. The rag-heads in the Middle East are coming to take over. Arabs and fucking Muslims. And the race traitors working with Ukraine. The Marxists and Communists. All of them. They're planning an invasion of the States. Why do you think there's so many of them coming through the border? You think they're really wetback asylum seekers? Please. They've been bringing in their troops every day while those assholes in Washington sit around with thumbs up their asses. But Mr. October's a *real* patriot. We're getting trained and armed, and when the word comes down, we're going to take America back. And don't give me any of that insurrectionist shit . . . We're patriots, too. We're God's warriors, and He wants us to take back *His* country."

The speech was interesting. Insane, unbearably naïve, and downright stupid, but interesting. I glanced at Top and the others. No one said anything, but their expressions spoke volumes.

"And you can't tell me where *any* of these camps are?" I asked Stewie. "The one near Philly? No idea?"

"You kidding, man? Security is the most important thing; otherwise, the government Marxists would shut them down before we're ready."

Then I hit him with a key word we'd acquired from an operation Church ran in Canada. "When's Firefall?"

He looked at me. "What?"

"Tell me about Firefall."

"What's that even mean?"

The truth was that we did not know what it meant. In the context given during the Canada thing, it was used as if it were the name of an upcoming operation. That was a few months ago, and so far, all we've heard is the name. No one that any RTI team had so far interrogated knew what it was. Nor, apparently, did Stewie.

Not knowing was giving me a real itch between the shoulder blades, like someone was out in the weeds with all of us in the sites, adjusting for windage and elevation, getting ready to take a clean shot.

Firefall.

Sounded ominous as hell.

And we still had no idea what was coming.

INTERLUDE 11
THE MANSION
UNDISCLOSED LOCATION
NINETEEN MONTHS AGO

"I have another present for you, my dear," said Mr. October.

Mary looked up from the cat she was petting. The cat crouched in her lap, frozen to immobility with terror. Too frightened to scratch or yowl or struggle. Her fingers clawed through its fur in a parody of affection.

"A present?" she asked, then frowned, suspicious of Mr. October's sense of humor. "What kind of present? Not more injections. Not more drugs that are *supposed* to make me feel better but only turn my stomach into a cesspool and give me shits for hours at a time."

October held up a finger. "Manners," he soothed, though it sounded like a warning.

There had been incidents over the last few weeks. A few small fires Mary had set. Graffiti on the walls—usually the phrase *Burn to Shine* but often the sloppy, drippy capital letter *A* overlapping a circle. The thing with the gardener, that required payoffs and a burial where the body would never be found. What was *left* of the body.

The drugs he gave her actually did help, controlling the rage, the bouts of irrationality, the psychological shifts that manifested dozens of brief, strange moods and personalities. A lot of that was settling down, but Mary resented it. She resented everything. She resented being alive and resented having been dead.

But when October reached into his jacket pocket, he did not remove a pill bottle or a syringe. Instead it was a Kingston Data Traveler two-terabyte thumb drive. Mary eyed it with blossoming interest.

"Is that a game?"

She loved games, the harder and more challenging, the better. Even though her emotional IQ was skewed downward to something akin to a naughty six-year-old's, her intelligence was unscalable. The psychologists October had flown in from around the world could not agree on an exact number, but they did agree that she was in the same basic ballpark as the early-twentieth-century child prodigy William James Sidis, whose genius could only be estimated and was likely in the 200–300 point range. October knew of only a few people in the world with a mind like hers—one of which was Bug, the computer genius who worked for Mr. Church. Doc Holliday and Church himself were each super geniuses, and that was because St. Germaine tended to scout and hire the very brightest minds.

Even so, Mary was a freak, and they both knew it. No one with a mind like hers could ever hope to be normal, and no one with a lesser mind could hope to predict the ways in which that staggering intellect would follow. The burden of it, and the dread of all things ordinary, was ponderous, and Mary had cracked beneath its weight. Cracked, but in useful ways.

October tried to entertain and distract that mind. When a new high-end video game came onto the market, October obtained a copy before it was even launched, and Mary usually beat it within a day. Often less than that.

"It's a game of sorts," he said. "And one I believe you will be quite familiar with."

She put on a pouty face. "I don't want to play anything I've already beaten. You *know* that."

October came and squatted down in front of her. She was at her favorite spot by the fireplace. He reached out with one hand and took the cat away from her. Mary's pale fingers resisted but for a moment, and then she let the animal go. October kissed its head and then released it. The cat raced for the french doors, which stood ajar, and bolted into the yard, never to be seen again.

Then he crossed his ankles and sat, holding the thumb drive between his fingers.

"This isn't that kind of game, my pet," he said. "This is how we are going to set the world ablaze. And . . . I know how you like to see things burn."

Her eyes brightened as if there were actual fires burning inside. She made a grab for the drive, but October pulled his hand back for a moment. Then he handed it to her, and as she took it, he used both hands to fold her icy fingers around it.

He began to rise, then paused and leaned forward to whisper in her

JONATHAN MABERRY

ear. He said a single word, but it filled Mary's eyes with both intense fear and joyful tears.

The word he said was, *"VaultBreaker."*

CHAPTER 30
COMFORT SUITES ATLANTIC CITY NORTH
ABSECON, NEW JERSEY

We spent a total of four and a half hours with Huberman, and when he ran dry, I let him go shower, then as soon as he was clean, Belle shot him with Sandman. The dart caught him as he was bending down to pull on a pair of Walmart tighty-whities—part of the set of clothes Remy had run out to buy so when the team came to transport him, they didn't have to deal with poopy drawers. As soon as the Sandman hit him, Huberman toppled instantly and struck his cheek on the edge of the nightstand. He had a small cut and a massive bruise that swelled visibly as Bunny hauled him back onto the bed. Belle never misses or makes a clumsy shot, so we all knew the timing was intentional. But none of us had an opinion that was worth sharing. Not out loud and within her hearing.

We left him in briefs and socks. The other clothes were in a neat pile on the corner of the mattress.

The soiled stuff was bagged, and then we sprayed the living hell out of the room, blowing through a whole can of Lysol. Then I moved my gear to a different room. Remy drew short straw and ran out again, this time for pizzas, beer, and—for Belle—Smartwater. Everyone retreated to their private rooms for some much-needed rest.

I called Church on my cell, wanting the conversation to be private. He answered on the third ring.

"Boss," I said, "did any of that help?"

"Knowing that our mysterious Mr. October is behind Tenth Legion confirms a theory, and that is very useful information."

"So, you think he's buying weapons in quantity from whomever is now running Kuga?"

"Perhaps," said Church. "What does your gut tell you, Colonel?"

"I think October and Kuga are in bed together. Not sure how, what, or why, but that's what I feel. October came out of nowhere after Bolton was killed. We've been hearing rumors that the Kuga organization did not so much as collapse as go through reorganization. We know that Aydelotte was selling arms, too, and he's also dead. This clears the way for someone to come in and take over the Kuga group and make a real killing as the premier arms dealer for the terrorist community. October could be Kuga's new number one client."

"Yes," said Church. "Though a case could be made that October *is* the new Kuga."

"Really? You know this how?"

"I don't *know* it, Colonel. Call it *my* gut feeling."

We thought about that for a moment.

"Well," I said, "whether they're one guy wearing two hats or two guys working together, I am nominating October as our Big Bad here. Tenth Legion is on the field, and they're running us ragged."

"Agreed. We all monitored your interrogation with Huberman, and Bug and his team are digging deep on October and on the Tenth Legion. Gun sales on the dark web, all of it. We need to give them time to do their jobs before we can begin working out a strategy."

"Does Homeland or the Pennsylvania State Police have anything on possible bases north of Philly?"

"None on record," said Church. "But Bucks County has a history with radicalization, religious extremism, and white nationalism. There are, if you remember, more Ku Klux Klan groups in Pennsylvania than any other state."

"Which is why we call everything between Philly and Pittsburgh *Pennsyltucky*," I said.

"There have been several incidents of race-related violence in eastern Pennsylvania," said Church. "Including the Trouble back in 2006."

"I remember."

The Trouble still held the record as the worst incident of domestic terrorism in US history. It happened in Pine Deep, a town whose economy is split between farming and tourism built on their status as "the most haunted town in America." That's what all the tourist brochures say, and Pine Deep celebrates Halloween pretty much all year.

As for what happened, there are a lot of theories. The official line, though, is that a group of white supremacists spiked the local drinking water with hallucinogens and then went on a killing spree that left something like eleven thousand residents and tourists dead. A man named Vic Wingate was the ringleader, and he died in the catastrophe he started. No chance to get the full story out of him. None of his asshole minions survived, either.

Funny thing is, since then, all kinds of wild-ass conspiracy theories have sprung up. The most popular one is that the white supremacy thing was a smoke screen for a real attack by an army of vampires. I know, I get a chuckle out of that. Lot of people buy into it, though. A local newspaper reporter wrote a book about it—*Hell Night: The True Story of the Pine Deep Massacre*. Vampires, werewolves, ghosts—pretty much all of it. Total bullshit, of course. Every year around this time, all the streaming services play the movie based on that book. I've seen it a couple of times, too. Pretty good flick if you're into the fang gang.

Mind you, Pine Deep is a pretty creepy place. Remote and strange, but the only ghosts that haunt it are the memories of all those deaths.

"Pine Deep's not the only place that has white knights charging around trying to purify America," I said.

"Sadly, no, it isn't," agreed Church. "But that area is fertile ground for recruitment. And with I-95 and an interstate parkway close by, it's strategically valuable. I'll have Nikki put two of our best pattern search techs to work looking for online chatter, unusual purchases, recent construction, and so on. If it's there, we'll find it."

"Sooner than later, I hope. From the way Huberman was talking, it sounds like they're ready to make their play. Though even he didn't know what that play will be."

"Did you at least get an impression of its purpose or scale?"

"Not a real purpose unless this October freak is as much a racial purist as it seems. As for scale . . . Stewie seemed to think it was going to be big. He said it would be the real start of the war. Could be hyperbole or him regurgitating the propaganda he was fed, but . . . given the recruiting center we busted here in Jersey and the thought there might be twenty or more actual training camps . . . let's just say that I'm choosing to take him seriously."

"Yes, I am inclined to agree."

"Tell Nikki and Bug and all to put some topspin on this."

"I have made it clear that this is a priority," said Church dryly.

"Okay," I said. "We get anything from the trailer park?"

Church said, "The prisoners are in the process of being handed over to Homeland. That will make it easier for us to get whatever intel is collected. We have more friends there than in local law."

"What do you want Havoc to do? I'd like us to stay local and be ready if we locate that camp near Philly."

"Do nothing at the moment," he said. "Stay at the motel. Get some R & R. Huberman will be picked up shortly."

"We turning him over to the cops?"

"Hardly," said Church. "He will be taken to an off-the-books site and undergo more extensive interrogation, though given your thoroughness, I doubt there's much more we'll get from him. As for Kemmer . . . his body will be discovered in a ditch somewhere well away from your location. So, take the night and maybe all of tomorrow to decompress. Go to Atlantic City and spend your paychecks at the casinos. Take in a show."

It was as close to lighthearted chitchat as he gets.

Then he said, "You did good work today, Colonel. You and your whole team."

He ended the call.

I clicked my tongue for Ghost, who jumped up on the bed and demanded head scratches and cuddles. I was entirely good with that.

INTERLUDE 12
THE MANSION
UNDISCLOSED LOCATION
TWENTY MONTHS AGO

Mary sat for hours with the computer.

With Haruspex.

She was delighted that it remembered her.

She remembered it. Remembered designing it. Remembered building it on the bones of other computers that had come before it, though it took some moments to pull each name of its forebears out of her mind. There was wreckage in the way. There was dust and spiders in there.

Pangaea was its grandmother. She knew that for sure.

A master computer system created by Antonio Bertolini, an Italian genius who had pioneered early computer systems for a group of Cold War scientists called the Cabal. *Pangaea* was not the name of the actual computer—that was *Kiagyal*, the Hungarian word for *mastermind*—but was instead a search-and-destroy software package that allowed the computer to intrude into nearly any computer and steal its secrets without leaving a trace.

Kiagyal and Pangaea were stolen by . . .

Here her mind stumbled a bit. She could see only a shadowy figure when she tried to remember who had taken those systems from the Cabal. She knew the man was dangerous. Extremely dangerous. He had slaughtered some of the most feared terrorists in the world to stop them from using Pangaea from stealing missile science, defense information, and more.

His face was a dark blur, and the harder she tried to see through the brain fog, the denser the obscurity became. It was as if her mind did not want her to see the man's face. Or know his name.

And yet he had so many names. She remembered once doing a net search and coming up with nearly forty names. She'd also found photos of him dating back decades. Not merely a few, but far back. Too far back. Frighteningly far back.

The members of the Cabal had called him by a nickname.

The Alchemist.

They had feared him. Rightly so. She wondered what they thought and felt in the last moments when the boogeyman of their dread had appeared, gun in hand, to end them.

The Alchemist.

That was as far as she could get with trying to remember the man's name, and her heart was racing for fear that trying further would somehow invoke him. She got up from her desk and checked the bedroom and patio doors to make sure they were locked.

Not that locks could keep the boogeyman out.

Even so, it broke the trance, and when she sat down again, she felt she could move on.

Pangaea and Kiagyal. Grandmother and grandfather to Haruspex. After them . . . who? What?

She sat on her chair, rocking forward and back for nearly ten minutes as she fought to reclaim that memory. There was fear associated with its name, too. Just not as much.

Mind . . .

Mind something.

When it came, it burst like a light in her mind.

MindReader.

And its consort . . . Oracle.

Mother and father.

Oracle was actually first. A newer version of Kiagyal, built using the latest in emerging computer science. Sophisticated but imperfect. Not truly what it would become. Not yet the young god of computers. Not yet MindReader.

MindReader was so beautiful.

"God," she said aloud, just thinking about how powerful it was. The elegance of its design. The radical forms its software took. The power that blossomed within it.

And oh how it shared its power with her. It clarified her vision; it lengthened her reach.

Yet she was not content with it, because even that magnificent machine was not fully evolved. Haruspex had been its next incarnation. More powerful, more dangerous in its specificity of purpose.

Now she sat with Haruspex.

Wondering what *it* would become.

Wondering what new power it would give her.

She could almost feel the world shudder at the very thought.

CHAPTER 31
COMFORT SUITES ATLANTIC CITY NORTH
ABSECON, NEW JERSEY

Half an hour later, a team came to transport the prisoner and the corpse. They also brought a legit cleaning crew to sanitize the room

JONATHAN MABERRY

so I could move back into it. They even left a vanilla-scented candle burning to clear the last of the stink out of the air.

While they were working, I went outside to make a couple of calls. The first was, of course, to Junie.

"Joe," she said sleepily. "How are you?"

"I'm good, babe," I said. "Where are you?"

"At the moment, on the couch in the living room. I got home last night and decided to spend some time over at Rudy and Circe's. They need a break from screaming kids."

"Nice," I lied. Much as I loved Rudy and Circe, and the kids, they were both in noisy phases, and I hate the sound of kids screeching, either in play or teething distress. If some terrorist ever wants me to spill state secrets, just put on a video of screaming kids, and I will be happy to talk. Bunny, who has a little one, would likely agree whole-heartedly.

Even with the phone pressed to my ear, Ghost heard Junie's voice and began to wag his bushy tail and make keening noises. I held the phone out to him so Junie could tell him what a good boy he was and how many belly rubs he was owed when he brought me home safe. He danced around and smiled at me.

"When are you coming home?" asked Junie.

"Soon as I can," I said.

"Are you still in the States?"

"Yup." I paused. "Do you ever miss it? Being here, I mean?"

"Sure. America's beautiful, and it's home," said Junie. "But Corfu is home, too. It's where *we* live."

That made my shriveled, blackened coal-chunk of a heart glow. Our conversation went deep and went personal, and, no, I'm not going to share it.

When the call was over, I called Rudy, completely forgetting in the moment that it was 4:00 a.m. in Corfu. He sounded more weary than newly awakened, though.

"How are you, brother?" he asked.

"Getting by. Lights are on."

That was shorthand for no presence of the Darkness.

We talked about work for a while. My cell is encrypted, and so is Rudy's phone. I told him about the interrogation and what we'd learned. He said that he would watch the videos from our body cams and give me any assessments that came to mind.

"Let me ask, Joe," he said, "how many cases can you work at one time? There's the Tenth Legion, there's Kuga, there's Mr. October, and there's still those strange videos with the snakes and bats."

"That's the thing, Rude," I said, "Church and I are pretty much of the opinion that they're all threads on the same sweater. Well, maybe not the bats-and-snakes thing. We're nowhere with that. But the rest of it . . . yeah. October seems to be the bad guy here."

"Is that a theory, or a supposition built on evidence?"

I explained the conversation I'd had with Church and how we each shared our gut feelings.

"Both of you are known for good instincts and for making intuitive leaps," said Rudy.

As with Junie, Ghost wagged when he heard Rudy's voice. But I swear to god there was a slyness to his doggie grin because he knew he was on the outs at the Sanchez-O'Tree household. Despite attempts to prevent such an event, Ghost and their Irish wolfhound, Banshee, had gotten together and produced a large litter of enormous pups that were an even genetic split between wolfhound and shepherd. Most of the pups were in training with Jessica McNerney, the RTI animal trainer, and at least three would go into service as combat dogs. Circe, who was Church's estranged daughter as well as Rudy's wife, was unhappy about that. Lilith, Violin's mother and Church's lover, was *deeply* upset because Banshee was one of a very long line of pure wolfhounds. Neither Circe nor Lilith much cared for me without that, and the pups were reminders that I was a bastard.

I gave Ghost some dog treats. His current favorite was dried bison lung.

Rudy and I chatted for a bit longer, shifting eventually from work to family to our dogs to baseball. Then we said good night.

Before he disconnected, though, he said, "I have a bad feeling about all this, Joe. I'll light a candle for you."

I put my phone away. Like Toys, Rudy was a devout Catholic. He knew I had very little actual faith left in me, but his lighting a candle meant something to him. And therefore to me.

JONATHAN MABERRY

I took Ghost for a walk, letting him sniff everything and leave what Junie calls PeeMails. Then we went back inside.

Within half an hour, I was asleep, with Ghost's head on my stomach. We slept soundly.

Until Church called me at two in the morning.

INTERLUDE 13
THE MANSION
UNDISCLOSED LOCATION
NINETEEN MONTHS AGO

Mr. October did not want to be seen and therefore was not seen.

He wished he had great psychic powers like people in books and movies did. But prescience and clairvoyance were not among his many talents. Awareness, to be sure; some intuitive flashes. Some connections with the natural world, which existed in his mind on some nameless levels that he had never been able to properly and thoroughly quantify.

But he could not read minds.

Not *read*, as such.

His empathy gave him a degree of insight into most people. He could almost always tell when someone was lying. He was hard to fool when it came to motive, bias, or allegiance. People like Top Sims, Scott Wilson, and that overgrown oaf they called Bunny—they were easy to read. The average man on the street was as close to being an open book as he needed.

And yet.

He watched Mary as she knelt on the muddy bank of a stream, a raccoon caught in her hands. Blood dripped from the mangled animal, and its dying screams were so faint now that they did not even disturb the bees and sparrows.

October watched Mary as she chewed. Watched her eyes as she looked into the woods. Her eyes were intensely dark—black irises and pupils surrounded by vicious red sclera. It was her feeding look, he knew. Absent at all other times, but present when the hunger was on her with such scarlet intensity.

The raccoon squealed in terror, its broken body struggling still, even though it was far closer to death than it ever would be again to life. Dying. Mostly dead. Yet fighting. For each last breath. For each beat of its failing heart.

October felt a small pang of compassion for it. He wished he could snap his fingers and still that frantic heart.

They always think I'm cruel, he mused. *People think I'm the devil, that I'm evil.*

It amazed him that his reputation had always preceded him like the spreading tide of a plague. Yet he bore no animus to anyone. Not even the people who died during the machinations of one or another of his games.

To him, all of this was a game. He sometimes dreamed that he would be recognized and revered as a prince of games. Maybe *the* Prince of Games.

Not now, though.

Not while St. Germaine still lived.

Hate filled that man's heart, for sure. Or . . . so he assumed. St. Germaine—or Church or Abbot or John the Traveler or whatever name he used—was one of those few people October could not read. Not at all. Not even a little bit.

His pet scorpion, Joe Ledger, was nearly as bad. That man's mind burned like the heart of a nuclear reactor on the verge of meltdown. Hate lived in him, too.

He looked at Mary.

Her mind was a closed fist to him. A shuttered room in a haunted house.

What are you thinking, my beautiful monster?

She lifted the raccoon and crushed its throat with her teeth. There was a last spasm that made the animal shudder from whiskers to tail, and then it slumped limply in her hands.

What are *you, little girl?* wondered October. That thought was followed very quickly by another. *What have I wrought upon the earth by waking you up?*

The sparrows flitted from tree to tree as Typhoid Mary ate the raccoon. Blood and meat, hair and bones. Every last bit.

JONATHAN MABERRY

CHAPTER 32
COMFORT SUITES ATLANTIC CITY NORTH
ABSECON, NEW JERSEY

I thought the call was from Bug.

"Bugster, my man," I said sleepily, "give me some happy news. Tell me we have clearance to come back home and—"

But before I could finish, Church's voice said, "Colonel, I need you packed and rolling in ten minutes."

"What? Why? What's on fire?"

"Maybe the world," said Church. "Call me when you're on your way to the airport."

And the call went dead.

I heard the strain in his voice, the sharp tones, and something else. Was it fear?

We were in the truck in eight minutes and thirteen seconds.

CHAPTER 33
FISHERMAN'S PARADISE RV CAMP
RADFORD, VIRGINIA

The two killers lay deep in the shadows of a copse of sassafras trees, each of them studying the cottage through scopes. They both had Sako TRG 42s, superb Finnish bolt-action long-range sniper rifles chambered for .338 Lapua Magnum cartridges. Each weapon was fitted with ARIES sound suppressors.

The extra weight of the suppressor cans had some drag on the barrel, but each gun was steadied on a bipod. Both guns had been sighted in. The shelter of the trees cut down on windage, but the evening itself was calm. And at a distance of two hundred yards, each of the women was confident of hitting and killing whatever they shot at.

The woman on the left was the better shot, and they both knew it. It was a factor to be added to the equation of this mission. For this reason, the woman on the right was acting as spotter.

Just shy of the two-hundred-yard mark was a cottage with

whitewashed aluminum siding and a wraparound porch that looked out on a cedar-water lake. The vast Pine Barrens encircled the lake, with small cutouts into the forest to accommodate thirty similar cottages. Two men stood on the porch. One was smoking a cigarette, the burning end flaring every now and then as he took a drag.

The spotter's name was Tamileigh Squires—Tommy to everyone—and she was the younger of the pair by a good number of years. That age difference was in no way obvious, because her partner looked no more than five years her senior. Looks were deceiving in many cases, though in this instance, that deception was extreme.

Tommy was still fairly new to this line of work, having done it solo for most of her late teens and into her adult life. She had been recruited by her partner—a foreign woman who went by the call sign of Violin—during a rescue situation in Orlando, taking children away from human traffickers. It had been a bloody fight, and Violin's ex, Colonel Joe Ledger, had been a big part of it.

Since then, Tommy and Violin had been everywhere—all across America, up into Canada, and with several trips to Europe, Africa, Asia, and South America. Now they were in Virginia, following people like the two men in her scope. Following them. Sometimes just watching. Sometimes with Tommy spotting for Violin, and sometimes pulling the trigger herself.

She had not yet learned the seemingly unbreakable cool her friend and mentor always maintained. In fact, Tommy could not even imagine Violin losing that cool. Sure, she knew that Violin had been badly affected by the Shiva hallucinogenic bioweapon in Israel months before, but that did not count.

Beside her, Violin was as silent as the shadows in which they lay. Silent, patient, cold as ice. They watched the men talk, listening to their conversation via the live feed from a starling drone that was pretending to sleep on one of the beams of the porch roof.

"—be here soon, Donny, " said the smoker.

"Not sure this is all that smart, man," said Donny. "After that shit show in Tuckerton . . ."

"Not our circus, not our monkeys," said Smoker. "Those button-dick gun nuts probably shot each other. News reports say that no one

JONATHAN MABERRY

else was found dead or taken alive. Just those idiots. We're the A-team. They're all a bunch of incel retards."

They both chuckled at that.

Donny was still nervous, though. "I don't like it. We should have bumped this handoff to at least tomorrow. That Firefall thing is supposed to happen soon, and we have the party favors. Those little cunts in there are sure as hell not in any hurry. Not juiced as they are."

"Boss says deliver tonight and let the legionnaire fucks play tomorrow," said Smoker. "Maybe it's to soothe everyone's prelaunch jitters. From what I heard, Firefall's going to be huge."

"So people keep saying," muttered Donny, "but we don't even know what it is. Firefall? Sounds kind of faggoty, you ask me."

"Hell if I know, man," said Smoker. "And no, I haven't asked, and I'll tell you why. Couple weeks ago, I heard one of those militia asswipes ask about it, and his CO came down on him like a ton of bricks. Gave him the whole 'loose lips sink ships' speech."

"Huh," grunted Donny. "Between you and me, brother, *not* knowing what's coming makes my asshole clench tighter than a nun's cooze. And it doesn't make me feel better about doing *this* shit."

Smoker laughed. "Have another beer and calm your ass down, dude. How many times have we done this stuff? It's clockwork."

There was the faint hiss of beer bottle twist-off caps being turned, then both men lifted Budweisers to their mouths and drank deeply.

Tommy knew they could have taken them both right then. Violin could have done them both before either man could yell out. Tommy was pretty sure she could, too, but this wasn't the time to experiment.

An SUV drove past on the dirt road, a pair of canoes on a trailer behind it, wheels thumping and bumping. It headed farther north along the lake and vanished out of sight. The two men had watched it pass without otherwise reacting to it.

Eight minutes later, another vehicle came up, moving slowly, swerving gently to avoid the potholes. It was a two-year-old Ford Transit cargo van with smoked front windows. No side or rear windows. A sign on the side read: SUBURBAN PROPANE.

Tommy tensed up, but Violin touched her shoulder, letting her fingers linger until the younger woman relaxed.

"Hop frog," said Violin. Those were the first words she'd spoken since they had arrived early that morning.

Tommy nodded, shifted away from her rifle carefully so as not to disturb its placement, and picked up a small, flat tablet. The screen display showed an image of a benign *Mona Lisa* smiling her secret smile. Tommy activated it with a thumb on a sensor, and the screen saver dissolved to reveal a set of controls, each labeled with the name of the kind of drone they'd put in place that morning—starling, owl, rabbit, and hop frog.

As the cargo van pulled up to the house, Tommy activated one of the waiting hop frogs. It looked exactly like what it was supposed to be—a common Pine Barrens tree frog less than two inches long. Most of its internal machinery was designed for movement and battery storage, but in its belly was a transponder.

The tree frog hopped from the side of one porch railing baluster and leaped onto the back of the van. It crept up the side, and Tommy guided it to a concealed place behind the bumper. The frog's feet deployed an adhesive that set within seconds, permanently adhering the drone to the metal. Then it shut down all functions except the transponder and battery. With no other drains on its energy, the signal came in strong and clear on Tommy's tablet, and it had an effective range of five miles.

She set the tablet down and regained her position as spotter.

Waiting was the second-toughest part of this mission, and it was more than twenty minutes before the two men from the porch and the two occupants from the van accomplished their task. A fifth man stood out by the road, a cell phone to his ear, reporting on any traffic. There was very little, it being late in the season.

Then Tommy tensed again as the four men each came out of the house with a small figure. The largest and perhaps oldest of those figures was a tall ten-year-old boy. Three boys in all, the others much younger and smaller; and seven girls, ranging in age from six to eleven. They each staggered as if drugged, and were held upright by one of the men. Ten children. Their mouths were covered with duct tape, and there were sleep blinders over their eyes. Their hands were fastened with plastic flex-cuffs, but Tommy noticed that the cuffs were padded to prevent chafing. She knew this was not for the comfort of those kids but to prevent damage to skin. Damage to property.

The children were listless, except for the tall boy, who struggled and fought. Perhaps they had not given him enough tranquilizers. But the man holding him pulled the kid close and whispered something in his ear that the starling drone could not pick up. The boy froze, then began trembling. He offered no new resistance as he was handed up into the back of the van.

All of this was done with the kind of quiet efficiency born of many repetitions.

Tommy had to fight to keep her finger outside of the trigger guard. She saw herself in each and every one of those little kids. She remembered men like these. Men—and even women—who held absolutely no regard for the pain, the fear, the humiliation, the horror that children like her endured. People who saw young flesh as a commodity, even to the point of scheduling surgeries to repair hymens ruptured by sports so that every little girl was a verifiable virgin. People who fed erectile dysfunction drugs to the boys so they were able to get and maintain erections—even the very young ones. People who, in Tommy's view, were soulless. Evil people who could not blame their cruelties on any cause or factor of upbringing. Even before she'd met Joe Ledger, Violin, and Dr. Rudy Sanchez, Tommy understood that the nature-versus-nurture equation was fundamentally flawed. It omitted choice.

These people chose to be this way. That was what made it evil.

Tommy's finger caressed the welcoming curve of the trigger.

"Wait," murmured Violin.

That one word.

Tommy closed her eyes for one full second, then opened them, nodded, and kept watching.

The van did a turnaround in front of the cottage and headed back to the road. Violin leaned over to watch the tablet screen. They saw the strong signal from the transponder make a turn onto the highway and head north, eventually merging onto I-81 heading north.

Without a sound, the two women rose, put their rifles into a padded gear bag, and ran silently through the trees to where their vehicle waited—a smoke-gray Toyota Highlander. By the time they were on the highway, too, the Ford was miles ahead. Tommy drove quickly enough to close the gap to two miles, but she got no closer. With a transponder, line of sight wasn't necessary for an effective tail.

They settled in for the long chase.

CHAPTER 34
WESTCOAT ROAD
EGG HARBOR TOWNSHIP, NEW JERSEY

It was technically a ten-minute drive to the airport in Atlantic City. Remy was driving, so . . . figure six minutes.

I had Church on comms before we had the doors closed.

"I will give this to you quickly, Outlaw," he said. "Shirley has been prepped and is waiting for you. All clearances have been handled. Once you arrive at the terminal, you will be met by a local asset who will take you directly to your jet. Bug will download a complete briefing package once Havoc is airborne."

Shirley is more or less my personal property. Not legally, but no one is ever likely to contest it. She's a sleek Gulfstream G650 that was big enough to accommodate all five members of Echo Team, along with Ghost, two logistics guys, and the flight crew. It had a range of seven thousand nautical miles and could hit a maximum speed of Mach 0.95. A zippy little bird that once belonged to a Colombian billionaire who thought it would be a quick cash grab to set up a bioweapons shop in the same lab he was using to make coke and heroin. I thwarted that plan by throwing him out of the hatch while we were in flight. He made a tiny little splash and probably gave some sharks indigestion. I confiscated his ride, and Bug fudged the ownership paperwork.

We were all synced with the TOC, so everyone could hear Church's rundown of the situation.

"You will fly to Penn Yan Regional Airport in upstate New York," he said, "where Bird Dog will be on deck with a vehicle and equipment. The vehicle's GPS will be preset to take you to a location near Canandaigua Lake, in the Finger Lakes region. To Autumn Nest, a bed-and-breakfast."

"And why do I want to go to take my team of highly trained special operators to a romantic B&B in the Finger Lakes district? I mean, we're pretty close, but . . ."

Ignoring that, Church said, "Autumn Nest is a cover and is manned by two agents who used to work for the DMS and now work for a joint international bioweapons research group known as Serket—that is S-e-r-k-e-t—named for the Egyptian goddess of healing venomous stings and bites."

"Never heard of it."

"No reason you should have, Colonel. Until now, that is. Serket oversees a number of containment facilities around the globe, all of them well hidden and on a need-to-know basis. None of your previous cases has involved any of those facilities."

"And now I *do* need to know because they have some kind of mad scientist lab under the bed-and-breakfast?"

"In a nutshell," agreed Church. "The facility to which I'm directing you is code-named Gehenna, and it operates with a charter agreed upon by a special nonpolitical group within the US government."

"Again I ask, why is Havoc going there?"

"Because as of 8:22 this morning, local time, Gehenna has gone dark."

"Okay, fair enough. That's ominous," I said. "But correct me if I'm wrong, boss, the US of A has a lot of alphabet groups who have both the knowledge and jurisdiction to handle this kind of thing."

"They do, but it is in our best interest that they are not involved. The level of secrecy involved here is considerably above top secret, Outlaw. No president since Kennedy has needed to know about its existence, and for that, we can all be thankful."

"Even so, why us?" I asked. "I'm as patriotic as the next ten baseball-loving, beer-drinking devourers of Mom's apple pie, but I'm not working for Uncle Sam at the moment. Not unless there's been a policy change I haven't heard about."

"Fair question, but you won't like the answer," said Church.

"Try me."

"Gehenna was set up to serve several key functions. Foremost among those are various kinds of forensic biological research projects in which the corpses of persons infected by exotic bioweapons are kept. Designer weapons of the kind the DMS and other groups have encountered but which cannot be safely studied at ordinary laboratories for a number of reasons. Primarily the secret nature of bioweapons developed for and/or by criminal or terrorist organizations requires more safeguards. Just the knowledge that certain disease forms have been able to be mutated for specific purposes makes them targets of theft."

"Sure," I said. "Everyone wants to copy their homework from Frankenstein's notebooks."

"Precisely."

"Coming up on it," said Remy.

"I heard," said Church. "Once you're in the air, activate the ORB so Doc Holliday and I can give you that full briefing."

"Copy that," I said.

CHAPTER 35
OFFICES OF FOX 5 ATLANTA
1551 BRIARCLIFF ROAD NE
ATLANTA, GEORGIA

The call came in overnight and left on the voicemail. An assistant producer listened to it over her morning coffee.

> *I am calling on behalf of the Sons of Fuentes, the militant arm of the Juárez Cartel. I will not give my name. That does not matter. What matters is that we will no longer be persecuted by the bloated pig that is the United States of America. You have seen what we did in Atlanta. Do not believe that we will stop there. America must bleed. America must burn. We hold the razor and a lighted match. Withdraw all of your agents from Mexican soil. Abandon all of your border checkpoints. Do this now. Do it to save your own lives. Do this in memory of Vicente Carrillo Fuentes, who was murdered by the CIA. The Sons of Fuentes will never forgive, and we will never forget.*

The AP listened to the statement, then had her computer print it out so she could read it again without having to navigate the caller's heavy accent.

"What the hell?" she wondered.

The typhus story was already fading from a headline to nothing much. There had been no spread, and the authorities another producer had spoken with said that it was believed the fleas carrying the disease were accidentally brought to the country, likely in food shipments or on animals. A dead end.

The AP sipped her coffee and thought about it. Then she dropped it in a tray of outgoing interoffice mail for a senior producer to consider for possible follow-up.

The senior producer barely glanced at it, then tossed it in the trash.

"More bullshit," he said.

CHAPTER 36
MONTGOMERY MUSEUM OF FINE ARTS
1 MUSEUM DRIVE
MONTGOMERY, ALABAMA

She wandered through the exhibit halls apparently without purpose or plan.

One of the security guards, Alfred Comings, watched her with growing interest and mild concern. The visitor was a nervous-looking young woman in her early twenties. She wore jeans and an untucked man's dress shirt that had some dull brown stains on it. Coffee, probably, thought Comings. The woman's hair was short and uncombed, though that kind of look was still in style. It made the guard wonder if the woman was one of those trendy hipster types.

The visitor was white and wore sunglasses, which was odd, given that the lighting for most of the exhibits was discreet. Again, maybe that was part of some attempt at looking cool or stylish.

What bothered Comings, though, was that the woman was sweating. Sure, it was hot outside, but the air-conditioning inside the museum was set low. Also, there was a splotchy red rash peeking up from the vee of the woman's shirt. It was on her chest and the sides of her neck. Psoriasis? That's what Comings guessed.

When the woman came into the same room for the third time, Comings decided to approach her.

"Can I help you, miss?"

The young woman turned to him. "What?"

"I asked if there's anything I can do for you? Is there something in particular you're looking for?"

Instead of answering, the woman turned aside to cough. It was a dry cough, but deep. And she moved like she was in pain.

That's when the first alarm bell went off for Comings. There was a new strain of COVID going around. God in heaven, was that what was going on here?

"Miss, are you feeling okay? Do you need to sit down?"

The coughing fit trailed off, and the woman dragged a forearm across her wet lips.

"I'm . . . I'm okay," she said. "Thanks."

She took a moment, straightened, pulled in a deep chestful of air, and exhaled slowly, nodding as she did so.

"Yes, I'm good." She took a short step toward Comings and, weirdly, patted him on the arm. "All good. I just came in to get cool. Is . . . is there a bathroom?"

Comings told her where it was and ghosted along behind as the woman went inside. She was in there for five minutes, and Comings was just about to call for a female docent to go in and check on her when the woman came out. Her face was flushed and her shirtfront spattered with water as if she'd vigorously washed her face. But the shirt was tucked in and she'd combed her hair.

"Much better," she said, spotting Comings. "Thanks."

The woman sketched a salute and headed for the door.

Comings watched her go, but then a busload of teenagers from a local school began pushing in through the doors, and the strange young woman vanished from his thoughts. He did not think about her at all until the following afternoon, when the ER doctor was yelling at him to provide details of *any* kind as to where he'd been, who he had been with, and other questions. By then, Comings was sinking down and down.

By the time the specialist in infectious diseases arrived, Comings was in a coma.

He died at 11:17 that evening. Twenty-eight hours after the museum visitor had patted his arm.

CHAPTER 37
MONTGOMERY MUSEUM OF FINE ARTS
1 MUSEUM DRIVE
MONTGOMERY, ALABAMA

David White had his bulky, ape-faced driver stop in front of the museum. White hopped out, caught up to the new Typhoid Mary, and, without touching her, guided her to the gray panel van.

"Where are we going?" asked the woman.

"Somewhere quiet, Mary," he said.

As she entered the van, the woman paused for a just a moment, looking at the heavy plastic sheeting. "What's all this for?" she asked.

Instead of answering her, White shot her in the back of the head with his silenced .22. Typhoid Mary, whose real name was Andrea Allessio, never saw the gun. She did not feel a flicker of pain. She merely ended.

He looked at her body for a moment, wincing a bit in disgust as her collapsing muscular control made her bowels release. He tossed the gun into the back, closed the van, went around to the passenger side, and climbed in. The driver with the gorilloid face handed him a blister pack of sugar-free gum. White took it and popped out two of the peppermint pieces and put them in his mouth. The mint aroma was strong, though he could still smell the faintness of fecal matter.

Neither spoke as the van drove away.

CHAPTER 38
AL.COM

While our jet was climbing into the wild blue yonder, the news services and internet were losing their goddamn minds.

I was following several stories on my MindReader laptop. I saw the articles about the Fuentes group—or someone pretending to be them—taking credit for a biological attack in Atlanta. Other groups—all small fringe groups in Central and South America—vying to say it was them.

There's some of that all the time. Tiny cells of disgruntled assholes who don't have the money, muscle, or savvy to orchestrate something like this themselves, so they try to borrow power by making false claims. Saw this when I was a cop in Baltimore after the latest kill by the serial killer du jour, and more times than I can count since coming to work for Church. Some people are demonstrably evil, and others are evil adjacent.

Stuff like this makes my nuts itch.

They also scare me, because someone *did* get hold of a bioweapon and *did* release it, and that means there is a serious player out in the weeds. Maybe that person or group was among those who took credit—which confuses the search. Or maybe they're staying silent and letting the loudmouths draw all the attention from the investigative groups. My gut told me it was the latter case, but that was instinct and not confirmation.

As we rose to cruising altitude, Nikki Bloom at the RTI sent me something that came in to the news desk of a multi-platform cable news service in Alabama. It read:

> *America supports genocide in the Gaza Strip. They fabricated the Hamas invasion of the false state of Israel. The atrocities that followed prove that there is no compassion, faith, or humanity in Israel and America. We will not abide this any longer. In the heartland of America, in the city of Montgomery in the state of Alabama, we have shown that there is nowhere safe from reprisal. America must denounce the government of Israel and deny them any further financial or military support. This is not a negotiation. This is the will of God.*

The note was unsigned, but Nikki used MindReader to determine that the email originated in Qatar.

The message blew up on the net and social media, and everyone at the RTI started sweating bullets. Two biological weapon incidents. Two different pathogens. And—strangest of all—two completely different groups taking credit. A cartel sympathizer and now a militant group in the Middle East.

What the actual fuck?

I could feel every part of me all the way down to my molecules bracing for what *else* was going to happen.

INTERLUDE 14
THE MANSION
UNDISCLOSED LOCATION
SIX WEEKS AGO

"My dear girl," said Mr. October, "I think I have something you may find both entertaining and a challenge."

Mary was at her usual spot on the floor in front of the fireplace. There was no fire, and the ashes looked cold and dreary. Her modified Haruspex computer sat on a plump decorative pillow, and Mary had been working through some new code for VaultBreaker. She looked up slowly, her face a study in comprehensive disinterest.

"Oh," she said in an utterly flat voice, "goodie. What is it? An updated copy of the white militia screed?"

"Ha! Hardly," laughed October. He was dressed in god-awful checked golf trousers and a polo, and the outfit was so bad that Mary decided not to comment, because it was very low-hanging fruit.

"Then what is it?" she asked.

"Come and see," he suggested and walked back to the foyer and out to the front of the house.

Mary gave a low, long sigh, stood up, smoothed her jeans, and tugged her Disturbed T-shirt down, then followed.

Parked outside was a late-model white Ford F-250 with several crates filling the bed. At October's invitation, Mary came and peered over the side at them. The driver was using a pinch bar to pry off the lid. When it came free, he took it and stepped back. October told him to go get some coffee inside.

When they were alone, Mary watched as October pulled away

handfuls of plastic packing straw to reveal three metal devices of a kind unknown to her. Each was shaped like the tip of a retro science fiction missile, with a conical cap that reminded her of the funnel hat the Tin Man wore in *The Wizard of Oz*, but with no finger ring. October bent down and carefully unscrewed the cap and handed it to her.

She was surprised by its weight and upon examination saw that it wasn't metal but a kind of plastic coated with silver metallic paint. With the cap—or, she supposed, nose cone—removed, she saw that the upper shaft was ringed by ten clear plastic cylinders filled with a golden liquid.

"What is all this?"

"It's called a Gorgon," explained October. "A new kind of warhead developed by Marco Russo—the Italian software genius. You've heard of him? Yes? Good. He designed it, and it was constructed by a special team working for the late and much-lamented Jason Aydelotte."

Mary brightened. "Whoa . . . wait . . . Is this the Shiva delivery weapon?"

"The very same. Those cylinders are separate warheads with the fungal bioweapon in a preservative suspension."

She ran her fingers over them very lightly, then glanced at him. "For what? Is this what we're going to deploy on Firefall?"

"Mmmm, yes and no," he said. "Ideally, I'd like to add something nasty—but not *too* nasty—to the contents. Maybe MERS . . . ? Do you remember?"

"Don't be a dope," she snapped. "Middle Eastern respiratory syndrome. You said they have a lot of it at Gehenna. It's on our shopping list."

"Indeed it is."

She studied the cylinders. "Should be easy enough, once we have the MERS samples."

"Ah," said October, "getting the pathogen is one thing, and we should be ready to hit Gehenna in a month or maybe a bit more. That isn't what concerns me. These warheads are controlled by what I'm told is a 'master chip.' I assume you know what that is?"

"Sure. A chip loaded with security software to prevent tampering."

"Right again. We can't dismantle or tamper with the warheads, nor access the contents, without them blowing up in our faces. At this range, the blast would be fatal, and even if it didn't kill you, it would give you a super-dose of Shiva, and you'd go quite mad for a very long time."

"Mad-*der*," she said, and they both laughed at that. Then she bent and studied what she could see of the mechanism.

"It's supposed to be unbreakable or, I suppose, unhackable," said October.

"Bitch, please," she said.

It was the first time in months that Miss Mary looked genuinely happy.

CHAPTER 39
DOUBLETREE BY HILTON HOTEL
1000 EASTPORT PLAZA DRIVE
COLLINSVILLE, ILLINOIS

It was a convention of mid-level cybersecurity experts. Three hundred of them. They were a chatty lot and tended to start conversations with anyone handy about their computer and social media safety policies.

Gil Foehner, the day shift assistant bar manager, had listened to hours of it and was pretty sure that being run over by a slow bulldozer would be very much more pleasant. He was not actually at the point where he wanted to go into the back and start doing shots of Drano Max Gel, but it was tempting. The waitress on shift kept throwing him increasingly desperate glances.

In a rare moment of quiet, when both were in the back cleaning glasses, she said, "I swear to the lord baby Jesus that if one more of them asks me how often I change my password, I'm going to start putting Ex-Lax in their food."

"After that guy from Des Moines kept leaning over to *accidentally* press his shoulder against your boobs, I'm surprised you didn't *accidentally* spill his martini in his lap," said Gil.

Fanny, the waitress, sighed. "I almost did, but it's a big order and I need the tips. But I did give him *the look*, so he knows that I know. And if he doesn't leave a tip significantly north of twenty percent, I'll be serving spitters the rest of the day."

"What is it about conventioneers that turn ordinary people into raging assholes?" wondered Gil. "I mean, it's not like they can blame being drunk."

"Oh, hell no," Fanny agreed. "They come in like that. And the jackass who was leaning against my chest has a wedding ring on. He didn't even have the self-respect or empathy to take it off, like his buddies all did."

Gil shrugged. "I don't see anything wrong with spitters. A little in a martini, well-stirred . . ."

"I'm considering it."

They smiled at each other, but neither would really go that far. It was nice to speculate on small and subtle acts of revenge, though.

Someone else came into the kitchen—a member of the housekeeping staff responsible for keeping the lobby orderly, the hand sanitizer dispensers filled, and bathrooms stocked with paper products. She was a new hire, which is why she was that low on the staff pecking order. But she did not seem to mind.

"Hey," she said.

"Hey," said Gil. "It's . . . Mary, right? Not Maria?"

"Yes. Mary. And you're Gil and Fanny." She was a Latina in her early twenties, a bit heavy for the off-the-rack uniform, but pleasant and friendly.

"What can we do for you?" Gil asked.

"Oh, sorry." She held up the gallon jug of the off-brand hand sanitizer the company used. "Just making the rounds."

Gil nodded and gestured to the dispensers in the back. There was one near the prep sink and another by the kitchen door. Mary gave them a smile, refilled the units, nodded, and left.

Once she was gone, Fanny said, "That was weird."

"What was?"

"Did you look at her face? She was sweating like a pig."

"It's hot outside. Maybe she just came in from having a smoke."

"I guess," conceded Fanny. "Anyway . . . I'd better get back to it."

She reached past Gil, pumped a dollop of the clear sanitizer into her palms, rubbed her hands vigorously, then wiped the residue on her apron. The stuff usually evaporated quickly because of the ethanol in it, but the company had been through half a dozen vendors of the stuff in the eight years she'd worked at the hotel. She gave it almost no thought as she picked up a plate of appetizers and headed out to deliver them to the cybersecurity conventioneers.

The guy who had been so inappropriate earlier gave her a big smile and even—god help her—an actual wink. Who the hell really winked anymore?

Fanny served them all and went off to take orders from another bunch who had come in while she was chatting with Gil. The day got busier, and as evening came on, she began to feel a little shaky.

She clocked out and went back to the one-bedroom where she lived. A small place that was neat and tidy and comfortable. On the way, she stopped at a CVS and picked up some Nyquil just in case it was a cold coming on. The Nyquil dropped her into a deep sleep halfway through an old episode of *Justified*.

Fanny woke late, having forgotten to set the alarm. As soon as she stood up, she knew it was more than a cold. The room immediately swung around and her knees buckled, and she sat down hard on the bed. The headache was bad. Worse than bad. It was like someone was trying to kick his way out of her skull. The cough, when it started, was even worse. She all but crawled to the bathroom for Tylenol and a COVID test kit.

The test was negative, which was a sort of relief, but not really. She felt truly awful.

Her temperature was climbing, and the cough was getting bad. So, Fanny called the manager at the hotel.

The phone rang twenty times.

She tried again. No answer.

Then she called Gil's cell. He answered on the fifth ring, but his voice sounded like someone else—it was gravelly, rough, phlegmy, and wrong.

"God, Gil . . . are you sick, too?"

He laughed. Maybe it was a laugh. Hard to tell because it sparked a coughing fit.

"Hey," he said at last, "I feel like death. Tried to come in, but everyone's got it. Some kind of bug. Damn. Coughing my lungs up."

"Did you see the doc?"

"No," he said. "Sally took the car, and she can't get off work to come take me until later. What about you?"

"I tried to call in, but nobody's answering at the desk. Weird."

Gil was silent for a moment. "No one picked up?"

"No. I tried twice. I'll send a text message to Connie. She's on morning shift."

She listened to Gil coughing, and then she was coughing. The shivers started then, and they were bad.

"Gil," she said, "I'm scared."

"Can you drive?" he asked.

"I . . . guess."

"Go to urgent care. I mean right now. This isn't right. Call me once you know something."

"I will," she promised.

She showered, which helped a little, then dressed and drove to the urgent care in Collinsville. A nurse met her at the door.

"Do you have the symptoms?" she demanded before even asking her name.

"I . . . yes . . . I think so . . ."

The nurse wore a mask and kept her distance. She turned and yelled in through the open door, "We got another one."

"Another?" asked Fanny.

Or, she tried to. By then, she was falling down, and everything faded to black.

INTERLUDE 15
MISS MARY'S LAB
THE MANSION
UNDISCLOSED LOCATION
EIGHTEEN WEEKS AGO

"MERS?" Mary stared at October. "MERS, really? All of these plots and plans, all of these wheels within wheels, and you want to give people the flu?"

"It's not the flu. MERS is Middle Eastern respiratory syndrome. It's a coronavirus closely related to COVID-19. And it's nothing to look down your nose at, dear girl. You *slept* through the pandemic, but there were over seven hundred million cases of infection and more than seven million deaths."

Mary only grunted at the numbers.

October said, "In fact, the group that developed the mRNA vaccines used to fight COVID-19 was working on a vaccine for MERS when COVID hit. So, yes, it's a very serious illness. If we can get MERS cooking out there in the public—and Gorgon will light that match very nicely, thank you—then we'll have another pandemic. I mean, sure, they could use Paxlovid, but that isn't really specific enough. There's a group in Norway working on something, and one of the best treatments on the horizon is from a research group in Saudi Arabia, where they are using a combination of lopinavir and ritonavir supplemented with interferon beta-1b, but it's not FDA approved here yet. Nowhere near. We may not get the same death toll, but think of the chaos."

"God, there you go with chaos again."

"Chaos is what it's about, Mary," October said sternly. "Disruption to supply chains, overloading hospitals, messing with national and international travel and business. And the politics! That's where it gets really fun. COVID set the stage for a comprehensive lack of agreement and lack of cooperation between the major political parties and even sowed the seeds of dissention within each party. With Firefall, we'll launch Gorgon rockets into the fifty biggest and most crowded venues in the United States. The blame will fall to terrorist cells, and you've already seen some of the AI videos we've prepared. More are being made now, and there are teams ready to tweak the news feeds to amplify the doubts, the fears of foreign attack, all of it. We'll have families ripping each other apart as well as turning the borders into new versions of the OK Corral. God, Mary, we've gone over this. You used to be happy about all this."

"I used to be alive," she said.

October leaned against the wall and folded his arms. "Are we bringing that up again? That has nothing to do with this. What you are now is a gift. Billions would kill to have what you have."

"And I'm an ungrateful little snot, I get it."

"No," said October patiently, "you are caught up in your own drama, and I would appreciate it if you would focus on what *we* are trying to do."

Mary looked into his eyes, then she sighed, smiled, and nodded. "Sorry, Daddy. I'm just tired."

"'Daddy' . . . ?" he echoed.

"Slip of the tongue," she said. "Tell me, though, how do you plan on getting the right strains of MERS? Not the Wuhan ones but something spicier? Maybe . . . weaponized . . . ?"

"Glad you asked," he said. "Why do you think I gave you a copy of VaultBreaker?"

She smiled at that, then walked over and gave him a chaste kiss on the cheek. Then she walked up the stairs and out of her lab.

October stayed where he was, ignoring the questioning looks of the scientists and lab techs. Then he used a shrug to push himself off the wall and followed her up into the house.

CHAPTER 40
DOUBLETREE BY HILTON HOTEL
1000 EASTPORT PLAZA DRIVE
COLLINSVILLE, ILLINOIS

David White chain-smoked Newports and watched the staff entrance. When he spotted the newest Typhoid Mary, he had his driver start the van.

The Mary came tottering over, drawn by White's beckoning hand.

"Where are we going?" she asked as he held the rear door for her to climb in.

"Somewhere quiet," he said as he drew his pistol.

CHAPTER 41
THE MANSION
UNDISCLOSED LOCATION
TWO WEEKS AGO

"What's Lady Frankenstein doing down there?"

"Hmm . . . ?" Mr. October looked up from the sheaf of sales reports Toombs had handed him. It took him a moment to disconnect from the papers and track what his manager was saying. Then he saw that Toombs was looking at the heavy oak door that led down to the basement. "Oh. . . . *things.*"

Toombs waited, one eyebrow raised.

October smiled and set the papers down on the kitchen table. "Sorry, was that a serious question? Yes? Well, it's Mary's big secret."

"Computer lab?" queried Toombs.

"No. That doesn't require that much space. Apart from the cold room where the mainframe is kept, but that's the room off the front bathroom upstairs. No, my friend, what Mary has downstairs is her lab."

"Lab? It's my understanding that she's a computer super-whiz. What's she need a lab for? She also a scientist suddenly?"

October shrugged. "She could be if she wanted to. Mind like hers? Yes. And in truth, she picked up quite a bit of knowledge about a great many areas of science during the years she worked for the Department of Military Sciences. Anatomy, physics, physiology, genetics, organic chemistry, biomechanics . . . it's a long list. Not that she's an *expert* in those fields, but she has a flypaper brain. Everything sticks, and even now, even with the—how should I phrase this?—changes to her cognitive abilities, that knowledge is wonderfully organized."

Toombs said, "But . . . ?"

"But she is not doing anything downstairs. Her team is."

"Team? What team?"

"Dear Mary has been scooping up a number of top minds in useful fields and has set them to work on a variety of special projects."

Toombs walked over and touched the door lightly with his fingertips. "Are we talking weapons development?"

"Not in the way you think," said October. "No guns, no bombs, no guidance systems. Nothing like that."

"Then what? Or is this going to be one of those need-to-know things?"

October drummed his fingers on the sales report. Then he went and stood by Toombs. When he leaned close to the door, Toombs did, too.

"What are we listening for?"

"Wait. Shhh . . . There it is."

He heard it then. Very faint, muffled by the heavy steel-core oak door. It was a sound. A kind of moan or growl—it was hard to distinguish which. Deep, filled with pain, heavy with misery and anger. Toombs recoiled.

"The *fuck* is that?"

"Call it a competitive edge."

"What's that supposed to mean?"

"Rogue Team International is hunting us. They'll likely find the camp in Black Marsh. My sources tell me that the prisoners from the trailer camp have been moved to a secure facility that certain people in Homeland have, in the past, shared with Mr. Church. That means they will be *encouraged* to cooperate."

"They know about the bonuses for silence, though," countered Toombs. "They know we have an army of lawyers."

"What is that to someone like St. Germaine? He is not above using drugs, coercion, and other methods to facilitate open conversations. No, Mr. Toombs, they'll eventually locate the Black Marsh camp, and likely the depot in Upper Black Eddy and the holding pens near here."

Toombs mouthed the words *holding pens* but saved his questions for later. October drifted off point too easily as it was.

"And if they do?" he asked. "That idiot running the Black Marsh camp has a constant hard-on for a real firefight. He has the manpower, the weapons, and the fortifications to take on an army. If he gets hit, he can hold off any field team long enough to get word to us, and we can be in the wind. I mean, it's not like he knows our address all the way out here."

"Not my point," said October. "This house has its own defenses. No, no, no, what Mary is cooking up downstairs will be shipped to the camps and other facilities later today."

"Are we talking Berserkers?"

"In a way," said October. He cocked his head. "How much do you know about what the Jakoby twins were doing at their lab on Dogfish Cay?"

"You mean the Dragon Factory? Not much. That's where the Berserkers were first developed. I know that much. And some kind of weird-ass designer animals. As I recall, they did some kind of DNA stuff to turn regular test animals into convincing fakes of shit like unicorns and dragons."

"In a nutshell, yes," said October, nodding his approval. "But the Jakobys had a lot of other surprises. The living specimens were killed, of course. However, their bodies were transported to a facility called Site 44."

"That's where you got Mary from," said Toombs.

"It was. Her, four Berserkers, and a lot of other very useful samples. Tons of research. Enough raw materials and hard data that when Mary asked to set up her own lab and production floor, I said yes. She's been at it for nearly two years, and . . . well, let's just say that if anyone *does* attack us here, we can open a door at the end of a tunnel that runs from the basement to the woods. We can release the hounds, so to speak."

Toombs backed away from the door.

"Does that disturb you, my friend?" asked his employer.

"Of course it does, for fuck's sake," Toombs fired back. "This is . . . this is . . ."

Words failed him, and he shook his head. He rattled the doorknob and beat the side of his fist once on the door. It was as solid as a fortress. When he turned back to October, he caught just the smallest swirl of colors in the man's eyes. When October blinked, his eyes were entirely normal.

But the world no longer was.

CHAPTER 42

CHICAGO TRIBUNE
TRIBUNE TOWER
435 NORTH MICHIGAN AVENUE
CHICAGO, ILLINOIS

Louis Allan Harper, reporter, was young, but his upward mobility was nearly vertical. He had gone to Temple University Department of Journalism, and from there to Harvard for his master's. He knew he didn't have the looks for TV news, and he rather liked the semi-anonymity of being a name on a byline.

Like all good reporters, Harper had racked up kudos for his unique approach to any story—finding not only experts to reinforce the data but a really good POV person involved in the matter. He built on the individual, making his stories read with the strong personal touch that encouraged empathy on the part of the readers. He was a natural mimic when it came to voice, tone, and phrasing, and he often put more words into the source's mouth—and better phrasing—than was there in the interview. No one ever complained because his verbiage made the source look smart, insightful, and aware.

When Harper took a call from a friend of his in Homeland Security, he thought it was going to be something to do with a story he had been building about the rise of militia groups throughout the region. It wasn't.

"Lou," said Diego Vázquez, "have you been following the ricin thing in Montgomery?"

"I'm aware of it," said Harper, "but my editor put Huck Foster on it. He handles all the terrorism stuff. And the crackpots."

"Well, maybe this isn't a crackpot thing."

"What, Montgomery? Some chick spreads a poison around a museum and fucking Hamas takes credit? Come on, D, that's bullshit, and we both know it."

"Whatever it is, Lou, it's not bullshit," said Diego. "We got another one. Hotel in Collinsville."

"Another what? More of that ricin stuff?"

"No. This is different, and you'd better hold on to your seat."

Lou laughed. "Sure. Hit me."

"Plague."

"What . . . ?"

"*Yersinia pestis*. Bubonic plague. The Black Death. Call it what you want."

"You're shitting me."

"I shit thee not, brother," insisted Diego. "A hotel maid at the DoubleTree in Collinsville must have been covered in fleas. They bit some other staff members and a few guests."

"Wait, slow down. I thought it took days for something like that to show up. For symptoms, I mean."

"That's one of the things that has everyone freaked. It *is* usually three to seven days. Sometimes shorter, but rarely. And this was like twelve hours from exposure to symptoms presenting. The people who were bit started getting headaches at around eight hours, but by twelve, they had full-blown flu-like symptoms—vomiting, swollen and painful lymph nodes nearest the bite sites. Skin discoloration—wait, here's the proper term—*acral necrosis*, kicked in by hour fifteen. By the time it took local hospitals to realize what they were dealing with, three of the infected had already died."

Harper stared at the wall, seeing nothing.

"Jesus Christ," he said.

"I owe you like five favors, Lou," said Diego. "No one has this story yet, so I'm giving this to you. And there's one more thing, but you can't print this part yet. It's not public and they'll know it came from me or someone in my office. But I want you to be ready to submit your story once this goes public. Ready? I'm going to read it. I can't risk putting any of this into an email or voicemail, you dig?"

"Yes, I do," said Harper as he opened his laptop and pulled up a blank Word document. "Tell me."

"This is from a note found in the maid's locker. Mary Olivera. She's gone. Local police and our boys are doing a coordinated search for her. Looks like the name is phony. So is the address she gave. All we have are a photo and fingerprints. Some DNA from a hairbrush in her locker. But this is the note, translated from Spanish."

"Go," said Harper.

"'My mother and two little brothers fled Mexico because of poverty and the constant danger from the cartels. America is supposed to be the Land of Freedom, the Land of Opportunity. There is that statue that calls to people like me, people like my family. The statue says, "Give me your tired, your poor, Your huddled masses yearning to breathe free, The wretched refuse of your teeming shore. Send these, the homeless, tempest-tossed to me, I lift my lamp beside the golden door!" And yet when we come, we are beaten and arrested, sexually abused, put in cages, humiliated, denied the basic human rights. My mother and brothers died on American soil, trying to be free, to be accepted as human beings worthy of compassion. Instead, their bodies were shipped home for burial without even a note of apology. So much for America being a shining light. Like so many people, I cannot sit quietly and let hurt and harm come to those I love. And so, I—and many like me—will continue to cross your borders. Not to find sanctuary but to punish all Americans for their cruelty. You will need to buy many shovels to bury all of the American dead. Do not expect people like me to weep for them, for none of you have wept for us.'"

"God damn," said Harper.

"I wanted to share this with you, to give you a scoop, but promise me one thing."

"If I can."

"I know how you can frame a story so that people understand what's at stake. You were good at that even when we were in school together. Maybe there's some way you can, I don't know, maybe *flavor* it so that people don't rush down to the border to start killing Mexicans."

Harper promised he would do his best.

When the call was over, he reread what he'd written. A dozen approaches to writing the piece occurred to him, though not one of them would keep from pouring gasoline onto a fire. This was going to break big and break bad.

"God help us," he said.

Then he began to write.

JONATHAN MABERRY

AT HELL'S GATE
PART 2

Everybody is going to be dead one day, just give them time.

—NEIL GAIMAN

It is easy to go down into Hell; night and day, the gates of dark Death stand wide; but to climb back again, to retrace one's steps to the upper air

—there's the rub, the task.

—VIRGIL

CHAPTER 43
THE POWER STATION WITH LIZ POWERS
MSNBC CABLE NEWS

Scott Wilson called to tell me that the ORB conference was going to be delayed for a bit because Church was on calls related to the bioweapons releases.

"What's the nature of the call, though?" I asked.

"He'll tell you," said Wilson, then hung up.

Dick.

"Outlaw," called Top. "You should be watching this."

He had the news on the main viewscreen on the jet, so I swiveled my chair to watch.

"We're back with Dr. David Birnbaum, principal deputy director of the Centers for Disease Control and Prevention in Atlanta," said Liz Powers. She was a midforties woman with thick black hair parted in the middle and carmine earrings that matched her lipstick and the small flowers on her blouse. "Dr. Birnbaum, what can you tell us about the biological attacks that have taken the lives of so many Americans over the last week? Are these natural mutations, or are they, as many believe, genetically engineered bioweapons?"

Birnbaum, sixtysomething with a precisely trimmed beard and half-glasses that perched on the end of his nose, nodded soberly. "It's fair to say that these incidents are suspicious, but I can't personally say that they are bioweapons."

"Even though terrorist groups have claimed responsibility?"

"That's complicated, Liz," said the scientist. "There have been three separate incidents—Atlanta, Montgomery, and Collinsville."

I cut a look at Top and mouthed, *Collinsville?*

"Oh, you'll love this, boss," said Bunny. "Someone released a fast-acting version of the plague."

"Plague . . . ?"

"Yup. Our old friend *Yersinia pestis*. Keep watching."

I watched.

"—each case, a different infectious agent or poison was used," continued Dr. Birnbaum. "Typhus, ricin, and *Yersinia pestis*. Admittedly the *versions* of each that we've seen—particularly the typhus and plague—are new variations. Both were dependent on insects—what we call *vectors*—to deliver the diseases. And yet each case is unique. The fleas in Atlanta are different from those in Collinsville. And the ricin incident in Montgomery is a poison that doesn't require insect vectors."

"And yet terrorist groups *have* taken credit . . ."

"Have they? In the Atlanta case, it is a previously unknown splinter group that is possibly tied to Hamas, possibly tied to the war in the Gaza Strip. For Montgomery, it was a cartel group—again, an unknown splinter group—that took credit. And the plague in Collinsville was claimed by a woman who said she was seeking revenge for the deaths of her mother and younger brothers. There is no connection in terms of the biological threat, the targets, and the people ostensibly taking credit."

"All three were strikes against America, though," insisted Powers. "That is the connective tissue, surely."

Dr. Birnbaum said, "Well, so it appears, but we don't know if any of the claims are legitimate." He paused, then added, "It might even be a copycat."

"How so?"

"Well, a lot of people around the world—individuals, groups, even nations—are on record as hating America. When one group took credit, another group—seeing the outrage in the news—might have used that as a window of opportunity to air their own grievances. If that's the case, I fear we might see more such attacks."

"Oh, ouch," said Bunny.

"Shit," agreed Top.

What Birnbaum said was exactly the *wrong* thing to say. Unscripted, indelicate, and easily misunderstood. Social media influencers pulled parts of his comments and used them like Molotov cocktails to set the internet ablaze.

We watched in real time as everyone with a device and a social media account went absolutely apeshit.

JONATHAN MABERRY

CHAPTER 44
TRANSCRIPT OF SESSION NOTES
DR. RUDY SANCHEZ AND COLONEL JOSEPH EDWIN LEDGER

SANCHEZ: How are you feeling?

LEDGER: You mean how many voices are in my head?

SANCHEZ: That wasn't my question. Nor my intention.

(A long pause)

LEDGER: Yeah, okay. Sorry, Rude. It's just everyone is asking about the Darkness.

Asking if it's back. If it's driving the car.

SANCHEZ: We have spent many sessions unpacking that, Joe.

LEDGER: No shit.

SANCHEZ: But it's not the reason we are having this session.

LEDGER: Then what?

SANCHEZ: Jerusalem. Ashdod. The Cave 13 case.

LEDGER: Shit.

SANCHEZ: And before you ask——because I know you will ask——I'm not singling you out. I am conducting a series of interviews with every member of RTI who was there. Particularly everyone exposed to the Shiva and God's Arrow ergot bioweapon variants.

LEDGER: Yeah. Okay. Shit.

SANCHEZ: When we spoke directly after the event, while you were still in the hospital, you mentioned that you had visions of various kinds. Mostly unpleasant ones. You said you heard your father speak to you. And you said that Jason Aydelotte told you things that he could not possibly know.

LEDGER: I was out of my head. That was all hallucinations.

SANCHEZ: I would like to explore elements of that.

LEDGER: Why bother?

SANCHEZ: Because there are things that are left unresolved.

(Another long pause)

SANCHEZ: Joe . . . ? Sure you're willing to have this discussion with me?

LEDGER: Do I have a choice?

SANCHEZ: You always have a choice.

LEDGER: You say that, brother, but what I hear is that I can choose not to talk about it and you can choose to have Church bench me.

SANCHEZ: We both know that mental health is a component in any assessment of combat readiness.

LEDGER: And I went crazy once already. Crazi-er, I mean. You cleared me for the old DMS when you——more than anyone——knew that I had a head full of bees.

SANCHEZ: You were able to effectively function, and function at a higher-than-average level, with all three of those aspects working in harmony.

LEDGER: Still makes me a nutjob, and you were okay with me going to work for Church.

SANCHEZ: Joe, you have never quite understood my reasoning about that. At another time, I would be delighted to explain it point by point, but——

LEDGER: Yeah, yeah, but it's me on the couch. I get it.

SANCHEZ: You're also deflecting.

LEDGER: Is it working?

SANCHEZ: Not very well.

LEDGER: Crap.

SANCHEZ: There are three specific things I want to discuss. The first of which is your statement that

during the Tenth Legion attack on the safe house in
Jerusalem, you heard your father's voice giving you a
warning. A warning that saved your life.

LEDGER: Yes.

SANCHEZ: You still hold to that?

LEDGER: Yes. And before you write the order for them
to put me in four-point restraints, let's not forget
that you're Catholic and you are literally required to
believe in ghosts.

SANCHEZ: I'm not criticizing you, Joe. Nor am I casting
doubt on what you believe you heard.

LEDGER: That's a squirrelly way of putting it.

SANCHEZ: I am a psychiatrist, Joe. We are a rather
squirrelly lot.

LEDGER: Ha ha. But . . . sure. Okay. Do I believe my
dad's ghost is watching over me?

The truth is I don't know, because I generally don't
believe in ghosts. I know I said I saw the ghosts of my
whole family when I was being run by the Darkness. I'm
not saying that was real. But I heard my dad's voice at
the safe house, and it did save my life. That happened.

SANCHEZ: What do you feel about that?

LEDGER: Christ on a pogo stick, Rude, how am I supposed
to feel? My dad was my hero. He stood by me after Helen
and I were attacked. He helped me when I found Helen
after she killed herself. He was my rock. I don't fool
myself by pretending that I've gone through the whole
process of grief. Not sure I ever will. So, is that PTSD,
family edition? Is it me losing more of my shit? Or is
the ghost of my father, who loved me, still lingering
around on this side of the light, watching over his last
surviving blood relative?

SANCHEZ: No one can answer those questions, Joe. If
you believe it's a ghost, then how can anyone prove

otherwise? If, as Mr. Church so often postulates, the spiritual world——the **larger world**, to use his phrase——is real, then it is likely an area of science that we have not yet learned how to measure, quantify, and understand.

LEDGER: I'm willing to lean into that. Now more than ever. What's the second thing you wanted to ask me about?

SANCHEZ: We're jumping ahead.

LEDGER: It's my hour on the couch. Jump with me.

SANCHEZ: It involves something you said someone told you. You said you imagined it was Helen. You said she whispered the names of the teenagers who attacked you both.

LEDGER: Which is bullshit.

SANCHEZ: Is that what you believe?

LEDGER: How can it be anything else, man?

SANCHEZ: Do you believe it was only a hallucination brought on by the ergot weapons?

LEDGER: What else can it be?

SANCHEZ: Well, we have already discussed the fact that you now believe in ghosts . . .

LEDGER: Are you fucking with me?

SANCHEZ: You know I'm not.

LEDGER: How can I even answer that question, then? I was out of my head, and the ghost of someone who died a long time ago appears to give me information neither she nor I ever had.

SANCHEZ: Do you remember those names that she said?

LEDGER: Yeah. So? What of it?

SANCHEZ: Have you looked into it? Have you asked Bug to search them and see if there is a connection?

LEDGER: No.

SANCHEZ: Why not? It seems to me that temptation would be difficult to ignore.

LEDGER: I . . . Fuck, man . . . I think doing that would prove that I'm crazy.

SANCHEZ: Will you give me those names?

LEDGER: Why? So you can go look them up?

SANCHEZ: It would be one way to verify the information.

LEDGER: Christ, you're crazier than I am, you know that?

SANCHEZ: Humor me. Give me the names.

LEDGER: And what if they're somehow real names? It's not like we could ever connect them to what happened.

SANCHEZ: Then it won't matter if I looked.

(Pause lasting nearly one minute)

LEDGER: Jesus fuck, Rude. Shit. I shouldn't even be doing this. Hell, **you** shouldn't be doing this.

(Another pause)

LEDGER: Okay, the names she said——or that I imagined while comprehensively fucked up by that ergot stuff . . . Christ, I can't believe I'm doing this. The names are Joe Listopad, Jamie Stanton, Danny Beck, Bob Reilly, and Greg Murphy.

CHAPTER 45
ROUTE I-81 NORTH
NEAR LACEY SPRING, VIRGINIA

Tommy drove the car while Violin reviewed the photos and video data they had collected in Virginia.

Tommy tried not to catch glimpses of her companion in the mirror.

Although they were friends, the two women seldom spoke much while on a mission, even an information-gathering gig like this one.

Tommy listened, though, as Violin spoke to her mother, Lilith. The call was on speaker.

"Make sure you do not lose them," said Lilith.

"I won't, Mother."

"And don't take that tone with me."

Tommy clenched her teeth to keep all reactions from her face. Violin was widely regarded as one of the most dangerous assassins active in the world, and her work with both Arklight and Mr. Church's various organizations was spoken of with awe by other Arklight members. There was no hint of praise or anything approaching it in Lilith's voice.

Lilith, the strange woman who had founded the Mothers of the Fallen and its militant arm, Arklight, was rumored to be in love with Church. Tommy found that hard to accept, because there seemed to be no passion or compassion in the woman. She was made from cold steel and polar ice.

And she treated Violin like a clumsy child—often scolding or upbraiding her, even in front of other Arklight members. It was shocking to hear those derogatory tones used in even so simple a conversation. It made her want to do something—take Violin's hand, pat her shoulder, hug her. But even if she weren't driving, none of those things seemed like they would be welcome. Not in that context.

"Tommy ran facial recognition on the men at the park and the two who took the children," said Violin, apparently unperturbed.

"And . . . do I have to ask?" said Lilith with asperity. "Or will you go ahead and make a clear and full report?"

"Two of the men are in our files," said Violin. "They're part of the larger group involved in the video ring Joe Ledger and his friend Monk Addison broke up a few months ago. Those two were not onsite, and until today, there was no evidence to share with local law enforcement. I passed their information to Baba Yaga, though."

Baba Yaga was the code name for one of Arklight's older field agents, and one known for her merciless and appalling interrogation practices. Tommy was able to slit a throat or pull a trigger, but torture was something she did not think she'd ever be comfortable with.

"And the others?" snapped Lilith.

"The two in the car were not in our files, but they both have military backgrounds. As did one of the men at the cabin. All three served in either the army or marines. Two have dishonorable discharges, and the other left after two tours in Afghanistan. The item of special note, though, is that two of them worked for Blue Diamond Security. I will not be surprised if they are now with Tenth Legion."

There was a silence on the other end of the call. Then Lilith said, "Continue with the pursuit. Gather all information you can."

And that was it. The line went dead.

Violin sighed and tossed her phone down into the tray under the dash.

Tommy let a mile or two go past before she asked, "You okay?"

Violin just looked out of the window and shook her head.

Another few miles.

"That thing with Joe and the other guy . . ."

"Monk," said Violin. "Gerald Addison, known as Monk to everyone. What about it?"

"Was that case tied to this, then?"

"Seems so."

"Joe won't be happy that some of those guys slipped through his fingers."

"No," said Violin, "I don't suppose he will."

INTERLUDE 16
MISS MARY'S LAB
THE MANSION
UNDISCLOSED LOCATION
FOUR WEEKS AGO

Miss Mary had a small private studio behind heavy doors down in the lab. It was tucked under the stairs. Soundproof, snoop-proof, with a lock keyed to her voiceprint and the fingerprint of her left ring finger.

Her computers were in there, and when she needed to work—really dig deep into the software of the Gorgon master chip—that's where she went. Bose speakers provided such fidelity that Slipknot, Falling in Reverse, Drowning Pool, Korn, Avenged Sevenfold, Five Finger Death Punch, Sevendust, and Staind sounded like they were in the same room. That was her current playlist, built for her for this project. The bass rattled the walls and the guitars beat at her in just exactly the right way.

The master chip was beautifully crafted. Russo's sophistication, his ability to adapt existing targeting software and anti-tampering programs was unparalleled. Mary could only think of one person who could crack it. One person apart from her. Bug could do it, but it might even push him to his limits.

Despite everything that had ever happened, Mary admired Bug. She liked him. While working for the old DMS, she had flirted with him a few times, but he always seemed immune to her, even as beautiful as she was back then. For a while, she thought he might be gay or, worse, one of those asexual people. Gay she could understand, but a lack of sexual drive made no sense to her. It felt unnatural. Her own hungers ran very, very deep.

She wondered what he would be like in bed. He was thin, nerdy, not exactly a stud. Yet his brain was soooo sexy.

Almost as sexy as her own, and she turned herself on several times every day. Mary loved being brilliant.

Now, at least.

Back in her worker-drone days at the DMS, she was often bored by mundane life and mundane people. Now, with her intellect unchained and all of October's money for her to use to buy scientists and toys and whatever else she wanted, Mary could indulge every whim. Every need. Every desire.

She tapped away at the keys, crafting code. Getting closer and closer to breaking the Gorgon master chip.

And then what?

October wanted this task completed so he could either replace the Shiva in the warheads with MERS, or perhaps with a blend of the two. Potentially lethal, but not necessarily so. A scare tactic. A panic inducer.

Which, she knew, would work.

For what October wanted.

She smiled as she worked, knowing that what October wanted and what *she* wanted were not at all the same thing.

Not even close.

CHAPTER 46
TRANSCRIPT OF SESSION NOTES
DR. RUDY SANCHEZ AND HARVEY "BUNNY" RABBIT

SANCHEZ: How are you feeling?

BUNNY: I'm good.

SANCHEZ: Is that true or an offhand remark?

BUNNY: You know me.

SANCHEZ: I do, and my question stands. How **are** you?

BUNNY: **(Laughs)** Where do I start?

SANCHEZ: Let's start with what happened in Chad.

BUNNY: Shit. I **knew** you were going to bring that up.

SANCHEZ: It is rather germane to how things unfolded in
the weeks leading up to the Cave 13 case. To be frank,
it was the beginning of it for RTI. The official mission
to investigate the incidents with the scholars who
killed themselves and the Boko Haram prisoner and his
interrogators who died by snakebite. Mr. Church and
Scott Wilson believe those events to be part of some other
investigation, and Havoc Team is likely to take point on
field research. You are aware, I believe, of some leads in
New Jersey that the team may be sent to follow.

BUNNY: Sure.

SANCHEZ: But in Chad, when you entered the basement
cells where the teenagers were kept, you had an
experience.

BUNNY: I guess.

SANCHEZ: It was in your report, Bunny.

BUNNY: And it was a side effect of that ergot shit. Shiva
or whatever.

SANCHEZ: Except that there wasn't much of it in the air,
according to the data downloaded from the BAMS units.

BUNNY: There was enough of it. Those kids were freaking out.

SANCHEZ: They were victims of drug therapy and had been injected with a solution containing ergot. You were not. And only one other person has so far admitted to having experienced a hallucination.

BUNNY: I know. Outlaw thought he heard Grace Courtland. Took him a while to admit it, and I can understand why. When you say shit like that, people look at you funny. They treat you like a mental case.

SANCHEZ: That is, perhaps, an unfair assessment of how the other members of RTI react to extreme events.

BUNNY: Maybe. Whatever. But you already know what I saw.

SANCHEZ: Tell me again.

(Several seconds of vulgarities followed
by a very long sigh)

BUNNY: I thought I saw Lydia holding Brad, and the baby was . . .

SANCHEZ: Tell me, Bunny. Saying it doesn't make it real. It won't call in bad luck.

BUNNY: Maybe. And maybe not. Since I signed on with Mr. Church, I've seen some wild shit even without ergot.

SANCHEZ: Tell me anyway.

BUNNY: Lydia was there and she was holding Brad, and the baby was . . . was . . . fuck. He was dead, okay? Does that make you happy?

SANCHEZ: Of course it doesn't. But every time you say it and then know that it isn't true is a step toward taking agency over the memory.

BUNNY: Headshrinking 101. Got it. But listen, doc, there's nothing more to say. It was that fucked-up image, and then it was gone. It hasn't come back except in some dreams, but none for weeks now. Whatever I inhaled did

JONATHAN MABERRY

its work. It kicked me in the balls, but I'm fine now. And
I would like to change the goddamn subject.

> (There is a pause as both men take
> a break for bathroom and coffee)

SANCHEZ: Now that we're back, let's talk about how things
are at home.

BUNNY: Jeez. Okay.

SANCHEZ: You seem visibly stressed about the subject.
Tell me why.

BUNNY: Well, when Lydia and I got married, it was right
out of a storybook, y'know?

SANCHEZ: How so?

BUNNY: Oh, we were all huggy-kissy twenty-four seven.
Couldn't keep our hands off each other.

For like the first six months, we were fuc——I mean, we
were making love a lot.

Every day. Sometimes three, four times a day.

SANCHEZ: And what changed?

BUNNY: I don't know how to put it. That all kind of slowed
down.

SANCHEZ: There is a documented phenomenon called the——

BUNNY: The honeymoon period, yeah, I know. So I guess
that was it. We kind of settled down after a while. I
mean when I was home. RTI keeps me pretty busy. So,
when I got back from a gig, we'd have a nice reunion.
That was great. But then it would be watching TV on the
couch. Sitting on the beach reading shit on our phones.
Like that. Like we'd been married twenty years.

SANCHEZ: And how do you feel about that?

BUNNY: Honestly?

SANCHEZ: You know from our many past sessions that
honesty is the only policy with me.

BUNNY: Yeah, yeah. I know. I get it. It's just that I feel weird saying this.

(There is a pause)

BUNNY: I'm split on how I feel about it. Half of me wishes we could rock the same vibe we had when we first got married. That excitement. That constant hunger, you dig?

SANCHEZ: Of course. I know it firsthand.

BUNNY: Yeah, guess you do. You got two kids now. So, I guess you had the same thing. That honeymoon period thing. And my guess is it cooled down for you, too. Maybe it does for everyone. Anyway, I miss it. The intensity.

SANCHEZ: We all do.

BUNNY: But . . . And don't judge me here, okay? And don't think this is **any** reflection on Lydia. But for a while there, I was coming home from the job, and we'd just kind of **be**. No trying to qualify for the sex Olympics. Not trying to beat the world record for most orgasms. We started that being-normal married-folks thing.

SANCHEZ: And does this change disturb you?

BUNNY: That's what I mean about not judging. The god's honest truth is that I came to start looking **forward** to that. Just being, I mean. No expectations. No demands. Nothing to prove. It was better in some ways than sex. Does that make sense?

SANCHEZ: Yes, it does. And it's a sign of a healthy relationship that you look forward to those quieter moments. The stablest relationships have that as a foundation. The other things—the passion and intensity—are wonderful and healthy, but they are not strong enough to be the framework for the whole of your bond with Lydia.

BUNNY: So you **do** get it.

SANCHEZ: I do.

BUNNY: Cool. But then she got pregnant.

SANCHEZ: How did that impact your relationship?

(Another long pause)

BUNNY: Well, there were changes. I guess it's the
hormones and shit. And maybe Lydia feeling fat and
ugly. Lots of moods all over the place. One minute she's
the woman I'd knee-walk through broken glass for. Next
she's yelling at me for not setting the table right.
Bam—that fast.

SANCHEZ: As you observed, hormones cause mood swings.
It's entirely normal. And with first pregnancies, the
woman is substantially unprepared for it, no matter
how many books she reads or bits of advice she hears.
Hormones are an engine that sometimes races out of
control.

BUNNY: Sure, sure . . . but some of the things she said
were harsh as fuck. Hard to like . . . **Forgive** isn't the
right word. Forget, maybe.

SANCHEZ: We can spend some time on that. And trust me
when I say that I have both personal and professional
experience with exactly that.

BUNNY: Yeah. So, we go through that, and it's no fun. I
felt hurt sometimes, but then I'd see how hurt she was.
Not just with something dumb I might have said but
hurt because of the things she knew she said. I saw it
in her eyes, but she didn't talk about it. Lydia is the
stubbornest person on God's green earth. She's never
been much for apologizing. And that's a thing, because
I'll own up to any dumb fucking thing I say or do. She
either can't or won't, and it leaves the things she said
kind of hanging in the air.

SANCHEZ: Would it help if we arranged a session with the
two of you?

BUNNY: Probably would, but I don't know how to suggest it without losing a limb.

SANCHEZ: We'll go over some verbiage that might be useful.

BUNNY: Sure. Then there's the other thing.

SANCHEZ: Which thing?

BUNNY: The baby.

SANCHEZ: Bradley?

BUNNY: Yeah.

SANCHEZ: Are you in any kind of conflict with your son?

BUNNY: He's a baby, dude.

SANCHEZ: With having a son at all. With a baby in the house.

BUNNY: Oh yeah. Kid's a challenge. I can infiltrate a high-security facility, fight half a dozen guys, and, let's face it, following Colonel Ledger, I've been up against zombies, Red Knights, killer drones, fucking aliens . . . but a screaming baby who will not stop? A little shit machine who produces more crap than is possible based on how much he eats? Man, I'm way out of my depth.

SANCHEZ: You have a nanny . . .

BUNNY: Yeah. Your niece. Maria.

SANCHEZ: How is she working out?

BUNNY: Lydia loves her. Brad loves her.

SANCHEZ: And you?

BUNNY: Dude . . .

SANCHEZ: Meaning?

BUNNY: Look, I know she's your niece, and maybe she's the nicest person in the world to everyone else. But . . . fuck, man, as far as she's concerned, I can't do **anything** right. Forget how much I fuck up putting

Pampers on the kid. I can't wash a dish right, I can't warm formula right. I can't say or do anything right.

SANCHEZ: (Laughs) Sounds like Maria.

BUNNY: Wait . . . what? You **knew** she's a demon from the outer darkness?

SANCHEZ: She was the nanny for my firstborn, too.

BUNNY: Oh shit. I didn't know.

SANCHEZ: She's not the nanny for our second child.

BUNNY: And you turfed her over to me? You total motherfucker.

SANCHEZ: Don't worry. I have some useful strategies for dealing with her.

BUNNY: Do any of them involve gunplay or unarmed combat? I ask because I don't know if I can take her.

CHAPTER 47
INTEGRATED SCIENCES DIVISION
PHOENIX HOUSE
OMFORI ISLAND, GREECE

Church did a quick knuckle tap on the door, did not wait for a reply, and went in. Doc Holliday was at a computer workstation, eyes darting from one to another of a row of monitors arranged in a half circle around her. Some screens showed muted talking heads—clearly physicians and scientists; others scrolled with data; and one had many smaller windows showing the faces of people who were in oxygen tents, intubated, and connected to blinking machines.

"Doc," said Church, and she held up a finger. He realized that she was on a call and listening to someone in her earbud.

"Send me everything you have, Barney," she said. "All of it. No . . . I don't care if it's a lot. Send it all. Okay, doll face. Thanks. I'll get back to you."

She tapped her bud and swiveled her chair toward Church, giving him a quick, wry up-and-down appraisal.

"You look like you're having as bad a day as I am."

Church frowned. "What trouble are you courting? A new RTI matter?"

"Not sure yet," she said. Then she yawned so wide that he could hear her jaw creak. "God, I would blow the pope for five hours of uninterrupted sleep." Then she shook her head like a wet dog and focused on him. "Short version is that Nikki Bloom convinced Ronnie Coleman to take a peek at those disease outbreaks in the States. You're familiar?"

Church pulled a chair over and sat. "Yes. Typhus, ricin, and bubonic plague. With different groups vying to claim credit."

"Yep. And those attempts to claim credit are making a lot of people very goldurn nervous. An old drinking buddy of mine from ATF says that gun sales are on a crazy rise over there. And before you say, 'That's not news,' I'm talking a sales spike in the triple digits. And with that a commensurate increase in xenophobia and calls for America to move away from globalization toward a fiercer version of nationalism."

"That *has* been a trend for over a decade."

"Not with the numbers we're seeing." Doc searched among the stacks of papers on her desk and pulled out a thin sheaf on Nikki Bloom's distinctive pink paper. She handed them to Church, who sat back and read through. When he paused on the next-to-last page, Doc said, "From the look on your face, I can tell you got to the part where Nikki's tracked the rise of new Tenth Legion groups."

"Yes . . ." murmured Church.

"Truth to tell," said Doc, "when Nikki first came to me, I thought she was off her rocker. Doing the paranoia two-step of trying to connect conspiracy theories. Nor did I think this was going to be an RTI thing. After all, Homeland, the DEA, NSA, and all of the other agencies over there can handle some spite crimes. But . . . designer pathogens, the disease equivalent of suicide bombers, spikes in gun sales, a three hundred percent rise in militia groups . . . ? Sounds like this is putting more than a big toe over the line into what Joe Ledger and his boys are already working on. Maybe Bedlam, too."

"Yes," he said again. "That does sound like something we need to put more resources on. Colonel Ledger seems to think a number of our active cases are connected, and I've been leaning toward his viewpoint." He tapped the papers. "I think these disease attacks *are* connected."

"There's pretty obvious cause and effect," agreed Doc.

Church rose. "Thank you, Joan. And pass along word to Coleman and Nikki. Thanks to them and my permission and encouragement to dig deeper."

"Do we all get cookies?"

"You do." He looked at his watch. "Havoc Team should be halfway to Gehenna by now. I have an ORB call pending."

"May I join you?"

"Please do."

They hurried out.

INTERLUDE 17
THE MANSION
UNDISCLOSED LOCATION
THREE WEEKS AGO

"Close your eyes and hold out your hand," she said.

Mr. October was still dressed for travel and had not even entered the house. Mary met him at the door and blocked his entry.

"I'm very tired, dear girl," said October. "I need a drink, a bath, and a meal."

She repeated her demand, saying it with slow patience. "Close your eyes and hold out your hand."

October sighed and did as he was instructed. Small muscles bunched impatiently at the corners of his jaws.

Mary placed something very small and hard on his palm.

She said, "Ta-da!"

He opened his eyes. On his palm was a small piece of plastic a half-inch square. It was unmarked and looked unremarkable. October frowned for a moment, then his eyes went wide and a huge smile blossomed on his face.

"Is this . . . ? Did you really . . . ? Oh my stars, sweet girl, is this what I think it is?"

"You wanted a chip," she said brightly. "You have a chip."

He clutched it to his chest, used his other hand to pull her close, and planted a huge, loud kiss on her forehead.

"You are the best of the best, my girl," he said, overjoyed. "You are my goddess."

Mary, for all her cynicism and damage, smiled like a happy child.

CHAPTER 48
IN FLIGHT OVER NEW YORK AIRSPACE

"ORB call incoming," said the pilot over the intercom.

Bunny immediately closed all the window covers and lowered the lights.

Top tapped some keys on a wall-mounted pad, and the cabin went pitch dark for a moment, and then thousands of little points of lights flared on. It was like standing in deep space. But those lights were really holographic projectors, and the inside of the jet gradually transformed into a conference room. Our own chairs were worked seamlessly into the overall image, with software making adjustments so that no one was seated on anyone else's lap. The holography was so dense it looked totally solid, as was once demonstrated when Bunny tried to set a can of Coke down on the table only to have it pass through the faux oak and splash all over the floor. We were all used to it now and kept our physical movements to a minimum.

Aside from Havoc Team, there were four other people in the ORB call with us. Church, of course, in one of his exquisitely tailored Italian suits. He was a big, blocky, powerful-looking man who looked sixty-ish but was likely a good deal older than that. Maybe a bit too much older, which had long since sparked all kinds of rumors and speculation around Phoenix House.

Next to him was a smaller, thinner, younger man with a medium-brown face, intelligent eyes, and a perpetually amused smile. That was Bug, an unparalleled computer geek hired by Church and Aunt Sallie when the DMS was formed. He looked sixteen but was closer to thirty, and behind his charming and friendly face was a magnificent if eccentric brain. It is no exaggeration to say that his computer wizardry had saved everyone's life more times than I could count. He wore skinny jeans and a T-shirt with Spike Lee's face on it and the phrase MAGICAL NEGRO screen-printed across the chest.

The woman who sat on his left was Doc Holliday. Actual descendant of the OK Corral gunslinger and arguably the smartest person on the planet. Not joking. Rudy told me that her IQ was not measurable by any standard model. Physically, she looked like a six-foot-tall version of Dolly Parton from back in the *Best Little Whorehouse in Texas* era. Gorgeous, outrageous, and weird. We all loved and—I'll admit it—feared her.

Rounding out the quartet was Dr. Ronald Coleman, a molecular biologist who had a wall full of degrees. He had a fierce black beard, ice-pale eyes, and wore black jeans under a Hawaiian shirt covered in *Star Wars* spaceships.

All of this would make a great company Christmas card from Nerds-R-Us. Or possibly an asylum. It's fair to say that eccentricity was not only common in the RTI but in its various science teams it flourished.

"Let's get right to it," said Church curtly. "We have been putting together disparate pieces of what we now think are parts of the same puzzle picture."

"Day must be ending in a *y*," muttered Top.

Church actually smiled at that. "It has become a pattern lately, but that's the nature of being a reactive organization. Things happen, and groups like ours and a few others—Sigma Force, MHI, Chess Team, and other allies—often have to look for patterns that ordinary law enforcement and intelligence groups can't see in order to assess the scope and plan a response. Or, often, the standard organizations are too mired in conventional thinking to believe that such extreme and isolated incidents could possibly fit into any recognizable shape."

"Which is why we exist," said Bug, and everyone nodded.

"The case in point here involves a number of our more pressing open investigations," continued Church. "So we're all on the same conversational page, let me itemize. One item, actually the one that brought us into this earlier this year, involves the apparently inexplicable deaths of CIA agents and their prisoner in Djibouti who were killed by cobras, and scientists in Jerusalem studying Dead Sea Scrolls who died from bat bites."

"Still twists my nuts into the wrong shape," said Bunny under his breath. If Church heard it, he chose to ignore the commentary.

"The research into that is being handled by Bug and Yoda," Church said. "Expect a report later."

"Are we going somewhere right now to restart that investigation?" I asked.

"No," said Church. "It's back burner, relatively speaking."

"Copy that."

"We are more actively investigating Tenth Legion activities around the world in general and in the United States in particular. Something big is coming, and we believe it is this *Firefall* project that we keep catching mentions of. It's disappointing that Mr. Huberman did not have information on whatever Firefall actually is."

"He blanked out," I said. "Don't think he was faking it."

Bug said, "Firefall's popped up a few times in net chatter, but then gets taken down right away. They're hiding it really well, and they have some smart people keeping their eyes on the net. Given the lack of substantial information, we can assume they're using word of mouth and eyes-only info rather than sharing critical stuff digitally. That sucks, but it's becoming more common. Not just because of MindReader but because of the overall sophistication of forensic computer sciences. Bottom line is that we've made very little progress in understanding what it is."

I made a face. "I hope that means it's part of long-range planning and not something they're going to spring on us tomorrow."

"Agreed," said Church. "I've reached out to a number of my contacts in the international intelligence networks. Firefall has popped up here and there, but always in oblique references that tell us nothing. We will keep looking. And, of course, Nikki Bloom's pattern recognition team has it added to all of their keyword searches, especially in research on Tenth Legion, Kuga, and Mr. October."

"We don't know who *he* is, either," I complained.

"Work in progress," said Wilson with more optimism than I think he actually felt.

"Nikki has been instrumental in making certain connections," observed Church.

"Some of her guesses are just that at this point, but we all know her track record for identifying patterns."

"Hooah," said Top.

"Yeah," said Doc. "She's cute as a button and scary as all hell. She's the one who brought the info to us about the three outbreak cases."

"The bioweapons?" I said. "Yeah. Is that our case?"

"Possibly, though not immediately," replied Church. "Nikki and Dr. Coleman are taking point to gather information. I have feelers out to a number of my colleagues and have mentioned to the right people that we are available if needed."

I nodded. Even though we'd left the old DMS behind a couple of years ago and were no longer on Uncle Sam's payroll, I still had the knee-jerk reaction of thinking all such cases belonged to us. In truth, agencies like Homeland had become very damn good at getting on top of threats like this. We were hired guns and no longer the default agency for weird shit.

Weird as it sounds, I half-ass resent that.

"The groups claiming credit are of the kind that would trigger overreactions in certain civilian and political demographics," said Wilson. "Hamas and ISIS trigger anti-Muslim responses, and a Mexican woman reminds people of all of the years of infighting about US and Mexico border security."

Bunny said, "So someone is doing this to ramp up hatred of non-Christian and non-whites?"

"So far, that seems to be the purpose," said Church. "The next link in that chain of supposition is the effect of this increased xenophobia."

"Let me guess," I said. "People bombarding their representatives and senators to do something, and while they're waiting for that to happen, those people are going out and buying a shit-ton of guns."

"As I keep saying," remarked Doc, "he's not just tight buns and washboard abs."

I ignored that. "We know who likes to sell guns. Starts with a *K* and rhymes with *Tuga*."

"And what kind of groups like to play with guns?" asked Top.

"I'll take militias for six hundred, Ken," said Bunny.

"If this theory holds water," said Church, "then we need to step up our search for Mr. October and whoever else is running Tenth Legion, and—if possible—establish a connection between them and Kuga. It could be client and vendor, or it could be two sides of the same coin."

"How do these weaponized diseases fit into that scenario?" I asked. "I mean, I know that when he was running things, Harcourt Bolton had the Rage bioweapon created. But that was an original. A one-off. Made from those squids."

"Squids?" asked Remy. "I thought Rage was a virus."

Coleman fielded that one. "So did we at first. But it turned out to be Loligo beta-microseminoprotein, a protein. Loligo beta-MSP for short. It's found in the longfin inshore squid—*Doryteuthis pealeii*—a species common in the North Atlantic."

"Oh," said Remy with a straight face. "*That* squid."

Belle elbowed him.

"We don't know if the pathogens in question originated in a Kuga lab," said Church. "We do know that several of their labs were taken down by Havoc Team and later by Colonel Ledger."

That resulted in a moment of utter silence. We all knew what he meant with that last bit. When I was under the control of the Darkness, I did a substantial amount of damage to Kuga's science network.

Plowing on, Church said, "There is another possibility, however. And it's why you are on a fast jet to upstate New York."

"Oh," Bunny said, "I can't *wait* to hear this."

INTERLUDE 18
MISS MARY'S LAB
THE MANSION
UNDISCLOSED LOCATION
THREE WEEKS AGO

Miss Mary became obsessed with the Gorgon warhead. She spent whole days just sitting and staring at it or walking around the one that had been brought down to her basement lab. She had her own office down there, and now her door was closed and the blinds drawn.

The song "Down with the Sickness" was playing on a continuous loop. Not only the original by Disturbed but the full range of covers by Vitamin String Quartet, Violet Orlandi, We're Wolves, Melodicka Bros, "Weird Al" Yankovic, Jonathan Young, Twinkle Twinkle Little Rock Star, Drewsif Stalin's Musical Endeavors, Beyond the Black, Anthony Vincent, and the lounge-lizard Richard Cheese version from the Zack Snyder remake of *Dawn of the Dead*. Over and over, day after day.

Mary wore denim shorts and a black halter with pink fringe, and for once, her clothes and her body were clean. This level of intense work had worked a transformation on her.

Everyone left her alone. Meals were set on a table outside the office. And even Mr. October texted before coming to see her. Except for a few brief outings to Camp #18, which was close by, she spent twelve hours a day in with the Gorgon.

Much of that time was spent at her desk, hammering away at variations of a piece of software that was gradually taking shape. She typed a series of commands and then sent the latest code to a simulation program she designed based on some of Marco Russo's data that Toombs had been able to recover. Russo was one of those code monkeys who all but created his own language forms, and the material from Toombs was as close to a Rosetta stone as she could get.

It was enough, though. Once Mary understood the slants and twists of Russo's design philosophy, she was able to get into his head, to see things the way he did. It was the same process she and Bug had used when writing the original version of VaultBreaker, and it was somewhere between computer forensics and psychological profiling.

She took a party-size bag of Twizzlers from a drawer and began eating them, one after another, taking many small bites, chewing until the candy was mush, swallowing, starting over again. Obsessive, compulsive, delicious, and calming.

Then a green bar appeared in the middle of her screen. She spat the candy into a trash can and leaned forward, reading the message.

SIMULATION SUCCESSFUL

Two words.

Mary screamed so loud people came running, but when they opened her door, they saw her sitting there, laughing.

CHAPTER 49
IN FLIGHT OVER NEW YORK AIRSPACE

Doc Holliday took the reins for the next part of the ORB call.

"There are three kinds of facilities in which the world's most dangerous bioweapons, and their component pathogens, are stored," she began. "One kind is very much out in the open, and the Centers for Disease Control and Prevention in Atlanta is the clearest example. Everyone knows about the CDC. Everyone knows that they have everything from ten thousand variations of the common cold to recent variants of Ebola there. There are scores of them around the world, and they conduct research on all manner of communicable diseases, with some internal labs studying natural mutations and modified pathogens. Those places are known to both the authorities of each host nation and appear in official budget reports and official oversight. With me, kids?"

Remy shrugged. Belle just sat there.

"Taking that as a yes," said Doc with a happy smile. "The second kind range from the old biological warfare sites like the one that used to be in Umatilla, Oregon, and Building 470 in Fort Detrick, the Institute of Virus Preparations in the old Soviet Union, Noborito Research Institute run by the Japanese way back when, and scads of others. All *officially* shut down following the Biological Warfare Convention and subsequent agreements, though since none of us here arrived on the short bus, we know that they were just moved elsewhere and renamed."

"Nice," said Remy.

"That's where the third kind of facility comes into play," Doc continued. "Every country with a budget has a shop set up to study germ warfare in all its many and varied forms in a more proactive way. We're talking about *off-book* sites. Biohazard R & D black labs and storage facilities. Places where some one-term political stuffed suit in Congress will never hear about them and try to use them as career currency."

"Correct," said Church. "These off-book sites are of the kind that even many presidents and prime ministers are unaware of. Places where the level of security is so critical that they are hidden from the political process. Their budgets are funded by deliberate misappropriation of funds and otherwise padded on the books' budget items."

"Sure," snorted Bunny. "Nine-hundred-dollar toilet seats, three-hundred-dollar hammers . . ."

Doc turned her thousand-watt smile on him. "Proving once again that you are not just a mile-high stack of pretty beefcake but actually have a brain."

"If these sites are illegal according to American and international law, then why are they being funded at all?" demanded Remy. "Doesn't the world have enough problems?"

"There are two answers to that," said Church. "One is the usual official line about doing research on existing or potential bioweapons in order to have response protocols on file. There is some validity to this, because—unlike the movies—the response, research, development, mass production, and distribution of either prophylactic methods or disease treatments can take months or years. If, in fact, such cures are ever found. We saw that with COVID. There's no magic wand or silver bullet for bioweapons, and the people who want to use such weapons know this. They count on the lag time to increase the body count and therefore reinforce whatever ideological stance they are prosecuting."

"Well," said Remy, "that sucks."

"It's the world we live in," observed Church. "The other reason they do the R & D is because many nations still believe in the concept of mutually assured destruction. It's the reason no one started using nukes when Russia invaded Ukraine. It's why Pakistan and India have never gone to total war."

"I get it," said Remy. "I just don't much like it."

"Join the club," said Coleman.

"The point is that these bioweapons exist, and they are an increasingly dire threat," said Doc. "I *do* believe the research needs to happen because we all know that some radical or corrupt ass monkey will try to use them. I mean, how many have the old DMS and RTI stopped so far? It could be happening right now. Sure, we've been able to spank those bad guys, but something big and bad gets off the leash and none of us have done our homework, this world is going to be populated by nothing but disgruntled ghosts."

"I wish I could say I entirely disagree," said Church wearily. Even I had to nod. "It is a necessary evil."

"With a capital *E*," added Coleman.

"Okay," I said, "so there are mad scientist labs out there, and their closets are full of microscopic monsters. What's happening right now that puts us on a plane?"

"Too much," said Church. He nodded to Coleman, who tapped a few keys, and floating screens popped up, each crammed with data.

"This is the current list of off-books sites," Church said. "The sites shown in bold black typeface are those currently believed to be stable and which have reported no recent incidents."

It was a long list. Next to about twenty of them was a question mark.

Coleman anticipated our response, though. "Those are sites we *suspect* exist but can't confirm. Likely, though."

Top gestured to a second, much shorter list with entries in red. They had names ranging from nondescript, like *Site 11*, *Room 73*, *Site 266*, *the Barn*, *Brighton Paper Storage*—to some with more dramatic, even lurid, nicknames such as *Deep Ice*, *Inferno*, *the Vault*, *Red Door*, and others.

"And those?" he asked. "They're active off-book sites that we *do* know about?"

"They are," agreed Church. "I expect you recognize a few."

"Too damn well," said Top.

"I see that the Vault's on the list," I said. "So is Site 44. Those have been shut down, though. I mean, *we* shut the Vault down."

"Yeah," said Bunny. "That was fun. Dealing with insect super soldiers is why *I* don't sleep all that good, either."

"Insect super soldiers?" echoed Belle, looking deeply unnerved.

"Before your time, sister," said Top. "Bunny, the colonel, and I dealt with that."

Remy shook his head, grinning one of those what-the-actual-fuck grins. "If I can interrupt for a sec—what's with all these super-soldier programs? I've only been with you cats for eight months, and we took down three."

Coleman fielded that. "We're not talking Captain America and the Winter Soldier here. These are programs designed to enhance individual operatives in a variety of ways. It's not always strength and speed. Sometimes it's resistance to bioweapons likely to be employed by their enemies. Sometimes it's PMCs who want to be Superman for a couple of years and then retire rich. Point is, these programs are almost always used by groups that are resource poor—no backing government, no million-man armies, no chance of putting a substantial ground force on the field. Enhancements of one kind or another intended to level that playing field."

"It's not only bad guys," said Doc. "Sometimes it's big governments who want to reduce the risk of overall casualty numbers by using alternate tech. Drones, those robot combat dogs, biomechanical enhancements, nootropic endurance drugs to fight fatigue in fighter pilots and soldiers on long missions. It's a long list."

"I did say *almost always*," muttered Coleman under his breath.

"It's okay, snuggle bear," soothed Doc. "Everyone gets a participation trophy."

He pretended to scratch his nose but used a forefinger. Doc laughed. Then she glanced at me. "Uh-oh, Outlaw is about to make some sarcastic crack about us taking the long way around the block to get to the point."

I merely spread my hands. "My point is that the Vault is shut down, right?"

"It is," said Church.

"And Site 44? Hasn't that been closed for something like two years?"

"It has."

"Inferno's on the list, too," said Top. "I heard about that one. It went down right after we got back from Israel, right? Some big accident or something. I thought that was a total loss."

"Also true," said Doc. "It was more of a storage facility, though. A place to keep very bad things until we knew what to do with them or could safely dispose of them without having to do more of the R & D we talked about. That site suffered a catastrophic failure of their hot room containment, and that resulted in a witch's brew of advanced bioweapons being released into the ventilation system. No chance at all of cleaning it up. It was a goldang tragedy resulting in the deaths of seventy-some people. A total loss."

"And now we're going to another one of those," said Bunny.

"Yes, but we'll get to that," said Church. "Most of the others you may not recognize, because they are on foreign soil and have not factored into any DMS or RTI cases."

Top nodded. "And I suppose some of the ones with question marks are in countries belonging to folks who don't like us. North Korea, China, Russia, and Iran . . . ?"

"Correct."

"And," said Coleman, "that's just vault storage and official labs. There's a much longer list of grab-and-go groups."

"Grab and go . . . ?" asked Remy, frowning. "You talking terrorists with portable labs?"

Doc nodded. "A gold star for the pretty Cajun stud muffin. Yes, there are plenty of those, but it's impossible to know how much of any specific biohazard they have—raw pathogen or designer monster. Being mobile and lacking the billions of government funding and the necessary obfuscatory infrastructure, they are unlikely to have large enough or *secure* enough storage for a vast number of biohazardous materials. Also, there's no real way to track them, so let that rock you to sleep tonight."

"I ain't ever going to sleep again," said Remy.

"This may be cold comfort," said Bug, "but the software package created to protect the established sites from actual forced entry is what resulted in Site 44 and Inferno being shut down so hard. Tragic as the loss of life is in terms of staff, our VaultBreaker software's counter-intrusion protocols were designed to burn them down rather than allow for even the possibility of theft of those bioweapons. Sad, but better than releasing weaponized diseases that could wipe out most or all of humanity."

"That's very cold comfort," said Remy.

"To put a button on this," continued Doc, "the Vault went into hard lockdown after you three gangsters paid your visit. Site 44 and Inferno both had catastrophic systems failures. Both are very old facilities, so those by themselves are not red flags."

"That is what we were led to believe via reports from our friends in the US governments," said Church. "However, as we are not a government-sanctioned organization, we don't have full access to reliable intel on all such sites, and some of the allies we've relied on have either retired, died, or moved on to other jobs. There are gaps in our flow of intelligence." He immediately held up a warning hand. "Let's skip the obvious jokes about that."

I swear to god I heard both Doc and Bunny clack their jaws shut at the same time.

"Aside from mechanical or noncriminal human errors," said Church, "there have been a number of attempted break-ins and security breaches with other facilities of their kind—both at official sites and off-book labs. Luckily, facility security is naturally top of the line, and those attacks have been repelled."

"But not all of them," I said. "Else we wouldn't be flying to New York."

He looked grave. "Yes. There are two extraordinary incidents underway right now."

"Hit me," I said.

And he did. He hit us real damn hard.

CHAPTER 50
FORESTED AREA
ROCKINGHAM COUNTY, VIRGINIA

From under cover of a camo blanket and cut brush, Tommy and Violin watched the children being unloaded from the truck and transferred into the backs of three four-wheel-drive Jeep Wranglers. A black Escalade sat twenty yards apart, half-hidden by trees.

Three exceptionally large men stood several yards from the Jeeps, their faces hidden by shadows thrown down by ball caps with large bills.

Tommy studied them. "Jeez Louise, look at the size of those guys."

Violin's only reply was a nod, though she looked troubled.

Other men, more normal sized, were handling the actual transfer of the children, while a woman stood watching, her back to the sniper scopes. She seemed to be in charge down there.

Tommy used crow drones to deliver hop frogs to the turnaround where the Jeeps were idling. It took careful maneuvering to get the bird drones to drop the smaller ones. Once that was done, the crows flapped up to sit on tree limbs while the hop frogs made their way to the Jeeps and the Escalade, leaped up, and hid inside the rear bumpers. A fifth hop frog wormed through the grass, and Tommy paused it as close to the people as possible. There was a freshening breeze that rustled the leaves in the trees, which smothered most of the conversation.

Tommy cursed under her breath, but Violin touched her arm. A calming gesture that suggested patience.

The men did not take particular notice of the four silent crows in the towering pines. The clicks of their camera shutter eyes were too soft to be heard beneath the constant hiss of the autumn breeze in the trees. The images were sent to Tommy's tablet, and she ran them through facial recognition software.

The software was connected to a variety of databases, including the FBI, CIA, Homeland, DEA, Interpol, local law, various branches of domestic and foreign military, scores of state and federal prisons, and the Department of Motor Vehicles. No trace of the data mining was left, because Arklight's computer system—Oracle—had been greatly modified by software engineer Annie Han, who liaised with her close friend and sometimes lover, Bug. Those people with the kids were each in one database or another.

All but one.

The exception was an Asian woman, a bit taller than medium height, wearing a pink Bettie Page–style wig and white plastic sunglasses. She had notable facial scars, but so far, no system pinged her. The closest approximation was of a deceased woman Tommy had read about in the news. She slid the tablet over to Violin and pointed to the face of the woman with the kids and the dead woman from the news.

Violin glanced at it and shook her head. However, she hesitated before sliding the tablet back to Tommy.

"Something?" asked Tommy very quietly.

"I've been doing this too long," said Violin with a small rueful smile. "I'm seeing ghosts. But . . . our mutual friend killed that one. That one down there isn't her."

They went back to watching.

When the breeze momentarily dropped, they heard one of the handlers speaking.

"—comfort camp," he said. "Everyone wants to party before Firefall."

The Asian woman turned slowly toward him and then stepped forward and got up in his face.

"You have a very big mouth for such a little man," she said.

The man visibly stiffened. "But it's just us here. Everyone here knows about Firefall and—"

The woman hit him.

It was shockingly fast and so powerful that it spun the man halfway around and sent him crashing against the side of one of the Jeeps. He rebounded, though, and whirled, his hand diving under his jacket. If he had a gun, though, it never appeared because one of the brutish sentries grabbed him. The big man moved with alarming speed, and one huge hand clamped down on the reaching arm and the other caught the smaller man by the throat. With no apparent effort, the brute lifted the man to tiptoes and then completely off the ground.

Tommy gasped. She'd seen that kind of thing in movies, but never in real life, and she marveled at the amount of raw strength required. Her deep knowledge of martial arts tried to insist that it was not possible for *anyone* to accomplish a one-handed lift of an adult male who had to weigh at least 175.

The Asian woman stepped closer and looked up into the man's face, watching with apparent fascination as it went from red to purple. Then she reached inside her own jacket and produced a knife.

What she did next was not merely murder, it was abomination. As the giant held the struggling man, she stabbed and slashed and hacked at his chest and groin, then stepped away, nimble as a dancer, as a red mass of intestines bulged and then flopped out onto the grass.

Inside the Jeeps, the children—drugged as they were—began to scream.

The other handlers cringed back against their vehicles, staring in utter horror at what the woman was doing. The captured man kept screaming—though his cries were choked to terrible whispers. He screamed longer than Tommy thought possible.

The woman kept cutting, though, until long after he was an empty, bloody, and lifeless hulk. Then she stepped back and . . .

. . . licked the blood off the blade.

Tommy gagged and had to clamp a hand over her mouth to keep from screaming. Or vomiting.

The brute dropped the corpse and walked behind the woman as she went over to the other handlers. The hop frog caught her words.

"Anyone else have a fucking word to say?" she asked. Her mouth was smeared with crimson.

The men cowered back, shaking their heads, making promises, trying not to look at the horror sprawled in the dirt.

"Then do your jobs, boys," said the woman. "And keep your mouths shut or what happened to him will happen to you and everyone in your family." She took her sunglasses off. "Look at me and tell me if I'm joking."

They looked.

They stared.

One of them began to cry.

The woman spat onto the ground between. A big, fat glop of saliva and blood. She turned away toward the parked Escalade, snapping her fingers for her three huge bodyguards. They fell into step behind her, obedient as dogs. One stepped up and opened the front passenger door for her and even offered a supporting hand as she climbed in. She handed him the knife.

For a single moment, she looked up at the crows in the trees and frowned slightly. Then she was inside, and the Escalade drove away. After a few minutes, so did the Jeeps.

Tommy sat up, her face wan and troubled.

"What the hell was *that*?"

Violin did not answer. Her brow was furrowed, and she looked both confused and worried.

"The crow she looked at," she said. "Pull up that feed. I want to see her face."

Tommy did, but unfortunately, there were leaves obscuring the image.

"What is it?" asked Tommy. "Do you recognize her?"

Violin replayed the video ten times, then shook her head in resignation.

"I'm seeing ghosts," she repeated, smiling ruefully.

Tommy thought Violin's eyes looked genuinely haunted.

CHAPTER 51
IN FLIGHT OVER NEW YORK AIRSPACE

"Two of the most critical active sites have been *potentially* compromised in the last twenty-four hours," said Church. "One is Das Feuerwehrhaus. Scheduled communication ceased eight hours ago. The no-name group within the German government reached out to me because they are not legally allowed to exist and would prefer not to call on their nation's security services. Heads would roll, and we would lose valuable contacts in that country." He paused. "Before you ask, they have been conducting research that contravenes both German and international bioweapons agreements."

"Ah," I said.

"Shit," said Top.

"I've sent Bedlam Team to investigate Das Feuerwehrhaus." Church looked off to his left and cocked his head as if listening to someone who was not on the ORB call. He nodded, then turned back to us. "They entered the facility three minutes ago, and we are waiting for their report. Scott Wilson is coordinating that action in the TOC."

"How do we know that place is compromised and not just dealing with some technical glitch?" asked Bunny.

"We don't know anything for certain," said Church. "However, there have been some unusual glitches with comms and different kinds of crucial internal automatic systems. This morning, both facilities went down entirely. Given the number of redundancies built into such sites, a total comms failure resulting from purely technical errors is virtually impossible. There has to be some deliberate action, either inside or outside. Possibly a coordination of outside attackers and an inside mole. Additionally, the bioweapons attacks in the States makes me less inclined to assume this is just a tech glitch."

"Fair enough," I said.

"I received a call from Oskar Freund asking that we provide an assist," said Church.

Oskar was the son of one of Church's old spy buddies from back in the day. He was a captain in the GSG 9 der Bundespolizei, a police tactical unit of the German Federal Police. Despite the public perception that the GSG 9 focused on hostage situations, kidnapping, terrorism, and similar threats, they had a special unit known as Sturmfest that was modeled along the same lines as the old DMS, thanks to Church's having been an advisor.

"Why is Sturmfest not already there?" I asked. "They're more or less as off-book as we are, and they're the home team."

"The timing is unfortunate," said Church. "Freund's entire team is in Taiwan at the moment handling something that cannot be put on hold. He asked for Havoc, but as you are in the States and Leopard's team was available for quick wheels-up, I sent Bedlam."

I nodded. *Leopard* was the combat call sign for Major Mun Ji-woo. She was sharp as hell, and so were her team members.

"Which leaves us with Gehenna," Church said. "No alarms have yet been rung in the American halls of power, mainly because there are only a handful of people in the States who are even aware of it. One of those who does keep an eye on it is a friend of mine, and she reached out right away. Gehenna's nature and location have been kept at this level of secrecy because presidents and members of Congress come and go, and too often, they are in the pocket of Big Pharma and interest groups whose lobbying funding may come from foreign sources."

I glanced at my team. No one was smiling.

"Gehenna is rated as a very secure facility, but like the Vault and Site 44, it's aging out, and the sophistication of thieves often rises faster than governments can respond."

"Sure," said Top. "Installing a lock's a hell of a lot more time-consuming and labor-intensive than picking one."

"Precisely," said Church. "Gehenna has been due for a system-wide upgrade for some time. It needs more than new software—the supercomputer upon which everything relies has become incompatible with advances in security software. That isn't a critical threat, but it is arguably just enough out of date to make it vulnerable to certain kinds of cyber intrusion. And now it's gone dark."

"Fuck a moose," I said.

Doc snorted. Church bit a piece of vanilla wafer.

"What makes this Gehenna joint so scary?" asked Remy. "Or is that a stupid question?"

"No such question is stupid," said Church. "Gehenna contains a large number of samples of some of the most dangerous and virulent designer pathogens ever created."

We sat with that for a moment.

Bunny said, "Even if it was ready for an overhaul, boss, it's still gotta be a hard nut to crack. Nobody's going to waltz in there with a cold chisel and can of liquid nitrogen."

"True. It has many layers of security and redundancies on their fail-safes. It was *designed* to be unbreakable."

Remy smiled. "Sounds to me like a bucket-list challenge for a cutting-edge vault breaker."

There was a slight pause as the words *vault breaker* hit Church, Doc, Bug, Top, Bunny, and me harder and in a different way than it did the others.

"Wait . . . what'd I say?" asked Remy, looking around.

Bug took a very long pull on a can of Red Bull. Into the silence, he said, "That's what I mentioned earlier. There actually *was* an ultrasophisticated computer program once called VaultBreaker."

"Oh," said Remy. "I thought that was just a phrase."

"Nope. Real program," Bug said. "It was, at the time, the absolute bleeding edge of cybersecurity technology. It had several protocols. One was to serve as an advanced counterespionage program to keep China, Iran, Russia, and North Korea from hacking into our energy grids and shutting them down. The other thing was to attack our *own* security systems. Sounds insane, I know, but it had a solid basis in logic. Once a new, ultra-secure facility was designed, VaultBreaker would be used to try to crack its defenses. Each time it found a hole, the designers of the facility would then be able to address that vulnerability. Reset and replay until there were no holes left to find. Smart stuff."

"Oh," said Remy. "I get it. Like when SpecOps teams are deployed to try to break into a secure facility so they can evaluate the security."

"Yup, just like that," agreed Bug. "Industry people call it 'penetration testing.' *I* don't, for all the obvious reasons."

Bunny and Remy cracked up at that.

"I prefer 'ethical hacking,'" said a grinning Bug. "Look, Vault-Breaker was designed to play like a video game. We even hired some top game nerds to play versions of it—in very controlled situations, you understand—to see how good it was. What freaked everyone out was that these gamers, most of whom were teenage kids, were better at using VaultBreaker than most of our security people were. In fact, only two people in the DMS were better than those geeks for hire. Me, because . . . well . . . I'm me."

"Modesty is your superpower," said Doc. Bug bowed.

"Who else could beat this VaultBreaker?" asked Belle.

"The only one who ever did was the woman who codesigned it," said Church. "Dr. Artemisia Bliss. She was recruited by Doc Holliday's predecessor, Dr. William Hu."

Bug nodded. "She wrote the largest chunk of the code and oversaw the gamers we hired to test the security."

"Sounds like the kind of person we want in on this," said Remy. "Where's she now?"

"Very, very dead," said Top.

"Bad guys took her out?" Remy asked.

Bunny gave a hard grunt of a laugh. "The colonel put two center mass when she was on a high balcony at the Marriott Marquis Hotel in Atlanta. They scraped her off the floor with a spatula, and yeah, she was dead."

"Okay . . . ouch," said Remy.

"The takeaway there, kid," I explained, "is that Bliss turned out to be a complete five-alarm fire of a maniac who wanted to kill the world. Fair to say we drifted as friends."

Remy looked around at us all. "So . . ." he said slowly in that Louisiana drawl, "how far up the dirty bayou does that put us, and do we have a paddle?"

"We are confused and apprehensive," admitted Church. "Given what's happened with Site 44 and Inferno, and now with Gehenna and Das Feuerwehrhaus, we have to assume a larger and more far-

JONATHAN MABERRY

reaching program of attack than was earlier apparent. Moreover, whoever has been attacking these facilities appears to be on a par with Artemisia Bliss and Bug."

"It's not me," said Bug, and there were a few smiles.

"The list of software designers on that level is understandably very short," said Church. "We don't know who is in play here or how they discovered the locations of these facilities."

Belle asked, "Does this mean someone else has a copy of Vault-Breaker?"

"That is the most logical assumption," Church said. "It is why Havoc Team is en route to Gehenna."

Remy frowned. "Maybe I missed something, but y'all are talking like VaultBreaker is still being used. If this Bliss chick helped design it and used it to do crimes, then why is anyone using it at all?"

"Not as simple as that," said Bug. "The version of VaultBreaker Bliss worked on is one form, and that's been swapped out with revised software. But VaultBreaker as a *concept* is still cutting edge. If someone on par with Bliss had the notes and if they were familiar with the design *philosophy*, they could adapt it for use. That would create a serious threat."

"Right," said Remy, still treading water, "but she *is* dead, and Bug's one of us. So why's that making everyone stand on chairs like there's scorpions on the floor?"

"Because Das Feuerwehrhaus, Inferno, and Gehenna—along with the others we mentioned," said Bug, "were built using VaultBreaker as a security check. They're the oldest facilities on this level, and it's *possible* that someone using VaultBreaker could manage a way to beat their security. Even with some routine upgrades and software patches that have been used since Bliss died. You with me?"

"With you," said Remy, nodding. "Scared as balls, but with you."

I said, "And Gehenna's aging mainframe isn't up to the task of fighting back against someone who's maybe as smart as Bliss or who somehow got a copy of VaultBreaker and is somehow using it?"

Bug waggled a flat hand in the air. "Iffy at best. A lot depends on who is using some pirated version of VaultBreaker or has something newer and better."

I said, "I probably don't want to hear the answer to this, but what *exactly* do they have at Gehenna? Are we talking weaponized rabies? Modified Zika? Quick-onset Ebola?"

"Yes," said Coleman. "All of that. But . . ." He let it trail off as he turned to Doc.

I jumped in and glared at our boss. "Is this the part I *really* won't like?"

"Without a doubt," said Church.

"Tell me anyway."

Doc's maniac smile was even brighter. "It's the only facility that has all sixteen strains of *seif al din*," she said.

Bunny made a soft, deep, ugly noise. Top hissed liked he'd been sprayed with boiling water. I sat there and felt my skin go numb.

INTERLUDE 19
MISS MARY'S LAB
THE MANSION
UNDISCLOSED LOCATION
NINE WEEKS AGO

Miss Mary walked through her lab as her scientists watched her. They were silent, attentive, and a little afraid, all of which were ideal.

Fear was a tricky thing to manage, though. Fear of her reprisal should never reach higher than desire for her approval. Earning their love and respect took more effort, requiring her to be more . . .

She had to fish for the right word.

Human.

She nearly missed a step when she realized that was the correct term, but it was a word that became less of a personal definition and more of a memory.

There were two doctors on her staff—Singh and Cooper—who had done thorough examinations of her. Not just surface examinations but blood work, DNA sequencing, and samples of every conceivable kind. Mary went along with all of it, though she seldom shared the test results with her patron. She did not care to share that with him.

Actually, as she moved through the lab for her daily inspection, she considered all of the other things that she opted not to share. Her views on his Firefall project. Her views on the comfort camps and other entertainments provided for October's troops.

Fucking swine, she thought. *Pigheaded shitheads who wouldn't piss on me if I were on fire.*

Their racism was palpable, and she knew she was tolerated and given deference because of the power she represented. Most of which, alas, was borrowed from October. *He* was the one they worshipped. He was the one they would follow to the gates of hell. Not Toombs and certainly not she.

October was a rich white man with lots of money. He paid for their training, uniforms, transportation, equipment, housing. Some of them—possibly Commandant Furman, who was the brightest of a dull lot—probably guessed that October was also Toombs's boss, which meant he was selling and buying his own guns. It was comedy, as far as Mary saw it, but the legionnaires ate it up. What, after all, did they care where the weapons came from as long as they got to own them and use them?

Mary stopped by the largest of the three glass-enclosed hot rooms. The one on her left was filled with the various diseases they had collected and which she used for her legion of Typhoid Marys. *Her* private army. The hot room on the right housed the MERS her scientists were scrambling to produce in large quantities for the Gorgon weapons.

In the middle, though, given the largest chamber, the thickest shatterproof glass, and the most sophisticated locks, was the real prize. The jewel of her collection.

Seif al din.

Only the earliest generations of it, but even so . . . it was beautiful.

She stared at it, wishing—not for the first time—that the disease could take a more substantial physical form. Something she could hold in her arms. Something she could kiss and fuck and be in love with.

No, she thought, *that's not crazy at all.*

Mary made herself turn away. With a straight face that was only a mask over her real feelings, she continued with the morning inspection. There was so much still to see. The latest litter of SDs were whining and snapping in their cages. And there was a table covered with Gorgon warheads.

CHAPTER 52
PHOENIX HOUSE
OMFORI ISLAND, GREECE

Rudy Sanchez moved like a ghost through the halls of the RTI complex. There were all manner of things happening, a plethora of crises in all of their various flavors and intensities. Every now and then, a runner would find him with questions from Scott Wilson or Mr. Church, and Rudy would reply—in person or via cell. But he rarely visited the TOC these last few days.

His most recent therapy session with Joe Ledger troubled him more deeply than he expected. His heart pulled him one way, his mind another, and the ethics of his job wrenched him yet another direction.

He finally went outside and walked well away from the main building. Despite the lateness of the hour, the last of the sun still shone brightly over the blue sea, sparkling in that way it does when it wants the world to look happier than it is. Rudy was never fooled by it. It was probably sunny that morning on Golgotha.

Gulls floated along the island's coasts, looking down through crystal water for something to eat before bed. They were pretty, too, even though they were about to kill. It was the way of the world. Predators and prey, and that depressed Rudy, pushing him beneath the surface of his professional objectivity.

When he could not bear it any longer, he sat on a wooden bench with an eastern view, took his cell from his pants pocket, and then stared at it for ten full minutes. Eight times he began to make the call. Eight times he did not.

Until he finally did.

She answered on the fifth ring, sounding breathless.

"Junie . . . ?" he asked. "Am I interrupting anything?"

"Oh, just my usual battle with how pizza goes straight to my hips," she said with a laugh. "Was on the treadmill. And before you apologize, I hate the treadmill with a fiery intensity."

"I feel the same about all of the exercise equipment Circe has bought for me over the years."

"Loathsome monsters, aren't they?"

"Despicable bullies," he said.

Junie took a beat, rising to her empathic intuition. "What is it, Rudy? Is something wrong? Is it Joe . . ."

"What? Oh, no. It's not anything urgent."

She laughed again. "*Lead* with that next time."

"Sorry."

"But . . . this is about Joe, isn't it?"

He did not ask how she knew. She knew, and that was Junie.

"I need some advice, Junie. Friend to friend."

"Of course."

"It's complicated."

"What isn't these days?"

Rudy smiled at the ocean waves. "True. Yes," he said, "this is about Joe. But more to the point, it's about something Joe told me in therapy."

A beat.

"Is it about the Darkness?"

"No, no," Rudy assured her. "It's not that. It's . . ."

"It's about Helen," she said abruptly.

"How . . . ?" he began, then caught himself. "Yes."

"It's the names, isn't it?"

Now it was Rudy's time to take a moment. "He told you?"

"Yes," she said. "He tells me everything."

"He told me the other day," said Rudy. "Right before he left for the States."

"Those names," said Junie.

"Those names."

"Did he tell you who told him? And under what circumstances?" she asked.

"Yes. Jason Aydelotte told him."

"While they were both whacked out of their heads on that psychedelic mushroom thing."

"Shiva, yes," said Rudy. "Or I suppose it was the stronger version. God's Arrow. Aydelotte gave him five names."

Junie said, "Joe Listopad, Jamie Stanton, Danny Beck, Bob Reilly, and Greg Murphy."

"Yes."

"Did you look them up?" asked Junie.

"Yes. Did you?"

"Yes," she said. "All of them match men who were seventeen or eighteen and who lived in the same part of Baltimore."

"Yes." He took a breath. "That alone means nothing. Joe's personal history is a matter of hospital and police records. Someone with Aydelotte's resources could have dug deep enough to learn about what happened to him and Helen. Aydelotte could have grabbed names of any boys of that age and in that area."

"Sure," she said.

"There's no proof that it was them," said Rudy. "Joe never knew their names. He never found them in mug shot books. His Identi-Kit drawings yielded nothing."

"Rudy," said Junie quietly, "you know more about that even than I do. Joe said no one was ever named, sought, or caught."

"That's right."

"Did the police or hospital staff use a rape kit to collect DNA?"

He paused. "Yes. They collected DNA and ran it. Nothing came of it."

"That was twenty years ago," she said. "Makes me wonder if they've ever run that data since."

Rudy felt like her words had hollowed him out. He felt old and frail.

"I have been thinking the same thing," he admitted. "But what can I do? Joe spoke to me in confidence, in the privacy of our therapy sessions. It's not like I can go to Mr. Church with this. Or Bug. Not without Joe's approval."

They sat in silence for several long moments. One of the gulls dove down, struck the water like a missile, and rose again with a baby crab wriggling in its beak. Rudy watched the bird fly away to find a private place to kill and feast.

"Rudy . . . ?" said Junie. "I have something to tell you."

"Do I want to hear it?"

"You might. Not sure how Joe will feel if I decide to tell him."

"Are you sure you want to tell me?" he asked.

"I almost called you forty times on this."

"Ah. Well. Tell me . . ."

"I told Violin."

"What?"

"I told Violin. She, more than Church or anyone at the RTI, understands what it means to be the victim of male hatred and violence. She's Lilith's daughter, born from rape, raised in a breeding camp. She's with Arklight. She's their most aggressive agent."

"Yes, she is."

"She also loves Joe. Not in a romantic way," said Junie. "Though maybe there's still some of that left over from when they were together. No, what I mean is that she loves who he is and what he is. She understands his damage and how he's spent all this time fighting to stop people like those boys who attacked him and Helen. She knows that he sharpened himself like a sword *because* of what happened, because he wasn't able to stop them at the time."

"Yes," said Rudy softly.

"Arklight has its own computer team. Annie Han runs it. She's as close to being Bug as anyone. Maybe better in some areas."

"She's brilliant."

He listened and could hear Junie breathing.

"Are you going to tell me Annie found them?" he asked.

"Yes," she said. "I haven't told Joe or Church or anyone. But . . . yes."

"And . . . ?"

"She obtained the DNA from the Baltimore police. Don't ask me how, because she wouldn't tell me. Rudy . . . the cops had lifted five sets of DNA from Helen. From her . . . body. Her clothes. Five sets. They ran all five."

Rudy braced himself.

"They match, Rudy."

"*Ay, dios mío.*"

"I haven't told Joe," said Junie. "I don't know if I should. Does that make sense?"

"Yes," he said. "It does."

"Explain it to me, please."

"It has to be Joe's choice," said Rudy. "He's had those names for months now. He told me about it in therapy, but he omitted it from his after-action report. I don't think he told Top or Bunny."

"I know that, Rudy, and that's something I can understand. My question, I guess, is what would Joe do if he found out that they *are* the five who attacked Helen and him? He has to be thinking about it. He may even have used MindReader to learn what Annie Han found out. What really scares me is what he might do. If he goes after them, what kind of damage would he do to himself?"

"They should all be brought to justice," said Rudy.

"They all have families. Four of the five of them have kids of their own."

"Abusers seldom make safe parents, Junie."

"What about repentance? What about redemption?" she asked. "You're Catholic. Three of those five men are Catholic. If Joe goes after them, how can he know if he is going after men who may have regretted what they did?"

"Maryland has no statute of limitations for felony sexual crimes, regardless of the age of the victim. They are criminals, and their actions led to Helen's suicide. Joe would not be crossing any legal or ethical lines in having them arrested."

"I know that," said Junie. "I lived in Maryland and looked up those laws. If I thought that the worst Joe would do would be to contact his friends in Baltimore PD, then it wouldn't scare me."

"I see where you're going with this," said Rudy. "You are afraid of what Joe might do if he took the law into his own hands."

"He worked for the cops and he worked for the US government during the DMS days. He works for RTI now. All of those groups are some kind of law enforcement. Sure, we both know he's broken a lot of laws hunting the terrorists he fights, but this is somehow different."

"This would be actual murder," said Rudy.

"Yes. And so much of who and what Joe has become is built on what happened. If he crosses a line for revenge, what will happen to him? That's the fire that burns in him. His hate and regret are his fuel. The need to set things right in the world is his *cause*."

"And you're asking what, Junie? Are you suggesting that closure might cause that internal structure to collapse? That he'd lose his sense of purpose? Surely you know he's stronger and more self-aware than that."

"When his family was murdered, he became the Darkness, Rudy. Do we want to know what will happen to him if he breaks the law, focuses on revenge, and becomes a murderer?"

"That isn't the right word for what he would do," said Rudy. "And before you ask, I don't know if there is a right word. Joe is not in any way a typical example of multiple personality disorder. He's unique in so many ways."

"You're dodging the question."

"That's because I don't have an answer," said Rudy.

"I know," said Junie with a note of despair in her voice. "Neither do I."

CHAPTER 53
DAS FEUERWEHRHAUS
GÖRLITZ, GERMANY

They moved like shadows. Like specters.

Six figures who came out of the night, running low and fast, making no sound. They broke from cover and separated, coming at the building from different angles, while pigeon drones flapped overhead, providing real-time video, thermal scans, and other telemetry.

When they stopped, it was as if they became part of the background. Nothing they did drew the eye. They wore black clothing, black weapons, black masks. Nothing was reflective, nothing clinked or rattled.

In its way, the building they approached was as nondescript as they were. It was a squat, two-story blockhouse with only two windows—both in front, on either side of a brown metal door—and a sign outside that read:

KLIEG DOKUMENTENSPEICHER

It looked exactly like the kind of building in which bulk documents were stored.

An L-shaped parking lot wrapped around two sides, with the rest of the perimeter taken up with dumpsters, a big industrial air-conditioning unit, and indifferently maintained decorative shrubberies. Cars—a three-year-old white Opel and a two-year-old green Volkswagen—squatted next to each other on the east side of the building. Everything was boring, quiet, of no obvious consequence.

Major Mun Ji-woo, topkick of Bedlam Team, crouched down beside a nondescript door and tapped the tactical computer strapped to her forearm. Instead of igniting with a bright screen, the display appeared on the inside of her Scout goggles.

"Leopard to TOC," she said quietly.

"Go for TOC," said Scott Wilson. "Grendel on deck."

"We're at the west door. All is quiet."

"We have you on live feed, Leopard. Yoda has control of all exterior cameras and sensors."

"Any word from Dr. Arnz?"

"Negative, Leopard. No communication from anyone inside the facility."

Mun took an Anteater—a portable electronic detector—from her belt and ran it around the entire door, considered the readings, and stowed the device. Then she tapped into her team channel. "Pond, on me."

Amy Neal—combat call sign Pond—the only other woman on Bedlam Team, materialized as if by magic. She was a tall woman and served as the team's field tech.

Mun nodded to the door. "Run a bypass."

Neal crabbed sideways and quickly removed a small device the size of a bottle cap from a belt pouch. She removed a strip of adhesive film from the back and then gently pressed it to the underside of a key card reader. Nothing seemed to happen for a five-count, and then the front of the key card reader flipped upward on hidden springs, revealing a far more sophisticated ID scanner below. This device had a key card slot, a rubber cup for retina scans, and a sensor pad for ring fingerprints.

Neal pressed the small machine she'd adhered to the reader and then sat back on her heels as the MindReader Q1 uplinked to a satellite that bounced its signal to Phoenix House in Greece. A digital display on her goggles read the steps, and Neal repeated them to Mun.

JONATHAN MABERRY

"The false codes have all been changed," she said. "MindReader's inside now. Rewriting the target software to allow me to play."

As they watched, small lights above each of the three sensors went from red to green. There was a very faint *click*.

"We're in," said Neal, shifting back out of the way.

"Copy that. Stand by, Pond."

Major Mun left one of her team—Luke Ward, call sign Gimli—to work the perimeter and called the rest to her. They were there in seconds.

"Enemy infiltration confirmed," she said. "They got in and changed the security codes. But we own the system now."

"Proceed with caution, Leopard," said Wilson. "There are friendlies inside."

He did not say anything as plaintive as "*I hope,*" but Mun and the rest of Bedlam Team heard it all the same. It was what they were thinking.

Das Feuerwehrhaus—the Fire Station—was a relatively small facility staffed by seven doctors, thirty-six assorted technicians and researchers, eighteen support staff, and a twenty-person security team. Eighty-one people, all designated *friendlies*.

Yet not one of them had managed to get a message to the outside world. Not a word or text or call. Not a peep.

Mun paused for a moment. She had joined Rogue Team International after the Rage case. The Kuga organization had abducted her and replaced her with their own agent who had then tried to sabotage the mission Havoc Team was running. During her incarceration, Kuga's people had brutalized her, tortured her—tearing out fingernails and pulling out her teeth—and inflicted terrible beatings in an effort to get her to divulge critical information. Despite their vicious enthusiasm, Mun had refused to speak. Later, she engineered her own escape and killed the men who had been abusing her.

Church had recruited her and—impressed with her intelligence, ferocity, courage, and skills—offered her the leadership of Bedlam. Since then, Mun had led her team in nineteen missions, ending each with a decided win. Das Feuerwehrhaus was the twentieth, and it came with a lot of risks. She did not know what kind of threat she was leading her team into, who had taken control of the facility, or even if it was an invasion rather than some currently unidentified catastrophic technical fault. The lack of useful intel was intimidating, even to the best field operators.

And . . . in truth, RTI had no legal jurisdiction to operate on German soil. They were there as part of Mr. Church's network of "friends" who tried to sidestep national bureaucratic red tape and operate with maximum efficiency on behalf of the greater good. Illegal by any metric, though it was how Church often waged his war. A "better to get permission than approval" approach that had kept the world from catching fire many, many times.

All of this was a heavy burden to carry—and an equally ponderous distraction—when breaking into one of the securest and most dangerous facilities on the planet.

I could have retired to Dojangpo Maeul and spent the rest of my life fishing and reading trashy novels, she mused. That was something she'd thought about during her captivity—leaving it all behind, buying a small fishing boat, and retiring to the ease and oblivion of civilian life. She had a couple of friends who lived there, and none of them knew what she really did for a living. It would be nice to become *normal* and to discover what she had spent her entire adult life fighting for.

"Call it," murmured Pond.

That pulled Mun back to the moment. She squared her shoulders, set her chin, took a steadying breath, and said, "Let's move."

And Bedlam Team followed her inside.

Into the Fire Station. Into the place where god knew what kind of monster waited.

The room directly inside the door looked exactly like the fiction the German government was trying to sell—utilitarian desk and chairs, file cabinets, a calendar showing scenic shots of air balloons over mountains, and fluorescent lighting. It was drab and relentlessly nondescript.

Except for the bodies.

There were two of them. Both male, both dressed in brown-and-gray commercial security guard uniforms. Both bound by plastic cuffs at wrists and ankles. Both with two bullet holes in their heads. They lay in pools of their own blood. Shell casings littered the floor, and the walls were spattered with blood sprays and bits of brain and bone.

Pond said, "Ahhhh . . . shit."

They were the only words spoken as the team moved into the building and began clearing the side rooms—bathroom, utility closet, and five larger rooms of actual records storage for local businesses. Like all such places, there was a legitimate operation aboveground.

When it was determined that there was no one else on the ground floor, Mun sent half the team to the second level, but that was also empty of everything except tens of thousands of carboard boxes filled with stored paper.

They regrouped on the first floor, and Mun tapped into the command channel.

"You see all of this?" she asked.

"Affirmative, Leopard," said Wilson.

Mun and Pond stepped into the utility room, located another high-end scanning terminal, sicced MindReader Q1 on it, and raised their weapons as the access door swung silently inward.

Outside, Gimli patrolled the perimeter, keeping to the shadows. He was alone except for a half dozen pigeon drones, two owl drones, and a rat drone that scuttled along the outside of the building. Each sent video feeds to the tactical computer strapped to Gimli's forearm. The data reassured him that there was nothing and no one in the area apart from him and the little machines. No heat signatures of anything larger than a small family of moles who shivered in their nest.

Gimli had been on Bedlam Team since it was founded when Mr. Church shuttered the old DMS and formed RTI. Before that, he had run with Omega Team in the Twin Cities, mostly hunting down players in the illegal weapons trade in the rural areas. There were some moments of drama, but overall, the Cities were a quiet station, with state and federal law—particularly Homeland—doing most of the heavy lifting.

He liked working for Church, and though he had seen combat several times, he had never taken a serious injury. Not in body, at least. His heart ached for friends who'd fallen in one or another battle in this war. One of his closest friends had been Brick Anderson, and Gimli was not even close to being over that. It freaked him out that it had been Church himself who'd killed his friend.

Not that Gimli harbored animosity toward Church. The Big Man, like everyone else caught up in the Cave 13 case, had been freaked out of their gourds by the Shiva and God's Arrows ergot-and-psilocybin bioweapons. But it made Gimli feel awkward around the boss. And it gave Gimli some nightmares he was working his way through with Dr. Sanchez.

He had been dwelling on that before the video feeds from inside showed the bodies of the two security guards. Now he was stiff with tension and had his rifle ready, a finger laid along the trigger guard, teeth grinding. The lingering grief was suddenly seasoned with outrage and anger. And fear.

He moved cautiously, taking no chances, allowing no assumptions to color his observations as he moved.

Even so, he was totally unprepared for the explosion that blew the back half of Das Feuerwehrhaus high into the sky, propelled by a fireball the size of the devil's fist.

CHAPTER 54
IN FLIGHT OVER NEW YORK AIRSPACE

Remy and Belle looked back and forth at the rest of us. The words *seif al din* seemed to hang burning in the air.

"I heard of that," said Belle. "But I don't really know what it is."

"You guys are scaring the crap out of me," said Remy.

"With good cause," said Doc Holliday. "*Seif al din*—sword of the faithful—is one of the most dangerous bioweapons ever developed. Possibly *the* most dangerous. In second place is Lucifer, developed during the Cold War by a group led by Dr. Herman Volker, and a close third is Vijivshiy Odin-Vasemnatzets—developer unknown but also cooked up in a Soviet lab. These latter two are in the class of endgame bioweapons."

Remy frowned. "Endgame? Is that an *Avengers* reference?"

"I wish," said Coleman. "But no. That's the class of genetically engineered pathogens intended for use as a doomsday weapon, to be used when the Soviet Union was engaged in a shooting war with the United States and was in danger of losing. The philosophy was that if they lost, then everyone else should lose, too. The biological version of mutually assured destruction."

Remy rubbed his eyes with the heels of his palms. "People are really that insane?"

No one felt the need to answer the question, and I think to all of us it was a measure of how young Remy actually was. Young in age and young in the process of having his optimism and general empathy sanded off by the real world.

"Of the three," said Church, "*seif al din* is the most communicable. It has an infection rate of nearly one hundred percent."

"More precisely, 98.99712," said Coleman, sotto voce.

Church smiled thinly and handed him a cookie.

To Belle and Remy, he said, "You likely heard about it without knowing what it was. It was released at the pop culture convention Dragon Con in Atlanta some years ago."

Remy snapped his fingers. "Sure. But I thought that was weaponized anthrax combined with some kind of hallucinogen."

"Cover story," said Top. "Same as when it was released at the Liberty Bell Center in Philly. That was the case Bunny, the colonel, and I signed on to fight. Our first gig. God damn near our last."

"That was this *seif al din*?" gasped Remy. "The news said it was . . ." He stopped, took a breath, and tried it a different way. "There's a lot of this kind of stuff going on all the time, isn't there?"

"Welcome to the war," said Church.

Bunny raised his hand. "Permission to go home and hide in my closet."

"Denied," said Church.

Doc Holliday said, "Following the release of the modified *seif al din* pathogen at Dragon Con, samples of that weapon were sent to Gehenna for study, along with the bodies of four infected. Other sites sent *seif al din* variant samples there as well, including versions salvaged from the original lab in the Middle East. The idea was for Gehenna to be the sole repository for the bioweapon and therefore provide easier overwatch and a quicker, cleaner disposal site."

"Okay . . ." I said cautiously.

Doc said, "The semi-good news was that the science team there was close to developing a prophylaxis for it. Not a vaccine, per se, since *seif al din* is a misfolded protein and not a virus or bacterium. Their reports were encouraging, but incomplete. We very much want to recover that data, most of which is encrypted in their on-site computers."

"Was Artemisia Bliss one of the infected corpses sent to Gehenna?"

Church shook his head. "Her body was transported to the Site 44 facility. The attack on that site—we believe—was made by people who knew her and were part of her old organization. Hackers and perhaps Berserkers. However, she and all of the hazardous materials stored there are presumed incinerated and the ashes sealed inside the facility."

"Okay," I said, "but am I correct in assuming that *seif al din* is another reason that *we* are getting involved? I mean, I get the fact that we're conveniently located and all that, but there really are groups here in the States that are trained specifically for this."

"Yes," said Church, "your presence here is fortunate, and I'm using that bit of luck. That said, my contacts in the US government are quietly preparing a more official response. However, the usual red tape is slowing things down. More to the point, you, Top, and Bunny have faced people infected with it on multiple occasions and prevailed. However, you also know the learning curve for first-time operators facing it. We lost multiple teams."

That was true enough, and it was the reason Church put together a new team composed of combat veterans who were far less prone to hesitancy than the average.

Into the silence, Belle asked, "What is a Berserker?"

I glanced at Top, who winced. He explained that Berserkers were originally engineered by the Jakoby crime family, using modified lowland silverback gorilla DNA to transform already huge PMCs into brutish killers. That was on my second DMS gig, the one at the Dragon Factory. Then later, while Bliss was working for the DMS, she stole the Jakoby research as well as samples of *seif al din* and tried to launch the bioweapon at Dragon Con. To make it even more entertaining for me and my guys, Bliss infected her Berserkers with one of the *seif al din* variants. That was a real hoot.

Belle just closed her eyes and shook her head. Remy looked around as if trying to find a parachute.

"There is a glimmer of optimism," Church said.

"Well, hell," I said. "*Lead* with that next time."

"It is possible the team that breached Gehenna is trapped inside and are working on escaping. If so, then we may have an opportunity for containment, apprehension, and interrogation."

"I'd be very happy to *apprehend* these cats," said Remy.

"Dibs on interrogation," said Bunny.

"What kind of window are we talking about?" I asked the crew at the TOC. "What's our timeline?"

"The internal security systems at Gehenna use a multi-phasic lockdown," said Bug. "When communication is cut off, then the facility goes into a *soft-lock*, which blanks out general key card use and seals the air locks and hot rooms for up to twelve hours if no cancel order is requested from the staff there. Dr. Sammie Trinidad is the lead epidemiologist, and it's her call. That allows time to assess the problem and work through the steps of containment verification and then unlocking. We're halfway through that phase now. It's a short flight for you and an equally short drive from the airport to the facility."

"What happens when the clock runs out?"

We all looked at Church. "If we cannot reestablish communication with the staff within," he said gravely, "phase two is a hard lockdown, where thermite charges seal the air locks. These are connected to the station's biohazard alert system. If the clock has run out but there are no active pathogens in the air, then the staff shelter in place and a team goes in to unseal the doors."

"And if there *are* pathogens floating around and this Dr. Trinidad doesn't pick up the phone?"

"Then *burn-lock* is initiated."

"Sounds ominous as hell."

"It is," said Church. "A second set of incendiary charges permanently flash-weld the air locks, and the internal emergency system incinerates everything. The entire facility becomes a tomb. Like the Vault, Site 44, and Inferno. And I will make very sure no one ever drills their way into it."

The way he leaned into that, I believed him. We all did.

Top asked, "This burn-lock thing . . . could that have anything to do with Firefall? Burn? Fire? Or am I just fishing without bait here?"

"It's a fair question," said Wilson. "We wondered the same thing and have added that to the keyword pattern search."

"Now hear me on this," said Church firmly. "If Havoc Team is able to secure the facility without staff oversight, you have my permission—even my blessing—to burn every sample of it they have. And if other bioweapons fall into the same bonfire, then that would make us all sleep a lot better."

"Hoo-damn-ah," muttered Bunny under his breath.

Top asked, "What are the rules of engagement for this little jaunt, sir?"

"Best-case scenario is that this is a technical fault and you and Havoc are angels of mercy helping them get out alive."

"And worst case?" I asked.

"Under no circumstances can we allow *seif al din* to escape from Gehenna. You may remember what I told you during the hiring process when I brought you on board the DMS. That still applies and—"

Suddenly, Church turned away and I could hear Scott Wilson's voice speaking very fast and sounding very upset, but I couldn't catch his actual words. Church turned back to us.

"Outlaw," he said sharply, "there has been an explosion at Das Feuerwehrhaus. Waiting on intel. Will get back to you soonest."

That fast, the ORB hologram disappeared, and the lights came on inside the cabin.

"Well," said Bunny, "that just made my nuts shrivel up."

Top took the matchstick from his mouth, studied the chewed stump, and put it back. "Major Mun's top grade and runs a tight fucking team."

It was meant as comfort, but it did not feel like it.

Remy turned to me. "What'd he mean by what he said, boss? What *did* the Big Man tell you back when you guys first ran into this *seif al din* thing?"

I stared out the window at the clouds flowing below us at five hundred miles an hour.

"He said that he would burn down heaven itself to keep this thing from spreading," I said softly. "He wasn't joking."

"Jesus," he said.

CHAPTER 55
DAS FEUERWEHRHAUS
GÖRLITZ, GERMANY

Major Mun lay in darkness, wrapped in pain, leaking blood. Her head hurt so badly it sickened her, and she turned over and vomited. There was blood in it, and that scared her.

Nearby, Amy Neal knelt and worked by the glow of a penlight as she tried to stanch all of the many deep cuts that covered Billy Robinette—call sign Kingsnake. The man was gray with pain and dangerously silent, not even grunting as Neal moved his limbs to apply the bandages.

"How is he, Pond?" asked George Yazzie—Mountain Man—who knelt by the air lock door, rifle ready, his face streaked with dust and blood.

"Let me work," said Neal.

And that said a lot.

The fifth member of their team, Felix Howard, an affable and good-looking soldier whom Neal often flirted with, was gone. Buried beneath a thousand tons of debris. That loss was going to hit Neal at some point, but she could not allow it yet.

Mun listened to the creaks and grinding noises as the shattered concrete groaned under its own weight. She tried to stay professional, forcing herself to do an objective damage assessment. Her right leg was broken, that much was clear. Several ribs, too, and at least three bones in her left hand. There was a deep pain in her stomach, and it felt hot and very wrong. A puncture, though she was too hurt and too badly covered with debris to look. Internal bleeding was her biggest fear. Rolling over to throw up had done her no damn good at all.

But . . . Kingsnake was much worse.

"I think they heard you at the TOC, boss," said Mountain Man with more confidence than any of them felt. "The Big Man knows we're in the shit. He's sending people. Just you wait."

Major Mun said nothing. The pain was so red hot and urgent that she was afraid that if she opened her mouth at all, only a scream would burst out. So, she waited with the patience of the damned.

They were in the first air lock.

What was left of it. The gigantic five-ton steel door leaned drunkenly on one twisted hinge. The mechanics and computer built into it were slag.

The lights inside the facility were on, though, suggesting that at least one backup generator was still operational. Somewhere an alarm buzzed continuously, but it was distant and muffled.

There were no shouts. No cries for help. No wounded begging for someone to come and do something. There was nothing.

Just the alarm and the muttering of the mountain of debris over them.

Mun had not prayed very much in her life. Not even when she was being tortured by Kuga's thugs.

Now, though, she closed her eyes, and in her private darkness, she prayed with all of her heart and soul.

CHAPTER 56
MISS MARY'S LAB
THE MANSION
UNDISCLOSED LOCATION

"How fast can you reproduce this stuff?" asked Mary as they strolled through her lab for her morning inspection.

Her senior lab tech, Singh, shrugged. "For the MERS, a couple of weeks is enough time to make all you need. It'll all be ready well before the event date."

The event was Firefall, but the scientists down in her lab did not know the code name. Their job was to mass-produce the Middle East respiratory syndrome pathogen in sufficient quantity to fill all of the Gorgons they had.

Singh gestured to a row of devices. "For the virus, we're using a continuous tubular bioreactor system. It helps to avoid the von Magnus effect that's often seen in continuous-stirred tank reactors. This will get us twice the yield in half the time."

"Good, good," said Mary, her tone a bit distracted. "And the prions?"

"Well, we only have enough of the early generation to mass-produce right now. We have PMCAs as you can see, and—"

"What are they?"

"Oh, sorry, ma'am. Protein misfolding cyclic amplification setups that we are using to mass-produce it."

"And that will take how long?"

"Well . . ." hedged Singh, "in order to mass-produce prions, we need an ample supply of the substrate protein. The obvious source for this would be ground-up human brains, but since those are hard to find without raising eyebrows, we're making a recombinant version using CHO cells—Chinese hamster ovary cells—in a protein production bioreactor." He paused. "We can scale this up by having more bioreactors. With those, we can take the product of the first one and then seed several new ones. But . . ."

"But what?"

"They're expensive."

"How expensive?" asked Mary.

"For the number we need? A couple hundred thousand at least."

Mary walked a few paces in thoughtful silence. "Buy them. Send the bill to me, understand? Not to Mr. October. Directly to me. I'll pay for them out of my own funds."

Singh looked puzzled. "But I was told that all purchases had to go through—"

She stopped and turned toward him. "Let's be very clear, Dr. Singh," she said in a not unpleasant tone. "This is my lab. October paid to have it built, yes, but he gave it to me. I own it. I have a discretionary account for private research. This is a side project, and so I'll fund it."

The scientist lingered. "This isn't for Firefall?"

Mary smiled. "Don't be silly. *Seif al din* is far too dangerous to put into a warhead. We're trying to get rich, not kill the world. God, Singh, I'm crazy, but I'm not *that* crazy."

Her smile looked genuine, as did her little self-deprecating laugh. The scientist looked greatly relieved.

"What was I thinking," he said, chuckling.

"So, you'll get those bioreactors?"

"Of course."

"Expedite the shipping, and set them up as soon as they're here."

He nodded and turned to go, then paused. "If I may ask . . . what is the prion weapon for, then, if not for Firefall?"

"Oh, that's something I'm working on. A long-range project. It won't interfere with Firefall."

He nodded and headed back to his cubicle to order the machines. Mary lingered, watching him, and then turned to gaze at the glass-enclosed hot room. It bothered her that they only had samples of the earlier generations of Amirah's beautiful and elegant *seif al din*. Mary only knew of one place that had all of the strains, including the strain that had given her the strange and wonderful life she had now.

"Gehenna," she murmured.

CHAPTER 57
IN FLIGHT OVER NEW YORK AIRSPACE

Shirley is a very fast jet.

And yet it seemed to take forever to get to upstate New York. Each moment became an hour as we waited for a status report on Bedlam Team.

To keep everyone from sinking inside their own speculations as to what was happening to our friends, Top, Bunny, and I explained the realities of *seif al din* to Belle and Remy. We were barely into the science of it before they started looking for parachutes to get the hell off that crazy bird. I can't blame them one little bit.

Here's the shorthand.

Some years ago, a British pharmaceutical billionaire named Sebastian Gault partnered with a religious fanatic from Yemen called El Mujahid and his wife, Amirah. She was the molecular biologist who conceived and created a new kind of spongiform encephalopathy, particularly the fatal familial insomnia version that, unlike mad cow or other variants, had two really terrifying designer qualities. The first was that it was not just rapid-onset—which all bioterrorists love—but was nearly immediate. It was transferred mainly by bites, but Amirah also developed a version that could be loaded into darts similar to what the Snellig fires. The second major difference from other prion diseases of that family was that it reduced higher brain function to practically nil while also reducing the body's metabolism to nearly undetectable levels. The upshot was that the infected appeared to die and the disease reanimated them in ways that made them ultra-aggressive and driven to spread their infection through bites.

So, yeah, pretty much zombies.

Not *actual* living dead, but close enough. More like the insane infected in flicks like *28 Days Later*. Alive, but because Amirah's vicious microscopic monsters also modified the body's automatic repair processes, the victims could withstand incredible injuries and still attack. You had to not only get a head shot, but in order to stop them, one needed to destroy either the motor cortex or brain stem. That kind of thing is always a piece of cake in *The Walking Dead*—everyone seems able to get a clean head shot.

In real life? Yeah, not so much. The attrition rate was alarmingly high.

Seif al din was developed to be a weapon against the West. Or at least that's what we thought. Turns out, Gault wanted to use it in limited ways, with no real chance of it becoming a true pandemic, as a way of scaring all governments into shifting lots and lots of money away from the military and into pharmaceutical R & D. Since Gault knew the science and had some response protocols ready to go, he was poised to make an obscene amount of money. It didn't matter to him that the larger groups among Big Pharma would make more. That was fine, because as he would be viewed as merely a small profiteering opportunist, he wouldn't be anyone's first choice as the Big Bad.

Unfortunately, his partner, Amirah, was playing him. Her husband, El Mujahid, wanted to legit bring about the end of the world. Kind of. Amirah had developed newer versions of the pathogen that would allow very specific people to retain their higher functions and be less, well . . . zombified.

The DMS and my own crew, Echo Team, shut them down hard. But it was a close thing. Very, very close.

Then some years later, Bliss stole that research and some samples of the pathogen. It was her way of making the biggest possible splash as she spiraled downward into total out-of-her-mindedness—and, yes, *mindedness* is a word—and she tried to release it at a pop culture convention attended by upward of eighty thousand people.

Again, Echo Team was on deck, and I parked a couple of bullets in Bliss's black heart. That, I thought, was the end of it. And now Church goes and dumps Gehenna on us.

There are times when I really and truly hate my job. Case in point.

Belle and Remy sat in silence for quite a while after we dumped all this on them. Belle said nothing, but then again, she rarely does.

Remy said, "Is there even a little itty-bitty chance you boys are just messing with us?"

He looked at Top, then Bunny, then me.

"Well . . . kiss my ass," he said.

CHAPTER 58
PENN YAN REGIONAL AIRPORT
PENN YAN, NEW YORK

The RTI logistics man, Brian "Bird Dog" Bird, was waiting for us, lounging against a black, late-model Cadillac Escalade, arms folded, holding a Dr. Pepper and looking unhappy. Granted, he looks unhappy a lot of the time. He's a tall guy, balding, bespectacled, with a goatee going gray. He insists that every single gray hair is somehow my fault. He may not be wrong. His attitude, though, was far more upbeat than his demeanor.

He gave me a long up-and-down inspection as he sipped the soda through a straw, his gaze lingering on my visible bruises and the black eye that was now spectacular.

"Nice face," he said. "Looks like someone took a dislike to it."

"They did."

"Can't blame 'em."

"Bite me."

We shook hands. Bird Dog dug a couple of little crunchy dog biscuits out of his pocket, raised his eyebrows to me for approval, and when I said it was okay, he fed them to Ghost.

He leaned in a bit and lowered his voice to ask, "Any news on Bedlam?"

"Nothing concrete," I said. "When we were taxiing, Bug pinged me to say that they don't know anything. But at least there's one hopeful sign in that the RFID chips for everyone on the team are still active. Doesn't mean they're alive, but if they were blown up or crushed under the collapsing buildings, there's a chance those chips would have been damaged."

"That's slim," said Bird Dog, wincing.

"It's something, though."

He leaned back, sighed, sipped his drink. "Got your gear in the back, Joe. Pluto and Goofy off-loaded it from Shirley."

Those are not the real combat call signs for his two assistants, but it's what he always called them. So much so that they called each other by the names, and everyone else seemed to pick them up.

"Speaking of the dogs," I said, "where are they?"

"Loitering outside of the airport. They'll drop in behind you at some point to watch your six. Look for a dark blue Chevy Silverado. That'll be them. They'll be on the main channel if you need to talk to them, and they're armed and armored in case you need backup."

"Good to know."

He held out the keys, and Remy plucked them away before I could even move my hand. He's a very good driver, though perhaps a bit insane.

Everyone got in, but I lingered for a moment.

"Always appreciate you, brother," I said.

He gave me a long, searching look. "Big Man sounded a little fritzed when he called me earlier to set this up. And he never sounds fritzed."

"It's that kind of day," I said.

"Should I be worried?"

I smiled. "Keep happy thoughts."

And then we were on the road.

I tapped my comms. "Outlaw to Bug."

"Go for Bug."

"We're going to break some speed laws," I said. "Do what you can do to make sure we aren't pulled over for speeding."

"Ha! I'm way ahead of you. We own all traffic cams between here and the B&B. If you blow through a speed trap, those officers will receive an urgent call to be anywhere else but in your way."

"If I had a sister, I'd let you marry her."

Gehenna was forty miles from where we left Bird Dog, and Remy's sense of urgency was evident. He peeled away from the curb like we were fleeing the scene of a bank heist.

CHAPTER 59
THE TOC
PHOENIX HOUSE
OMFORI ISLAND, GREECE

"We got something!"

The cry rang out, and every head in the TOC whipped around toward a technician at a workstation near the far wall. Church and Scott Wilson hurried over.

"Talk to me," demanded Wilson.

The tech took his screen display and threw it onto the main screen that dominated the room. It appeared as a pop-up window inside a larger image of police and firefighters dealing with the disaster at Das Feuerwehrhaus. A third of the building was a smoking pile of shattered stone, twisted metal beams, and burning debris. The rest was fully engulfed in flames that burned so brightly it turned the German night into noonday brightness.

The smaller inset window showed the display from a helmet cam. This display was littered with small data feeds from various drones.

"Gimli received a weak signal," said the tech, and Church and Wilson bent over him. "Not talking about the RFID feeds. This came in over comms."

"Play it," ordered Church.

The tech tapped a key, and everyone hushed as a familiar voice spoke.

"—down and the exit . . . Leopard . . ." There was a long burst of static, and the voice came back again. "Have to . . . inside . . . facility . . . stay safe . . ."

There was no more.

"Who was that?" asked Wilson. "That's not Major Mun."

"Amy Neal," said Church. "Pond."

Wilson had the tech replay the audio clip three times.

"I think she's saying that someone is down," he said.

"Or that the team had to go down into the facility to avoid the fire," suggested the tech.

"I think she is saying that the team itself is down," Church said. "They are trapped inside the facility. Scott, liaise with anyone we have in local fire and rescue. I'll get on the phone to someone higher up the food chain. We need to protect Bedlam from arrest."

CHAPTER 60
THE MANSION
UNDISCLOSED LOCATION
THREE MONTHS AGO

"Boss," said Toombs, "I feel compelled to ask . . ."

"Say it," said October. They were on the patio outside of the house, each with a glass of good whiskey.

"What's with Miss Mary?"

October sipped.

"Let's be real," said Toombs, "she's a bit much."

"She is what she is."

"That's evasive."

"Less so than you think," said October. But before Toombs could pursue the point, there was a sound, and they both looked back through the open french doors to see Mary come into the room. She wore a T-shirt and soiled leggings, and there were suspicious stains around her mouth. Dark and red.

October covertly touched Toombs's arm and gave a tiny shake of his head. *Not now*, it said with quiet eloquence.

Toombs drank his whiskey as a way of hiding his reciprocal nod. *Not now*, it agreed. *But not never.*

Then he caught a rare unguarded look in October's eyes. They were filled with sadness and . . . something else. Some other emotion he could not yet name.

All around them, the trees were filled with birds whispering to one another in their ancient, knowing, secret voices.

CHAPTER 61
EN ROUTE TO AUTUMN NEST BED-AND-BREAKFAST
UPSTATE NEW YORK

We took the fastest safe route. It wasn't a long drive, but Remy made a few random turns while checking the rearview to make sure we weren't being followed.

"Got that Silverado five cars back," said Remy as we crossed the state line into Georgia. He tapped his earbud. "Gator Bait to Goofy."

"Got you, Gator Bait," came the answer.

"We in a parade, or are we good?"

"Clear as my grandma's colon," said Goofy.

"Copy that, Goofy," said Remy. "Hope your grandmama gets her full share of fiber."

The answer we heard was a pig snort of a laugh.

I saw Top lean over and quietly bang his head on the rear passenger window. Only once, but it was eloquent.

I only work with the very top professionals. It's how I roll.

"I don't get why this is out in the middle of nowhere," said Remy. "I thought these kinds of places were behind electric fences, with guard dog patrols and tower guards with fifty-caliber guns. How's this safe?"

"Each is different," Top said. "The official sites are in places like you describe. Or, about half of them. The ones the oversight committees in Washington keep their eye on. But Bunny, the colonel, and I . . . we've been to sites—biohazard, weapons R & D, no-name prisons— that are hidden in plain sight. One had an entrance in the back of a used bookstore in Encinitas, California. Tiny-ass place called Artifact so crammed with books you got to go outside to scratch your dick. But when no one else is in the place—and for a little store, that's a lot of the time—you pull the right two books at the same time and one set of mystery shelves folds back and you're at the top of a stairway."

"Guards and all?"

"Guards, cameras, scanners like you never saw. The facility is something like two hundred thousand square feet, spread out under the basements of all the stores on that block."

"Rad," said Remy.

"Yeah," said Bunny, "and there was this one in Michigan where you have to be at the Uber and Lyft pickup spot outside a hotel. The rides pick up whoever and drive off, and who the hell looks at someone else's ride?"

"And," Top continued, "there are a couple where employees get on a shuttle bus that goes through some rural spots and then vanishes down a tunnel that looks like it's going to take you to the Batcave. Whole series of tunnels down there and maybe three hundred people."

"Nobody thinks it's strange that buses go out filled with tourists or some shit and don't bring 'em back?"

"Not like that," said Bunny. "The staff work on six-month shifts, with three tracks rotating. Anytime a bus goes out fully loaded, it comes back loaded. Just not the same people."

Remy, however, did not seem overly impressed. "Whole buncha James Bond shit right there."

"Works, though," said Bunny.

"Most of the time," countered Top. "Seems to me somebody's been selling star maps to all the best biohazard dumps. Ain't all that happy about it."

Behind me, Belle was kneeling on the seat and pulling stuff out of equipment bags in the back. "There are ChemRigs back here," she said. "We will need to pull over somewhere and kit up."

"Got you, Mother Mercy," said Pluto. "Sending GPS for a side road that goes nowhere. We scouted it. Plenty of foliage for privacy. We'll patrol the road while you all get into your party clothes, then fall back to a standby position."

"Copy," she said.

The pull-off was perfect. A dirt road that led to an abandoned bait and tackle shop that had about six years of dead leaves in front of the doors.

We piled out, stripped down to skivvies, and reached for our hazmat gear. Even though none of us are leering hound dogs, we were sensitive to Belle. Not in terms of modesty but because of all the horrors that had been inflicted upon her. So, as he always does in such moments, Bunny stood with his back to her, his mass providing a considerable privacy screen. The rest of us turned away, too. No one needed to be told.

The ChemRigs are the latest generation of MOPP 4 chemical warfare protective overgarments. Not as clumsy as hazmat suits, and with all of Doc Holliday's upgrades. They were several generations above the Saratoga Hammer Suits we used to wear. Exceptionally durable but also incredibly light, thanks to the special polymers used in construction. Doc Holliday and Ron Coleman had designed them to allow the wearer to move fast, be agile, and fight at full efficiency while being safe from whatever nightmare biological or chemical threat filled the combat arena.

What made the ChemRigs even better was the Kevlar and spidersilk body armor built into it—and that was also latest generation—with graphene composites built in to reduce the foot-pounds of impact from most calibers of handgun and long gun. A sniper bullet would get through, but not much else. And the dense weave prevents most stab and slash wounds, which Kevlar does not.

They fit snugly and could be easily adjusted for body types. Belle, the smallest of the team, was about 100 pounds, while Bunny was 270 and built like a taller version of Dwayne "the Rock" Johnson. Bird Dog had set us up. No idea how he'd managed it, given the short time frame, but then again, Mr. Church tends not to hire anyone who only gets honorable mentions. It's also possible Bird Dog can do magic. I have no proof to the contrary.

Once the ChemRig suits were on, we strapped on gun belts, ammunition vests, and what pretty much amounts to Batman's all-purpose utility belts that have everything from pouches for lockpicks and MindReader links to things that go boom. I'm pretty sure mine included a pregnancy test and a turkey baster. Bird Dog went whole hog.

Ghost did not have a suit and was going to have to wait in the car. He would not like it, and Bird Dog anticipated this because there was a Petco bag with dog treats and a chew toy. There's a reason he's pretty high up on my Christmas list. He thinks of everything.

Once we were in our gear, we climbed back into the Escalade and got back on the road. Goofy assured us it was clear, and in truth, we saw maybe three cars the rest of the way.

That's when Bug contacted us with an update on the disaster in Germany. Some or all of Bedlam Team were down. Local first responders were on scene, and Church was finessing things with the government. I'd like to have been a fly on the wall for *that* call. I've seen and heard Church in action, and though RTI had zero legal justification for being in country and at a secret facility, I knew the Big Man would manage something. Hell, I've heard him push around two different US presidents in the past.

I told Bug to keep us in the loop, and he promised to do so.

Top, who'd heard the call—as had the others—leaned toward Remy. "Any reason you're driving like my aunt Selma?"

"Two things," said Remy. "Fuck and you." But he hit the gas even harder.

About four or five miles later, he began humming "Diggy Liggy Lo," a lively Doug Kershaw song that was old before anyone in that car was born. Top was the only other one who knew the words, and he sang along with him in a surprisingly melodic baritone. We picked up the chorus and sang with him.

There are surreal moments like that in this kind of work.

The Autumn Nest was set well back from the road, around a couple of bends that were screened with thick stands of trees and a lot of bushy shrubs. The only thing visible from the road was a small sign with the name on it. There was a wooden gate across the driveway. It was closed and locked, but Bird Dog had provided the key. Belle hopped out, opened it for us, then secured it once we were inside. Then she faded into the woods and paralleled us as we drove to the building.

Night was falling, and the darkness was our friend. Remy pulled up at the end of the driveway, and we sat, the engine idling, studying the place.

"Woods are clear on the east side," reported Belle. "Going west."

"Copy," I said. Then I tapped Remy's arm and pointed to a spot on the far side of a turnaround where towering pines threw heavy shadows across the tarmac. "There."

He pulled into place and killed the engine. We got out, weapons up and ready. There was no sign of Belle, but I'd have been surprised if there were.

Top, Bunny, and I stood together in the shadows of the pines. The B&B looked like what it was supposed to be—a quaint faux chalet that had fallen on hard times. The parking lot was crisscrossed with cracks from which a variety of weeds grew. There were two cars in the lot, tucked into a corner by the back door—a white Camry and a dark gray Escape, neither new. Some leaves had fallen onto the hoods of each. Maybe two days' worth.

Our in-flight intelligence briefing told us that a two-person team operated the B&B and that the staff of Gehenna arrived via a regularly scheduled tourist bus to work four-month tours. Between drop-offs, that bus did legit tourist transportation to legit locations.

"Looks quiet," said Bunny.

"So does a morgue," Top replied dryly.

"Fair point."

I said, "Gator Bait, let's get some birds in the air."

He was ready for the order and began scooping out drones made to look like common grackles, each with a dark bill, pale yellow eyes, and a long tail. Their wings deployed as soon as he tossed them, and the little machines flapped off with an extremely convincing pattern of flight. Then Remy tapped the tactical computer strapped to his wrist and began sending the birds into different quadrants of the search radius.

"All clear," he reported.

"Give me thermals."

He did, and we saw nothing larger than a raccoon in the surrounding woods. Remy adjusted the search for body masses above eighty pounds. That would pick up deer, but none were in the area. No people, either.

Or so we thought.

"Outlaw," he said, "got two signatures inside the station office. Don't look good."

I bent over and looked. There were indeed two heat signatures, but they were only a few degrees above room temperature. Cooling meat. Not a surprise, but still a bitter disappointment.

"Mother Mercy," I said, "you watch our backs. Pappy, on me. We'll go in the back. Donnie Darko, you and Gator Bait come in the front. If all's clear, then, Gator Bait, I want you to fall back and play with the drones. But get ready to come running. Put an owl in that pine tree over there and another on the gable above the back door. Then get ready to deploy some vermin."

"Gotcha, Outlaw," said Remy and fished more machines out of his bag.

Vermin were a specific class of non-avian drones. They ranged from cockroaches to mice to rats, and Church spent a lot of money to make sure they looked like what they were supposed to be.

Ghost, in the back of the Escalade, glared hot death at me. The kind of look that promises a smelly surprise in my shoes if I wasn't back soon. He did not like to miss the fun. But we were going into a potentially toxic environment, and even though Doc made one for him, the suit's impermeable nature nullified his sense of smell. Sure, he still had sight and hearing, but a dog's best tool is his nose. Also, in a full ChemRig, Ghost couldn't bite, either. So, cute as his suit was, he never rolled out in one. I think Doc made the one he has just to make Ghost feel better. She's beyond brilliant but also equally weird.

The ChemRig goggles were a variation of the Scout glasses developed by one of Church's many friends in the industry. One lens was rigged to show feeds from the drones, real-time data, info from facial recognition software, GPS, and other tactical information. They could also be cycled for everything from thermals to infrared. We all tested the feeds to make sure everything worked, then Top initiated a mission clock, and the display appeared as a discreet digital timer in the lower left of the lens.

"Havoc Actual to TOC," I said.

"Go for TOC," said the chief of operations, Scott Wilson, in his clipped Eton accent. "This is Grendel, and we have the full team on deck here." That meant that Church, Bug, and Doc Holliday were all on the active call, though I guessed they had two sets of screens going, with half the people at the TOC working the Germany case. In any other circumstance, I would have asked about Mun and her guys, but I had my own shit to deal with.

"Two down inside."

"Copy that," said Scott. "We have the drone feeds."

"Going in now." I tapped Top's shoulder. "Moving."

And we moved.

CHAPTER 62
THE MANSION
UNDISCLOSED LOCATION
THREE MONTHS AGO

The words were spray-painted in garish red across the outside glass of the french windows. Three words that seemed to scream.

BURN TO SHINE

"What's with the graffiti?" asked Toombs.

He and Mr. October were strolling across the lawns that surrounded the Mansion. October smoked a 2017 Cohiba Talismán Edición Limitada cigar. One of the better Cubans, and Toombs—who did not smoke and did not enjoy the raw-sewer stink of cigars—surreptitiously rubbed lip balm under his nose. It helped, just as it helped when he was around Mary. Her personal hygiene was, at best, indifferent, and Toombs wondered if October smoked for the same reason.

Toombs held a balloon of Courvoisier XO Royal and took micro sips. He was more of a bourbon man, but Mary had recently smashed all of the best bourbon in one of her fits of pique. The cognac was full-bodied, with notes of summer truffles and wild mushroom risotto, so that made a nice compensation.

Summer was at its height, but the evenings were cool enough. The first bats of twilight were out, devouring the hordes of Pennsylvania mosquitoes.

October took his time before responding to Toombs's question about the words. The same phrase had been spray-painted on several exterior walls of the place, as well as in various places inside.

"Oh," he said offhand, "one of Mary's whims."

"No," said Toombs, "it's not."

October blew gray smoke up at the bats. "What makes you say so?"

"You forget that I know who she is," said Toombs. "Who she *was*.

I followed that news story when it was still breaking. I remember the catchphrase . . . *Sometimes you have to burn to shine*."

"Ah," said October. He tapped some ash from his cigar and kept walking.

"That's it? 'Ah'? I asked a serious question."

October nodded. "What did you infer from its presence in all those news stories?"

"That she was flying her anarchist freak flag," said Toombs. "Or, at least, that was part of her schtick. Mother Night. Cultivating and radicalizing all those disaffected gamer kids. Giving them money and toys and pretending to give a shit about them, then sending them into sports events and other places to do some ultraviolence. Very *Clockwork Orange* in effect, but . . ."

"But what?"

"But it was bullshit," said Toombs mildly. "She had another agenda, and the people who worshipped her were cannon fodder."

October smoked for a few paces without commenting on that.

"Now she's painting it all over the place," said Toombs.

"It amuses her."

"It must, but I don't get the joke."

October stopped and turned to look up at a window on the second floor. The house was six years old, but already ivy had begun its ambitious crawl up the exterior windows. The ceiling height on both floors inside gave the outside a sense of grandeur. October and Mary called it "the Mansion," but it was really a modern country home built to resemble a Tudor. At a glance, it appeared older than it was, and Toombs wondered if that was a feature or a bug.

"Mary is a troubled young woman," said October quietly.

"Uh-huh," agreed Toombs.

"She is also brilliant on a level that leaves most of the human population in the dust. She is so smart that ordinary life—the simple crudities and mundanities of it all—and boredom is kryptonite for a mind like hers."

"And cryptic graffiti's the answer?"

October shrugged. "She says it reminds her of happier times."

"Like before she went to jail or before she turned into some kind of *Resident Evil* mastermind zombie chick?"

Mr. October took a very long drag on the cigar, held the smoke in his lungs, and then exhaled while studying Toombs's face. "You seem to know a lot about her, my friend."

"Should I tremble in my shoes because you're *aware* of how much I know? How much I've guessed?"

However, October laughed. "Not at all. Frankly, I'd have been disappointed if after all the hype you turned out to be a dullard."

They resumed their walk. A raccoon watched them from beneath a rhododendron, a small apple held in its little hands. Toombs smiled at it for no good reason.

"Mary is my ward," October said. "I treat her like my daughter, but I've never had any actual children. Blame my rather unusual biology. She is important to my work. Very important."

"Selling arms to bonehead militia goons?"

"That's part of my work, my friend. I have a more extensive agenda."

"Firefall?" prompted Toombs.

"Among other things," said October.

"Which you don't feel the need to tell me about."

"I tell you what you need to know, my friend. Forgive me if I keep some of my secrets to myself."

CHAPTER 63
AUTUMN NEST BED-AND-BREAKFAST
PENN YAN, NEW YORK

We ran across the parking lot in a tight line. I had an HK416 with a thirty-round STANAG magazine and a sound suppressor, and a Beretta M9 holstered on my hip. Top had the same, and so did Remy. Bunny had a Benelli M4 Super 90 shotgun. Yes, since you ask, we actually *did* plan on both kicking ass and taking names.

Bunny and Remy split off and took up positions on the front porch while Top and I ran back. It was a small building with a big deck running around it. We crept up carefully. Top covered me while I knelt and aimed my gun along the exterior wall. The back door was also ajar, but I'm not the "fools rush in" kind of cat. I have my issues, but rampant stupidity isn't one of them. I plucked a miniature Anteater from my belt, tore off the adhesive, and pressed the gizmo to the doorframe just above the strike plate. Anteaters are a kind of scanner that sweeps for all manner of electronics. They've saved my life several times by alerting me to listening ears or electrical IEDs. But this time, it was quiet.

I used the toe of my boot to nudge the door open but faded back in case there was a trip wire that I couldn't see.

Nothing went boom.

So I pulled a soft-light grenade and tossed it inside. It's like a flashbang but without the bang. It pulsed out a painfully glaring light, and anyone in that room was going to be blind for a good twenty seconds.

Nothing. No sounds of human reaction.

"Quiet entry," I murmured and heard a soft *Hooah* from Bunny. I tapped Top on the shoulder again as I moved inside. He rose and followed. I broke right, and he went left.

The rear door opened into a mudroom, and that spilled out into a large country-style kitchen. Big table, charmingly mismatched chairs, tablecloth embroidered with chickens and cows. Lots of cabinets and open shelves, big sink, and all of the other things you'd expect to see in a bed-and-breakfast.

Except that there was a body on the floor.

It was a white man of about forty, fit-looking, blue jeans and a brown-and-green flannel shirt and Timberlands. Short hair, clean-shaven, and a line of bullet holes that started above his belt buckle and stitched upward to the ruin that was the top of his head. Flies crawled on his face. I made sure my body cam was angled for a good look at his face.

In my ear, Bug said, "Owen Elliot. Federal agent."

I said nothing but moved toward a door in the back of the room. It opened into a powder room that had a toilet, urinal, sink, cabinets, and a second corpse. A mixed-race woman in dark green tights under a floral-patterned dress. She had beaded hair, tan skin, green eyes, and she had been shot only once. But whoever killed her had worked on her for a long time. Eight of her fingernails had been pulled out and laid with care along the edge of the sink. Both thumbs lay there, too, the cuts very clean. Blood spatter was everywhere. The woman's face had been beaten into inhumanity by a ball-peen hammer, and the bloody tool was in the sink.

"Brittney Hopkins," said Bug. "Damn."

Top leaned over Hopkins. "They fucked this poor lady all the way up."

"She didn't want to give up what they wanted," I said. "She made them work for it."

"Yes, she did."

"Tough lady."

Top looked at me with the coldest eyes in town. He said nothing, but that look promised awful things.

Bunny came through from the front. "All clear," he said, then stopped and looked down at the dead woman.

"If whoever did that is still here," said Bunny and just waggled the shotgun, "I'm going to ram this up his ass and pull the trigger."

"Get in line, farm boy," growled Top.

We turned to the wall opposite the sink. It had a row of pegs on which were hung street clothes, rain slickers, and a couple of ball caps—Mets and Yankees.

In our ears, Scott said, "Pull the second peg out and down while rotating the third anticlockwise."

I placed another Anteater on the wall, and its little light stayed green.

"Stairway down with four landings and then the main entrance at the very bottom," I said. "Two guards at each level and an air lock at the bottom to access the facility with a four-man team."

"Guards didn't hear the gunfire and screaming up here?" murmured Bunny. "That doesn't fill me with enthusiasm."

Top snorted. "I hear Taco Bell's hiring, farm boy."

"You joke, old man, but I'm waiting for a callback on my application."

He slung his shotgun, and we stepped back to offer cover, rifles snugged into our shoulders as he followed Scott's directions. There was a soft *click*, and that part of the wall opened inward.

As a noun, *Gehenna* most often refers to a large fire that's dangerously out of control, and that was true enough. But the meaning that hung burning in my mind was the one from Dante's *Divine Comedy*.

It was another name for hell.

And into hell we went.

CHAPTER 64
IN FLIGHT OVER PENNSYLVANIA AIRSPACE

"They're inside," she said. "I can *feel* it."

The way she said it was intended to be salacious. Toombs looked across the aisle at her as October's jet—once Bolton's aircraft—tore through the skies heading south. His stomach was as foul and polluted as a sewer drain. For once in his life, he was glad that his complexion tended toward a ghastly white; otherwise, Mary would see him go pale.

With horror.

With disgust.

He had not gone into Gehenna but had watched as much of it as he could on the computer screen in the jet. Everything was over the top. Beyond over the top. Everything had been insane.

October had warned him that Mary's personality had become *extreme*. That had been a short conversation before Mary, Toombs, and the strike team boarded the Dassault Falcon 8X, a gorgeous long-range executive jet. October took Toombs aside while the gear was being stowed and they spoke in low voices.

"This isn't her first field op," said October. "But it's the first one where she will be essentially in charge and therefore off the leash."

"I thought the objective was an in-and-out theft of germ warfare stuff," countered Toombs.

"And it is. But before the big event, I want you to see what her *range* is."

"Range . . . ?"

"Her ability to stay on task while at the same time having fun. Her brand of fun."

Toombs unwrapped a stick of peppermint gum and put it into his mouth, chewing softly for a few moments. "Why are you giving her that much freedom at all?"

October shrugged. "Various reasons. Mainly so I can see if she'll do her part during the event without knocking it all off the rails."

"And if she can't?"

"I have a cell in the cellar of the Mansion," he said. "I had it built very quietly when she was out on other errands."

"To what end? To keep her as a pet?"

"To study her. She's . . . different. We both know that. Unique."

"*Unique* isn't a very comforting word. Nor is *different*."

"They are not meant to be comforting, my friend. They are, however, accurate."

Toombs chewed. "Permission to speak freely? And I do mean *freely*."

"Granted," said October with a faint smile.

"We both know she's crazy as fuck. Dangerously erratic. Unpredictable. That's inarguable."

"It is. And . . . ?"

"And you hired me to run your sales operation. I am *not* crazy as fuck. I'm not erratic or unpredictable. I'm careful and efficient, and I dislike dealing with extreme personalities. Yes, I know you overpay me to compensate for—how shall I phrase this?—her excesses."

"Good word choice."

"But I don't know how objective you're being here. She's like your daughter. You indulge her. You allow her way too much freedom. Hard to say whether it's some kind of field research or science experiment or some shit. What I do know is that I do not for one minute believe that she is to be trusted."

October nodded but made no comment.

Toombs said, "I know you're hooked on the whole 'chaos is fun' thing, but there's chaos and then there's fucking ourselves up."

"What is it you're suggesting, Mr. Toombs?"

"Just between us?"

"Yes. All truth, no penalties."

"I think you should run her through a goddamn wood chipper. She wouldn't come back from that."

They stood for a while, watching as Mary oversaw the last of the gear being stowed.

"I will take that under advisement," said October.

Now, on the flight back, Toombs sat alone in the cesspool of his thoughts. Hating her. Disgusted by her.

Fearing her more than he had ever feared anyone.

CHAPTER 65

GEHENNA BIOLOGICAL RESEARCH AND CONTAINMENT FACILITY

PENN YAN, NEW YORK

There was a nondescript set of stairs leading down and down.

I tried not to infer anything from that or take it as the universe's attempt to set the stage for drama. We knew it was going to be bad. It couldn't *not* be bad, and yet the stairs were not covered with blood spatter. There were no bullet holes or bloody handprints on the concrete walls. Instead, the stairwell was brightly lit, and there was a mix of small posters on the wall. Some were standard policy things like *Safety Begins with You!* and *Rules Are There for Everyone's Protection . . .* and inspirational pap like *Believe and Succeed!* and a photo of a group of skydivers holding hands in a circle before chute deployment and the word *Teamwork!* written below.

Gosh, we all felt suddenly so empowered.

There was a wide first landing that had two doors. One was a closet in which were emergency kits to repair hazmat tears and lots of spray bottles of disinfectant. The other was an elevator. We ignored them both.

"Where are the guards?" asked Bunny. "Supposed to be two on each of the four stairwell landings and four at the bottom by the air lock."

"No bodies," observed Top. "No signs of a fight."

There was an elevator, but all of the lights were off, and the doors firmly closed.

In my ear, I heard Bug say, "Elevators go into lockdown if there's a fire or security breach. They can also be switched off from the security desk."

We checked and saw that that the control switch was still in the ON position.

"Cutoff was either done at the security office in the main complex," said Bug, "or by the automatic security protocols."

"Can't you tell which?" I asked.

"Not until you reach the bottom level and plug MindReader into the data port beside the key card scanner. Right now, it's all offline as far as remote access on my part."

"Copy that."

But Top drew our attention to the small security cameras mounted to cover every possible inch of the stairwell. They were black, their cup-shaped lenses shattered.

It was troubling because it was in that shadowy zone of uncertainty between clumsiness and enigma. Even having stolen entry protocols from the dead couple upstairs, someone would be monitoring the feeds from the cameras. Even before the bad guys began smashing the cameras, the security officer would have seen hostiles in the stairwell and would have rung all kinds of alarms. Those alarms had not run at all.

"You think our bad guys had a man inside the security office?" asked Top.

"That'd be my guess."

A mole in the facility security, especially if his monitoring shift coincided with the intrusion, would not have been able to open the outer doors, nor would he have had the codes for the two dead minders. That explained why the codes had to be taken by brutal force and could explain why no alarms were triggered.

"Why smash 'em?" mused Bunny, then answered his own question. "Seems like closing the barn door after the horses skedaddled. It's bass-ackwards."

"Sure as shit is," said Top.

We proceeded slowly.

The second landing had another closet of emergency stuff, and there was a small, tiled emergency shower with large tanks of chemical disinfectant. Again, an empty security desk. We looked in the toilet cubicle to see if there were bodies, but they were clean and empty.

It was the same story on sublevel three.

"I don't see any signs of struggle," said Bunny. "No bullet holes, no

JONATHAN MABERRY

spent brass, no blood. Giving me a weird itch between my shoulder blades."

The fourth landing changed the shape of the day.

Top, who was on point, paused, crouched, and shined the flashlight on his rifle onto the floor. The glow caught on the curved husks of scores of metal cylinders. Shell casings.

He picked one up and showed it to us. It was a Ruger 9mm.

"Found your brass, farm boy," said Top. "Bad guys got down this far. Hate to think they got all the way down to where the goodies are."

Bunny pulled up the floor plan of the Gehenna facility so we could quickly assess our options. There was a much larger room at the bottom that was basically a concrete box with an air lock and a couple of guards. Beyond that was a series of decontamination chambers, each with techs and soldiers stationed there to ensure all protocols were strictly adhered to. Once past those, there was a large central space filled with computer workstations. Administrative offices lined one side, with various kinds of labs on two other sides, and a row of hot rooms, each of which had its own decontamination cubicle. There were also bathrooms, showers, meeting rooms, and a whole wing of apartments for the long-term staff.

"Big damn place," Bunny said. "Football field long and half that wide and a whole lot of places for bad guys to hide."

"If they're still down there," said Top, "I'm going to find their asses, and they had better be right with Jesus."

"Hooah."

"BAMS," I said, and Bunny immediately pulled a device from his belt about the size of a TV remote, flicked it on, and held it up, waving it back and forth through the air. These portable bio-aerosol mass spectrometers draw in ambient air and hit it with continuous wave lasers to fluoresce individual particles. Key molecules like dangerous viruses, fungi, bacillus spores, and certain vegetative cells are identified and assigned color codes.

The row of little green lights stayed green.

"I hope that's a good sign," he said, his tone dubious.

"Don't believe nothing, farm boy," muttered Top, then he stopped to watch me because I'd squatted down to give the shell casings a closer look. "What are you seeing, Outlaw?"

"Effect without obvious cause," I said. "Put on your Junior Crime

Scene Investigator hats and take a real good look. There are a lot of shell casings here, but not a single bullet hole in the wall. No blood, either."

"Noticed that, too," Top agreed. "Kind of looks like they were just dumped here. Or, maybe it's closer to say they were *placed* here."

"What's it mean?" asked Bunny. "Someone trying to set a scene?"

"That'd be my guess," I said. "Not sure to what end, though."

I rose and looked down the next set of steps.

Top squinted at me through the goggles of his ChemRig. "If I were a gambling man, Outlaw, I'd put my whole Christmas bonus on the line they placed that brass here so it would draw our eye."

I nodded. "So we'd miss something else and go galumphing down there waving our Vorpal swords in pursuit."

We were still on the landing. I tapped the suit's goggles to infrared, and suddenly, there were red lines crossing back and forth on the lower stairs of the next landing.

"Laser trip wires," I said. They switched to infrared, too.

"Wonder what happens if we break one," mused Bunny. "Alarms or booby traps?"

"Let's find out," I said. "If it's alarms, that's not as bad, because if they're still here, then they probably know we are, too. And if something goes boom, let's be smart Cub Scouts and stay well away."

"Drone?" asked Top.

I nodded. "Drone."

He dug into a thigh pocket and removed a handful of small Busy Bees—drones that looked like overfed honeybees but were high-efficiency, short-duration machines. The energy expended to allow it to do all sorts of functions drained the tiny batteries quickly. When used only for surveillance, they'd be active for a couple of hours; but delivering a payload of Sandman or other toxins, evading capture, and so on used them up quickly. They were expensive, efficient, and actually kind of adorable. I sometimes mess with Ghost by having them harass him in the yard.

Top selected two, sending one high and having it land on a wall over the landing in order to send a video feed of whatever happened, and once it was in place, we crept up two flights of stairs and crouched down well out of the anticipated blast radius of any antipersonnel mine.

"Go," I said, and he sent the other to fly through the laser beam.

We got our answer right quick, because a microsecond after the Busy Bee passed through the beam, there was a sharp *bang*. The air around the landing and halfway up the stairs was instantly filled with a few thousand ball bearings the size of dried peas. They pinged and banged in a maniac flurry of ricochets as we scuttled halfway up the stairs.

"That would hurt," said Bunny when the last of them stopped bouncing around. "Wouldn't kill, though."

"At the speed they moved, they'd tear holes in any normal kind of hazmat," observed Top. "Maybe even our old Hammer Suits."

"Won't get through these," said Bunny, tapping his ChemRig.

"Yeah," said Top, "good thing nobody outside the family knows we got them or they'd have planned better."

"Let's make no assumptions," I warned as I crept down the stairs and squatted over some fallen pellets. Something about them really bothered me. Ball bearings or ordinary shrapnel would do a better job of tearing apart protective overgarments and would cripple or kill pursuers. A quarter pound of wood screws would work even better. So why smooth, round balls?

As if reading my mind, we heard Doc's voice over the comms. "Would one of you pretty boys gather up some of those little darlings? I've love to take a look at them to see if there was a plan B tucked inside."

"Inside?" asked Bunny.

"Be a nice hunk of beach-boy beefcake and just collect 'em real careful like. Good, now hold one up so I can take a closer look," she said. Bunny did, leaning close so his Scout glasses could get a tight focus. "Yup. Just what I thought."

"What are they?" I asked.

"Short answer is 'bad.' Longer version is that they are platinum-iridium spheres used for delivery of a disease form or toxin."

I leaned close to look. The ball was tiny, but by dialing up the zoom on my glasses, I could see that there were tiny holes all over them.

"Back in the Soviet days," Doc explained, "they used this sort of thing for assassinations. First that comes to mind was a Bulgarian dissident, Georgi Markov, who defected to the UK and wrote a lot of very dang sarcastic pieces to fry the grits of the Soviet government. They sent someone to snuff him using a poison-tipped umbrella back in 1978. During his autopsy, they found this l'il ol' pellet in the tissue of his leg. Weren't no bigger than one-point-seven millimeters, composed of ten percent iridium and ninety percent platinum. Had a couple little holes in it packed with ricin. And before you embarrass yourself by asking what that is, ricin is a carbohydrate-binding protein called a *lectin*, a toxin produced in the seeds of the castor oil plant. Now I know that your mamas always told you castor oil was good for just about anything that ails you, but mama dear would be wrong."

Bunny waved his BAMS unit over the thing and we watched the little light switch from a comforting green to a weak orange.

"That make any sense to you, Huckleberry?" I asked, using Doc's combat call sign.

"Sure. The pellets have ricin in them, but most likely it's discharged on impact and otherwise contained, likely by a micro-wall of wax or cellulose. BAMS is picking up trace elements. Even so, handle with care and keep your flies zipped. Bag a few and bring them back to mama."

We did.

Church came on the line next. "Outlaw, what is your assessment of the situation thus far?"

"I believe we are walking into someone's game," I said. "The shell casings, the laser trip wires—neither makes sense. They are set up as distractions, though to what end is unknown."

"Agreed," he said. "And there may be more of the same."

"The ricin pellets are clever and dangerous, but we're not the only biohazard response team to use BAMS units, especially in situations like this. It's almost like they don't have a lot of faith in modern military tech and protocols, or they think we're stupid. So . . . anyone at the TOC have any theories?"

"Grendel and Bug are working on it."

"Suggest they don't stop for coffee. This one has a weird feel to it."

"It does," said Church.

"Call the play, then, Merlin. Do we hang tight and wait for something from the brain trust or proceed with the mission?"

"We need to know whether Gehenna is secure," he said. "We need to know if anything of critical importance has been taken. See if you can manage that without incident."

"Copy that," I said and silently flipped him the bird. Yes, I know that Top's and Bunny's body cams both picked it up.

It was one of those situations where there is no good choice. We couldn't just walk away, but pushing forward into a situation where the bad guys were playing some kind of game presented all of the obvious dangers.

I tapped comms for Remy. "Gator Bait, I need your whole bag of goodies. Leave the owls in place for overwatch, and bring Mother Mercy with you."

"On the way, Outlaw," came the reply.

We hunkered down on that landing and waited.

CHAPTER 66
IN FLIGHT OVER PENNSYLVANIA AIRSPACE

Toombs sat with his back to the bulkhead as far away from Miss Mary and her remaining soldiers as he could. She had left one of her Berserkers behind to give Ledger a message.

He texted October and gave his boss a quick update, doing his best to avoid histrionics and hyperbole. Not that exaggeration of any kind was needed. Not after what she'd done.

When he got to the point where he relayed what Mary had told her infected Berserker to tell Ledger, there was a very long pause before October replied.

When the message came through, all it said is, "That's unfortunate."

"Oh, you think?"

"We'll talk when you return, my friend."

Toombs erased the conversation, closed his phone, and put it away. Then he sat back and pretended to be asleep.

As if sleep were ever going to be possible for him.

CHAPTER 67
PHOENIX HOUSE
OMFORI ISLAND, GREECE

There were few lulls in Mr. Church's day, and that was how it had been for a very long time.

Wars run on paperwork. He'd seen that on a coffee mug once and almost bought it. It was a truth as old as civilization. Half of the ancient texts, scrolls, and clay tablets were some kind of recordkeeping.

Despite everything going on in America, Canada, and Germany, he found small islands of quiet. He treasured them. When one came his way in the gap between briefing Havoc Team for their mission and waiting on a report about Bedlam Team, he retreated to his office, closed the door, took off his tinted glasses and rubbed his red-rimmed eyes, then poured a glass of ice-cold spring water and sank into the welcoming cushions of his leather chair.

His desk was covered with neat but dishearteningly thick stacks of folders, each representing something that would require his permission, his advice, his financial backing, or his opinion. Church glanced at the pair of chairs on the opposite side of his desk. Brick Anderson usually sat in the right-hand chair, his bulk filling the seat. Now Brick's absence lent a quality of bleak loneliness to it.

Brick had been more than a bodyguard. Far more. His high intelligence, insight, and calmness had transformed him into a colleague rather than employee. And he had been a friend. A true one. Brick was one of a very small group of people Church had trusted with his secrets. With his personal secrets. He'd known nearly as much about Church's past as Lilith did.

"Damn it, Brick," said Church softly. "I will never forgive myself."

For a moment, he swore he saw Brick sitting there, glasses pushed up on his shaved head, eyes filled with skeptical amusement, mouth smiling.

"Wasn't you who killed me," he seemed to say. *"You weren't yourself, and we both know it. Tearing yourself up is giving a win to the bad guys."*

"I wish you were here," murmured Church. "If it would not be an insult to your own path, I'd pray that you haunted me."

"*What, you think I'd ever leave you high and dry, St. Germaine?*" asked the phantom. "*You know I'll always have your back.*"

Church blinked and the specter was gone, and he was alone. So alone.

He had not told Dr. Sanchez that he sometimes saw, heard, and even spoke to Brick Anderson. The only one he trusted with that was Lilith. As he sat there, he remembered her reply.

"You keep trying to make this world into something quantifiable, my love. But it never was and never will be. Or do I need to quote Hamlet at you?"

"I know there are more things in heaven and Earth, Lilith," he'd replied, getting testy with her.

"Then act like it," she'd snapped back. "Do you think it was Jason Aydelotte who conjured the names of the five men who hurt Ledger and his girlfriend and not that poor girl speaking through him?"

Church said nothing in reply, and the rest of that morning had been filled with cold silences.

Now Church unlocked the bottom left-hand drawer of his desk and removed a file folder sealed with a thumbprint lock. He unlocked it, placed the file on his desk, and opened it. There were five sets of papers, each fastened with a clip. Each with a single name. The folders were thick, filled with every single bit of useful data about five men who lived in and around Baltimore.

Church sipped his water and looked at the papers without touching them.

CHAPTER 68

GEHENNA BIOLOGICAL RESEARCH AND CONTAINMENT FACILITY
PENN YAN, NEW YORK

Each of us carried more of the Busy Bees, but they were not adequate for what we needed. They were good to help us get down the rest of the stairs, but that would be about it. Remy had bigger drones with more functions, including thermal, infrared, and other scanners across the light spectrum, but also more powerful cameras and mics for sound pickup, and they could be set in place to act as motion detectors. And he had bat drones that had BAMS technology built into them.

He and Belle came in fast. Bunny went up to the top of the stairs to meet them, and soon all of Havoc was on the landing.

"I called in the dogs to watch the outside," said Belle. "Remy keyed them into the drone feeds."

"What's going on in here?" asked the young Cajun.

"Somebody is playing games," I said and brought them up to speed. "They are either inept enough to think that we'd fall for their tricks, or they are using some kind of misdirectional sleight of hand leading to a bigger reveal."

"The latter," said Remy. "Trying to psych us out."

None of us questioned his judgment. Remy had come to RTI with a pretty good skill set that included all kinds of electronics and explosives. Andrea had deepened that well of knowledge, particularly in the psychology and philosophy of setting traps. His understanding of how to rig sequential traps that played off anticipated reactions made him of exceptional value, especially in situations like this. If you are an expert in setting traps, then you are likewise an expert at spotting them.

Remy removed a bunch of drones and double-checked that the floor plan of Gehenna had been uploaded. Then we watched as he sent two bats and two rats down through the smoky, bomb-damaged stairwell. The bats scanned the air and sent back green safety signals. The rats scampered around looking for electronics that might indicate other booby traps.

The video feeds they sent were gathered and collated by Mind-Reader into a cohesive 360-degree image of the room at the bottom of the stairwell. It was a twenty-by-twenty chamber with steel-reinforced concrete walls, floor, and ceiling. Against one wall was a row of hazmat suits, complete with rolls of duct tape to reinforce all the arm and leg seals, and lockers for any clothing that needed to be left behind—jackets, work boots, and such. On the opposite wall was a sink and emergency shower. On the wall directly across from the stairs was an air lock. Very large and very expensive and set securely into a steel wall.

Top quality in every way, beside which was a retina scanner, handprint scanner, breath scanner, a microphone, and a key card reader.

The protocol was to use the first three scanners before donning the hazmat suits, then use the mic to speak the day code and personal ID number, and then swipe a key card. Complicated and time-consuming, but smart. There were other scanners inside, but anyone breaking in had to pass every level of security outside first.

There was one more trap, another laser trip wire, but Remy grunted when that came up on his tactical forearm computer.

"What have you found?" I asked.

"They used ultraviolet light for that trip wire. Same basic frequency as they use in better home security systems."

"That going to be a problem?"

"No. Just not what you expect to see with someone savvy enough to break into a high-tech facility."

Bunny leaned over his shoulder. "Can you disable it?"

"My grandmama could disable it," said Remy. "And she's blind, deaf, and drunk."

He withdrew the other drones and then sent one down the stairwell that was not painted to look like anything. Just a miniature drone. He linked its guidance system to the GPS signature taken by the bat. The device was something new—he calls them NoSeeUms, taking the nickname from the nearly invisible biting insects, midges that are found on every continent and hated everywhere they are encountered. Remy's little critter was designed to emit a limited-range electromagnetic pulse whose dispersal pattern could be adjusted. It wouldn't reach us where we were, but everything in range that had any electronics would go dark all at once.

"Give the word, Outlaw," said Remy.

"*No, wait,*" I barked, raising a clenched fist.

Everyone stopped where they were, all eyes on me.

"Do nothing," I ordered. "That's a trap, too, just not the one we're thinking."

They all looked at me.

"How do you know it's a . . ." began Remy, but then he got it, too. The others were only a short half step after him.

"They're setting us up for a sucker's play," Bunny said.

An EMP blast would fry those scanners, which in turn would trigger the facility's security protocols and possibly initiate a hard shutdown. If that happened, four-foot-thick steel walls would drop from the ceiling on the *other* side of the air lock, each of them with spikes on the bottom that would, upon impact with the floor, detonate thermite charges that would flash-weld the steel in place. This would happen throughout Gehenna, essentially turning it into a steel box.

And then a set of six hundred vents would discharge intense flames that would incinerate everything inside. Wood, paper, metal, glass, and plastics. Anything organic would be turned to ash, from the smallest amoeba to the largest animal specimen. And every human being inside.

"I feel like I'm inside a damn video game," complained Bunny. "*Resident Evil* or some shit."

That comment, meant as a throwaway, made something skitter across the inside of my mind. I fumbled for it—for what it meant or some connection to a memory—but it scampered out of sight. Even so, the words lingered.

Like a damn video game.

Without saying another word, Remy hit recall on the NoSeeUm.

"What's *our* plan B?" asked Bunny.

"Two options as I see it," said Top. "We send a drone to trip that trap and hope it doesn't do more than go bang. Or we go down there and try to bypass it but leave it in place."

I said, "There a play you like best?"

"No."

They all looked at me. "Personally, I don't want to go down these stairs at all," I said. "Remy, let's see what's under those metal steps. Look for pressure triggers. Maybe the point of this trap is to make us step over the trip wire and step down on the stair below it. If so, the greatest pressure exerted would be on the step above as you take a step and below as you step down and then the pressure two steps down. Both potential weight triggers."

He cut me an approving look. "Dang, boss, you ever work countersabotage?"

"No, I'm just tired of having things blow up in my face."

"Not a fan of that, either," agreed Bunny.

Top said, "Hooah."

He sent a cockroach because it had the least weight and a good camera. We watched as the video feed filled Remy's computer screen.

I think we all said, "Oh shit," at exactly the same time.

The undersides of the stairs were wired with Semtex. A quarter pound on each of those two stairs, and a full pound under each of the next five steps. Had we tried to creep down, our first step would have sent us to Jesus.

CHAPTER 69

GEHENNA BIOLOGICAL RESEARCH AND CONTAINMENT FACILITY

PENN YAN, NEW YORK

Remy set about de-arming the bombs.

All of us offered to help, but he waved us off.

"Always work better alone, guys. Too many cooks."

We retreated halfway up the steps and tried not to backseat drive. Or flee. I called into the TOC to see if they knew anything about the kind of bomb that went off in Germany, but they had nothing. Wilson told us that the local authorities were in control of the scene and all RTI presence had withdrawn. Before I could ask about Mun and Bedlam, he said there was nothing new.

Swell.

So, we watched in a tense silence, and I don't think any of us took a full breath all that time.

Once Remy figured out how the bombs were rigged, he got the first couple done quickly. Then he paused, studying the third.

"Well, kiss my sweet ass," he said.

"What?" I asked.

"These sons of hogs are tricky bastards," he said. He was hanging from a rappelling line attached to the railing on our landing, dangling there and looking at the underside of the stairs. "What they did is rig the first two with what y'all might call a mid-level sophistication.

Stuff that would make most first-year bomb squad jocks sweat all the way down to their ass cracks but wouldn't do much to raise the blood pressure of a pro. You follow me?"

"I do. So what's the twist?"

"On the third one, it's rigged to *look* like the same kind of pressure switch, but it's not. The third one's a dummy. The Semtex is real, but the wiring is phony baloney, and it's exposed wiring like you see in movies. Bomb makers who know their shit hide the wires so there's no nail-biter as they decide to cut the red one or the blue one. Then we get to the fourth step, and this one has the pressure switch setup, but it's really a trembler switch that would go ka-bloom if anyone tried to de-arm it the way I did with the first two."

He lowered himself another ten inches and studied the next step.

"Yeah, and the next one has a motion sensor set against the inside of the riser."

"Jesus. Can you de-arm them all?"

"Not that fourth one, no," said Remy. "It's a doozy. All kinds of safeguards, and that's just what I can see. It's specifically designed to kill anyone who tries. And, yeah, that EMP would have set it off, too. Looks like there's a radio link on it, so if it blew, all the bombs would go off at once. I don't dare get closer for a better look because then we'd all be having coffee and beignets with Satchmo and Fats."

Belle turned to Top. "Who are Satchmo and Fats?"

"Two famous dead guys," he said.

"Ah," she said. "Got it."

I asked, "Are there enough explosives there to do the kind of damage like what happened at Das Feuerwehrhaus?"

Remy considered for a moment. "Yeah. Maybe. Enough to blow the B&B upstairs to the far side of the damn moon."

"May I be excused?" asked Bunny. "I think I left the stove on back home."

I ignored him and leaned over the rail. "Gator Bait, what's the floor like? Is it safe if we rappel down?"

Remy hung there and studied the concrete floor. "I don't see nuthin'," he said. "Hold on."

He fished a rat drone from his pouch, tied a string around it, and lowered it, pausing a few inches from the floor.

JONATHAN MABERRY

"Switching on the Anteater."

We all waited, then Remy lowered it the rest of the way. Remy dropped the string and let the drone scuttle around, poking into every corner.

"Looks clear. Going down myself."

"Be careful," I said.

"Dying ain't nowhere near the top of my to-do list, Outlaw."

His boots brushed the concrete, and we saw him take a deep breath before he put any real weight on them. He walked around a bit, taking steps like a tai chi practitioner, slowly easing weight onto each foot. Then he crouched and looked under the stairs, made *tsk–tsk* noises, and finally went and stood next to the air lock.

"Come ahead," he said. "One at a time. Drop down past that fourth step before you even think about touching the side of the stairs."

We were very careful.

I don't think I breathed at *all* on the way down. My nuts had crawled way up into my chest cavity, and I was half a heartbeat away from reciting prayers when my feet landed on solid ground that did not go boom.

"Good job, Gator Bait," said Scott Wilson. His voice had a bit of a nervous tremolo to it. "Proceed with the utmost caution."

Remy looked at the rest of us. "Really? I was going to do some Cajun two-step moves."

"Keep focused," was Scott's retort, but it landed flat.

Bunny flipped Scott the bird but was wise enough to do it outside the radius of anyone's body cam.

We moved very, *very* cautiously to the air lock and stood clustered around it.

"If they went to such pains to blow us to bits with those stairs," said Top, "what are the odds they rigged something cute here?"

"That's not easy to do," said Remy. "There's ten thousand ways to fuck up your day with trip wires and bombs and all that, but rigging this kind of electronics is next level."

"Could you do it?" asked Bunny.

Remy considered. "Sure, I could rig it . . . but why would I? This doesn't follow any kind of logic I can see. If they wanted to kill a team coming to the rescue, there are better ways than this. Andrea and I used to story-top each other over beers thinking up bad-boy ambush scenarios. This feels more like someone just showing off."

"More like someone fucking with us in a different way," suggested Top.

"Say it," I said.

"All of this . . . what's it accomplishing other than pissing us off and making Remy want to scratch his head?"

"It's slowing us down," I said.

"You think that's the point?" Bunny asked.

Top said, "What else could it be?" But there was still some hesitation in his tone. "That and something else."

"It's showing off," said Remy, but Top shook his head.

"It's someone *playing*," said Belle, and we all looked at her.

"Think about it," she said. "It's childish but on too high a level. This is like a child but a *godly* child. Someone with too much power, too much knowledge, but too little maturity."

It was a striking observation, and it crystallized a lot of what had been scratching at my mind.

"It's a game," I said.

Belle nodded. "With rules being made up as they go."

"So . . . instead of terrorists, we're facing a psychotic?" asked Remy. "That's a comfort."

"Havoc Actual to TOC," I said.

"TOC here," said Church.

"Merlin," I said, addressing Church by his call sign, "there might be another reason for all the fun and games. I think they're running down the clock to *burn-lock*."

"Agreed," he said. "You have fifty-eight minutes left on the mission clock."

Bug came on the call. "Outlaw, I'm watching your feed in high-def, and the port looks good. Go ahead with MindReader."

"What about a software-based trap?"

"Negative, Outlaw. Once MindReader Q1 interfaces with the facility computers, we're driving the go-kart. I don't care how smart their guy is, MindReader is smarter *and* tougher. She'll have your back."

"Let's all hope you're right," I said.

I took a breath, held it, and let it out slowly as I inserted the little uplink.

We waited there. Tense. Nervous. Uncertain as all hell. None of us actually said as much, but we were all expecting something very bad to happen.

But MindReader Q1 tore through the Gehenna's ultrasophisticated security, and the big steel door suddenly hissed and swung open. There were no trip wires attached to it, and nothing went bang.

That should have been a comfort, but given the circumstances, it really wasn't.

Weapons ready, eyes open, and hearts thundering, we stepped into the heart of hell itself.

CHAPTER 70
GEHENNA BIOLOGICAL RESEARCH AND CONTAINMENT FACILITY
PENN YAN, NEW YORK

Once the four of us were in the outer lock, the door closed behind us and powerful detox jets bombarded us with disinfectant spray. The stuff was so intense that for a few seconds even the lights on the handheld BAMS units went green.

Then MindReader opened the inner lock, which opened into an empty preparation area, with more racks of hazmat suits, clipboards on the wall with duty rosters on them, another key card reader for employee tracking in and out, and several doors marked for different kinds of research or containment. There was also a rack of syringes prefilled with antitoxins and other chemical mixtures that were for use in accidental exposure situations.

Every syringe was smashed.

On the floor were the bodies of the security guards who had been assigned to guard each stairwell landing. All zip-tied, all shot in the head and stacked like sacks of garbage.

"God almighty," breathed Remy. His hand twitched in the direction of his chest, and I wondered if he was going to cross himself.

"Keep your shit wired tight," I snapped.

We had our goggles set to full spectrum, but there were no laser trip wires in sight, and so we passed through the last lock and stepped into the Gehenna for real. Guns up and out, each of us fading left or right to cover the big room.

"Shit, shit, shit," said Bunny. He had his BAMS unit out, and every light now glared a furious red. But his words faded out and died.

We stood in the entrance to a large, brightly lit room set with rows of metal tables and computer workstations. The wall behind us had only the air lock; the other three walls were lined with heavy-duty glass doors leading to different kinds of labs, examination and dissection rooms, storage units, and meeting rooms. None of those doors should have been open.

All of them were.

Propped open with chairs, wheeled carts, or bodies.

That was bad enough. But it wasn't what made us stare in horror. Everywhere we looked, there was death.

Scientists, technicians, ordinary workers, security guards, secretarial staff.

All of them . . . dead.

They were sprawled in ugly ways. Some had wide sickly crusting around eyes, nostrils, and ears—victims of the countless germs filling the air. Others, though, lay in small lakes of congealing blood, their bodies torn by gunfire. Shell casings were everywhere. But the dead had clearly not all died from bugs or bullets.

Some of them were torn to pieces. Arms ripped from shoulder sockets. Legs hacked off. Heads lolling on partially severed necks.

"Fan out. Clear these rooms. Two by two."

Top and Remy paired up and went left; Bunny took Belle right, while I prowled down the middle of the room, using the workstations as cover. There was no way to avoid walking through the spilled blood. In places, we had to step over bodies . . . or parts of bodies.

"Look for trips and traps," I said.

Havoc Team went room by room, peering in through glass windows or open doors. They took turns providing cover while the other cleared each room—looking under desks, in closets, in bathrooms, behind rows of cabinets. Calling *clear* each time.

After about ten rooms and ten scenes of utter carnage, Remy—in a tremulous voice—said, "*Why?*"

"Don't worry about why, son," said Top, his tone filled with that mix of mature control and combat sharpness. "Do your job and stay sharp."

"Copy that," Remy replied with a bit more firmness.

On the other side of the big room, Belle and Bunny worked in silence except to announce a cleared space. Bunny had seen too many scenes like this since we first rolled out together during the original *seif al din* case. In fact, the day I met him, we had almost no time to even get to know each other before Church sent us to a meatpacking plant in which a bunch of technicians were systematically infecting children with the pathogen to study them in hopes of discovering usual variations on reactions. It was like being awake inside a nightmare. Top was with us, along with two other people—all of us strangers before that day. Top, Bunny, and I were the only ones left from what had been Echo Team. That scene marked us as surely as this was marking Remy.

As for Belle . . . her internment in the genital mutilation camp was its own ring of hell, and the effect on her ran much deeper than the scars visible on her skin. There were ghosts in her eyes, as there were in mine. In Bunny's and Top's. And after today, those ghosts would scream behind Remy's eyes.

There is a moment when seasoned soldiers have to process the deaths of other soldiers, and that is one kind of hell. Then there's the moment when you can see the realities of war take a scalpel and cut the innocence and a lot of optimism and faith in humanity out of a younger fighter. What he'd been through at the Stronghold in Israel was one level of madness; but this . . . this was far worse. This was abomination. This was the mark of the beast forced upon the innocent.

I wondered how he would survive it. *If* he would survive it. I know for sure he'd need to spend some time with Rudy. And maybe with Junie. She's been through the storm lands herself.

Once the main room and the smaller offices and labs were clear, we gathered together and went in search of the hot room indicated on the holographic map on our forearm-mounted tactical computers. It was through another set of security doors and down a short corridor. Top sent some Busy Bees ahead of us, but the corridor was clear.

"Had to be a bunch of them," observed Top. "Caught everyone by surprise."

"Yeah," said Bunny. "This wasn't an exchange of gunfire. They came in hard and fast and just opened fire. Efficient as hell. Like they knew the layout ahead of time. This wasn't hunt and search."

"And these cocksuckers worked fast," growled Top. "Hardly any shell casings under or around the guards, which meant they fell first."

"Bug," I said, "can you hack into the video feeds?"

"Seriously? Hack? Nobody ever uses that word anymore unless they're hijacking your Facebook account."

"I will personally snap the arms off every single one of your action figures next time I see you."

"Yeah, yeah, give me a second," he said, then, "Oh . . . crap. This is weird."

"We're ass-deep in weird," I said. "Can you be a little more specific?"

"There *is* no video feed," said Bug. "Everything's been wiped."

"Isn't there some kind of magic you can do to find it?" I asked. "I thought all of that stuff is impossible to erase. Like stuff on the net."

His sigh was long and eloquent. "Let me work on it," he said. And I swear I heard him mutter, "Luddite."

We moved through the room.

"Count seventeen dead," said Top. "Zero hostiles."

Once the big room was cleared, we began taking the offices one by one. There were corpses in nearly every one. Some were simply dead, marked with the bullet wounds that had killed them. But suddenly, Bunny called us over, and we clustered in a doorway, looking in at a different kind of horror.

A man sat at a desk. He wore a lab coat with the name tag DONNER. Deputy director of the facility, according to the mission briefing. He was dead, of course. But someone had gone the extra mile to desecrate the corpse. His hands had been cut off at the wrists and lay palm up in the center of his desk blotter. In the palm of each hand was an eye.

"Fuuuuccck," breathed Remy. Through the lenses of his goggles,

I could see that he'd gone paste white. Beads of sweat ran down his face. Or maybe they were tears.

The body in the next office was a woman of about forty. Her body was whole, with no missing parts. But she had been crucified against the wall with at least forty knives. Someone had dipped a finger into the lake of blood at her feet and drew a smiley face on the wall.

It got worse from there.

Bodies dismembered. Bodies torn to rags by hundreds of bullets fired into them. Bodies missing heads. A room with all of those missing heads laid out in a circle around a man who'd been lashed to a wheeled chair by electrical cords. He had no marks of bullet or blade, but someone had wrapped duct tape around his nose and mouth with such thoroughness that he had suffocated.

"This isn't crime," said Top. "This is madness."

I said nothing.

Madness was something I understood, both professionally and personally. There was a word for this that was more precise than madness, and it was Belle who finally put it out there.

"No," she said, "this is evil."

Evil.

A lot of people think that's an abstract concept. People like us, we know better.

CHAPTER 71

GEHENNA BIOLOGICAL RESEARCH AND CONTAINMENT FACILITY
PENN YAN, NEW YORK

"You think anyone's still alive down here?" asked Remy.

"We don't know *what's* down here, Gator Bait," Top said. "Stay on my three o'clock and don't touch nothing."

Weapons hot, we moved along the passage.

The hot room was marked with every kind of biohazard warning there is. Two security guards lay in a heap to one side of it. Both of them had drawn their weapons, and there were enough mixed shell casings to show that they'd defended their post. Didn't do them or anyone any good, but they couldn't have known that this was their Alamo.

"The hot room door's still closed," said Bunny. "Did we finally get lucky here?"

I tapped my earbud. "Bug, do we have eyes inside that room?"

"Negative, Outlaw. The entire video surveillance network there is down."

"Is there an access log?" I asked. It was common with hot rooms in high-end facilities to automatically register every entry based on codes entered and scanner data. All of those entries included a register of interior cabinets opened. Most of the cabinets had scales on them, too, that indicated which vials or other samples were lifted from their slots. That meticulous attention to detail was intended to track all movements of the pathogens and connect it to whomever entered the room.

Bug was ready with that data. "Says the last person to access the room was Gehenna's chief virologist, Dr. Sammie Trinidad, at 7:13 eastern time. That's—"

"—forty-one minutes ago," I said. "Nine minutes before we pulled into the parking lot."

We stood looking at the door. It was a large slab of deeply uninformative stainless steel, and we did not want to open it.

Yet we all knew that we had to.

The lights on the BAMS unit glared at us.

"Outlaw," said Bunny, "what if some of the staff locked themselves in there to stay safe? What if that closed door is all that's keeping them alive? Not just the guns who tore up the place but from what's in the air. If we open it and they're not in biohazard suits, we could kill them."

It wasn't a *could* situation. If he was right, then opening it *would* kill them. I thought about the smashed syringes of emergency meds. Though, given how many of the world's deadliest bioweapons permeated every cubic inch of air all around us, there would be no way on Earth to treat anyone we infected. It was a no-win situation.

I glanced at my guys. I saw the truth of it, the understanding of it, in their eyes.

"This is their last little trick," said Remy darkly. "They left this—exactly this—to mess with us. Maybe thinking we'd try to save whoever's inside or wait for med team backup or something. Basically run out the clock. But . . . we can't, can we?"

I didn't answer because his question was rhetorical.

"Bug," I said, "can MindReader open this vault without our help?"

"Yes."

"Do it."

We spread out, each of us settling into shooters' crouches.

Not sure what I was hoping for. Best-case scenario was a bunch of scared people in hazmat suits. Every other option was a sad one.

The clock was ticking in my head.

The lights on the scanner array next to the door flashed and clicked and pinged. There was a soft *click* and a softer hiss of air, and the door swung open.

The room was filled with people. At least thirty of them—techs, scientists, general staff, security, even maintenance. All crammed together. The one in front was a small Asian woman with a plastic name tag that read TRINIDAD.

She was not wearing a hazmat suit. None of them were.

None of them were alive.

But all of them were on their feet. They stared at us with eyes that were green and veined with red. Their mouths were smeared with blood. Their flesh was torn, and red-black blood ran in thick viscous lines down their limbs.

They were all infected with *seif al din*.

With a howl of bottomless, savage hunger, they rushed at us, hands reaching and teeth snapping.

CHAPTER 72
GEHENNA BIOLOGICAL RESEARCH AND CONTAINMENT FACILITY
PENN YAN, NEW YORK

"*Back!*" I roared as the woman lunged for my throat.

The attack was so fast and so shocking that she was on me before I could pull the trigger. Her small hands locked onto the fabric of my ChemRig, and her teeth snapped an inch from my windpipe.

I pivoted as hard as I could, and that lifted her completely off the ground. She was petite but very fit, and I used that weight and mass to slam the scientist into the open air lock door. Despite the hungry roars of the other infected, I could hear bones snap with gunshot clarity.

"Head shots, head shots, head shots," yelled Top as he faded to one side, brought up his rifle, and opened fire. Despite his own instructions, he hosed the infected with at least half a magazine. Remy and Belle yielded ground, each caught in that crushing vise of indecision—these were civilians in their minds, and not the monsters these people had become.

Belle shook it off first, probably because she'd encountered a similar situation with the Rage bioweapon in Korea. Her sniper rifle was slung, and she had a Sig Sauer P226 in a two-handed grip. The one slip I could see in her composure is that she held the handgun in a teacup grip—with the butt of the pistol resting in her palm—which is an old revolver method. Between her second and third shot, she seemed to realize her mistake and switched to a far stabler grip with her left wrapping around the handle at an angle to avoid the slide while providing a more stable platform.

I think it was the first mistake I'd ever seen her make.

That is fear. That's shock and horror, stripping away layers of training. It was what got far too many soldiers and cops killed when things suddenly went south.

She edged to one side and began firing at the heads of the mass of scientists, aiming at the motor cortex at a roughly midway point in the skull. Her next three shots instantly dropped infected.

Bunny kicked one of the living dead techs in the hip, knocking her back against the rest, then he opened up with his Benelli M4 Super 90 shotgun. He was firing solid slugs that did terrible damage.

Trinidad was down but trying to get up despite the broken bones. Gravity kept pulling at her, and I finally put her all the way to the ground with a shot to the head.

Gunfire and screams filled every inch of the world. The moans of savage hunger that drives anyone infected with *seif al din* were awful to hear. They tore holes in our hearts and shredded our souls as we fought.

　　　　　　　　　　　　　　JONATHAN MABERRY

Top was firing as he walked backward, and suddenly Remy was right beside him, taking cues from Top. He wasted a whole magazine shooting center mass, dropping only a couple of the infected when his rounds hit their spines. Top snarled something at him, and his barrel rose, finding more useful targets.

"Reloading," growled Top as he swapped out his magazine. Remy echoed and slapped in a new mag. When their guns came up, Remy seemed more stable. He's lucky because a lot of very good soldiers of one kind or another never survived their moment of understandable pause. It's not called *fatal* hesitation for nothing.

For my part, I had backed up to the opposite wall and with my rifle snugged into my shoulder so I could make spaced shots that counted. Bunny switched from shooting head-high now that the monsters were in the hall and instead aimed at hips and knees, blowing off legs and shattering bones. As the zombies collapsed, Belle took them with head shots, her gun moving smoothly from target to target.

It was brutal work.

There was no glory here, no thrill of victory. This was survival in a fight that would gouge scars in all of us we would never—*could* never—erase. Not sure if it was worse for Remy, who was new to this, or Belle, whose familiarity was growing. Or maybe it was worse for Bunny, Top, and me because we've done this. We have had to kill innocent people time and again. Civilians. In the past, sometimes even children. It was like being in hell for real, reliving a sinful act over and over again, shattering that ultimate taboo of taking an innocent human life.

We'd all need Rudy. We'd all need our loved ones. We'd all need alone time to throw up, scream, cry it out, fight for rationalization. But this is the kind of war we fight. The real monsters were not in the room with us. They were the ones who caused this. They were the villains who turned the innocent into monsters. They forced us to deal with their crimes but denied us the chance of punishing the actual culprits.

It was how they could fight groups bigger than themselves. Like ISIS establishing headquarters and training centers in the basements of active schools and daring the coalition of nations to bomb the place. Knowing we sometimes had to make bad choices and do those strikes. It helped them create martyrs useful for recruitment.

It happens over and over again. It's not new, either. That kind of cowardly guerilla warfare goes way, way back. It's one of the many reasons veterans reach for a bottle or pills or a syringe or opt out by eating a gun.

The knowledge of that was present in my mind as we fought.

The hatred it ignited was a terrible thing. I could feel it burn me. And I knew it was scorching the souls of the good people fighting at my side.

I swapped in a new magazine and continued to be the necessary executioner that was my assigned role.

CHAPTER 73
THE TOC
OMFORI ISLAND, GREECE

Mr. Church stood between Doc Holliday and Scott Wilson. The whole big room was as silent as the grave as they watched the body cams of Havoc Team.

Firing into the undefended flesh of doctors and scientists, technicians and staff down in the hell that was Gehenna.

Death after death.

Atrocity after atrocity.

After a long while, Wilson asked, "Doc, is this *seif al din*?"

Doc, who usually wore a broad, bright smile when things were really bad, had no expression at all on her face. "Yes," she said in a ragged whisper.

"Yes," echoed Church.

"God almighty," breathed Wilson.

Church looked at him for a moment and nearly said something about the lack of the presence of God in that place or anywhere on the field of battle. But he left it unsaid.

The gunfire filled the air, made far too real by the cruel fidelity of the speakers.

"There is order in this chaos," explained Doc after a moment.

"What?" asked Wilson. "Order? In this?"

"Yes," she said. "The infiltration wasn't done by anyone out of control. The killing of the guards was efficient. These killings are gruesome, but there is a kind of childish structure to them. I doubt either of you boys have seen many Batman movies or read the comics, but this is the kind of thing you'd expect of the Joker. It's showy. An attempt to make some kind of statement."

"Statement?" asked Wilson, appalled. "Political?"

"No. Artistic. *Bad* art, to be sure, but some of those rooms are clearly staged. And I'll bet a whole dollar it was done once the whole complex was secured. When there was time to play while the rest of the team was doing whatever they came there to do—steal diseases and bioweapons, download files from the computers, and like that."

"Art," mused Church. "Yes."

"I don't see it that way," said Wilson. "This is wholesale murder, torture, and obvious insanity."

Doc ignored him, directing her comments to Church. "And I'm going to go out on a limb here and say that those statement pieces were done—or ordered done—by one person."

"What kind of person?"

She shook her head. "That's something you need to ask Rudy Sanchez."

Wilson began to say something, but Church cut him off. "Get Dr. Sanchez in here. Now."

CHAPTER 74

US CUSTOMS AND BORDER PROTECTION—VAN HORN STATION
VAN HORN, TEXAS

David White sat in a white power company truck parked near the corner of Laurel and West Fire Bush Streets. The border patrol station was half a block away. There was a low cinder block wall around it, though what good it did, White couldn't guess. If anything, the low and easily scalable wall seemed to make a statement about how effective any walls are at keeping out determined and clever people.

The coyote who had brought in the latest Typhoid Mary had used a portable ladder that allowed his customers to go up and over with ease. The fact that some of them were caught shortly after crossing from Mexico to the States was not a flaw but a feature in his plan.

The Mary was eighteen, pretty, but hollow-eyed from poor food, poverty, and the drugs given her by Mr. October's contacts over the border. They wanted her stoned and staggering so that her symptoms wouldn't easily be noticed.

The Van Horn station was over fifty years old and looked it. Weathered, brutalized by the sun and by sand driven by desert winds.

It was a small station, built in the '70s and staffed with five officers who had responsibility for thirty miles of the border and 3,775 square miles of land. It left them with a huge area that included all of Culberson County. They were efficient, though, and rounded up as many undocumented migrants as they could.

Mary was gathered in a sweep at three-thirty in the morning. She and eleven others were brought to the office for inspection and processing. She had no idea that she had been *made* ill, only that she felt it. Her fever came on like a tidal surge and brought with it an intense headache. She asked for aspirin, but the officers ignored the request.

Malaise came next, and she all but collapsed onto a metal bench, cowering into herself as pain flared in her muscles and in every joint. There was a metal seatless toilet in one corner of the holding room, and Mary staggered to it, barely getting there before the first round of intense watery diarrhea seemed to rip through her. It brought its own pain, with severe cramping and what felt like a stomach full of razor blades.

The other women in that room moved away from the smell and from someone who was clearly ill. They called out to the agents and were told to be quiet.

That quiet lasted for three hours, and then Mary began vomiting blood. She slid off the toilet, trailing bloody feces, then collapsed on the floor.

The agents rushed in to check on her, their humanity rising above the cynical disdain of the people who kept making their lives so difficult. Once they saw how bad she was—shivering from the fever, eyes glazed and vacant, her body twitching and spasming—they called a doctor.

From the moment the doctor agreed to come over until she arrived, it was only twenty-one minutes. By then, Mary was dead, and four of the other women were complaining of headaches and stomach cramps.

The EMTs arrived just as the first of the border patrol guards began feeling feverish.

A rapid-response team sent by the CDC arrived within hours. It was the first of a parade of RRTs. Watching through a pair of high-power compact binoculars, David White logged eleven separate agencies and by that understood that this was finally the full-blown response. These were multiagency, multidisciplinary teams that operated using Incident Command System (ICS) and the National Incident Management System (NIMS) principles. The gathered agents waited, though, until an unmarked black midsize cargo truck pulled up and six people wearing Level A hazmat suits stepped down and hurried inside.

"Time to go," White told his driver. The big ape-faced man grinned, showing too many sharp teeth for White's comfort. Their truck turned and went the opposite way.

They drove in silence for nearly two hours before pulling into a garage next to one of Mr. October's safe houses. The driver killed the engine.

"Hey, boss," said the driver, "can I ask you something?"

"Try me."

"I was reading up on these diseases those Typhoid Marys have been delivering, and I noticed something. Back in Atlanta, the first one spread typhus, right?"

"You know the answer to that," said White irritably. "Of course it was typhus."

"Right, right, but Miss Mary calls all of these chicks 'Typhoid Mary.' And I read that typhus and typhoid are different. Typhus comes on those fleas. Vectors, I think they're called. But typhoid fever is what people in poor countries catch from raw sewage, or dumbasses in restaurants spread from not washing their hands after they take a dump."

White studied him. "So, you want to go ask Miss Mary why she used the wrong word? Is that what you're telling me?"

"What?" asked the driver, suddenly looking scared. "No, I was just wondering. I didn't mean nothing by it." He paused, eyes wide. "You're not going to tell her I said anything, are you?"

"No," White assured him. "Just keep stuff like that to yourself."

The driver nodded. Then, after a few moments, he asked, "How many more of these do we need to do?"

"This was the last one," said White, and he shot the big man in the temple. As the huge simian driver collapsed against the window, White shot him twice more.

David White sat in the truck for ten minutes, looking at the dead man. He weighed the .22 pistol in his hand, wondering what it would feel like if he shot himself.

He nearly did and even got as far as pressing the cooling barrel beneath his chin.

"I'm going to hell," he said.

But he did not pull the trigger.

CHAPTER 75

GEHENNA BIOLOGICAL RESEARCH AND CONTAINMENT FACILITY
PENN YAN, NEW YORK

We stood there.

Still as statues.

Our heads ringing from the gunfire.

Our eyes dry from staring. Except for Remy, who was openly weeping. He kept trying to blink away the tears because the seals of our ChemRigs prevented him from wiping them away. His nose was running, and his lips trembled.

"I'm sorry," he said, staring down at the corpses all around us. "I'm so sorry."

Then he said something else, and it changed the moment. Maybe it was the strongest part of his mind exerting itself in a way that said what he *meant* and always what he needed to hear himself say.

"I'm so sorry this happened to you."

Top caught my eye and held it. We both knew that if Remy had said anything like *I'm sorry I did this to you*, then the young Cajun might have suffered a fracture. Taking on guilt of that immensity was crushing, crippling. It could ruin someone, even if they had therapy immediately after. But Remy had self-corrected. He said, very specifically, that he was sorry it had *been done to* them. Taking no personal blame.

That was going to matter to Remy now, and it would be the first piece of psychological ground he would need to stand on as he processed and healed.

Top gave me a small nod, which I returned.

Belle went over to Remy and punched him on the shoulder. She understood, too.

Worlds turn on moments like that. Remy had been staring into the abyss, but he did not see any version of himself staring back. I knew at that moment he would survive this.

I knelt briefly beside the torn and broken body of Dr. Sammie Trinidad. She was young, with an entire future stolen away from her. Her eyes were open, and her dead lips formed an "Oh" as if in surprise at all of this. It was almost childlike in its apparent wonder.

I closed her eyes and straightened, feeling very old and empty.

"Boss," said Bunny, "ticktock."

It jolted us all back to the moment. I tapped my earbud. "Havoc Actual to TOC."

"Go for TOC," said Church.

"Is Bug still there?"

"I'm here, Outlaw."

"Can MindReader shut down the burn-lock protocol? We need time to continue our sweep and gather intel."

"Hold on," said Bug.

While we waited, I went into the hot room and studied the germ storage systems. My body cam fed it all in high-def to Doc.

"Looks like they cleaned it out," she said.

"Affirmative," I said. "What they didn't take, they smashed." Bunny leaned into the shot and showed her his BAMS unit, with all of its glaring red lights.

"Huckleberry," I said, "are you getting our readings?"

"Yes, I am, Outlaw."

"I don't think there's any way for us to estimate how much they actually took. Once they infected some of the staff with *seif al din*, they probably just put a few sick ones into this room with any staff still living. The infected did the rest."

"Without doubt."

"Then they smashed everything they could, every vial and flask and whatever, and let the air circulation spread it around so it *looks* like this was some kind of wild vandalism. Something to sell the idea of crazy violence."

"Like the Joker in *Batman*," said Doc. "I just explained that to the boys here."

"Yeah, like that," I said. "But not *actually* that. There's some sick and insane stuff, like what was done to some of the staff. But if you act crazy enough, people stop looking for the logic behind it. You following me? Like the protest stuff you see when eco-warriors trash an animal-testing facility. But I think what they were really trying to do was hide what they stole."

"I entirely agree, Outlaw. But I do think at least someone in that team *is* crazy. Maybe he's a pet psycho on a leash that they let out to play while the smarter ones do what they came for."

"Copy that. Even so, there's a hole in that."

"As in, why are you still breathing?" she asked. "Why didn't they rig a simple trip wire to a detonator with a ten-second delay so Havoc could use MindReader to bypass the air lock and step inside before it all went boom?"

"Like that," I said. "There's another shoe ready to drop, and I don't think it was this shit we found in the hot room. There's something else."

"Keep your eyes open," she said, and Wilson echoed it, though in an uptight Eton sort of way.

"Doc, based on the BAMS readings," I said, "is there any way of determining what's been taken? Maybe something with particles per cubic feet of air density?"

"If we were able to do a particle analysis of the entire facility, maybe, but I doubt it."

"Then they really *did* know what they were doing here."

"Yes," she said.

"Yeah," I said. "I'm definitely reading this as more stage dressing."

"And that kind of thinking is very disturbing because it's almost certainly the case," said Doc.

"There's another thing," I said. "Shouldn't there be a fail-safe protocol in play here? Aren't there sensors that would crash this whole lab if certain toxics were released into the shared atmosphere?"

"Yes. And that earns you another gold star. That had to be sabotaged, and even though I'm no computer stud like Buggy dear," said Doc, "I bet it isn't something just any ol' person can do."

"Absolutely not," agreed Bug, coming back online. "It takes mad skills. I mean *deep* knowledge. Not only about those kinds of systems in general but of the specific software that governs the fail-safes there at Gehenna. I mean, *I* could do it. A couple of my guys could, but we're talking dense code. You can't do that on the fly. You'd have to bring the software with you, and that is a whole new kind of weird because that software is proprietary. Very hard to obtain and harder by like a million times to rewrite because the software itself has anti-intrusion subroutines built in."

"So . . . someone crazy *and* smart," said Bunny. "This gets better and better."

"Bug, I need the answer to my question about the burn-lock."

"Outlaw, I can slow it down, but it's already initiated. When they accessed the computers inside the place, they did very precise damage. The fail-safes are already in final countdown. You have maybe thirty minutes . . . and that means by then you have to be out of the building."

I saw Top wince. That meant leaving the facility, going through the sanitizing sprays, climbing the ropes up past the booby-trapped stairs, and out of the B&B. There was barely enough time to do that.

Church said, "Havoc Team, we have missed the window on this. There's no time left for a sweep. Assess the damage. Leave MindReader Q1 uplinks in every terminal, laptop, and cell phone you find, and get out of there. Do it now."

We backed away from the hot room, then turned and began hurrying back to the main room.

Which is when the lights went out and the hallway was filled with the sounds of terrible, animalistic roars of rage and hate.

And laughter.

With no time left, we were trapped in the utter blackness with some new kind of monster.

CHAPTER 76
PATRIOT NEWS PAGE
X (FORMERLY TWITTER)

First post:

> Illegals did it again! America is under siege.
> Another bioweapon and more Americans dead.
> #RIPVanHornStationBorderPatrol
> Vengeance is mine sayeth the lord.

Follow-up post:

> Deuteronomy 32:35
> "It is mine to avenge; I will repay.
> In due time their foot will slip; their day of disaster is near
> and their doom rushes upon them."

> Likes: 164,928
> Retweets: 1,928

CHAPTER 77
GEHENNA BIOLOGICAL RESEARCH AND CONTAINMENT FACILITY
PENN YAN, NEW YORK

"Combat circle," I yelled, and we formed a ring, guns outward. "Lights."

The ChemRigs had small but powerful LED lights on the helmet—like the kind miners and spelunkers used—and they flashed on, building a bubble of white light around us.

The hall was silent for a moment.

"What was that sound?" asked Remy. "Where'd it come from? 'Cause I don't see shit."

Bunny raised his shotgun. "If it's what I think it is, kid, it's going to come in fast and hard."

He was right.

It stepped up to the very edge of the light and paused. It wore the shredded remnants of a high-end hazmat suit. No helmet, no respirator. The thing's body was so grotesquely packed with corded muscle that it looked like a cartoon figure. Like the Hulk, except that it had a distinctly simian face. It held a fire axe in one hand and most of a human arm in the other. The arm was covered in blood that matched the crimson smears around its mouth and on its oversize incisors.

The thing stared at us with eyes that were too wide and too strange—the irises burned a greenish red, and the sclera a deeper scarlet. Those eyes glared at us with a terrifying mixture of humor, hunger, and malevolence.

It was a Berserker.

And it was infected.

It was a zombie.

Remy said, "Mary, Mother of God."

The creature laughed, and in a voice that rumbled with malice, it said, "God ain't here, motherfucker."

I pointed my rifle at the thing's face but did not yet pull the trigger.

"Listen to me," I said carefully and clearly, "we can get you out of here. We can get you to doctors. They can help."

It took a small step forward. Not exactly threatening in itself, but everything about it and the moment screamed warnings at us.

"I have a message for you, asshole," said the creature. "Miss Mary wanted me to deliver it personally."

"Who's Miss Mary?"

"An old friend." Moving slowly so as not to spook us, it reached into a pouch on the utility belt strapped around its waist. Bunny's shotgun rose to point at the thing's face. But with two deformed fingers, the Berserker removed a small blue Bic lighter. The kind you see in every 7-Eleven from coast to coast. He showed it to us the way a magician does before pulling a dove out of his sleeve.

"What's the message?" I asked, my finger beginning a slow move from the underside of the slide to the trigger guard.

He thumbed the little metal wheel and popped a flame. A tiny thing that underlit his simian features, making them even more horrific.

"She wanted me to tell you," said the beast, "that sometimes you have to burn to shine."

And he touched the flame to his chest.

The ChemRigs cancel the sense of smell, because smell is particulate. None of us could smell the gasoline in which the Berserker had doused himself. His entire body burst into a furious blaze. The heat tore a scream from the creature, and he rushed at us.

We all fired.

Most of us screamed, too. I know I did.

Our bullets tore into the burning, running, howling, undead monster. In the space of two seconds—in the space of two running steps—we probably hit it twenty times. No one missed. Chunks of flaming meat flew from its body and it still came on. Then Bunny fired from eight feet, and the heavy shotgun slug exploded the Berserker's skull.

Its legs failed and it fell, but it was moving with such shocking speed that it slid almost to where we stood.

There was one full second of silence, and then we were running. Racing. Tearing down the halls toward the main room and the air lock. I don't know if there were more of the infected Berserkers in Gehenna. We didn't wait to find out.

We crowded into the first of the sterilization chambers, pointing our guns the way we'd come. The sprays blasted us, and we ducked and peered to see if those monsters were going to attack us while we were half-blinded.

Then the jets stopped and we walked backward, weapons hot and high, into the next chamber. And the next.

All the time, I felt those words burning in my mind.

Sometimes you have to burn to shine.

No.

No way.

No goddamn way.

My brain was stuck in that gear until we were outside of the main air lock.

JONATHAN MABERRY

No.

But the creature had said those words. Those exact words. *Sometimes you have to burn to shine.*

CHAPTER 78
SIDNEY STRAIGHT UP
FOX NEWS

The reporter's name was Sidney Selicec, and she was a pretty blonde with a lot of frosted hair, sparkling blue eyes, and just the right shade of lipstick—nothing overtly provocative, tending toward a business-like shade of dust red.

"And welcome back," she said into the camera. "We're here with Congressman Jeffrey Ormond to discuss the latest terrorist attack. A brutal biological warfare incident at the Border Patrol's Van Horn Station. Congressman, will this latest attack finally be what sparks the president to take appropriate action?"

"I can't see how it could be any other way, Sidney." He was the junior senator from Michigan and a member of the Homeland Security Committee. Although generally a centrist, over the last seven months, he had become a fierce advocate for tougher border controls and harsher punishment for any migrants—documented or not—who committed felonies in the United States. A month earlier, he had added his name to a bill demanding that the border be closed completely until a package of security measures could be worked out in a way that would garner support from both sides of the political fence.

"What would that look like?" asked Sidney.

"In the short term, we need to close all ports and borders to migrants," said Ormond. "Particularly migrants from certain countries."

"Are you talking about a new Muslim ban?"

"Look, Sidney, I was never a fan of that before because it's too sweeping. So, no, not a ban on Muslims. A ban on migrants from Mexico and Central and South America. And from the four countries where terrorist groups have taken credit for the previous attacks."

"Iran, Russia, North Korea, and China?" promoted Sidney.

"Maybe less so with Russia."

"Why give them a pass?"

"Oh, not a pass. By no means. No, Sidney, it's simply that the video purporting to be from a militant pro–New Soviet splinter group was routed through Syria. Some folks—and I can't name names, you understand—in our intelligence communities believe the group who actually *is* behind the attack in Collinsville is likely Syrian."

"So, more Muslims . . ."

"As I said, this is not a Muslim thing. It's more likely Hamas, Boko Haram, or ISIS."

CHAPTER 79
MISS MARY'S LAB
THE MANSION
UNDISCLOSED LOCATION
THREE WEEKS AGO

The warhead lay on the table.

Each of the six plastic canisters attached to the Gorgon was filled to the brim with amber liquid. Small wires connected each canister to a triggering device that would detonate if anyone tried to tamper with them. The designer, Russo, had gone to great pains to make the weapon immune to tampering. The master chip governed everything, and if it were triggered, not only would the canisters of Shiva explode but thermite charges throughout the entire device would also detonate, reducing the whole thing to slag.

Mary knew this. So did the group of scientists and technicians who surrounded the table. Everyone wore level one hazmat suits, which would protect them from Shiva but were still vulnerable to shrapnel.

"Here goes," said Mary, her voice trembling a little as she bent to connect leads from her laptop to the housing of the master chip. "This is either going to work, or we're all going to have a really bad day."

It was said as a joke, but no one laughed.

Once the leads were in place, all that remained was to depress a switch on the master chip housing at the same time she pressed the Return key on the laptop keyboard. Two actions that had to be done simultaneously. She could not even trust doing it remotely because there was always the risk of a signal delay, no matter how brief.

A sound made her turn, and she saw Mr. October come into the lab. He wore no protective clothing.

"What are you doing?" she demanded. "There are plenty of suits on the rack."

"I'll be fine," he said.

"But—"

"I have faith that you've cracked this, my girl," he said smoothly. October pulled a stool over, and the scientists shifted away to make room. They exchanged covert and very nervous glances, but none of them ever questioned Mr. October. It was simply not done.

Mary looked at her patron for a long time, seeing his kindly smile and those strange eyes of his. The colors weren't swirling as they sometimes did, but she could feel his unnaturalness. It was palpable. She wondered if the others felt it, too, or if they were simply intimidated.

Focus, she told herself and shoved all of her attention back in the direction of the Gorgon warhead. *If I do this, if this works, then I am better than Russo ever was. Better than Bug.*

She drew a breath, exhaled half of it the way a sniper would, and then pressed the switch on the master chip housing and the Return key on her laptop.

And absolutely nothing happened.

Which is when everyone started cheering.

CHAPTER 80

GEHENNA BIOLOGICAL RESEARCH AND CONTAINMENT FACILITY
PENN YAN, NEW YORK

We climbed up the ropes, careful even in our fear and panic to avoid the booby-trapped stairs. As I steadied the rope for Top, Bunny—who stood beside me—kept saying the same thing over and over again.

"No way. That can't be what I heard. No fucking way. She's dead."

I said nothing. My brain was reeling.

Bunny went up next, then Remy and Belle. I was last, and I paused to look at the closed air lock. I tapped into the command channel, so it was only the people at the TOC on the line with me for a moment.

"You heard that," I said, making it a statement.

"We heard, Outlaw," said Church.

"By the time I get my people out of here, I want some goddamn answers, and I don't want to hear, 'I don't know.' You reading me on this?"

"Copy that, Outlaw."

I cycled back to the team channel before I climbed. It was the longest fucking climb of my life. When I reached the landing, Remy and Bunny both grabbed me and pulled me over the rail.

"Out, now," I snapped, cutting off any chance of conversation.

We raced up the stairs, out through the hidden exit, past the bodies of the two dead caretakers, and out of the building into the last of the day's dying sunlight.

"Outlaw to dogs," I yelled via comms. "Kick the tires and light the fires. We are out of—"

My sentence burst apart as I skidded to a stop in the parking lot. Pluto and Goofy were there, but they were crouched down behind the SUV, both of them with their rifles switched to rock and roll as they fired up into the air. I ducked and wheeled and looked up to see a pair of unmarked black helicopters hovering just above the B&B. The choppers immediately opened up with 3mm chain guns.

We dove for what cover there was, rolling as we dove, firing up at the deadly birds.

The car the dogs had been driving was ripped apart, sending hailstorms of glass, splinters of metal, and torn fiberglass everywhere. I saw Goofy reel back, his face and shoulder erupting with blood. Pluto grabbed him by the collar and belt and dragged him to the far side of the SUV.

The rounds chunked into the second car, too, but did little damage. It was heavily armored. At least we had that much grace.

"Covering fire," I yelled, and as soon as all guns were firing upward, I broke from cover and ran to the SUV. Goofy looked bad, but he was still alive. Pluto was covered in blood, but most of it was his friend's. "We have anything heavy?"

He wiped blood from his eyes and tapped the rear hatch. "Couple snakes in a box," he gasped. That meant we had a pair of SMAW II-85s, a new generation of the Raytheon shoulder-launched multi-purpose assault weapons. But the cases were in the back of the SUV, and it was going to take more time than we had to access them and prepare them for fire.

It was clear that the pilots of the enemy's helos considered the armored SUV a threat. Above us, the choppers had risen to weaken the effectiveness of our rifle fire and to allow them to hose us. Armor only goes about so far before constant heavy-caliber impact and metal fatigue took its toll. I considered trying to get inside the car and driving over to pick up my guys, then hiding beneath the forest canopy. That would buy us time to get the Serpents out and blast those bastards out of the sky.

I said as much to the team, but before I finished my sentence, one of the helos canted sideways. The body of the chopper speeded around, and for a moment, the gun was firing at the front of the bed-and-breakfast. Then the helicopter slanted downward into a fatal sideways fall. It crashed down atop the building and blew up.

Pluto and I looked wildly around, and in the same moment we saw the cause, there was a sharp crack and the other chopper was wobbling toward the trees. Belle had her sniper rifle braced on a large decorative boulder beside the front door.

Two shots.

Two fucking shots, and both helicopters died in balls of flame and fury.

"Holeeeeee shit," breathed Pluto. "Remind me to never, *ever* piss her off."

Top tapped Belle, and Havoc Team came at a dead run. Bunny and Pluto picked up the wounded Goofy and carried him as gently as desperate haste allowed, placing him in the back of the SUV. Belle, who was the smallest, climbed back there with him, and with Top's help began dressing the man's wounds. Remy slid behind the wheel and fired up the engine, and as Top and I piled in, he threw it into gear, did a wild gravel-spitting turn in the driveway, and then stamped on the gas. The SUV shot out of the parking lot and onto the road.

Exactly thirty-seven seconds later, there was a heavy *whumpf* that rocked the car and made the burning B&B collapse down.

Burn-lock had gone into effect.

I turned to look back as the place known as Gehenna become hell in very real terms. I knew that the facility itself was sealed and the fires inside would not escape—and not let any microscopic monsters out, either. But the internal forces of that fiery cleansing made the whole region shudder. The weight of a burning helicopter on the B&B brought the building down, and the second chopper had ignited a forest fire.

The speedometer hit one hundred and kept climbing.

We fled from the graveyard of a place, but we carried our ghosts with us.

CHAPTER 81
THE MANSION
UNDISCLOSED LOCATION

"What's wrong with you?" asked Mary. "You look like shit."

David White looked at the woman who had everyone who worked for Mr. October nervous. Scared, really.

She wore a lumberjack flannel shirt that was a mix of every shade of blue, and beneath that a skirt that was almost a tutu. She looked ridiculous. Her legs, particularly her knees, were filthy, and there were pieces of dried autumn leaves in her hair. He knew that meant Miss Mary had been out doing something awful in the woods. There were rumors that she had gone totally off her rocker and was hunting rabbits and raccoons with her bare hands—*and* catching them. Killing them.

Eating them raw.

His stomach lurched sideways at the thought.

What the fuck are *you?* he wondered, and not for the first time.

"Just tired, Miss Mary," he said quickly, giving her as convincing a weary smile as he could manage.

Mary walked up to him and stared into his face. He was not a tall man, and she was tall for a Chinese woman, so they stood nearly eye to eye. Her gaze was piercing, and she blinked too little and too slowly. Like a lizard.

Then she turned away. Abruptly, the action as effective a dismissal as if she'd ordered him to leave.

"Go away," she said. "Keep your phone on. Wait for my call."

He backed away, bending at the waist as if bowing before he realized he was doing that. Then he turned and fled.

CHAPTER 82
THE HOT SEAT
MSNBC NEWS

"Senator Harris," asked the reporter, "are we in a war?"

Niles Franklin had been a staple of the twenty-four-hour news machine for decades, having started with CNN, then migrating to Fox as a liberal panelist on a news discussion show, then to MSNBC. He had the wise eyes, graying hair, and firm jaw of a seasoned reporter and had a shelf in his office with two Pulitzers, several from the National Press Club, four Emmys, and a scattering of other journalism awards. He was known for provocative questions that put his guests in the hot seat, hence the name of his popular show.

"In a war?" mused the senator. "I never used to think so, Niles."

Bob Harris had always been a very soft-spoken, accessible, and gentle man who was never in a yelling match with colleagues on the Senate floor, never caught on hot mics talking trash, involved with civil and human rights issues. But over the last few weeks, he had come out with surprising vehemence after the typhus incident in Atlanta. What made people sit up and pay attention was the fact that Harris had always tended toward peaceful resolutions. A confirmed dove.

"And what is the nature of that war, Senator?"

"The short answer is terrorism," said Harris. "And I'm not talking violent acts by oppressed groups within different cultures or of ideologies. You remember that I was for ceasefires and peaceful resolutions in Gaza. But this . . . these attacks? This is sophisticated, well planned, and without a doubt well funded."

"Well funded? What makes you say that?"

"This isn't some politically disenfranchised individual sending powdered anthrax to people in Washington," explained Harris. "The version of typhus the CDC recovered from the Atlanta victims is genetically engineered. That isn't the kind of thing someone can do with a home chemistry set. Bioweapons of this sophistication require years—perhaps decades—of research under exacting conditions. We are talking about multibillion-dollar labs and topflight scientists. No, this isn't a band of extremists in a cave or hiding in an abandoned warehouse. These are weapons of war, created by nations with the budgets for research and development, and agendas that are more skewed toward the political long game."

"If that's the case, Senator, then who would risk open war with the most powerful nation on Earth? They risk retaliation by NATO and all of our allies."

"Fair point," conceded Harris. "However, with the terrorist mentality, they would see that as an acceptable risk."

"I see that," said Franklin, "but again . . . who are these terrorists? If it's, say, a nation-state like Iran, why attack us?"

"Reprisal for years of sanctions and for our efforts to suppress their nuclear programs. And in solidarity with other nations who feel that America should have used a stronger hand against Israel in their fight with Hamas."

"And yet the groups taking responsibility for the attacks are well-known but small radical cells."

"Sure. Iran would never declare an open war with America. That would be suicide and might likely trigger a world war based in the Middle East. No, Niles, I think what we're seeing here is bad-actor states manipulating smaller radical cells to do their dirty work and to let them take the credit. That keeps the blame off Iran—or North Korea, or whoever—while still hitting us hard here in the States. You've seen the extreme shifts in the stock market with each new incident. This is sly, secret warfare. A new kind of cold war. And as long as these states can manipulate radical groups, they can go on hitting America over and over again."

"Well," said Franklin, "that's pretty scary. What options do we have? If we can't prove it's Iran or any of the other countries, then we can't even rely on proportional responses."

"No, we can't. That would look like *we* are starting a war. America has been in too many wars, and no one wants a new one."

"Then what can the American people do?"

Harris's eyes turned hard as ice. "We can prepare," he said. "The Constitution is very clear on our options. Forming and training domestic response groups."

"You mean militia groups?" asked Franklin, his surprise evident.

"I prefer not to use that term, Niles. 'Militia' has been so thoroughly politicized. Domestic response as laid out in the Second Amendment speaks of a well-regulated militia. Very well. Let's help form them. Let's provide *them* with weapons, equipment, intelligence, logistical support, and whatever else they need so that if more attacks come—and they will—then Americans will be able to defend their communities, their towns, their states, and this great country."

CHAPTER 83
EN ROUTE TO PENN YAN REGIONAL AIRPORT
PENN YAN, NEW YORK

The drive from Gehenna to the airport was the first time I have ever been in a carful of RTI operatives who were absolutely silent.

Ghost kept poking his nose at me for comfort and maybe to see if I was okay. Canine empathy goes both ways. I sat in the shotgun seat and petted him and tried not to notice how badly my hand was shaking. He whined every now and then. I wanted to do the same.

A call broke the silence. It was Bird Dog on the team channel.

"Outlaw," he said, his voice filled with thorns and spikes, "an ambulance is waiting at a crossroads." He gave me the directions. "They'll take Goofy. Pluto will accompany him."

"Copy that."

There was a beat, then Bird Dog asked, "How is he?"

I looked over my shoulder, and although Belle's face was set into a grim frown, she nodded.

"Still with us," I said.

"Who's driving?"

"Gator Bait."

"Does he know where the gas pedal is?"

"He's standing on it."

"Good."

"Look, Bird Dog, I don't know if we were tracked there or if they had sensors at the site, but I don't want any new surprises."

"I got all my drones in the air, and police and fire at the B&B. Your road's clear. Bring my dog home."

"Be there in four minutes, brother," I assured him.

He dropped off, and I glanced at Remy. His face was stone, and he drove like the world was on fire behind us.

CHAPTER 84
ROUND AND ROUND
CNN

The four panelists sat liked armed camps, with the Democrats on the left and the Republicans on the right, and Milton Schick in the middle. Schick had hosted *Round and Round* through the last three presidencies, and he seemed able to rein in the vitriol and name-calling in favor of a reasoned debate. He invited members of each party with whom he had developed relationships and who could articulate their points with insight and concision.

Tonight's conversation was a discussion about the government's apparent slow-walking of a response to the terrorist attacks.

"Before we wrap, folks," he said, "I'd like each of you to give me—in one or two sentences—your opinion about what we need to do right now. Congressman Lyle, let's start with you."

Roger Lyle, one of the longest-serving members of the Senate and a fierce Democrat, said, "As much as it pains me to say it, Milt, I think we *should* close the borders. At least for now. After what happened in Texas? Yes. Close the borders for now."

Schick nodded and turned to the Republican house whip. "Congressman Martin Rumsicker?"

"First, I'm still processing what Roger just said," laughed Rumsicker. "And, of course, I agree wholeheartedly. But I think we need to go a step further and close all migrant entry."

"I think that's a bridge too far," said Senator Amanda Freer, Democrat from New York. "I could be persuaded to close the southern borders. But all migrations? No. That would hurt too many people, and it's bad optics. It shows us as scared rather than strong."

"But aren't we *already* scared?" asked Connie Ferguson, the Republican senator from Louisiana. "I know I'm scared. My constituents are scared. And the friends and families of everyone who has lost their lives in these attacks are scared. It's time we acted sensibly rather than sticking our heads in the sand and hoping for the best."

CHAPTER 85
TENTH LEGION TRAINING CAMP #18
PINE DEEP, PENNSYLVANIA
ONE MONTH AGO

They moved like machines.

Like wolves.

Like a plague.

Men and women running through intense movement prep and tactical drills. Bend and reach, around the world, squats, leg whips, windmills, balance and reach, push-ups of a dozen kinds, squat-reach-jump, dive and roll, buck and evade, twelve-mile runs, ruck intervals, grip-strength training, barbell-based strength training for performance and durability, chassis integrity for the midsection, low-back strength and strength endurance, loaded runs and carries, and dozens of others.

Never the same way twice and interspersed with surprise live-edge knife attack-and-defends and live-fire cross-field running.

Not all of the candidates survived it.

That was part of the training philosophy. Nothing inspires soldiers to go that extra mile, hoist the extra rep, or dance the jump rope in faster sets than seeing a fellow trainee fall into a bloody, ragged heap.

The camp commandant, Kurt Furman, had new recruits bury the

bodies of those who died in his drills. The morning run passed the cemetery on each lap. Nothing had to be said about it; the rows of crosses were eloquent in their silence.

None of the volunteers ever opted out and went home. That was not allowed in the agreement when they enlisted for the Legion. Join and fight. Quit and die. What more needed to be said?

And in the Gray House in the far corner of the camp, in the building the more seasoned recruits called the Monkey House—though never loud enough to be heard beyond their circle of friends—were the elite soldiers.

Forty-two huge men and eight towering women. Brutal, ugly, unnatural, and supremely powerful. Faster than the rest of the legionnaires. Easily twice as strong. Harder to hurt, harder still to kill. Men and women whose bodies could be seen to change day by day, moving further and further away from anything that fit the definition of *human*.

Sometimes a recruit who cheated on some of his drills or was caught dozing on watch would be given a set of brass knuckles and a sharp Ka-Bar and sent over to the Gray House. They were told to walk in the front door and walk out the back. If they did, they were allowed to rejoin their training unit.

After sixteen such events, only one soldier had regained his unit—and the respect of the whole camp. The others were in the cemetery, some shoveled into body bags.

Furman was pleased beyond words at how things were coming along.

There and in all of the other camps.

A war was coming, and he could not wait to lead his troops into battle.

CHAPTER 86
THE MANSION
UNDISCLOSED LOCATION

Mr. October stood looking at the text conversation on his cell.

The Mansion felt oddly large and empty around him.

He thought about the cell he had ordered built in the basement.

JONATHAN MABERRY

He thought about the tree outside where Mary had hung herself. He thought about many things.

Twilight was falling with unusual weight beyond the french windows. October went and built himself a tall gin rickey, a drink over which he had been obsessed a long time ago. Two ounces of very good gin, the juice of one lime, four ounces of club soda, and a lime wedge as a garnish. Yesteryear's drinks often soothed him, bringing him back to other, simpler times. Comfort food for the soul even for someone who had never been certain he *had* a soul.

A conscience, yes, though it lay dusty and disused for ages at a time. But a soul? That seemed oddly quaint. If he *did* have one, he mused, it must be tarnished and rust-eaten. Of little use to him in any of his aspects.

Yet now . . .

Sometimes you have to burn to shine.

That phrase belonged to Mother Night, not to Miss Mary. Not even, he thought, to the Typhoid Mary aspect his ward had been slowly constructing. Was that what Toombs saw today? The games of torture and murder? Sure, he understood that Mary was trying to slow down Havoc Team so the burn-lock would either kill them or cause them to fall too far behind the curve to be a threat. Like the business in Germany. Like the infected Marys released into businesses around the country.

The idea was to set the stage for the big event but to clear the audience of Church and his lot. Church and people like him. They were scurrying all over the world putting out fires whose flames were of no real consequence.

The event mattered.

So, what was the point of Mary leaving her message for Ledger?

Sometimes you have to burn to shine.

Was that her just being in the moment? Was it her simply being as mad as the moon? Was it a misjudgment, perhaps triggered by the brain damage she had suffered years ago in Atlanta or months ago in that noose?

Or was it something else?

Rebellion?

He did not want to think that was true. Or that it could be true.

"What are you doing, little girl?" he asked aloud. For maybe the thousandth time since he had brought her back to . . .

To what? Life?

No.

Unlife?

Probably accurate but far too corny, too pop-culture cliché.

Rebirth?

If so . . . as what?

October's life was uncountably long. Even he couldn't put a number to it. He could barely remember more than a dozen or so of the names he'd worn. Merlin, Elegga, Juha, Nicodemus, Baron Samedi, Anansi, Coyote, Renart the Fox, Flagg, Kappa, Mbeku, Yaw, Păcală, Cin-an-ev, Talihsin, Nanabozho. Most were forgotten.

Now he was October.

Until now, he had always been sure of his path. Chaos was his friend and his lover and his god.

Yet Mary seemed to *embody* chaos in a far more powerful way, a far purer way than he ever did. That angered him. But more than that, it saddened him.

And it truly terrified him.

He sat down and turned on the news, hoping to get lost in the outrage and panic. That sort of thing always calmed him and pleased him. He surfed from one channel to another. The politicians, political scientists, cultural anthropologists, and journalists who were being trotted out by every station were largely falling into alignment with his agenda.

He began to relax by slow degrees, even taking some amusement from how many of them supported total border closures, stop-and-search actions by police and Homeland, and other measures. What surprised him was how many of these people—including many leaning away from their normal political stances and humanitarian biases—were *not* among those his teams had bribed or coerced.

His phone rang, and he answered it and was both surprised and mildly disconcerted to hear Mary's voice.

"Are you *seeing* this?" she gushed. "The news? It's amazing."

"It'll spread even faster as the day goes on," October observed. "It's a win for us."

"Spread," she said, picking up his word. "You're right about that. It's like a disease spreading out of control."

"Yes," he said. "Like a disease."

"You have to burn to shine," she said. "And this is starting to burn really brightly. Can't wait for the full blaze."

"You mean Firefall?"

"Sure," she said with a laugh, then hung up.

October sat there, listening to the echo of that laugh in his head. He had not liked the sound of that one little bit.

AMERICA'S HAUNTED HOLIDAYLAND

PART 3

I do not fear death. I had been dead for billions and billions of years before I was born, and had not suffered the slightest inconvenience from it.

—MARK TWAIN

To the last, I grapple with thee; From Hell's heart, I stab at thee;
For hate's sake, I spit my last breath at thee.

—HERMAN MELVILLE

CHAPTER 87
FLIP'N'KICKS SKATE PARK
PENN YAN, NEW YORK

We pulled into the parking lot of a bankrupt skate park and handed Goofy off to waiting EMTs.

Bird Dog was there looking angry and scared. He pulled me roughly aside. "Tell me you put the sons of bitches who did this *down*."

I told him what I could of the events down in Gehenna. His face turned ashen, and he stood there, licking his lips. I could feel the intense waves of impotent rage he felt. He wanted blood for blood, but this was war, and that kind of cosmic scale-balancing wasn't always available.

"Tell you what, though," I said. "We're not leaving this alone. The Big Man and the whole team at the TOC are working on it. I'm keeping Havoc here in the States until we can start putting heads on pikes, you have my word on that, brother."

He nodded and blinked away some tears. Then he straightened and gave me an iron-hard look. "You need anything for that hunt, Joe, you call me first. No matter what you need, I'll get it for you, and that's not me blowing smoke. You call, I'll come running."

We shook hands, and I watched him climb into the back of the ambulance. Havoc stood together, watching it race away, lights flashing and sirens wailing like outraged banshees.

"Let's get out of here," I said.

We climbed back into our SUV and drove to the airport.

CHAPTER 88
TENTH LEGION TRAINING CAMP #18
PINE DEEP, PENNSYLVANIA
TWO MONTHS AGO

Mr. Toombs walked with Kurt Furman, the commandant of the Legion training facility.

Toombs was a patient man and made no protests or complaints when Furman had his troops fall in in full combat kit for a formal inspection.

Toombs had never served in the military and was not actually a fan of military rituals. He disliked being saluted to and was no kind of flag waver. His career had been about selling weapons and equipment to anyone with a big enough bankbook. But Furman was bursting with pride. He had a little boy's face on a body that clearly wanted to drift toward corpulence but which was held in check with brutal self-control. Even so, there was a softness about the man, and Toombs did not have to stretch far to connect that with his love of guns, uniforms, and the appearance of being a warrior.

Toombs stifled his yawns as vigorously as he did his sardonic smiles.

It was no different with Furman from how it was with a lot of militant types. He doubted any of them were earnest in their political or patriotic beliefs. More likely, they were addicted to the power borrowed from weapons and armies and the demonstrations of power.

The real fighters he'd met—whether military, private contract, religious fighter, or gangbanger—seldom needed to brag. Oh, they'd front one another and do all the big-dick-energy stuff, but as a schtick to impress the yokels. Privately, they were content in their power, and that made them both more dangerous and more reliable.

Furman was not that kind of man.

But he was the face of the Tenth Legion. Furman, and similar men and women who ran the other camps. The real fighters were the ones who went into the field, who ran operations, who took the lives of people who could shoot back. And it wasn't that Toombs idolized the genuine killers—it's just that he understood them. They were easier to work with because their confidence informed their business negotiations. They didn't need ego strokes, as Furman did.

"Very impressive," lied Toombs. "Very *damn* impressive. Tight."

The militia fighters stood like statues, jaws set, chests puffed, shoulders back, eyes looking through the walls of the world into nothing.

"Very tight."

Furman nodded to a sergeant, who had the entire group of two hundred soldiers turn like gears in a machine. Heels ground and stamped. Then the sergeant growled for a salute, and every hand moved in perfect synchronization. It was not the standard military salute but something Toombs was sure had been cribbed from an old gladiator movie. The soldiers' hands chopped toward their own chests and then shot out straight. As one, they yelled, "*Moritūrī tē salūtāmus!*"

We who are about to die, salute you.

Toombs nearly sprained his mouth keeping his expression neutral. The fake arm salute that started out as some faux Roman thing and ended with a gesture suspiciously Hitlerian was as comical as it was dangerous. But that catchphrase was downright absurd.

They're saying they are going to die. One of the many, *many* catchphrases used by political groups around the world, where it likely sounded good over too many shots of bad whiskey but sent entirely the wrong message.

Suck it up, he told himself. *The dumber and angrier they are, the more product they buy.*

"You should be proud of yourself, Commandant," he said in a voice so convincing he amazed himself.

"The Tenth Legion is the real deal, Mr. Toombs," said Furman, pitching his tone loud enough for some of his sergeants to hear. "There isn't a finer fighting force anywhere under God's green earth."

Toombs gave him a brief reappraising glance and wondered if Furman was a true believer after all. In a certain version of God, at least. That wouldn't be too strange among militia types here and abroad. He decided to ask October about it. The boss had a real knack for knowing what went on in both hearts and minds.

Toombs also wondered what Furman actually knew of the organizational structure in which they were both cogs. The Tenth Legion was owned and financed by Mr. October. That much was something all of the commandants in the Legion understood. Furman believed that Toombs worked for Kuga and not for October. The official cover was that Toombs was the field sales guy for Kuga International, which was publicly a legitimate dealer in weapons and technology.

What Furman did not know was that October *was* Kuga and that Toombs worked for the man who ran it all. The deception was part of October's fetish for compartmentalization, keeping walls between need-to-know people inside and outside of his organization.

October held a different position in Furman's eyes. Furman knew that October was the CEO of Tenth Legion. He believed that it was created to correct the downhill course America was taking. Furman believed the lie that the Legion was based in South Africa for—as October explained it—tax reasons; and because certain old-timers in South African power circles still longed for the good old days of apartheid. But the real goal of the Legion was to make that course correction by any means necessary. Reduce the numbers and influence by people who were not part of the ideal America. Black, brown, red, and yellow were all variations of pollution in terms of the gene pool as Furman saw it. October reinforced that, despite having Miss Mary with him on his own visits. Employees of white people were fine, but never the other way around.

October gave Furman a lot of speeches about how the nation needed to be saved from itself and that such a process could only be accomplished by cutting ties and involvements with other countries. America first and America alone. With that, October also gave speeches about how the process of repairing America was going to be both painful and bloody. But necessary.

That was the con.

It was a convincing one, because October had the master con man's knack for inspiring great confidence. He was knowledgeable and plausible, and he said exactly what people like Furman wanted— *needed*—to hear. It was how October sold Furman—and the commandants of the other Tenth Legion camps—to follow his dream.

Toombs did not like or trust Mary, but he did like his boss. October was a weirdo, but he was, as far as Toombs could tell, genuinely apolitical. For all his nationalistic speeches and shared racist jokes with Furman, October was really a businessman who convinced his customers they needed what he had to sell. It was working so well that October's big dramatic finale to this particular con—code-named Firefall—was going to go off in a few weeks, and then there would be a riot to buy more guns. More, more, more.

"Now," he said to Furman, "how 'bout we head back to your office and discuss the next shipment? I've got some new stuff in my catalog and want *you* to be the *first* to see it."

Furman grinned like a happy child.

CHAPTER 89
OVER NEW YORK AIRSPACE

Once we were aboard Shirley, we all retired to different bench seats that had MindReader workstations attached to swivel trays. I ordered everyone to draft preliminary after-action reports while the details were all sharp in our minds.

I didn't immediately do mine, however. With Ghost in tow, I went aft and snugged into the privacy pod. It's really made for one person, but the big fur monster always saw it more as a chance for snuggles and scratches. That was fine. Petting his shaggy white head always had a soothing effect on my nerves. Maybe on my soul, too. Dogs are like that.

For the record, I love my dog more than I love most people. In fact, it's hard for me to make any lifeboat list that doesn't include me pushing Ghost in first. I have never once encountered a mean dog that was not mistreated by people. He sat on the floor between my knees and laid his head on my thigh and looked up at me with those large, liquid eyes. Eyes filled with unconditional love, acceptance, forgiveness, and tolerance. I'd brought a Ziploc bag of dried goat treats with me to the pod and spent a few moments breaking off little pieces and marveling at how gently he took each one. His bushy tail went *thump-thump-thump* against the paneled wall.

I debated whether to call Junie, but instead called Rudy.

"Outlaw . . . ?" he answered.

"Scrambler's on, Rude," I said. "Is yours?"

"Oops . . . wait. *Mierda.*" I heard a triple click. "It's on. Joe . . . I was in the TOC."

"Then you know."

"Yes. It looked like an awful experience. How are you?"

Rudy doesn't deal in platitudes or deflection. We met when he was my therapist. Mine and Helen's. After I was no longer officially his patient, we became friends. But given the haunted house that is my head, I've been on his couch more than once. Maybe two million times? Feels like that. We can be goofy, baseball-fanatic, beer-swilling best buds, but when I need him to be *Dr.* Sanchez, he shifts at once. I make a similar shift to be an interactive and responsive client. There's no code between us for that. He knows. Rudy always knows.

"It was bad," I said.

"What is hitting you the hardest right now?"

"The pointless cruelty is always a challenge," I said.

"But you knew going in that the staff may have been killed," he said, gently steering the conversation.

"Yeah. And I've been to enough crime scenes and on enough battlefields to have seen the full fucking range of person-to-person atrocity. I've actually *seen* worse."

"Do you know why today's experience triggered you more than others?"

"You know why."

"I wasn't the one in that place, Joe."

"Yeah, yeah," I said. "It felt too . . . familiar. The booby traps, hacking the Vault, the random violence—anarchistic rather than strategic. The Berserkers. And what that one said."

"'She wanted me to tell you,'" quoted Rudy, "'that sometimes you have to burn to shine.'"

"Yeah."

"Key word *she*," observed Rudy.

"Yeah."

"You do know that Artemisia Bliss is dead," he said. "You killed her."

"I know."

"So what can you infer from what that Berserker said?"

"That's just it, Rude. It's her words. She used Berserkers. Gehenna stored all the different versions of *seif al din*. That's a lot of coincidence to simply dismiss. If I hadn't shot her back then in Atlanta, man, I'd swear this was her. But I saw them zip what was left of her into a body bag. She was dead as fuck."

"For what it's worth, Joe, I saw her body before it was processed and sent to cold storage in Site 44. I agree, she was completely dead. No brain activity, no respiration or circulation. Her skull was shattered, her back broken, and one of your bullets was lodged in her heart."

"Okay, so explain what that Berserker said."

"Joe, take a moment here. You were a police detective before joining the DMS. You are the senior field agent and case manager for RTI. What does your logical mind tell you?"

The "logical mind" was Rudy's shorthand for the Cop aspect of my personality. I understood that he was gently nudging me away from my bloodthirsty Killer and the panic-stricken Modern Man aspects.

"I wish I could see the body," I said. "And, between you and me, brother, I find it mighty damn suspicious that Site 44 was compromised in a way that triggered burn-lock. Even if we could somehow excavate that place, all we'd have as evidence of what was there and what might *not* be there would be ashes."

"Hypothesize on that," suggested Rudy.

I laughed. "Sure. The Cop in my head has investigated enough con games to know all the variations of a bait and switch. The most logical inference is that someone who knew Bliss and maybe worked with her on the Code Zero case—someone who was never on our radar at all, a lieutenant, ally, whatever—knows what happened to her. Someone deep enough in her confidence to know about the Department of Military Sciences and maybe RTI. Someone who knows about me. They tried and failed to retrieve Bliss's corpse from Site 44, perhaps to harvest the *seif al din* directly from the source. It's a prion disease, after all. It wouldn't have died with her. So maybe they wanted to harvest it. They either stole her body, which explains the Berserkers we met today who still had functional minds, or they destroyed Site 44 to create doubt. Then they went after Gehenna to get *all* of the *seif al din* variants to continue Bliss's work."

"But . . . ?"

"But that doesn't explain how the Berserkers were already infected."

"And what inference do you draw from that?"

"That's just it," I said. "As far as we know, there were no other infected people who had access to that variant."

"As far as we know," said Rudy. "Answer this, then. Was the perceptible intelligence level of the Berserker commensurate with Bliss's when you confronted her at the Marriott in Atlanta?"

"No," I said after some thought. "The ones today were brutal, savage, and simplified."

"An earlier variant of the bioweapon?" he asked.

"Probably."

"If Bliss were somehow alive, wouldn't anyone she infects have the same variant?"

"Yeah. Damn it."

We sat with that for a moment.

"That doesn't prove it either way," I said at last. "There could have been samples of earlier variants at Site 44 or Inferno. Variants advanced enough to allow the infected to retain some cognitive function. Which puts us back to square one."

"Sadly, I agree," said Rudy. "Tell you what, though . . . I'm going to ask Church and Doc Holliday to have another ORB call with you once you're at the safe house."

"Why not now?"

"It's my understanding they are rewatching the video from Gehenna. The full team. All of Doc's senior staff, with Bug's people helping isolate bits of the video to try to enhance for clarity. And . . . they're doing some necessary follow-up to what happened to Major Mun and her team."

"Okay, that makes sense," I said. "Try to set it up for today. If not, then first damn thing in the morning."

"I will insist," said Rudy. He paused. "Is there anything else you feel you want to talk about?"

Like Top, Rudy was always on high alert for the return of the Darkness.

I said, "If you have some updates on how the Orioles are doing, that would work."

Rudy, being Rudy, was prepared. "Do you really want to know what the Orioles did this afternoon?"

"Will it make me even a little happy?"

"They made a nice double play in the fourth inning."

"And . . . ?"

"It was a very nice play," he said.

"Ah," I said. "Don't tell me how it ended. I want to clutch the last shreds of my optimism for a little longer."

It was said as a joke, but it wasn't really very funny.

CHAPTER 90
THE MANSION
UNDISCLOSED LOCATION
ONE WEEK AGO

"You want the good news or the bad news?" asked Toombs from the doorway.

October lowered his newspaper and looked up. Most of a large breakfast was scattered around him. He was on his third cup of coffee and tenth newspaper.

"That's not a very fun way to start a conversation," he said.

Toombs came in and sat to his right. October set down the paper and poured his sales manager a steaming cup of coffee.

"It lays out like this," said Toombs. "Miss Mary has cracked four of the Gorgon rockets. Apparently, each master chip is a little different. A unique code tag or something like that. She tried to explain it, but I don't speak code monkey. Point is, she has to keep writing a new software patch for each. We have fifty. Firefall's in three weeks. At the rate she's going, we'll have *maybe* twenty by Firefall. That's three weeks from now."

"The four that she's already cracked, have the payloads been swapped out?"

"That's a slow process, too. Mary tells me that she's working as fast as she can. She says that the new MERS payloads will be ready on those four by the day after tomorrow."

October pursed his lips and stared at nothing for a moment. "Well," he said at last, "that's disappointing."

"My point, boss," said Toombs, "is that we may have to take a closer look at the Firefall timetable. Fifty Gorgons in three weeks is simply not going to happen. Twenty may even be a stretch."

October sipped his coffee. "Let me think about it," he said. "No schedule is ever set completely in stone."

We were wheels down at an airport north of Philly in no time. Bird Dog had called ahead and had one of his team secure an SUV for us, saving us the trouble of renting one. Then we drove to a safe house RTI shared with Arklight.

It was in the northeast part of the city, a detached house that did a creditable job pretending pretty effectively to be a nice, ordinary little three-bedroom place. There was absolutely nothing remarkable about it from the outside, which is pretty much the point. Two stories with an attached garage, attic, basement, and yard.

The good stuff was in the construction. There were steel panels in all the walls, the wood on the door was a veneer over more steel, and the basement had a smaller level below it made into a kind of bunker. In an emergency and if the house were actually breached, then the occupants could hide in the bunker, and it would take a whole lot to even find the trapdoor that led downstairs.

The guy running the safe house was a lean man with a poet's ascetic face. His name was Noah Fallon—call sign Gandalf—and once upon a time, he ran with Echo Team. Not long, though. The massacre in Atlanta when Mother Night released *seif al din* burned him out, and he switched to a training gig instead. He stayed with the DMS up until Church folded it, and transferred to RTI, but again requested a noncombat job. Since then, he had worked in a series of safe houses for us, but this was the first time I'd seen him in ages.

He gave me a warm but wary smile, and we shook hands. He gave Top and Bunny hugs. He shook hands with Belle and Remy, then knelt with Ghost and ran his fingers through my dog's thick white fur.

"Everything's ready for you guys," he said, rising. "Kitchen's stocked, there are three full baths, plenty of towels and whatever."

"Thanks, brother," said Bunny. "Good to see you."

Noah nodded. "Good to see you all looking well."

"How hard you looking?" said Remy under his breath.

"I got the briefing," said Noah. "I know enough. And last I heard, Goofy was in surgery and the docs were optimistic."

"Thank god."

Noah nodded. "You're Havoc's new gadgets guy, right?"

"Yeah, I guess," said Remy.

"Lucky you," said Noah. "When I ran with Echo Team, we didn't have all of the new stuff. Anteaters, drones of all kinds. The Toy Box, right? That's what they're calling it? We could have used some of that."

Remy shrugged. "Yeah, but you got through it without those toys. You must be a tough monkey."

"I prefer the quiet life."

To me, Noah said, "The Big Man wants an ORB catch-up call at 0800 tomorrow. He wants everyone to get chow and rack time. I've got a vat of pasta and a big pot of spicy meatballs going. Fresh sourdough in the oven. Everything'll be ready when you are."

We thanked him and headed upstairs. Belle took the room at the end of a hall. The four of us guys played rock-paper-scissors for who got first showers. Top and I lost, and we sat on one of the beds while the others sudsed and rinsed.

"You have any thoughts about that shit show back there?" asked Top as he unlaced his shoes and pulled off his socks.

"Which damn part? The killings? The booby traps? The zombies? Attack helicopters? Or what that Berserker said?"

He gave one of those smiles that looked like a wince. "All of it. But . . . yeah, that last part. Burn to shine? Are you shitting me?"

"Don't ask me, Top," I said. "Like I told Rudy last night, I killed that witch in Atlanta."

"So, what's all this, then? The Berserkers started a tribute band?"

I gave a rueful snort of a laugh. "Fuck if I know. We started out to spank some Tenth Legionnaires. Now this."

He studied my face. "This is me, Colonel. We been through this together from the jump. *Seif al din?* Berserkers and burn to shine? You can't tell me you don't see the connective tissue."

"I do, but dead is dead."

"Since when? No, serious question. Those zombie motherfuckers aren't dead by the rule book I read growing up. As I recall, you got hired by the Big Man after you killed the same terrorist twice in one week. Killed him dead the first time, and it didn't take."

"I parked two center mass, and she fell thirty stories."

"Uh-huh. But you didn't pop a cap in her head."

"So, what are you suggesting? That she's running this from whatever bucket they poured her into?"

"No, I'm saying science as we once knew it has gone way off the reservation. Think of everything we've faced, and I do mean *everything*. Those zombies are science, not fiction. The Berserkers are real enough. Ape men super soldiers? Seriously? You fought El Mujahid after he was infected. He was dead as fuck by every medical and legal definition, but he damn near had you for lunch. He's dead because you cut his head off. And you found Amirah after she'd been half blown up when Toys and Gault sabotaged her lab, and you *still* had to put one in her brain pan." He shook his head.

He was right. Of course he was right. What's more, I knew it on a deep level but did not want to face even the possibility of it. I think maybe Rudy was on the same page, too.

"Bliss was a gamer girl," I said, pausing by the dresser and leaning back against it. "Everything today was a game. The obvious tricks, the stage dressing, the real traps, accessing Gehenna. Bliss cocreated VaultBreaker, and if she's alive—or alive-ish—whatever we're supposed to call it—then she's had time to rewrite the software. Update it."

"Sure, but not completely," said Top. "Think about her target choices. She's been hitting the older sites, the ones whose security was mostly built on VaultBreaker but are aging out."

"Which makes them soft targets for her," I said.

We stared at each other.

"Well . . . fuck me blind and move the furniture," he said.

"And the choppers?" I said. "You thinking Tenth Legion?"

"Why not?" said Top. "They'd be useful muscle for hire. They don't like us worth a damn." He paused and gave me a crooked smile. "If any of this is even remotely possible, then Bliss and the Legion make for interesting bedfellows."

I went over and sat down next to where Ghost was sprawled and began slowly stroking his back. "Y'know, Top, I kind of think this is the main reason the boss wants an ORB session in the morning. They have to be following the same path of logic."

He nodded. "That'd be my guess."

Bunny came out of the bathroom with a towel wrapped around him, looking like a freshly washed Titan from Greek mythology. He really does have too many damned muscles.

"Shower's free," he said, "but you might want to give it a minute before you go in there. I had my own version of a toxic spill."

Top got up and walked to the bathroom door and leaned in, then recoiled. "Fuck me up, down, and sideways, farm boy. What the hell did you *eat*, and how sick was it before it died?"

"Yeah, well, I've followed you into the shitter more than once, old man. You don't crap wild roses and lilacs."

"When I take a dump, it doesn't contravene standing international chemical and biological weapons treaties acts."

I snuck out and went down to the other bathroom and waited for Remy to finish. There was almost no chance in hell he had polluted our shared bathroom as comprehensively as Bunny had.

I could still hear Top and Bunny yelling at each other.

CHAPTER 92
THE MANSION
UNDISCLOSED LOCATION
TWO DAYS AGO

"I was right," said Toombs as he and October sat with glasses of whiskey. "We have only four Gorgons ready and no real idea when the next ones will be ready."

Miss Mary was sprawled like a corpse on a stuffed chair, her legs over one arm, her head thrown back over the other. She was chewing gum deliberately loud.

"Is that the case, my dear?" asked October.

"If Lurch says it's so, then it's so," she said.

October considered. "We did discuss a contingency plan a while back, if you both remember."

"Which?" asked Mary without much genuine interest. "You always have fifty plans."

"The limited-release scenario," said October. "If we don't have the full complement of Gorgons, then we go with what we do have."

"And make a little tiny splash?"

"I see it more as throwing gasoline on a fire, sweet girl."

"Meaning?" asked Toombs.

"The Typhoid Mary project is coming along so nicely. People are already throwing stones at anyone who doesn't look or believe like them. All of the people on our payroll who need to be making speeches in Congress or reporting the news are slanting things in the direction of extreme nationalism. Toombs, you know what this is doing for our gun sales and for bulk purchases by corporations with factories in third-world countries. If you want to shake off your ennui, Mary dear, go look at our bank statements."

"But Gorgon on a small scale helps us how?" she asked.

"Once we do the thing down at the Texas border, sweetie, I'm thinking the simmering melting pot that is America will come to a boil. And let's face it—no one does righteous indignation better than the citizens of this great country. The irony of their outrage against immigrants while living on lands they stole *as* immigrants is hilarious."

"No speeches, please," said Mary between pops of her gum.

"No. Not a speech. Establishing context for a *possible* modification to the Firefall timetable. Four Gorgons filled with a disease from the Middle East deployed in one or two key locations will—I believe—bring us to the brink of a civil war."

"You actually *want* a war?" Mary asked.

October shrugged. "War or no war, I want people preparing to fight. We're not selling victory, sweetie, we're selling conflict."

Toombs sipped his whiskey as he got up and crossed to the french doors to look out at the mist crawling across the lawn.

"For the record," he said, "I'm okay with reducing the number of Gorgons we use, but I don't like messing with the timetable. The Tenth Legion guys are pretty well trained, but they've been pushing at the limits of our control. I particularly don't trust the biker gangs associated with official camps—like the ones in Arizona, Pennsylvania, and Central California. They're more outlaw bikers than well-regulated soldiers when it comes to following orders."

"Objection noted," said October.

"But if we do go with four Gorgons . . . where will they be deployed? Before you answer, we need to use those camps we trust the most."

"Furman's a loyal doggie," said Mary. "I was going to give him some SDs to play with."

"And what exactly are these SDs you keep bragging about?"

Mary just laughed and did not answer.

October finished his drink and poured another. "Let me look at the calendar of events. Where the Gorgons go will depend on which venues will give us our best bang for the buck."

"Okay, but where are you leaning?" asked Toombs. "Four targets with one Gorgon each, two for two, or all four at some big event?"

"Each has its pros and cons," conceded October. "Let me give it some thought."

CHAPTER 93

TENTH LEGION TRAINING CAMP #18
PINE DEEP, PENNSYLVANIA
SIX DAYS AGO

"They're ready to unload, sir," said a corporal after snapping off a Roman salute.

Commandant Furman looked up from the papers spread over his desk. He had joined Tenth Legion to fight against the globalists and blood traitors and Marxist scum. He prayed every night for God to give him continued strength and clarity of vision to see his holy purpose through to victory.

But the paperwork? The budget reports? He was sure they were the devil's work.

Unfortunately, Mr. October was adamant about it. Every *i* dotted, every *t* crossed. From an objective distance, Furman understood this policy. After all, no one ever wanted things to come crashing down because some asshole at the IRS saw a decimal out of place.

Tax irregularities were one of the things that tore down the old Blue Diamond group, and Mr. October was a stickler for precision with Tenth Legion.

He stood and stretched, then peered out the window.

The truck that had just arrived was carrying tractor parts, and if anyone dug around to determine why a paramilitary group needed farm equipment, there was an entire division of the Legion put in place to work with struggling American farmers—granted, only *white* farmers—who wanted to survive despite the villainy of large agricultural corporations, the FDA, and the Department of Agriculture. Americans helping Americans. It sold well, too. So, any official inspection of the contents would show that this was all part of the Legion's Patriot Families Project. Other shipments of different kinds of products were purchased by the American Church Alliance.

Bottom line—any scrutiny of the bills of lading, shipping manifests, and purchase orders were neat and tidy. The real cargo was hidden inside the tractor parts. Painted to match colors, shapes altered with modeling plastics that could be snapped or melted off. With some items hidden in cavities specially cut into the tractor engines, then sealed inside. The skills used to hide the cargo was on par with the weapons he was expecting.

"Very well," said Furman, closing his ledger and clicking his pen. "Is Mr. Toombs here yet?"

"He's out in the yard overseeing the unloading."

"Tell him I'll be there right away."

"Sir," said the corporal. He snapped a salute and left.

Furman went over to the mirror on the wall, studied his reflection, made a few adjustments to the hang of his uniform. Today's rig was a personal favorite, modeled after the Russian Special Forces Gorka-5 combat tactical uniform in a green-dominated camo pattern. He thought it made him look taller than his five foot six.

Smiling, he went out to see what kind of goodies Mr. Toombs had sent.

Commandant Furman was a well-pleased man and, as he saw it, all was right in God's favorite country.

JONATHAN MABERRY

CHAPTER 94

ROUTE 78
NEAR BETHEL, PENNSYLVANIA

"Where do you think they're taking the kids?" asked Tommy. She was driving, and Violin sat beside her, moody and mostly silent.

"You heard what I heard," said Violin.

"I heard something about a comfort camp."

"Yes."

"Which is what, exactly?"

Violin looked surprised. "You don't know?"

"If I do, then I don't know what it is under that name. Is it a rest stop somewhere?"

"No. A comfort station is where men—well, mostly men—have a chance to take their own kind of R & R."

"Meaning?"

"Remember what Hamas did to the Israeli women they captured?"

"Yes," said Tommy, wincing.

"And what ISIS did after abducting women and girls? The systematic rape and acts of sexual violence against Yezidi women and girls in northern Iraq?"

Tommy paled and nearly drove into a drainage ditch alongside the road they were driving. She corrected quickly. "You think that's why they took these kids?"

"Yes."

"And they call it a *comfort* camp?"

"Yes."

A number of miles passed before Tommy could speak.

"I'm going to kill those goddamn sons of bitches."

"Yes," said Violin.

Ahead, the target vehicles pulled into a cheap motel of the kind that is an outside row of one-story boxes with doors opening into a weedy parking lot. Tommy switched off the headlights and pulled over beneath a leafy oak.

"What are they doing?"

They watched as all the kids were led into the end unit, with a female legionnaire with them. One man sat outside on a desk chair he removed from the room. The other men went into the next two units.

"We have to do something," cried Tommy. "This must be the camp."

"No," said Violin. "I've seen this before. They're keeping the kids under female guard because they want them *pure* once they're delivered."

"Pure?"

"Untouched," said Violin.

Tommy actually growled.

"This tells me the kids are meant for special clients. Maybe Legion officers higher up the food chain. I think they'll actually be safe tonight. Most likely be made to shower and dress a certain way in the morning before they're taken to the actual camp."

"How sure are you?" demanded Tommy.

"Sure enough that I think we need to wait," said Violin. "Patience is going to give us a shot at more important targets."

"Even though we can rescue them now?"

"Rescuing them now saves these kids, yes. But it doesn't stop the process. And if we act too soon, then we interrupt the process. We'll sleep in shifts and be ready first thing. What we *can* do tonight is to sneak over there and put an earwig on the exterior wall of that end unit."

An earwig was a special listening device whose mic was powerful enough to hear through the stucco and drywall of an average home. The motel walls were cheap.

"I'll do it," said Tommy, but she said it too quickly. Violin smiled at her in the dark.

"No, sweetie," she said. "I will."

She dug the earwigs out of a bag, opened the door, and vanished into the dense shadows.

JONATHAN MABERRY

CHAPTER 95

Morning dawned clear and cool.

Noah had a mouthwatering breakfast for us—a mountain of scrambled eggs, crisp bacon, plump ham-and-apple sausages, steaming potatoes that had been pan-fried with peppers and onions, and a vat of coffee.

We ate like hungry wolves. Remy, by far the slimmest of the men, astonished us by the sheer volume of food he could stuff into his lean body. Belle, who pecked at her meal, stared at him with amusement and made what was for her a rare joke.

"I want to see you rappel *up* a line after all that."

"I'm a growing boy," he said. "Though what I really want for dessert is a plate of beignets covered in powdered sugar and some chicory in my coffee. No offense, Noah."

"None taken," said our host. "I've passed a lot of quiet mornings at Café du Monde, too."

They chatted about New Orleans for a bit, lapsing into a debate over whether jazz or blues was the true sound of that city. Top interrupted it, though, by tapping his wristwatch.

We rose and went down into the basement and waited while Noah did a bit of stage magic to cause a section of the floor to drop down six inches and then slide out of the way to reveal a short set of metal stairs.

"Very James Bond," said Bunny. "I dig it."

"The floor's got some kind of special wiring in it," explained Noah. "Like a Faraday cage. Once the door's closed, there's no way to detect any electronics from the ORB."

"How's the signal get in and out, then?" asked Remy.

"There's a fiber-optic hardline running through the foundation and then out in a fake water line. Goes to a tower down the street with satellite uplink. Perfect signal that nobody's going to even know how to find."

"Sweet."

Before we went down, Noah nodded to the various stacks of boxes arranged with deliberate casualness around the basement. Some were marked *Christmas Decorations*, others with *Games* and *Jimmy's Toys*. Even had a light layer of dust on them.

"Boxes are legit—or at least they'll look legit," said Noah. "Actual plastic wreaths, tree lights, board games, and stuff like that. Even found a working PS5 here and games—*Star Wars: Battlefront*, *Baldur's Gate 3* . . . ? If you're into that for downtime."

"Where's the armory?" asked Top.

"You just walked down it," said Noah. "Every step on the stairs is a locker. You activate the locks by pressing fingers under the left-hand lip of the stair. I uploaded your fingerprints already." He glanced at me. "After what happened to the safe house in Jerusalem, Scott Wilson ordered all safe houses to get an immediate upgrade. We have bird drones in every tree and telephone pole for three blocks in any direction. Nothing can get close without us knowing in good time."

"Hoo-goddamn-ah," said Bunny. He and Top shared a fist bump. Belle nodded her approval.

In my ear, I heard Scott Wilson say, "When you and your team are *quite* ready."

"On our way," I said, resisting the urge to give him the finger. I might have done it, but we were in civvies and not wearing body cams. Bunny scratched his balls in a significant way, though.

We went down into the ORB.

CHAPTER 96
THE ORB
JOINT-USE RTI-ARKLIGHT SAFE HOUSE

The basement lights dimmed, and immediately two hundred tiny lights ignited from discreet locations throughout the room. The ORB ignited, and Havoc Team was suddenly seated on one side of a large conference table that was so vivid we could see the wood grain and even a few stray cookie crumbs.

Across from us were Doc Holliday, Bug, and Scott Wilson. Church sat at the head of the table with a glass of water and a plate of vanilla wafers close at hand. Plates of other kinds of cookies—Oreos, animal crackers, and butter pecan—were closer to the others. Doc and Scott both had tea, and Bug had a tall Yeti travel mug that was almost certainly filled with his heart-damaging mix of Red Bull and espresso.

Ghost wagged his tail at everyone, but as he was in the center of the basement room, all anyone could see was his tail whipping back and forth through the wood of the table. I snapped my fingers twice, and he stopped wagging and lay down.

Church launched right in. "The survivors of Bedlam Team have been medevacked to St. Carolus Krankenhaus in Görlitz."

"How bad is it?"

"We lost one," said Church. "Felix Howard—Smoker—was KIA. Major Mun is in serious condition but is expected to make a complete recovery. George Yazzie—Mountain Man—is in stable condition. All of the others were treated and released. Staff Sergeant Amy Neal—Pond—is responsible for saving the lives of Mun and Yazzie, and she helped Bedlam Team get to safety."

"Pond's a damn hero," said Top.

"She is," agreed Church. "She will take temporary command of Bedlam for the foreseeable future."

"What do we know about the explosion?" I asked.

"It was incredibly intense, and so far, arson and bomb squad investigators have found only fragments of the device. Initial observation suggests that it is an improvised device rather than military. Chemical analysis shows that the C-4 used was part of a large batch stolen from the Miesau Army Ammunition Depot in Germany four years ago."

"Any ties to Kuga in that theft?" I asked.

"Suspected at the time, though not confirmed," said Wilson. "Call it likely."

"Okay," I said. "Gehenna. Top has a theory, and I think he's right."

I gestured to Top, who laid it out. I saw heads nodding before he was even a third of the way in.

"I'm afraid you may be correct, Top," said Church. "It corresponds with our own thinking and fits the facts as we know them."

Just saying that gave us all a moment of pause.

"Whoa, wait," said Bunny. "Are we saying that this is someone copycatting Bliss or that it *is* Bliss?"

"We have to be open to both options," said Church, but even though I couldn't see his eyes well through the tinted glasses, I could read him.

"So this *is* Artemisia Bliss?" asked Bunny. "I mean, we're all landing on that? Somehow somebody got into Site 44 and carted her off and did some kind of zombie CPR. Is that where we are?"

"Whether it's Bliss or someone on her level who has a similar agenda and identical skills is to be determined," said Church.

Bunny shook his head. "But you think it's *actually* Bliss?"

Church nodded gravely. "I do."

"Christ."

"And Top's theory for why Site 44 was destroyed holds water," added Church. "It also leaves us with no chance to prove it either way."

"That is the scariest thing I think I've ever heard," said Bug.

"Do we know who took her?" asked Belle. "Who . . . freed her? Who did whatever they did to bring her back?"

"Willing to bet my Christmas bonus that it's this Mr. October character," I said. "The hit on Gehenna was, at least in part, done with military precision. The sophistication of the booby traps Remy found was military. Advanced military. And those helos were military surplus. That sounds like Tenth Legion to me, and Mr. October owns Tenth Legion."

"Why would a bunch of PMCs want a zombie?" asked Remy.

"They didn't," said Bug, and we all turned to him. "Well, think about it, guys. They wanted a live, top-of-the-line computer expert. And not just for the vaults. When Toys was in Toronto, he bought Gorgons from an agent of October's, right? Well, if you guys remember, the Gorgons had those master chips in them that prevented tampering with the payloads. Buyers had to buy whatever payload Aydelotte was selling. Now, stir someone with Bliss's skill set into the mix. Marco Russo is pretty sharp, but Bliss is next level. October would need someone like her to crack that master chip. This would accomplish two things—the first is the payload. But the second is more important—once the master chip is disabled, the Gorgons can be disassembled without blowing up. That would allow October or Kuga or whoever to build more of them."

"How long would that process take?" I asked. "I mean, if they obtained Gorgons after we took down Aydelotte?"

Bug thought about it. "To reverse engineer something made with original parts? Nothing in that Gorgon is off the rack. So . . . figure one to two years for analysis, obtaining the right kind of materials, retooling a factory to make parts. It's not a fast process."

We thought about that for a moment.

"Does this mean that the Gorgons October somehow obtained from Aydelotte before or after his death are unable to be modified?" I asked.

"Without Bliss or someone like her?" mused Bug. "Yes. *With* her, cracking the master chip would only allow them to modify the contents of the warheads."

"Filling them with what?" asked Remy bleakly. "*Seif al din?*"

"I don't think so," said Church. "October is a businessman. And if he is, as we suspect, also Kuga, then there is no value in launching a doomsday weapon."

"Agreed," said Doc. "If that's what he wanted, then those hits in Atlanta, Montgomery, and so on would have been easier targets. No, I think our Big Bad wants to stir the political pot and then sell weapons to everyone who hates the other side."

"That's a lot of people," said Bunny.

"It's a lot of guns," said Top.

Church nodded. "There's money in this, without a doubt."

"Which means Kuga's back in operation, and this is the fall catalog," I said.

No one disputed that.

"And the Berserkers?" asked Bunny. "They up for sale, too? I ask, because if they're planning on turning whole camps of trained PMCs into those King Kong sons of bitches, I want a ticket back to Orange County."

"Hooah," said Remy.

Doc said, "There were Berserker corpses at Site 44, and that site also had copies of the Jakoby family genetic research and chemical-therapy formulae needed to create new Berserkers. That process of transforming a subject into one of those creatures takes quite a long time. At least six months, then there needs to be additional training for the subject to learn how to deal with the extra physical mass, muscular changes, increased bone density, balance, and coordination. If the Berserkers Havoc encountered at Gehenna were *not* revived corpses from Atlanta, then they're part of a new generation."

"Which means we can't know how many legionnaires have received that kind of treatment," I said. "Fun times."

"Really," said Bunny, "just a one-way ticket back to SoCal. I'll even fly coach."

"From where I'm sitting," I said, "I think we can stop guessing as to whether this is a dozen different cases or one. Tenth Legion is October, and October is almost certainly Kuga. The hits on the sites is PMC, which is Tenth Legion, which is Kuga. Tenth Legion hit us in Israel nine months ago and hit us again yesterday. I could go on."

"If all that's true," said Bunny, "and all this shit's Kuga making some big kind of play, then what's the actual game? Can it really be all about selling guns?"

"Arms are a very big business," said Wilson, who had been silent until now. "Arms sales were considerably north of a hundred and thirty billion dollars last year, and we're already on track to bump that by forty percent *this* year. The spikes in racial, national, and ideological hatred have energized the entire market."

"Personally," said Top, "I'd like to go after those Tenth Legion clowns, and I mean go hard. Pull out all the stops. We got some value out of the trailer trash. If we keep hitting them, maybe nab someone higher up the food chain, we might get lucky. Not talking taking scalps—Sandman and mind games are a winning combination."

"Hooah," said Bunny, and they bumped fists. Belle reached out and took a hit, too.

I said, "We can further assume Bliss is working for or with Kuga and has a version of VaultBreaker at least as good as the one she had before Atlanta and those other places. What can we do to counter that? I mean right now, for all of the other facilities? Here and everywhere? What can we do?"

Bug looked troubled. "In the short term? Not much apart from warning the facilities that are waiting for software and hardware upgrades. I'll take care of that right after this call."

"That's half the job," said Top. "What about *seif al din*? They *have* it now. We know that 'cause we've seen it. God damn near gotten eaten by it. What's our play? Call the president? Call NATO, the UN? Call the news?"

"Much of that is already in motion," said Church.

"Too right," agreed Wilson. "Once it was clear Gehenna had been compromised, Doc Holliday and I drafted a letter and attached a complete description of *seif al din*, with information on containment. And—ah—what you might otherwise call *best practices* for handling the infected. It is being sent to the White House, Homeland, and the DoD, with recommendations to share it with all other world leaders. We have most of Doc's staff working on new response protocols."

"I hope you warned them about the psychological reactions they should expect," I said. "If there's an outbreak, however small, some cops and soldiers are going to hesitate because these are going to be civilians. Some may go the other route and be so afraid of the prospect of facing actual zombies that they're going to shoot anyone who has a limp or a twitch."

"We covered that," said Doc. "And Dr. Sanchez gave us some verbiage."

"That's something."

Coleman cut in and said, "We're also working on adding something to suppress major nerve conduction to our Sandman formula. Probably going with a depolarizing neuromuscular agent. The hope is to get a knockdown drug that will stop the, um, zombies without killing them."

"Why bother if there's no cure?" asked Remy.

"Optics," said Wilson. "There have been instances in the past where it looked like one of our teams was gunning down innocent civilians."

"Artemisia Bliss used that strategy against us with *seif al din*," I said.

"Yeah, the subway thing in New York," said Bunny. The shadows in his eyes told me that he was recalling that horror show all too well.

"Harcourt Bolton used it during the Kill Switch case," said Top. "Mind-fucked us real good and then put it on the net."

"And they tried it with Rage," said Belle.

"Social media is a weapon of a heavier caliber than any gun," observed Church.

"We should expect more of it," I said. "So, yeah, Ron . . . a nonlethal alternative would be welcome. Especially since the Snellig has a higher-capacity magazine. That'll help us in the field."

"What about the medium and long term?" Top asked.

Church opened his mouth to answer, but at that precise moment, the house above us exploded.

CHAPTER 97
TENTH LEGION TRAINING CAMP #18
PINE DEEP, PENNSYLVANIA
FOUR WEEKS AGO

Toombs sat in Commandant Furman's office drinking whiskey.

He preferred to not drink with clients, but for some, it was as much a challenge as a pleasantry. Furman was like that, lots of unspoken little challenges that whispered to his deep insecurity. So, Toombs drank, though he sipped rather than shot the bourbon.

The main business of the day was concluded. Money had been wired to the right accounts and a timetable agreed upon.

"Commandant," said Toombs, "I overheard a couple of the fellows out there talking about Firefall."

"Yes, they're all jazzed up and ready for it."

"Notice that I'm not smiling," Toombs said.

"Why? Is something wrong?"

"You are aware that 'Firefall' is a secret, right? Even the name is a code only to be used with senior officers of the Legion, Mr. October, Miss Mary, and me."

Furman colored a bit. "It's just the name. The troops all have different theories, but as you instructed, only senior staff know what will actually happen during Firefall."

"And yet the name is out there. It's being used by soldiers trying to figure what it is. You don't see a problem with that?"

Furman's color deepened, and he looked nervous. "I will talk to my officers and get them to shitcan any mentions of Fi—of the *plan*."

"That would be much appreciated, Commandant," said Toombs with a touch of frost.

They sipped their drinks, and there was some useless chitchat initiated by Furman as a way of getting the taste of his own shoe leather out of his mouth. Toombs didn't pursue the rebuke and affected a degree of affability to normalize things. But Toombs's instincts told him that Furman had something else he wanted to discuss. When it came, it caught Toombs off guard only a little bit.

"About the comfort camp . . ." began Furman and let the rest hang.

"Comfort camp?" echoed Toombs.

"Mr. October said that one was going to be set up before Firefall launches."

"Did he?" mused Toombs, keeping his face straight despite the instant flush of revulsion in his stomach. "And what exactly did he say?"

Now that Furman had broached the subject and gotten a zero-emotion response, he looked uncomfortable. "Well . . . he said that it was a bonus. For the soldiers and all . . ."

"I see."

"Maybe I should talk to him about it . . . ?" suggested Furman weakly.

"That might be best," said Toombs. And then despite himself, he added, "I'm a salesman, not a pimp."

The conversation lagged. Toombs finished his whiskey, thanked the commandant for the hospitality, and left. By the time he got to his car, he was seething. And he was surprised. Something as vile as a comfort camp seemed out of keeping with the erudite October.

He wondered if this was really something Miss Mary had cooked up.

If so, it was one more log on the fire of his dislike for the strange woman.

"Everything okay, sir?" asked his driver.

"Sure," said Toombs, and he said nothing else all the way to the airport.

CHAPTER 98

JOINT-USE RTI-ARKLIGHT SAFE HOUSE
UNDISCLOSED LOCATION
PHILADELPHIA, PENNSYLVANIA

There was a huge *booooom* followed by all sorts of smaller bangs and pops. The lights went out and the ORB and all of the folks from Phoenix House vanished, plunging us into absolute darkness. Ghost shrieked and then began a fierce barking that was equal parts terror and fury.

"Lights," I yelled, but Top and Belle already had their cell phones out. Their cell flashlights cut through the darkness, turning the falling dust into swirling galaxies. I headed for the stairs, acutely aware that I was not armed. None of us were. Not down in the subbasement of a heavily fortified safe house.

Belle was trying to soothe Ghost, but he kept barking.

So I barked back at him, "*Ghost, no speak.*"

He went instantly silent. Funny thing about dogs—in a crisis, they'll panic like anyone else, but with a pack leader's command, they calm down almost at once. I just hoped his trust in me wasn't misplaced.

"Gandalf!" bellowed Bunny, using Noah's combat call sign, but there was no answer. Halfway up the stairs, I paused and listened, waving everyone else to silent stillness. We heard the weary groan of abused timbers, the crab-scuttle noise of debris tumbling over wreckage.

No yells or shouts. No gunfire.

"Go quiet," I told Bunny, and he stopped yelling.

I tapped my earbud. "Havoc Actual to Merlin. Repeat, Havoc Actual to Merlin."

Church did not answer.

"Can't hear that on my comms, either, boss," said Bunny. "Must be a jammer."

Top appeared at my elbow as if by magic and murmured, "Call it, Outlaw."

"We need weapons," I said quietly. "Church will know we're in trouble, and he'll take care of sending us help, but figure that's ten or more minutes out."

"Gandalf said there were weapons lockers on the stairs," said Remy.

We hurried over and began fumbling with the thumbprint scanners. The treads on three steps popped open, and everyone began grabbing handguns, long guns, and loaded magazines. Top handed me a Sig Sauer P226.

"One up," he said, indicating that a round was chambered.

The timbers made a louder and more insistent complaint.

"Don't want to wait down here to be dug out and buried," said Bunny.

"Copy that."

I stepped over the open lockers and began climbing the stairs with the gun held close to my chest in a center-axis relock position, my left supporting the pistol and keeping it steady against my body, right index finger stretched along above the trigger guard. It's a safety move that keeps me from banging gun or arm in close quarters, but it's also excellent for weapon retention.

There were more thumps from above that sent down plumes of plaster and brick dust. It sounded like falling debris, but I wasn't about to take anything for granted. Top was three steps down behind me, and the others were shadowy blobs.

At the top of the stairs was the door, and there was a very faint line across the top and parts of the lower frame, signs that the door was out of true. It had been a very big bang.

I leaned close and listened for noise.

There was nothing. Even the debris sounds had diminished. It wasn't a comfort. It meant that Noah was unable to respond. Silence did not prove absence of threat.

There was one sharp *pop*, and the cell lights went dark.

"EMP," I said.

Top said, "They're still gonna be up there."

"I know." I fished for a key Noah showed me. It was behind a false brick that pivoted on a hidden hinge. No electronics. I removed it and slid it very gently into the keyhole below the keypad, then turned it. There was the faintest *click*. "Moving," I said.

"On your six, Outlaw, then I'll jag left."

I counted down from three and then used my knee to push the door open as noiselessly as possible. That let some dusty light slip through. Enough to see the floor ahead. I went through at a rush, cut right, and knelt, bringing my gun up and out. Top came out and went left, rifle in hand. I felt more than heard Ghost behind me.

The blast had done a hell of a lot of damage. Part of the second floor had crashed down into the dining room. There was a bathtub amid the smashed remains of a breakfront, and a toilet upside down on a heap of rubble.

I saw no one, though.

No one alive.

Noah lay in the doorway to the kitchen. From the waist up, he looked perfectly fine, as if he had decided to lie down for a nap. Below the waist . . . that was different. There was nothing. No hips or legs. Nothing. The blast had cut him in half. His face, though, was totally unmarked. There wasn't even a smudge of dust.

I could feel my heart collapse under the weight of the loss. Noah Fallon was a quiet, good-natured guy who looked like he should be off writing poetry. He'd left the field because killing just wasn't his thing.

And now he was a broken scarecrow.

The heartache I felt turned to anger. Cold and mean and hungry anger.

I moved out, clicking my tongue for Ghost, who came out as silent as a cat.

He looked at me, and I gave him a couple of silent orders using hand commands. He crept off, sniffing, listening, training all of his canine senses on the disaster. Top and I moved deeper into the room, taking cover behind anything that looked solid. Behind me, I heard the soft tread of Bunny, Belle, and Remy. Then I heard the sound of hidden panels opening, and I knew they were getting weapons from the secret caches.

Bunny moved up, a pump shotgun in his hands. He went to what remained of the dividing wall between dining room and living room. Then Belle passed on my other side, an M4 carbine in her hands. And Remy followed with an HK416 assault rifle in each hand. He passed one to Top, and then came over to me and let me exchange his little FN 509 for a Sig Sauer M17 pistol and four magazines. I stuffed the mags into my pockets, jacked a round into the gun, and moved forward.

JONATHAN MABERRY

We found no one.

Bunny was at what was left of the front window. "Two vehicles," he said. "Ten men in combat gear with body armor and ballistic helmets. Shit, they're going after our SUV."

"The fuck they are," snarled Top, and he went through the front door, firing at the cluster of men who were trying to climb into a pair of Jeep Rubicons. One cried out and fell, the plastic front of his helmet disintegrating in a red spray. Bunny was right behind him, and as the attackers turned toward us, he opened up with the pump shotgun. It was loaded with lead slugs instead of buckshot, and one round hit a man in the sternum and flung him against the driver's door of one Jeep. That door crunched shut on the lower leg of a man who'd been trying to get in behind the wheel. He screamed the way someone does who just broke some important bones.

This team was all dressed for combat, but their reactions were wrong. They seemed surprised—even shocked—to see us come crawling out of a building they'd just blown up. That told me they didn't know about the subbasement. Did that mean they followed us here but knew little about the actual safe house? Had to be.

We all opened up now, and we each knew how to fight someone who is wearing Kevlar body armor. Their cars were thirty feet from the burning house. That was well inside the range of accurate pistol fire for my guys.

They tried to reorganize and return fire in some orderly way, but their surprise had stolen the only moments when that would have given them the edge. Had they laid an ambush and used the explosion to smoke us out, they might have had us. They squandered that advantage, and we made them pay for it.

Top hosed a knot of them, pinning them against the side of their own escape vehicle. Belle dropped to one knee and began squeezing off fast single shots. She targeted throats and joints and spots where an expert knows are vulnerable. Joints have to be flexible, and that makes them vulnerable.

Remy had found a pair of grenades that I hadn't seen in the stairway weapons lockers.

"Frag out," he roared and threw the first grenade at the lead vehicle.

The door was open, and the bomb vanished inside. One man already inside tried to fumble for the grenade, probably to do a scoop-and-throwback. The blast destroyed the front half of the Jeep and threw burning red pieces onto the twisted hood.

I went left, laying down my own cover fire as I skidded behind a pair of trees that were burning, their autumn-dry leaves bursting into flame. I crouched down to swap magazines, feeling the tree trunk shudder as bullets chopped into it. Somewhere, Ghost was barking. We'd become separated by the wildness of the moment. Then two things happened in the same instant—the bullets stopped hitting the tree and a man's voice rose in a towering scream of sudden agony.

I took the moment to move and ran as fast as I could past the burning Jeep, using the smoke and confusion of the grenade damage to try to come around on the blind side.

The gunfire was maddening. Bullets filled the air going in all directions, tearing apart the lawn plantings, the red-painted mailbox, and riddling already fallen bodies.

I crouched and duckwalked to the rear of the burning Jeep, did a quick peek around it, and then leaned out and opened up into a man who was drawing down on Top. He slumped forward, gun falling from twitching fingers. I rose and ran past him to get a better angle on another shooter, but before I got two steps, that man grunted and sat down hard on his ass. Most of the side of his neck was gone, and when he died, a silence dropped hard over the scene.

We had no working comms, so I found cover and yelled, "Havoc, count off."

They did.

Every single one. Then Ghost came bounding out of the smoke, his muzzle and upper chest red with blood and his tail wagging.

"Secure the scene," I growled, rising from cover. "Find me someone with a pulse."

Top came in from my right. "House lights are on," he said, gesturing to the surrounding homes. "Cops'll be on their way, and we don't have Bug to slow them."

"Got a live one," called Bunny. He materialized out of the smoke, carrying a limp form. "He's circling the drain, but he's still breathing."

The engine of our SUV roared to life, and Remy backed it up to meet Bunny. Belle opened the back hatch and helped get the wounded shooter in and secured. Then we all piled in, and Remy got us out of there. Eleven blocks later, we passed three police cruisers tearing along with lights and sirens. Remy did his very best civilian driving until they were out of sight, and then he hit the gas.

CHAPTER 99
TENTH LEGION TRAINING CAMP #18
PINE DEEP, PENNSYLVANIA
FOUR WEEKS AGO

When Toombs was aboard his private jet and taxiing down the runway, he told the cabin steward to go into the cockpit and close the door. Once alone, Toombs called Mr. October.

"How did it go?" asked his employer.

"In terms of sales and training, fine."

"Uh-oh," said October. "You sound like there's some kind of bee in your bonnet."

"Two words," said Toombs with tightly controlled anger. "Comfort camp."

The silence on the other end lasted for several seconds. "Ah," said October at last.

"You knew about this?" demanded Toombs.

"I did. And although I'm no fan of such . . . *things* . . . it's the cost of doing business."

"Are we talking hookers or what?"

"I left those details to Miss Mary," said October. He almost sounded embarrassed.

"Fuck."

"It's a small price to pay for what we will accomplish."

"Boss," said Toombs, "don't jerk me off here."

The plane lifted from the tarmac and clawed its way toward the cloudy sky.

"I make no apologies," said October, his tone firming up. "If you have issues with it, then I encourage you to bring it up to Miss Mary the very next time you see her."

That was the end of the call.

Toombs nearly threw his cell the length of the cabin. Instead, he forced himself to lay the phone down gently and position it precisely on the little wooden tray table. Imposing order into a chaotic moment.

October knew full well that Toombs was afraid of Mary. He knew he would never bring it up to her.

"God damn it," he breathed.

He leaned back and closed his eyes and tried to find a space of calm on which to stand. No matter how high or how far the plane flew, he failed.

CHAPTER 100
IN MOTION
KNIGHTS ROAD
BENSALEM, PENNSYLVANIA

"Where to, Outlaw?" Remy asked. His young face was streaked with dust and blood from several small cuts on his scalp.

"Find me a big store parking lot or a warehouse with a big yard."

What he found was a strip mall that was anchored by one of those big-box stores. Except the store was boarded up and only a third of the other stores had lights on. A failure for the local economy was a win for us in that moment. Remy drove around behind the box store and found two large industrial dumpsters of the kind they use during interior demolition before a big remodel. The dumpsters were piled high with old drywall, pipes, and other debris. He parked where there was no line of sight from anywhere back there.

We got out and gathered at the back of the vehicle. Belle peeled off to watch our backs. With the rear hatch up, I leaned in to look at our prisoner. Bunny had removed the helmet, revealing a young man of about twenty or twenty-two. Not the face of a villain . . . just a face of a person who knows he's right there at the end of his whole life. The realization of it was there in his eyes—a fear of death that rose above the pain in his broken and bleeding body.

Normally, this is a moment for Top. He's kinder and gentler than I usually am. And he has that fatherly reassurance and calm. But Top was black, and this kid was part of a group who saw anyone like him as something lesser. Something to be feared and despised.

So I leaned over him. "Listen to me, son," I said, even though I wasn't old enough to be his dad. "You know you're in bad shape. Your friends are all dead. You have one chance to do the right thing."

"G-G-G-God w-w-will hunt you d-d-down."

Hard to tell if the stutter was something he was born with or a manifestation of his fear and pain. On a weird level, it made me feel a sliver of pity for him. It humanized him.

"Remy, give me your lighter."

The young Cajun produced one. Red plastic. I jammed the bottom end between the dying man's back teeth. He fought me, and it was evident he was going to opt for the salvation pill hidden in his mouth. There was no time for pliers or anything like that. I held pressure, preventing him from closing his teeth at all. It did not prevent him from talking, but he had to use his mouth differently, his lips forming in distinct words. Actually helped with his stutter, though. Odd.

"You niggers and wetbacks and race traitors are all gonna burn," he said awkwardly, eyes blazing to emphasize his threat.

"Kid," I said, "we can have an ambulance here in ten minutes. Or we can drop you off at the closest ER. That's your call. That salvation pill isn't an option. It's not a knockout drop. It's poison. No, don't argue. Just listen."

"Fuck you, you lying sack of shit," he said, each word distorted as if he had a mouthful of macaroons.

"You're Tenth Legion," I said. "No need to deny it. Where's your camp?"

"Up your ass."

There was blood on his lips now. I glanced at Bunny, who gave a tiny shake of his head.

"Where is Mr. October?" I asked.

His eyes snapped really wide, then they immediately slid away.

"Where is he?"

The man shook his head, but the effort twisted his face with agony.

"Give me something, son, and we'll get you the help you need."

The pain of having moved must have made him acutely aware of how badly he was hurt. He could feel life seeping out of him. His eyes filled with tears. His lips moved with what I, at first, thought was prayer. I took a chance and slipped the lighter from between his back teeth. His mouth kept working, but now we could hear him.

"—tell her I w-was t-t-true," he said. "T-t-tell my m-mom that."

"I'll tell her you were a good soldier," I lied. "But only if you tell me what I need to know. Where is Mr. October? Where is your camp?"

He turned to me, tears running from the corners of his eyes. "N-n-n-not Oct-t-tober. He's b-bad. She's w-w-w-worse."

"She? She who? Are you talking about Artemisia Bliss?"

That elicited absolutely no recognition in his face.

"Are you talking about Mother Night?"

Again, no reaction.

Then he said, "M—M-Miss Mary." He shook his head. "She's a m-m-m-monster. Her dogs. God in heaven, those d-d-d-dogs."

"Where is the camp?"

"I d-don't know."

I tried another tack. "Tell me about Firefall."

The man smiled. His teeth were bloody, and the light in his eyes was fading.

"It's t-too l-l-l-late to stop it. G-God's wrath is c-c-coming for you."

"What is Firefall?" I demanded. "*When* is it?"

But the man looked at me, and through me, and through the walls of life into a vast and empty beyond. The back of the SUV was drenched with his blood, and his flesh sagged into utter limpness, looking smaller in the space than he should. Almost childlike in a sad and disturbing way.

Moments like this hit me strangely. Despite the attack, despite the tragedy of Noah Fallon's death, seeing this man die while talking about monsters and pleading for us to tell his mother he'd been a good soldier—a good boy—somehow separated him from the soldier and killer he'd been.

That mother had watched him pull himself up to stand in his crib for the first time and thought he was a terrific baby. Full of life and joy and potential. She had watched him take his first tottering steps, treasured the first word he'd ever spoken, had been patient with potty training and learning his ABCs and all of that. She had wrapped presents in bright paper for birthdays and Christmases; she'd filled wicker baskets with colored straw and chocolate eggs. She'd sat up probably worrying anytime he came home late.

Who was she? What were her politics? Did she know what that little baby had become? Would she mourn her soldier son killed in the wrong war? Or was she even aware that he had gone this far into some kind of cultural psychosis? How would the news hit her? How much of her would die when she learned of her son's death?

I banged my fist on the rear frame of the car and cursed softly between clenched teeth. The world should not be this badly broken, but I knew for sure it was. All of the scattered parts of me understood this.

At any given time, there are three people inside my head vying for control. One was the Modern Man, that version of me who might have been the sole and dominant personality had not those older teens attacked Helen and me when we were fourteen. His aspect was the one who believed the best in people and clung to the shreds of his optimism.

Then there was the Cop. Closer to the central personality in my current life. He's the pragmatist, the investigator, the efficient doer of things that must be done. I was an Army Ranger, but only for one tour—after that, I joined the Baltimore police and rose from patrol to detective very fast. I have a knack for figuring things out and, as Rudy so often says, making intuitive leaps. That Cop aspect was dogged, and I could feel him always at work trying the pieces of many scattered puzzles, looking for sense and order. Not unlike Nikki Bloom, I suppose. It's not a love of mysteries but an obsession for solutions.

The third aspect of my fractured mind was currently shouting. That was the Warrior part of me. Well, that "warrior" label was Rudy's choice. I tend to think of him more as the Killer. He comes out when the Cop is unable to control the situation and more extreme measures are called for. With every ambush, death, discovery, and fight in *this* war, I was feeling him edging forward out of the shadows where he usually lives. He is the savage part of me, and though he is capable of terrible violence, he never directs that at the innocent. Quite the reverse—he will go to total war against anyone who brings harm to the innocent. He is the one who has been trying to save Helen all these years. He emerged most powerfully after her post-assault PTSD got too big for her to handle and she killed herself. I found her, but it was the Killer who screamed himself raw that day. Partly for loss, but mostly because he could not save her.

All of this reminded me of the names Helen's ghost had given me when I was overwhelmed by Shiva and God's Arrow nine months ago. Joe Listopad, Jamie Stanton, Danny Beck, Bob Reilly, and Greg Murphy. The Modern Man did not want to ever see them or hear their names again. The Cop yearned to investigate them. But the Killer?

Well, his name says it all.

"Colonel?" said Top, and I realized it was the second time he'd addressed me.

"Yeah?"

"He said it's too late to stop Firefall."

"He was messing with us," suggested Bunny. "He knew he was done and wanted to kick us as he hopped the train."

"He did a good job with that," I said. "Told us next to nothing."

"Miss Mary?" Remy asked. "Dogs? What do you think that's about?"

"He was delirious," said Top. "He was talking shit."

I stepped back from the SUV. "I don't think he was."

Top frowned. "Wait . . . you think this Miss Mary is our girl? You think he was talking about Bliss?"

"Open to other suggestions, Top."

"And the dogs?" asked Bunny.

"I have a strong feeling we don't ever want to know what that means."

Bunny rubbed his eyes. "Every time we talk to one of these assholes, we come away knowing both less than we knew and more stuff we *don't* know."

"Then we'll have to keep asking questions," I said.

Ghost gave a small whuff.

I nodded to the closest dumpster. "Dump him in there. When we get comms back, we can tell the TOC where to come pick it up."

Remy shot me a look. "What do we do?"

"We get the fuck out of here," I said.

CHAPTER 101
TENTH LEGION TRAINING CAMP #18
PINE DEEP, PENNSYLVANIA
ONE DAY AGO

Miss Mary smiled as Commandant Furman hurried over to her. She had taken to wearing a pink pageboy wig and oversize white plastic sunglasses. It made her look like an Asian rapper with a Barbie fixation, and Furman found that very, very hot. He was okay with that desire. Sure, she was Chinese or Korean or some gook shit, but there was nothing wrong with fucking down as long as one married up.

"Miss Mary, what a surprise," he said. "I thought it was just a truck delivery day. Didn't expect you to come along as well."

"Oh, I turn up all sorts of places," she said airily.

"Isn't Mr. Toombs coming?" asked the commandant.

"Not today, no," said Miss Mary.

Commandant Furman looked past her at the two Peterbilt semis and their big trailers.

"Then what's all this, sir?"

As if in reply, there was a sudden sound—loud, harsh, disturbing. It wasn't barking, per se. Nor was it the roar of a big jungle cat. The noise held qualities of both.

"I . . ." Furman began and then let it trail off.

Miss Mary's grin showed a lot of teeth. "Don't worry, my friend. The SDs are well trained. More or less. And their handlers are with them."

Furman frowned. "SDs, sir? What does that stand for?"

"Oh, it's much more fun if I show you."

It amused Miss Mary greatly when the doors were opened and Furman saw what was inside each truck. He did not gasp or curse or yelp. Instead, he screamed.

Miss Mary closed her eyes and thought of all the fun her pets were going to have. She wondered what Joe Ledger would sound like when he screamed.

CHAPTER 102
IN MOTION
BENSALEM, PENNSYLVANIA

Remy burned thirty feet of rubber getting us out of there. He drove like a maniac for three blocks, then slowed and made a dozen random turns before finally pulling into the parking lot of a Target.

There was one bottle of water in the back seat, and Bunny took it and some Starbucks napkins left over from our ride from the airport and cleaned sweat, blood, and brick dust from his face and hands. Then he hopped out and went into the store.

Remy got out and quickly, quietly swiped a license plate from another SUV and put ours on that vehicle. It would likely cause some issues and confusion when that other car was pulled over, but that couldn't be helped.

When Bunny returned, he had a case of bottled water, energy bars, pre-moistened towelettes, and a burner phone. He tore the phone out of the plastic, got it running, and handed it to me.

Top looked at the towelettes. "Charmin Flushable Wipes?" he read aloud.

"It's what they had," said Bunny.

"Remy," I said, "drive us out of here."

"To where?"

"Just drive around. Look for a tail. I need to make a call."

I used the burner to call Church's private cell. He answered halfway through the first ring, proof that he was waiting for a call. I explained everything that happened, including Noah's death, Miss Mary, Firefall, and the rest.

"And no idea what this big event is?" he asked.

"Negative. You now have what we have."

I heard him murmur, "Miss Mary."

"Maybe I'm crazy, boss," I said, "but I think she's Bliss."

"I am inclined to agree," said Church. "When you go to ground and have the time, check the news. It has become clear that the disease attacks in Atlanta and elsewhere are more than terrorist incidents. Small groups—either unknown or previously marginalized—continue to take credit. They are evenly split between those ostensibly coming from Mexico, Central, and South America, and those purporting to be from radical Islamic groups."

"You say that like you don't believe either is legit."

"Do you?"

"Not really."

"The immediate effect is that this is the topic dominating the twenty-four-hour news cycle. That, in turn, has a strong ripple effect on domestic outrage, xenophobia, and militancy."

"Good for business if you're selling arms and renting out private military contractors."

"Indeed. The tricky part is convincing my contacts in the US government not to let themselves be fooled and to avoid making bold threats on the floor of either the House or Senate."

"Yeah, good luck with that," I said. "Have I mentioned recently how much I loathe politicians of any party?"

"As subtle as you are about that, I've managed to infer as much," said Church dryly. "In terms of the public's reaction to Islamic terror cells, that fire was stoked aggressively when the ISIS splinter group that stole the nukes in Israel took credit in an inarguably believable way."

"I thought Mossad had stomped that group flat."

"They did, and a clearer political picture was emerging, but that process has been largely ruined since Hamas launched its attack and sparked the invasion and taking of prisoners, followed by Israel's subsequent invasion of the Gaza Strip."

"Are we thinking ISIS or some other actual group *is* involved in the disease hits?"

"Not as such, no," he said. "Stealing the nukes happened because Jason Aydelotte and his organization helped make it happen. It was, in essence, an arms deal."

"Everywhere we turn, there's Kuga's footprints."

"Indeed," Church agreed.

"The more I think about what happened in Gehenna, boss, the more I think we caught the epilogue."

"Explain."

"It's pretty clear Gehenna was robbed long before we got there. They went to bizarre lengths to booby-trap it. I don't think it was their intention to actually kill us. There are fifty ways they could have done it. No, what they did was slow us down. Then they blew up the Firehouse in Germany around the same time. Splitting our focus, pulling on our resources."

"Yes."

"You said that Oskar Freund was in Taiwan working on something," I said. "Do we think it's another effort to drain our overall resources?"

"That occurred to me, too," said Church. "It's possible, even likely. I put feelers out through my network. There has been a noticeable spike in high-profile cases in key areas—the overall effect is that most of the teams that could be deployed have *been* deployed. Some are still working those cases."

"If they're that interested in sending us on wild-goose chases," I said, "it seems likely that this Firefall thing is going to happen sooner than later. Otherwise, all of this running us around is wasted."

"Fair point," said Church. "I'll put more people on that to see if we can get a clearer picture of how things stand and perhaps catch a glimmer of what's coming and when."

"Maybe move that to the top of your to-do list."

"Oh yes."

"On a related topic," I said, "because of the EMP, we weren't able to activate the autodestruct at the house."

"I'll take care of it," he assured me. "I'm truly sorry to hear about Gandalf. He was a good man."

"He was. And he deserved better," I said. "Look, we're out in the wind, and we need to go to ground and wait until Bird Dog can re-supply us. We got out with guns, but all of our electronics are dead. Can you take care of that?"

"As soon as this call is over. Once you are in a secure location, I'll have him load up with full field kits."

"Good. And truth to tell, boss, I'm getting really fucking tired of the Legion assholes finding us at our so-called safe houses. So, until you figure out where the leak is about those, I'm going somewhere off the grid."

"Do you have a location in mind?"

"I have friends in the suburbs," I said. "Folks who I know can keep secrets."

Church took a moment on that. "Understood. Call me when you are safe."

And he ended the call.

Everyone got back in the car, and Remy looked at me. "Where to, chief?"

"North," I said and gave him directions.

Remy frowned. "What's the name of the actual town, though?"

I said, "Pine Deep."

In the back, both Top and Bunny said, "Hooah."

CHAPTER 103
TENTH LEGION TRAINING CAMP #18
PINE DEEP, PENNSYLVANIA
THREE DAYS AGO

Kurt Furman sat in his office, an open bottle of Jack Daniel's on his desk and a cigarette smoldering in a tray.

His eyes were bloodshot and the skin of his face gray-green and pale.

When he ran fingers through his hair, they shook as if palsied.

He had not slept at all since Miss Mary delivered the two truckloads of SDs.

His command sergeant, Ryerson, sat across from him. They were both on that fragile edge of sobriety where one more drink would topple them into active drunkenness. Furman had his glass cradled between his palms and sat there looking down into the amber depths as if in the hope of finding some measure of sanity in a world that has lost its hold on reality.

"Fucking SDs," he said every now and then.

Furman nodded each time but said nothing.

"I mean, this is some kind of *X-Files* shit right here," said the sergeant. "I mean, sure, I understand what Miss Mary said. Genetics. Some surgical enhancements. All that. But even so. It's not normal. It's . . . fuck, I want to use the word *unholy*, but that sounds corny."

Furman nodded. "*Unholy* says it."

"This is some horror movie shit right here," said Ryerson. "Science fucking fiction, man. Lord of the motherfucking Rings and shit."

"And yet . . ." said Furman. He picked up his glass and gave an ironic salute with it, and they both knocked the whiskey back hard. Ryerson refilled the glasses.

"Can I tell you something, man?" asked Furman.

"You're the boss."

"No. I'm talking just between you and me. We've known each other forever. We've seen some shit. I want to tell *you* something."

"Anything you need to say, brother, you can say. It's just us here."

Furman nodded, sipped, nodded again. "I don't know how much of this kind of stuff I can take. I mean it. Those SDs . . . ? I . . . I . . ." He stopped and shook his head. "This ain't the war I signed up for. This ain't the *America* I know. That creepy Chinese chick? What's that all about? That Chink bitch is out of her mind."

"Yes, she is."

They drank. The ledge of sobriety cracked beneath their weight.

"Mr. October's pretty weird, too," said Ryerson. "Never met a man who smiles that much."

"Yeah. Toombs is the most normal of the bunch, and he looks like a zombie." Furman set his glass down and rubbed his eyes. "It's like they're trying to freak us out."

"It's got to be an act," said Ryerson, his voice slurring now. "Like a disguise. The Chink's goofy-ass wigs and all. Maybe Toombs is wearing makeup. I bet when they're not visiting the camps, they don't look like that. I think it's like the red cowboy hat thing."

"The what?"

"When I was at the police academy in Tulsa, we had some classes on how to be a trained observer. Part of it dealt with how to *fool* regular observation. If a guy robs a 7-Eleven wearing a big red cowboy hat— fire-engine red—every witness will be able to describe it down to the last crease and stitch. But ask them about the guy wearing it and you'll get forty different descriptions. Short, tall, fat, thin, black, white."

Furman thought about that as he sipped. "Yeah," he said. "Maybe."

"Has to be. Here we are talking about Miss Mary's wigs, October's smiles, and Toombs's skin color. Sit any ten of our soldiers down with a sketch artist and they'll dig in on the *look*. Has to be that."

"Maybe," repeated Furman. "But, yeah, I agree the three of them are freaks. I'll be happy once Firefall is launched so we don't have to deal with them anymore."

They drank and looked at each other over the rims of their glasses. Looking for confirmation of that theory. Looking hard. Furman's eyes shifted away after a moment. Ryerson looked down into his glass.

"But those SDs," said Furman. "Those aren't dogs in costumes."

Ryerson said nothing.

CHAPTER 104
THE MANSION
UNDISCLOSED LOCATION

"But, yeah, I agree the three of them are freaks."

Toombs reached across the dining room table and hit Pause on the tablet that lay between him and October. Furman's voice stopped abruptly.

"That's what they think of us," said Toombs.

October was leaning back into his chair, slowly running the pad of one finger along the bottom curve of his lip. His smile was still there, but it had dimmed.

"To be fair," said October, "we do make a comical trio. And God knows I've been called worse." His eyes were steady on Toombs. "Why, does this bother you? Being called names?"

"Of course not," said Toombs irritably. "I've looked like this since I was born. It's a skin condition. I'm used to assholes making comments, and in business, I've learned to use it. No, that's not it, nor what they said about you."

"Then what?"

"It's Mary."

"Dear lord, please tell me you're not offended on *her* behalf. Surely you have to realize that she is aware of her effect. She leans into that role for exactly the reasons they suggested. The red cowboy hat thing."

Toombs laughed. A short, sharp half snort. "You actually think Mary's doing all that, acting weird, acting *insane*, dressing like she stepped out of a comic book or a B movie horror thing?"

"I do."

"You're serious? I *live* here, boss. She's been like this since I first met her. Maybe I'll buy her playacting the psycho bitch thing that first time where she pounced on me. And her sometimes wearing next to nothing just to jerk me around. That was then. But why now? No, October, this isn't an act. Mary isn't sane by any yardstick I can think of. The phrase *batshit nuts* occurs to me, and that makes her dangerous."

"Dangerous is what we want, isn't it? She scares people like Furman and the other militia types. Rightly so. They've seen her excesses. They don't dare step out of line around her."

"Neither do I," said Toombs. "Neither, it seems, do you."

"Don't mistake indulgence with nervous concession," said October. "You know a little of what Mary's been through. We can't expect her to be normal. She is still exploring what she has become and what it means."

Toombs sat back and gave his employer a long look, eyebrows raised.

After a few moments, October said, "What? Speak your mind."

"You've always said that Mary is smart. Not just a genius but a certifiable super-genius. Smarter than just about everyone."

"She is. And . . . ?"

"And she acts like a deranged overgrown child just to mess with the heads of people like Furman and the commandants of the other camps. When she has moments of wild psychotic behavior, it's deliberate to keep the troops in line, to make them afraid of her."

"Yes."

"Here at home, she plays a different role. Much more childish and childlike. Naughty, but not in a way that makes you dislike her or want to abandon her. Joyful whenever you give her a new toy—a spiffy computer, a lab, freedom to go roam the woods like a wolf, all the shit you've taken from the biological warfare sites. If you're not trying to buy her cooperation and genius with presents, then you're rewarding her excesses. No rebuke."

"She is useful to my plan. To *our* plans. We're on the eve of Firefall, and her excesses have been useful in terms of misdirection. The authorities are looking for foreign agents. The blame game is causing

JONATHAN MABERRY

civil unrest, and those angry citizens are buying everything in our catalog. Ever since the typhus story broke, sales have risen—what was the percentage?"

"Five hundred fifty-eight percent."

"Exactly. She is accomplishing exactly what we want."

"That's all great, boss," said Toombs, "but I wonder if we've both been so starry-eyed over the profit margin Mary's helped spike that we're not looking closely enough at Mary herself."

"Toombs," said October with the first flush of impatience, "have you ever heard the expression 'If it's not broke, don't fix it'?"

"Yes. Have you ever heard the one that goes 'Don't judge a book by its cover'?"

"Sure, but I fail to see how it applies here."

"Let me put it another way," said Toombs. "When is Mary at her most extreme? When is she acting the craziest? Saying the most outrageous things and being the most demonstrably provocative? I'll give you a hint—it's not in front of our customers."

October's eyes darkened for a moment, and he looked away, apparently studying a Rosetti painting on the far wall. Without turning back, he said, "You think she is playacting here? For us?"

"Not all of it," said Toombs. "Not all the time. I think she really *is* nuts. But it's really easy to conflate wild eccentricity with a measure of—I don't know—*innocence*. Mary's your ward. She's like your daughter. You see her as damaged goods, and you tolerate it because that damage manifests in ways useful to the goals of the Kuga organization. And maybe your own goals of liking to stir the world up because chaos is good for our business. But given that we've seen Mary turn her crazy act on and off, dial it up and down—and knowing that she is fully aware of its effect on folks like Furman, David White, and the others who work for you—haven't you *ever* paused to wonder if she is using that same scheme on us?"

October said nothing.

"I *do* wonder," continued Toombs. "There's one more expression you might want to consider, boss."

"Which?" asked October, his tone almost listless.

"Crazy like a fox."

Mr. October turned away and looked at a painting on the wall for a few moments. Without looking back, he asked, "Aren't you supposed to be in Texas making final arrangements for the camp in Houston?"

Toombs studied the side of his face, then he rose and left the room.

A few minutes later, October heard the front door and then a car engine starting. He turned away from the painting and looked at the cushion on the floor by the fireplace. His dark eyes swirled with ugly colors.

CHAPTER 105
THE TOC
PHOENIX HOUSE
OMFORI ISLAND, GREECE

Mr. Church walked down the steps of the TOC, and as he passed, all of the chatter and noise fell away to leave an expectant silence.

"I just got off the phone with Colonel Ledger," he said. "The safe house was bombed, and the house resident, Noah Fallon, has been killed. They used an EMP weapon, so all electronics are fried, including the self-destruct. Their vehicle plates have likely been photographed by neighbors and have been called in to police."

There were soft gasps and curses from the technicians. Scott Wilson, Bug, Rudy, and Doc Holliday stood at the top of the stairs, all of them having hurried there after the ORB connection was severed.

Church looked grave as he addressed the rest of the staff. "Havoc Team is in crisis but safe at the moment. They are heading to the town of Pine Deep, which is in Bucks County. Some of you are likely familiar with it and its reputation. There was a terrorist attack there seventeen years ago."

Several people nodded.

"This was a Tenth Legion hit," he continued. "You all know what needs to be done to drop a blanket over the safe house. We need to be in contact with local law enforcement. We need to be tapped into any CCTV in that area to look for anything that might give us a lead. And we will need to get a full team field kit prepped and on its way to Pine Deep. I will make some calls to colleagues of mine to ensure that every legal roadblock is cleared, but timeliness is critical. Get to work."

And they did.

There was not one person in the TOC who was not a top professional in their respective fields. Each of them grabbed for a phone or began hammering on keyboards, setting into motion the considerable force of Rogue Team International. Although the group no longer worked for the United States government, there were many people in positions of real power—career professionals in those kinds of jobs that did not change with shifts of political parties—and within minutes, the wheels of effective power began to gain traction.

Rudy Sanchez hurried down the steps and stood with Church. "I'm so sorry about Noah," he said. "He deserved better."

"Colonel Ledger said the very same thing, Doctor, and I agree. He has family, and I will make sure they are cared for in every possible way."

"What about Joe and his team?"

"They are unhurt but understandably stressed."

"I wish I was there," said Rudy. "I know that town very well."

"If I thought Havoc could use you, Doctor, I'd have you on the first thing smoking," said Church. "However, everything is fluid right now, and you may wind up being of better use here. Now, if you will excuse me."

He was hitting speed dial on his phone before he even finished his sentence.

Church moved off and left Rudy standing there, watching as one of the techs populated the big screen with images of cell phones and body cams from the first officers on the scene. An aerial view from a news helicopter showed the smoking ruins of the safe house.

"*Ay, dios mío,*" said Rudy quietly, then he crossed himself.

CHAPTER 106
RED LION DINER
HORSHAM, PENNSYLVANIA

A couple entered the diner and paused to share some words with the hostess behind the counter. They laughed, and then the hostess plucked menus from a sheaf and led the couple to a table about thirty feet from where Mr. October sat drinking coffee at the counter.

The woman was tall, strongly made, pretty but with a hard beauty; there was very little softness about her. October knew the woman had scars. He could always feel scars, and he sometimes caught glimpses into how those scars came to be. For her, there were accidents—fast cars and motorcycles driven on rainy or snowy roads. That accounted for some of the scars. But others were marks of a different kind of violence—brutal hands, sharp teeth, wicked claws. As she sat, October caught the energy of a different kind of scar.

She's buried children, he thought. *Her own children, cut down by disease.*

As he sipped his coffee, he wrestled with an odd feeling of compassion for her. She was interesting and powerful and unusual, and he liked those qualities.

Compassion, though . . . that was something new, and it had been cropping up in him ever since he had brought Miss Mary into his life. It was interesting, but in the same way that a lionfish or black widow spider was interesting. For him, the danger was obvious and yet the feeling attractive.

He studied the couple.

The man with her was shorter, very thin in the way certain wiry people are—thin, not frail, though often mistaken for someone weak. He had black curly hair shot through with gray, and blue eyes that looked amiable but flicked here and there to read the room. A professional assessment backed with insight. October pulled his own energies in so that there was nothing for the man to read. This fellow was not a psychic man, to be sure, but one of those children of the storm lands—the ones whose scars ran very deep indeed and provided a certain radar for prey that had become predatory.

They sat across from each other, and he squeezed her hands for a moment before they picked up the menus.

Although Mr. October had never met either of them before, he knew them. Not because of his assessment of them, nor from any psychic flash. No, he'd read the books and seen the movies about what the people in the town of Pine Deep called the Trouble. October knew both versions of the story—the official one about white supremacists who spiked the local drinking water with hallucinogens and then went on a killing spree that resulted in the largest death toll

JONATHAN MABERRY

of any terrorist incident on American soil. That was almost twenty years ago. The anniversary was coming up fast, which was why all the streaming services were replaying the movie based on the book, *Hell Night: The True Story of the Pine Deep Massacre.*

In that bestselling nonfiction book, written by local newspaper reporter Willard Fowler Newton, the story presented—though widely discredited as sensationalist nonsense or absurd conspiracy theories—was much closer to the actual truth.

Mr. October knew the truth.

He even knew the person—long since dead and buried—who was behind the whole thing. Not Kurt Wingate, as the official story claimed; nor the serial killer Karl Ruger, who had been drawn to that town and became caught up in the Trouble. No, October had been well acquainted with the man who—in this town, at least—went by the name of Ubel Griswold. A fake name, of course. It meant "wolf of the gray forest." Even his older nicknames—Peter Stumpf, Peter Stumpp, Jan Le Loup, Jacques Roulet, Giles Garnier, Libbe Matz, Folkert Dirks—were all fakes. Names of convenience, often containing jokes. Like *Mr. October.*

He had known Griswold before that man moved from Austria to the United States. There were details about Griswold, though, that October did not fully understand. Like his death, which was credited to an itinerant blues musician named Oren Morse, who had come to the farmlands of Pine Deep seeking work while dodging the Vietnam War draft. *Hell Night* claimed that Morse—known locally by the nickname "the Bone Man"—had beaten Griswold to death with a guitar. That made no sense to October, who knew how difficult it was to kill someone like that ancient German.

Then, according to the book, Morse was lynched for the killing, but rose again as a ghost to warn of Griswold's return in a different form and with greater powers. That, October knew, was true enough. Griswold was the force behind the Trouble and was believed killed for good and all by the curly-haired little man and the stern woman in the booth. Those two and a red-haired boy named Mike Sweeney.

It seemed impossible that so humble a collection of normal people could destroy someone—some*thing*—as powerful as Ubel Griswold.

I wonder how they did it, mused October. *What is it about them that made them able to do such a thing?*

It intrigued him. Enchanted him.

He drank his coffee and watched Malcolm Crow and Valerie Guthrie-Crow order and eat, talk and laugh. It made him wonder if seeing them here, completely by chance, was some kind of a sign.

He rather thought it was.

CHAPTER 107
CAFESJIAN CENTER FOR THE ARTS
10 TAMANYAN STREET
YEREVAN, ARMENIA

His name was Hovsep Petrosyan, and he was a goldsmith.

His studio was in a distant corner of the Cafesjian Center for the Arts, where he spent most of his days doing restoration work on ancient objects made from precious metals.

Petrosyan was an apolitical old man whose personal bias was toward peace and a life lived in service to others. He was a widower with no children. Although there were other Petrosyans in Armenia, none of them were really kin, and when he died, his name would die with him. That was a sad thought, when he allowed it, but he was philosophic enough to accept that immortality through progeny was a selfish illusion.

The work he did occupied nearly all of his time, and at night, he sat in cafés and read books in four or five different languages, then went home to his cats and one very old dog. He rarely spoke to people, preferring the conversations in his own head. Every now and then, though, he would receive a call from an old friend. Someone he had known for quite a long time, though that time had carved lines into Petrosyan and far less so into his friend.

When his cell phone rang near midnight, he knew who it was. The people at the arts center never called him after working hours, and he had no other friends. He pushed up his black sleep mask and fumbled for the cell on the bedside table.

"Paron Yekeghets'I," he said, using the name his friend had been known by when they first met.

"Hello, Mr. Petrosyan," said Mr. Church. "My apologies for calling at this hour."

"I'm too old to need sleep."

Church gave a soft laugh of agreement. "We both are."

Petrosyan asked, "You got what I sent last month? The stars for Mr. Anderson and Mr. Bianchi. I read what you sent me about them. They seemed like good people."

"I did. And, yes, they were both very good people. Their stars are already on the wall. The craftsmanship is as beautiful as ever."

"Kind of you to say, but I'm old now. My hands are not what they were."

"It does not show in what you make."

"You're kind," said Petrosyan.

"I'm truthful," countered Church.

There was a small pause. "And now you are calling me to make another one." He did not ask it as a question, because he and Church seldom spoke for any other purpose.

"Two more, alas."

"Ah, such a sad thing. Who are they?"

"The first is for Noah Fallon."

Mr. Church told him about the gentle person who had died at the safe house. Church did not speak of Fallon's record as a law enforcement officer or as a field operator for the DMS. Instead, he spoke of Fallon the man. The quiet, introspective, kind man who was loved and respected by all of his colleagues.

"It is sad when the world loses someone like that," said the goldsmith.

"It is very sad," said Church. "And the second is for Felix Howard, a field operative who died only an hour ago." And Church told his old friend about the Bedlam agent. A tough, likable man nearing the point where he would likely step off the field and work behind a desk or at a training camp. Gone now. His body in a German morgue and his friends in surgical suites.

"I will begin on the stars tomorrow morning," said Petrosyan.

"Thank you, my friend."

"It is the very least I can do." After another slight pause, the old man said, "Tell me . . . how do you bear it?"

"What, in particular?" asked Church.

"The deaths of so many brave young people while we, the old and wicked, endure year after year. How can you carry the weight of it?"

"Because I must," said Church.

"That answer is evasive."

"It isn't, my friend. The truth is that I ask them to walk through the Valley of Shadows, and they do it willingly. They take up their swords and shields because they believe in what we do. If they fall, how much of a fool and coward would I be to retreat to the safety of ignorance or sophistry if they have given more than I ever have?"

Petrosyan sighed. "The war is the war."

"The war is the war," said Church and ended the call.

CHAPTER 108
RED LION DINER
HORSHAM, PENNSYLVANIA

"What . . . ?"

Crow blinked and realized that Val had asked him a question.

"Huh . . . ?" he asked.

"I said, what's wrong?"

"Wrong?"

"You went all still," she said. "When that guy got up from the counter, you turned and looked at him and then went all stone statue on me."

"Did I . . . ?" murmured Crow absently.

"Do you know him?" asked Val.

The man had left the diner, gotten into an electric-blue Range Rover, and driven away.

Crow blinked again, then shook his head. "No. I don't know him. Never saw him before."

"So, what was that, then? Cop radar?"

"Maybe." He considered, then shrugged. "I don't know."

Val studied her husband's face. He was smiling—but then Crow smiled a lot; it was his most effective shield—but the smile was half-formed.

"Then what is it?"

All Crow could do was shake his head again. "Beats me. There was something about him. Nothing specific. A feeling. Just . . . something."

They watched the SUV, which was at a red light. There was nothing at all exceptional about it. Without saying a word, Val took a mechanical pencil from the pocket of her plaid work shirt and handed it to him. Crow took it and quickly jotted down the license number on a corner of the paper place mat. He tore it off and put it in his pocket.

"You want to call it in?" asked Val, turning the place mat so he could see the numbers.

"Nah. He didn't do anything," said Crow, but a moment later, he picked up his cell and called it into the dispatcher. "Call me if you get anything twitchy."

He set the phone down, but it rang immediately. Crow looked at the incoming number and frowned. No one he knew, and he almost didn't answer, but something made him thumb the green button.

"Hello . . . ?"

"Crow," said a familiar voice.

"Joe . . . ?"

"Are you at the station?"

"No, I'm at a diner with Val. Why? What's shaking?"

"Heading your way," said Ledger. "Need a place to hunker down and get my ducks in a row."

"You bringing trouble with you?"

"Fleeing from it. No one on our tail, though."

Crow glanced at his wife. "How soon will you be here?"

"Forty minutes."

"Come to the office. I'll meet you there."

"Thanks."

"Joe . . . I'm serious here—don't bring trouble to my town."

But the line was dead.

CHAPTER 109
STATE ROUTE A-32
PINE DEEP, PENNSYLVANIA

We rolled across a narrow metal bridge, and Remy slowed to a stop before a big billboard that was stained from years of hard weather, scraped by debris blown by wind, threadbare and torn.

Remy leaned forward and craned his neck to look up at the message on that sign. I did the same even though I'd seen it before, and then the three in the back seat rolled down their windows and peered up at it. It told two distinctly different and conflicting stories. One that maybe predated the Trouble, as the locals called it; and another one more recent but still years old.

The original sign was an advertisement for the *Pine Deep Haunted Hayride—Biggest on the East Coast*, it shouted in happy orange letters. The accompanying art was so faded that it was hard to tell what it was. But I remembered the original sign and knew that it once showed a bunch of teens on the back of a tractor-pulled flatbed, all of them screaming in joyful terror as zombies, vampires, werewolves, and other monsters crowded around, reaching through the wood slats.

Pasted diagonally across it was a long white banner that had been carefully glued and smoothed flat. On that were two words spray-painted in the style of urban street taggers—3-D letters in a mix of Old English and cartoon styling, with lots of ombré shading. The message was simple and direct:

GO HOME!

The rest of the intended meaning was unwritten but still clear enough to understand.

Go home . . . because this isn't it.

"Well," said Remy, "that's welcoming as all hell."

"Yeah," said Bunny. "The colonel takes us to all the best places."

Ghost gave a single bark and then crawled off of Top's lap and into the footwell.

"Is the town really as unfriendly as all that?" Remy asked.

"Depends on who you piss off," said Top.

"No joke," agreed Bunny. "Take a tip—don't piss off the chief or his main deputy."

"Why? Are they your cliché asshole small-town cops who don't like strangers and get up all in your grille?"

"Malcolm Crow's the chief," I said. "Little guy. Looks like a strong wind would knock him over. But he's been through his full share of shit, and he's the one still on his feet."

"What is he?" asked Belle. "Ex–Special Forces?"

I laughed. "Hardly. Used to own a craft store before he ran for the cop job. He's just someone who makes a great friend but a really bad enemy."

"And his deputy?"

"Kid's Bunny's size, but he has his own—how should I put this—*skill set.*"

"Yeah, boss," said Bunny, "you've been making vague-ass comments about him for a while. I met him, and he's weird and all, but otherwise just a cop."

I said nothing to that. Top and Bunny met Crow and Mike during a case involving a material witness for Homeland. Things did get pretty bizarre, but they never really got to see Mike Sweeney in action. I did, though. I worked a solo gig right before Church closed the DMS. Crow, Sweeney, a Philly PI named Sam Hunter, and a local kid named Antonio Jones. It got very, *very* weird, and so far, Church has kept that file sealed. I agree with his reasoning because there's something about Pine Deep that always makes me feel like I stepped out of the real world and into some kind of SpecOps revisionist version of *American Horror Story.*

Instead, I said, "And there's another cat in town. Monk Addison. He's ex-Delta and ex-PMC, working now as a skip tracer. Quirky dude who looks like he would have fun dismantling an Abrams with his bare hands. He and I worked with Arklight on a human-trafficking thing just a couple of months ago. More to the point, he's earned the Arklight seal of approval."

"Hooah," Belle murmured.

"Hooah," agreed Top. Bunny nodded, though maybe with less enthusiasm. He was not a fan of his one trip to Pine Deep. He's talked about it on Rudy's couch a few times.

"Works for me," said Remy and put the car back in gear.

We rolled along a country road framed on either side by huge farms. Miles of cornfields, with the stalks standing tall and green, waiting for the harvesters to begin their slaughter. Other farms had countless acres of garlic and pumpkins, and groves of apple trees. The leaves on all the trees were succumbing to time's cruelties and were wrapping themselves in their most colorful funeral clothes. The canopy of trees lining the road was a riot of every possible shade of yellow, orange, and red.

"Looks like a postcard," said Remy.

In the rearview, I saw Top and Bunny share small, wry smiles.

At one point, we paused as an old man crossed the road in front of us. He was clearly homeless and was dressed in layer upon layer of mismatched castoff clothes whose only thematic connection was the presence of many pockets. He even had extra crude pockets sewn on those garments, and each pocket bulged with God only knows what.

His skin was filthy, his long hair and beard matted, and he looked skinnier than any cornfield scarecrow. The man moved slowly, limping, mumbling to himself and occasionally patting this pocket or that.

Remy inched the car forward and rolled down his window. He took two energy bars and two bottles of spring water and held them out. The old man stopped and looked at them, then raised his eyes slowly to the young Cajun's face. Top pulled a ten out of his wallet and handed it to Remy.

The tableau held for a strangely long time as he studied Remy and then each of us in the car. I had the weirdest feeling that he could see more than was actually visible. Don't ask me to explain that, because I can't. It was a sudden feeling that I will go to my grave believing.

Then the man limped toward the driver's window. He looked at the food and money without immediately taking it. When he spoke, his voice was low and growly and reminded me of the way Tom Waits sang songs.

"I asked for nothing," he said. "Is this freely offered?"

"If you can use it, man," Remy said. "Then, by all means, and God bless."

The old man reached out a nearly skeletal hand and took the water bottles first, shoving them into deep pockets. He took the ten after that and sniffed it, then tucked it away. The last thing he took was the energy bars, and he stood there, squinting at the labels and the ingredients, nodding to himself as he did so. Then he put those away as well.

I thought the transaction was over and was about to tell Remy to get moving, but the man put a hand on the side mirror as if to keep the car in place. With his other hand, he dug into a coat pocket and rummaged around for a moment before producing something that surprised us all. It was a little plastic pumpkin with orange feet. The windup kind that would walk clickety-click across any flat surface until the spring wound down.

"Better than any alarm clock," he told Remy. "'Specially when you really need to wake up." He leaned very gently on *really*.

Remy took it gingerly between thumb and finger. The toy looked old, maybe an antique, and was chipped and scratched and grimy. Remy turned the little arm twice and set the thing down on the dashboard. But it just stood there, still and silent.

"It ain't time to wake up," said the old man.

"Thank you, mister," said Remy with kind patience.

Top leaned forward. "You stay warm and safe, brother."

The old man turned toward Top and studied his eyes for several seconds, and we all waited. I actually held my breath, though I don't know why.

"Do you have any children?" he asked.

Top hesitated. "Got a daughter. She's disabled. Had a son, but we buried him."

The homeless man nodded, a strange light flickering in his eyes. "Call your daughter," he said. "Tell her you love her."

Before Top could reply, the man turned away and made his slow, painful way to the far side of the road. He ducked between the boards of a farm fence and then vanished into the dense forever of cornstalks.

We sat there a little while longer.

"What just happened?" asked Bunny.

No one answered at first. Then I said, "Welcome to Pine Deep."

Remy put the SUV into gear, and we continued driving.

CHAPTER 110

AMERICAN LIBERTY BANK & TRUST FIELD
STREET ROAD
FEASTERVILLE, PENNSYLVANIA

The facility director's name was Gary Bob Howard. He was in his forties, looked thirty, and wore a polo shirt over blue jeans with carefully pressed creases. His hair was an unnatural shade of blond and carefully sculpted and sprayed.

"As you can see," he said airily, gesturing to the tens of thousands of seats rising row upon row from the field, "we are more than ready for tomorrow's festival."

"Looks great to me," said the smaller, slightly plump man in the off-the-rack business suit who walked beside him. "And the permits are all in place for the fireworks?"

They walked on vinyl sheeting that kept the chairs on the ground level from damaging the Astroturf beneath.

"Oh yes," Howard assured him. "These ground pads are flame retardant, and the sprinklers have been tested. Your team can test-launch some fireworks tonight as planned."

"That's great."

They stopped and looked at the main stage. There were three steps up to the main platform, several podiums, comfortable bleachers for the choir, and looming above it all was a pristine white cross one hundred feet high. It dominated everything, even in an arena built for sixty thousand people.

Howard turned to his companion. "With all that's been going on around the country, I appreciate you offering to provide extra security."

"It's my pleasure. My teams will arrive early for a walk-through on the day of the event. They are all well trained, and they are all soldiers for Christ."

They shook hands.

Howard walked him out of the venue and all the way to his car—a black SUV. The driver wore a black uniform and wore a sidearm. The patch on his right shoulder was that of the three crosses on Golgotha. The patch on his right was the Roman numeral X in a circle.

"Thank you for everything you're doing to make this prayer extravaganza safe," said Howard.

"Oh, it's my pleasure," said Kurt Furman as he got into the car.

CHAPTER 111
STATE ROUTE A-32
PINE DEEP, PENNSYLVANIA

"That was weird," said Remy. He turned to look at the others. "We can agree on that, right? I mean, there's a consensus."

"Yeah," said Top.

Bunny said nothing. Nor did Belle or I.

We passed a big farm that had huge, orderly fields laid out in the geometry of the professional grower. There were scarecrows standing sentinel above every third post. Each of them had a Phillies baseball cap, and each had a necklace of garlic bulbs hung around its neck.

"What's the message there?" asked Remy. "Are the Phillies all vampires or some shit?"

"Hell if I know," I admitted. "Pine Deep's a strange place. It's a farm town, but for most of the last fifty years, it's built its tourism around Halloween. Haunted hayrides, a Halloween parade, scarecrow contests, pumpkin-carving contests, horror movie celebrities making appearances. The works. There was even a magazine article— *Newsweek* or *Time* or one of those—that labeled it 'the most haunted town in America.'"

"'America's Haunted Holidayland,'" quoted Bunny.

"Hooah," said Top.

"Sounds kind of fun," Remy said. "I mean except for that terrorist attack thing."

"Took a long time for the town to recover. Tourism tends to drop when psycho extremists start blowing things up and killing the clientele."

Remy nodded. "Fair."

The town of Pine Deep was a triangular wedge of land made up of upscale shops and lush farmland and bisected by Route A-32. It bordered the Delaware River that separated Pennsylvania from New Jersey and was framed on all other sides by streams and canals. Interstate Route A-32 wavered back and forth between the two states, across old iron bridges and then plowed straight through the town, becoming—for eleven blocks—the city's Main Street. Black Marsh was an even smaller burg just to the south; and miniscule Crestville was the next town heading north. A-32 was the only road that cut all the way through those three towns; the other streets were all small farm roads that led nowhere but to someone's back forty or to the asymmetrical tangle of cobblestoned streets in Pine Deep's trendy shopping and dining district.

I pointed to the big farm we were passing. "That belongs to Chief Crow's wife, Val. Good woman. They were here during the Trouble. Crow and Val fought back against the extremists. Took some hits doing it. Crow nearly died. He wasn't a cop then. He had been years before but drank himself off the job. Then he started going to meetings, earned his chips, fell for Val, and opened his craft store that sold everything from monster model kits to costumes. The entire police force was wiped out during Hell Night, so when the town got back on its feet and needed a chief, he put himself up. Ran unopposed, and they kept on reelecting him."

"Wow."

"And that big deputy? He was a teenager at the time, and his stepfather was the one who orchestrated the hit. Vic Wingate was the guy. He abused Mike's mom and used to beat the shit out of Mike every chance he could. Mike had been studying jujitsu on the sly from Crow, and he had one of *those* moments when he just couldn't deal with it anymore, so he stood up and fair beat the piss out of Wingate. When he was done with college, Crow offered him a job."

Remy whistled. "Well . . . damn."

"Like I said before, the town's got a complicated history. But don't ever get on the bad side of Crow or Mike."

"Hell," said Top, "don't cross Val Guthrie, either, because she will sit your ass down."

"Note to self," laughed Remy.

Belle, sitting behind Remy, was listening to all this, looking interested but saying little.

We crossed Dark Hollow Road, which separated the Guthrie farm from a corner of the mountainous state forest that gave the town its name.

As we drew closer to the town, the conversation changed back to the Tenth Legion.

"I don't get these militant Christian assholes," said Remy. "I grew up Catholic in New Orleans, and we all go hard for Jesus, but not to the point of kicking other people in the balls if they go to a different church."

"Or mosque," said Belle. "Islam has its own fools and killers, but it doesn't define us. There's half a million peaceful Muslims for every killer in Hamas or ISIS or whatever."

"With you on all this," said Top. "I was raised Southern Baptist, and sure, there's some Baptists who would think the Tenth Legion and crews like that are doing God's work, but I know for a fact there's more who think it's a sin seeing Jesus turned into a poster child for hate. Reminds me of a line from an old song by that Dumbledore actor, what was his name—?"

"Michael Gambon?" suggested Bunny.

"No, the first one. Richard Harris. He was a singer, too. Irish guy. Did one piece, kind of a spoken-word thing once. There's a line from it that stuck with me. Let me see if I can get it right. His song was from Jesus's point of view. He said, '*Shame on you for converting me into a bullet and shooting me into men's hearts.*' Something like that."

We all considered the sentiment, nodding in favor of its wisdom.

"I've been edging closer to agnosticism," I admitted. "I was raised Methodist, but after cancer took my mom, Helen died by suicide, and then Santoro killing every last blood relative I have, my faith in a loving God's slipped more than a few notches. And I've never been a fan of evangelism. Offering food and medicine to brown and black people but only if they ditch their own beliefs and become good little Christians."

"That's not fair," said Top. "There's a lot of Christian missions who don't put a price tag on generosity."

"If so," I said, "they sure as hell aren't making the news."

"Why would they?" asked Belle, and that made me think for a bit.

"Okay, maybe," I said. "Even so, I'm with you, Top, about turning religion into a weapon."

"That Jesus line from the song, Top," said Remy. "That's what the Tenth Legion is doing."

"Personally," said Top, "I look forward to going all Old Testament on every one of those motherfuckers."

"Hooah," said Bunny. "Only time I go to church is when someone gets married or gets buried. I never had much faith. None, really. Always thought religion—all that confession and acts of contrition stuff—was a handy way for bad people to do bad things, get a fresh coat of whitewash on their souls, and go back out and do more, because the confessional or communion or whatever was always there. Fuck that."

The conversation faded out as we topped the last hill and saw the town of Pine Deep laid out before us, the stores bright with orange and black decorative lights, ghosts hung from streetlamps, trees wrapped in netting that flashed all of the autumn colors.

"Welcome to Pine Deep," I said again.

CHAPTER 112
STATE ROUTE A-32
PINE DEEP, PENNSYLVANIA

The SUV climbed the long hill and seemed to pause as the last of twilight's fire burned on its windows and black skin. Then it vanished down the far side.

The old man came out of the corn and stood watching this.

He had one of the energy bars in his hand, and when the car was long gone, he looked down at it. He smiled a smile that might have given even the four tough men and one tough woman serious pause.

A bird landed on the fence near where he stood. It was a very old crow whose feathers were discolored and ragged with age and harsh weather. He had one ink-black eye and one that had turned milky white. The bird and the man stood there as the first of the night breezes came whispering toward them across the fields.

Then, they each turned and looked down the road that led to the bridge. There was no traffic at all, but they watched for a long time anyway.

"Storm's coming," said the old man.

The crow opened its beak as if in reply but made no sound. The clouds above them were turning purple as the sun fled beyond the hills. The breeze tore leaves from the tree and chased them in the direction of the vanished car.

"Going to be bad, too."

The bird once more made its silent caw.

Then it pushed off the fence, dipped for a moment until the beat of its wings lifted it high into the air. It flew toward town, following the car.

The old man once more regarded the energy bar. He smiled and then put the whole thing in his mouth, wrapper and all. He chewed it into mush and swallowed.

"Freely offered and freely accepted," he said as he dragged the back of his hand across his mouth.

He turned and vanished into the corn again.

CHAPTER 113

OFFICE OF PUBLIC SAFETY
PINE DEEP, PENNSYLVANIA

"Begone, poltroon. We're closed for the month of Ramadan."

I stood in the vestibule at the Pine Deep PD. Just me and Ghost. The rest of the guys were still in the car.

"Ramadan is in the spring, genius," I said.

Chief Malcom Crow shrugged. "It was worth a try."

"So much for small-town charm."

"Well, to be fair," he said, rising from his desk, "you never come here unless the poop has hit the propellers."

We shook.

Crow is a short guy—five foot six or thereabouts—and weighs maybe eight pounds carrying a five-pound bag of rocks. He has a tanned face creased with what the inattentive might call *laugh lines*. And, sure, he does laugh a lot, but I knew that most of the creases were from hard use, pain, loss, and bad luck. He had curly black hair that was a lot grayer than I remembered, and though small, he had a grip like a vise.

He smiled as he squinted up at me. "You're an uglier man than I remember."

"Miles, not years," I said.

"Yeah. Same here." He looked at Ghost. "How's the fur monster? Has he forgiven me for being a cat person?"

"He no longer pisses on your photo," I said.

In fact, Ghost was wagging his tail with considerable enthusiasm.

"May I?" asked Crow, pausing with a hand halfway extended to Ghost.

"Sure," I said and made a little covert finger movement to let Ghost know it was okay to accept a touch. Crow scratched Ghost's head and then took his face between his palms and looked into my dog's eyes for a three-count. Then he let go and straightened.

"You have a good friend there," he said to me.

"We get along," I said.

"Coffee?" suggested Crow.

"Sure."

He looked past me out the window. "What about your team?"

"They're doing a recon drive around town. Like I said on the phone, we're just looking for a safe spot to regroup."

Crow snorted. "And you came *here*?"

"'Safe' being a relative term," I conceded.

He got up and poured two cups of coffee, handing me one. "Don't you superspies have safe houses?"

"The bad guys found us *at* a safe house in Philly," I said. "You may have seen it on the news."

"What?" asked Crow. "The place in northeast Philly that got blown halfway to Mars?"

"That would be the one."

He studied my face. "All your boys get out alive?"

"All but one. The resident. You know what that is?"

"Sure. Guy who minds the safe house."

I nodded. "Our man in Philly was a good kid. Used to roll out with me when I worked for Uncle Sam. Took the resident gig because he wanted the quiet life."

"Damn, that's sad," said Crow, meaning it.

"It is." I sipped the coffee. I like a medium roast, but Crow likes his boiled, black, and bitter. It was like being mugged. However, I did not complain. Instead, I said, "My crew and I are hoping to gather enough intel on the bad guys and maybe go pay them a visit. We think they might be local, or at least have a local group. We had a run-in with a bunch in Jersey and—"

"*That* was you, too?"

"Yeah. They tagged us somehow, and the hit on our safe house was tit for tat. Before you panic, we switched vehicles since then, and we made sure no one was tailing us."

"Jesus. Please don't let this spill over into my town, Joe. We have enough of our own shit going on. Biker gangs, some human-trafficking stuff we're gathering evidence on."

"We'll keep a low profile," I said. "Won't get in your way, and since we're freelancers now, there'll be no jurisdictional pissing contests."

"Fair enough," Crow said, though he looked troubled. He sat back down, picked up an old Phillies baseball that had been signed by Mike Schmidt, crossed his ankles on the edge of the desk, and began tossing it high into the air between two idle blades of the ceiling fan and catching it with casual efficiency.

I took a hardwood chair, turned it backward, and straddled it, forearms crossed over the back.

Crow's dispatcher, Gertie, was trying to overhear us, but Crow had an Echo Dot on a file cabinet that stood between her and him, and it was growling out some late-sixties barroom blues with lots of electric guitars. A very effective privacy screen.

Every now and then, Gertie—who was fortysomething but looked sixtysomething—would shoot her boss a vile look. I knew from previous visits that Gertie hates blues music, doesn't think much of Crow, and was trying hard to be the town gossip. But Crow closed her out pretty effectively and is known to have fed her disinformation just for fun.

I sat for a moment looking at the cop. He sat there enduring the scrutiny, playing his game of solo catch. He did not look up when he threw and didn't seem to look when he caught the ball. That made it look easier than it was. I think he knew that I was able to draw a lot of inferences from it. Crow was savvy like that.

"Val's been taking cooking classes lately," he said out of the blue. "Want to come over for dinner?"

I paused. "Um . . . I've had Val's cooking. Don't take this the wrong way, brother, but I'd rather be shot in the nuts with a Red Ryder air rifle."

Crow laughed. "No offense taken. I think half my paycheck goes to DoorDash and the other half to dinners out. She does *try*, though."

"And points for that, but I'm not actually suicidal."

Crow snorted, but said, "Then do this, Joe . . . go out to the farm. Use the back entrance off Dark Hollow Road. You know the one. I'll call Val and say we have company and that I'm bringing Chinese. She will do virtually anything for General Tso's."

"If there's a sex joke in there, I don't want to hear it."

"Come to think of it . . ." he murmured.

"Look, I have a new kid with us," I said. "Remy. Cajun kid. Terrific cook if you like things spicy enough to melt your molars. We'll pick up some groceries and *he'll* cook. Providing Val gives him free rein in her kitchen."

"Pretty sure she can be talked into it. Val loves Southern cooking."

"Cool. But . . . what about the kids?" I asked. "I mean, no one followed us here, but . . . just in case?"

A shadow passed across Crow's face. He and Val have two teenage kids, but they had others buried in the family cemetery. Their son, Terry, and his sister, Abigail. Stolen from them by disease. Life seemed determined to go all fifteen rounds with Crow and Val. I can make a pretty long list of people I'd rather see get hit with even *half* as much pain and misery. And the list of folks I know who could go through what they've been through and still retain a sense of humor, optimism, and genuine empathy is a lot shorter.

"I'll tell Val to send them to stay with Annabelle Pish over in Black Marsh. She's Mike Sweeney's not-quite-girlfriend. Big house, lots of room, and the twins love her. The house, though . . . it's supposed to be haunted by a nice old lady, and she often babysits the owner's kids."

Crow makes jokes like that, and—truth to tell—I'm not always sure he's joking.

"I didn't come here to impose and shake up your life, Crow," I said. "Just looking for a safe place to go to ground and regroup."

"I know."

"Maybe Val should go with the twins . . . ?"

Crow's eyes seemed to glitter with something. Not mischief, though.

Something darker. "Maybe, but our place is pretty safe at the moment." He paused. "Sam's at the house. Staying over for a few days. He, Mike, and that kid, Antonio Jones, are planning on going hunting down in the Hollow."

"Sam . . . as in Sam Hunter?"

"Yup."

"And when you say they're going hunting . . . ?"

"Yup," he repeated, and there was that strange sparkle in his eye.

"Jesus."

"So," he said, studying me, "what kind of trouble are you in?"

"It's complicated. And it's a bit weird."

He spread his arms to indicate more than the office in which we sat. "You're in Pine Deep, Joe. Pretty sure we hold the original patent on weird."

CHAPTER 114
INTEGRATED SCIENCES DEPARTMENT
PHOENIX HOUSE
OMFORI ISLAND, GREECE

Scott Wilson and Mr. Church came into the lab at something close to a dead run.

"Tell me," said Church before he was all the way through the door.

Doc Holliday was hunched over a worktable with Ronald Coleman and Nikki Bloom. The tabletop was covered with maps, printouts from dozens of official sources, news stories, autopsy reports, and other materials.

Church scanned them and looked at Doc.

She said, "With all that's going on, boss, this damn near slipped through the cracks. Luckily, Nikki is a darling girl of a super-nerd with great hair; she's proof that OCD is a superpower."

Nikki flushed, tried to say something cool in reply, totally failed to do so, and turned a deeper shade of red.

"What's the nature of this emergency?" demanded Wilson.

"I take it you haven't actually seen the news."

"We've been a bit busy," said Wilson sharply. "We have one team in the hospital and one on the run. Our bad guys have *seif al din*. So, please, get to it."

"Short version," said Church. "Headlines first."

"Gird your loins, lads," said Doc. "There have been at least four incidents of unusual infectious disease outbreaks. Nikki believes, and I concur, that none of them are random."

She then recapped the incidents.

"Having seen the lab reports from our friends in the CDC," she continued, "I think we can safely say that these are strains taken from Site 44 and Inferno."

Church stiffened. "How high is your confidence on this?"

Doc rattled off the specific strains and then tapped some keys on a laptop and sent the results to one of the closest of a row of big monitors.

"How can you tell if these are deliberate or natural mutating strains?" asked Wilson.

"Mother Nature is a freak," said Doc, "but she's not *this* efficient. No, boys, these were cooked up in a lab, and I had Ron Coleman do a full and very deep analysis of each, and they match known strains restricted to the hot rooms at several on- and off-book sites. For that matter, there are versions of two of these at Gehenna, but it's too soon for those to have been used."

"As far as we know," said Nikki.

"She's right," agreed Wilson. "The team that hit that facility has had hours to play merry hob with whatever they stole."

However, Church shook his head. "The Gehenna hit was focused mainly on *seif al din*. That's the big win for Bliss. These other strains are, as you say, Doc, *known* to have been at Site 44 and Inferno, so let's assume that's where they came from. The timetables work."

Wilson thought about it and nodded. "What's the plan, then?"

"We don't have a useful footprint in the States," said Doc. "Told you that before. We need to create a new team, maybe. Like John Cmar's Bug Hunters, but working directly for RTI."

"Send me a proposal," said Wilson.

"It's been in your inbox for five months," said Doc with a dazzling smile. "Maybe check your spam folder once in a while."

"We'll get it done," said Church. "In the short term, what can we do to assist local agencies with this?"

Doc turned and leaned a meaty hip against the table. "Two things, actually. First, get some kind of channel open that will allow us to share information rather than stealing it. We can't even have these conversations with them, because we have not obtained any of this legally. Right now, I've been faking it—and I never fake anything—by telling them we're reaching out with an offer of help after having seen the news stories. But what's in the press lacks nearly all of the specific details Nikki lifted from CDC and NIH computers."

"I can do that," promised Church. "What's the second thing?"

Doc's smile was wicked, accusatory, scolding, and weirdly flirtatious all at once. "You can charm a girl by stopping the bad guys from stealing all those pathogens. That would make my heart go pit-a-pat."

CHAPTER 115
OFFICE OF PUBLIC SAFETY
PINE DEEP, PENNSYLVANIA

Havoc finished their sweep and came into the office. I introduced them to Crow. Top and Bunny did the handshake/half hug that guys do. Normal handshakes with Remy and Belle.

Gertie looked at them and made faint chicken clucks of disapproval. Belle replied with one of her very rare smiles. It was the kind of smile that makes people want to be somewhere else. Gertie suddenly developed an interest in some papers on her desk.

The door opened, and Patrol Sergeant Michael Sweeney came in.

Mike is about the same size as Bunny. Both were six foot six, and both packed with muscles. Bunny, though improbably massive, had a more sculpted look, with narrower hips and the legs of a beach rat who played a lot of volleyball. Sweeney, on the other hand, was thicker through the chest and had a different kind of solidity to his mass. Kong versus Godzilla.

Sweeney was around thirty, with dark and curly red hair, a collection of odd facial scars, and weird pale gold rings around the irises of his blue eyes. Like the kind of enhancement you'd see in AI-generated artwork of Tolkien's elves. That gold ring was—I noticed—brighter when his anger was up. Not sure if that was just a weird light effect in certain situations, but in the real world, it doesn't look cool or artsy. It's merely strange. And it gives Mike that otherworldly quality that has, according to Crow, given many a bad guy serious pause.

"Captain Ledger," he said to me. "Pleasure to see you again."

"*Colonel* Ledger," corrected Remy.

"Oh yeah? Well, congratulations, sir," he said, offering me his hand. I shook it. "And it's Joe, Mike."

Sweeney nodded. "Joe it is, then."

He turned to Bunny and Top, both of whom he had met on a case years back, in my early days with the DMS. They shook with a single pump accompanied by a nod.

"Dude," said Bunny.

"Dude," replied Mike.

Crow quickly explained the basics to Mike, who asked no questions. He merely accepted.

"Mike," said Crow, "run them out to the house. Then take the kids to Annabelle's."

Mike cut him a quick glance. "Crow . . . do they know about the, um, *hunting* trip?"

"They know you boys are going," Crow said and left it there.

We all went outside. Crow suggested I go with Mike. Havoc was in the second vehicle. We made a U-turn in the street and headed back out of town.

CHAPTER 116
THE PAN HEAD BAR AND GRILL
PINE DEEP, PENNSYLVANIA

There were thirty-two motorcycles parked slantwise to the curb.

The bikes were mostly Harleys—Road Kings, Road Glides, Heritages, Softail Classic & Slim, Dynas, Fat Boys, and some Harley trikes.

Two men sat outside the bar, sprawled on a wooden bench, smoking cigarettes, and watching the foot traffic that kept Main Street busy. The tall man was known as Buck, and his friend was King.

Both were Pine Deep locals, and both had been with the Cyke-lones Motorcycle Club for years.

Both were scouts for the Tenth Legion camps in eastern Pennsylvania and South Jersey. The bar was across the street at an angle from the police station. As a result, the Pan Head was the quiet one of a pair of taverns owned by the club. The other, the Rebel Room, was on a side road that split off Dark Hollow Road. That one was a lot rowdier.

Buck tapped his buddy on the arm, and when King looked up, Buck used an uptick of his chin to indicate the group of people coming out of the police station. Then he opened his phone to the pictures file and scrolled through. They studied the images and compared them to the people talking with Chief Crow and Sergeant Sweeney.

Buck and King exchanged a look.

"Jesus fuck," said Buck.

"Can't be him," said King.

Buck tapped the image on his phone. "Call it in."

King dug out his cell and made a call. After introducing himself using the current day code, he said, "I'm sending you some pics. Tell me if this is who I think it is."

There was a pause, then, "Jesus Christ. Where'd you take that photo?"

"Right here in Pine Deep. Sitting outside of the Pan Head across from the cops."

"Are you going to follow?" asked the voice.

"Follow Joe fucking Ledger?" laughed King. "Kiss my dog's ass. That guy's the angel of death. With his full team and those cops? Sorry, but my mama didn't raise a complete damn fool. Wait, they just left the police station. Ledger's in the lead vehicle with the big red-haired cop. Others are in an SUV." He described the SUV and gave the plate numbers of each vehicle.

"Where's he going?"

"Down A-32 toward the farms."

A pause. "Okay. I think I know where he's going," said the voice. "You guys stay where you are, and thanks for the heads-up. I'll send someone in a farm truck. Someone who won't draw attention."

CHAPTER 117
ON THE ROAD
PINE DEEP, PENNSYLVANIA

I turned in my seat and looked back at the biker bar across from Crow's office.

"Those two clowns sitting near the bikes . . ." I said.

"What about them?" asked Mike

"The vests they're wearing. The gray and red? Aren't they the Cyke-lones' colors?"

"Yes."

"Last time I was in town, Monk Addison told me that you guys had a big tussle with them. Gunplay and all that. Bunch of them went to the morgue."

"Yes."

"But the club is still going? Still allowed to operate in your town?"

Mike shrugged his big shoulders. "The ones who were involved in that scuffle are either in the ground or in jail. But they were just a small part of the group. There are hundreds of them spread across nine states. All up and down I-95."

"Running drugs up Cocaine Alley?"

"Affirmative. Different jurisdictions have arrested some, but the main group hides behind lawyers, the Fifth Amendment, and all that. They know how to play the game. So, to answer your question, yes, they are still in operation. We tried to shut them down, but the judge threw it back at us, saying that the actions of a few couldn't legally be used to take down a group that has existed for more than forty years. The majority of the members don't even have criminal records. So, we have to accept their presence."

"That can't be fun," I said.

"Frankly," said Mike, "they've been a pain in my ass for a long time. I thought they were finished after that fight. But they're like bedbugs—hard as hell to get rid of."

"They behaving?"

"Most are," said Mike. "Some aren't. Lots of them are being pretty vocal about what's been happening with the terrorist bioweapon stuff.

Waving Confederate flags, Nazi flags, and those stupid-ass *Don't Tread on Me* ones."

"Redneck stuff," I said.

Mike shot me a look. "This is small-town farm country, Colonel. We're *all* rednecks here. That doesn't make us all dumb fucks or jack-asses."

"I stand corrected, Mike. My apologies. Didn't mean to offend."

He almost smiled. "There's that old expression that city folks often overlook: *country* don't mean 'dumb.'"

"Duly noted." I ticked my head back toward the bikers. "You building a case against the Cyke-lones?"

"For a long time now, yes," he said. "You were a cop once, right? Then you know how frustrating it is to know more than you can prove."

"Yes, I do," I said. "Up to and including right now."

Mike turned the wipers to low intermittent to deal with the driz-zle. We drove to the local supermarket, and we waited in Mike's car while Remy ran in to shop.

"Just for the record," Mike said eventually, "I don't like this."

"Like what, exactly?" I asked. "Us being in your town? You afraid of us dragging trouble behind?"

Mike turned to study me for a few moments, then looked out at the sky. Dark clouds had covered nearly all of it, and the tops of the trees lining the parking lot were swaying in the pre-storm winds.

"Free country," Mike said. "Not stopping anyone from coming to Pine Deep. We're a tourist town, or haven't you heard?"

"Then what is it, Mike?"

I saw the muscles at the corner of his jaw flex a few times. "He's sending you *home*."

"Ah," I said. "Wasn't my idea, if that matters."

"It *doesn't* matter, actually," he said. "Look . . . Crow and Val's kids are civilians—innocents, which makes them vulnerable. You know they buried two kids out by the tree in front of the house. I helped dig those graves, Joe. Nothing I ever did hurt more or was harder to do. Not looking to dig more graves because of collateral damage in someone else's war, feel me?"

I looked at the side of his face and said, "I buried all of my family two Christmases ago."

He nodded. "Crow told me. And I'm sorry. Really sorry. But you, of all people, should know the danger of putting civilians in the cross-hairs."

"This thing we're chasing, Mike," I said, "it's not someone else's war. This is an international cabal of arms dealers who we think are behind all of the disease releases and probably behind the deepfakes on the net. They are selling WMDs to militia groups all through the States and training those groups to be combat ready for a war they want to start."

He gave me a skeptical look. "Creating a war just to sell guns?"

"Don't be naïve, man. This ain't the first time that ever happened."

He frowned and nodded, not liking it any more than I did.

"And there's more," I said. "And I'm taking you on faith because we've been in the shit together. You, me, Crow, Antonio Jones, and Sam Hunter. We fought terrorists right here in Pine Deep."

"I remember."

"You have Crow's trust, and that means you have mine," I said. "So let me tell you what the real stakes are."

I explained the basics of what we were facing. Kuga, October, Bliss, the Gorgons. He listened without comment. We watched Remy come jogging across the lot to the SUV, arms heavy with shopping bags and a big, lazy grin on his face.

Mike said nothing. Actually, he didn't speak again until he pulled to a stop in front of the big farmhouse.

Val Guthrie stood on the top step.

She was north of fifty, and you could see it in the lines around her mouth and across her throat. She was tall, strong, farm fit. Short black hair that snapped in the early-evening breeze. A Remington pump shotgun was cradled in her arms, held the way someone does when they know how to use it.

My guys clustered in front of the bottom step, standing in the light rain, looking up at her. She looked past us to Mike Sweeney.

"Kids are packed and in the kitchen," she said.

"Yes'm," he said, bobbing his head. Then he trudged around the side of the huge, old farmhouse.

Val looked down at us. "Joe," she said with no trace of a smile.

"Val."

Her expression softened slightly when she looked at Top and Bunny. The smile lingered, however falsely, as she gave Belle and Remy the up and down.

I put a foot on the lower step. "I know this is a lot, Val. We appreciate it. However, say the word and we will turn right around and go find a motel."

I watched her face. She really gave that some thought. Then she lowered the shotgun, stepped back a pace, and half turned. "You're all welcome to stay for as long as you need to."

She went inside and left the door open behind her.

No one on Havoc Team said a goddamn word as we carried our gear bags and Remy's groceries inside.

Ghost lingered on the porch, and when I glanced back, I saw him watching the endless rows of swaying corn. I thought I heard him utter a low growl, but he made none of the actions or sounds he'd been trained to make if there was a clear threat. I think it was just Pine Deep that spooked him.

Smart dog.

I clicked my tongue for him, and he turned slowly and walked past me, claws clicking softly on the hardwood floor. Inside, a veritable herd of cats was waiting—lying on the arms of chairs, perched on end tables, sitting like Egyptian temple guardians in the foyer. No idea how many. My senior citizen of a marmalade tabby, Cobbler, would have been right at home. Ghost felt as awkward and unwelcome as I did.

I closed the door just as the wind picked up and rain began hammering on the windows.

Welcome to Pine Deep, my ass.

CHAPTER 118
THE GUTHRIE FARM
PINE DEEP, PENNSYLVANIA

A man knelt between green stalks of corn. A battered old Dodge pickup stood nearby, its engine recently switched off for the day, the metal ticking as it cooled beneath the fall of cold autumn rain.

The man, known as Tuner to his friends, watched through a sniper scope, holding it to one eye, elbow steadied on the middle rail of a wood fence that separated the cornfield from the gravel turnaround in front of the house.

The big cop who'd brought Ledger and his team here had left, taking the police chief's two teenage kids with him. Tuner did not like that man, though he could not pin down exactly why. Just a feeling. It wasn't merely because Sweeney was a giant and a cop. No, this was something else, and as he watched, Tuner tried to sort out exactly what it was.

It most strongly called to mind a time back when he was twelve and his uncle Sean had taken him out for his first overnight hunting trip out in Potter County. They'd walked for hours, carrying heavy backpacks, the tent, and plenty of ammunition for their guns. By the time they reached the deer stand Sean had built, young Tuner was nearly weeping with exhaustion. Luckily, the tents were pop-ups, and soon Sean had a fire going and some canned beef stew beginning to boil.

Sean was no talker, and there were long hours of just sitting, watching the fire, listening to the woods become increasingly stranger as insects, night birds, small foraging creatures, and other things moved in the inky shadows. Long after they climbed into their sleeping bags, young Tuner lay awake listening, letting his young mind conjure monsters in the dark. His older mind was still feeble in its counterarguments, and so the night stretched on into a black forever.

When they woke, the tent was slashed all along one side. The food—hung high in the trees—was gone, the nylon rope shredded. Everything of value—everything that could be eaten—had been taken.

"Goddamn bear," growled Uncle Sean as he stalked around the camp, kicking ruined equipment. "Fat fucking son-of-a-bitching bear!"

But Tuner didn't see a single bear print. Not one.

Uncle Sean had taught him how to identify different animals, and bears had been a big part of that. The ground was more than soft enough to take any mark.

There was nothing.

Tuner remembered the exact moment when Sean noticed it, too.

He froze, one hand going to the holstered Ruger Blackhawk he wore gunslinger fashion on his hip. The woods went absolutely silent for a few moments, and Sean thumbed off the restraining strap.

Silence.

Sean began to draw that gun. Inch by slow inch. Deep in the woods, there was a sound. Soft. Heavy. Like something moving just outside of the line of vision. Moving around the camp. Slowly. Patiently.

Young Tuner could feel strange eyes upon him. Watching.

Watching with hunger.

And then . . . the birds started chirping and the insects buzzed.

They left shortly after, and Uncle Sean told tall tales about the bear that ruined their camp. Each time, he added elements he plucked out of the air—seeing a brown bear, prints everywhere, claw marks on the trees. All lies, and his occasional quick glares at Bob kept the boy silent, made him a coconspirator in a fiction that was the only one that made the world make sense.

It was no goddamn bear in the woods, but neither of them could ever admit it. Not aloud. Not even to each other.

Uncle Sean kept on hunting, but he never went to that part of the forest again.

The feeling that Tuner had for that big red-haired cop was similar to what he'd felt that morning in the woods. The same kind of doubt and uncertainty. The same feeling that there was something out there in the shadows that did not want to be understood or described or known.

Thunder grumbled in the distance, and the rain began to really hammer down.

Tuner debated calling in to Mr. October, and his hand even stretched toward the pocket that held his cell, but he left it there. Call and tell him what? He'd already reported the location where Havoc Team had gone to ground. What else was there to say? That he was afraid of an overgrown kid of a cop? That he was afraid of the dark?

So he waited and he watched through the sniper scope.

And the woods all around Tuner watched *him*.

CHAPTER 119
THE GUTHRIE FARM
PINE DEEP, PENNSYLVANIA

Val seemed pleased with the thought of Remy cooking up some Cajun-hot groceries and yielded the kitchen to him.

Remy sketched a faux elegant deep-swooping bow. "How spicy do you like it, ma'am?"

Val went and opened a cabinet in which were scores of bottles of hot sauces. We all leaned close and studied the colorful labels. Remy read them aloud.

"Sichuan Ghost, Backfire XL, Mad Dog Plutonium, A Little Funky, Anal Angst, Alice Cooper No More Mr. Nice Guy, ANALize This, Ass Blaster, Ass Kicker Carolina Reaper, Fire Ant Juice, Mean Green Motherfucker, Nuckin' Futs, oh . . . wait . . . I found it. The king of hot sauces. Oh *hells* yes."

He turned and held up a bottle of lethally dark red sauce with a black label and the face of a grinning Satan. The label read: *The Devil Hates Your Colon!*

We all approved, and Val laughed.

The meal Remy made was the best, most succulent, most suicidally hot concoction. Not sure it had an actual name, but we all agreed that it qualified as a weapon of mass destruction. We had seconds and thirds as tears streamed down our faces. My hair was sweating, and I could only guess at what Top was going to say if he had to share another bathroom with Bunny, who was shoveling the stuff in by the quart.

When Crow came home, he had three helpings. Watching his face go from pale to pink to five-alarm fire red was a treat. He tried to put out the fire with several bottles of Yoo-hoo. And failed.

Later on, Top, Crow, and I went outside to watch the storm. Thunder boomed like a tank battle, and the rain fell hard as bullets.

"Okay," Crow said, "so one last thing to clarify . . . what made you choose Pine Deep? Specifically, I mean. You didn't come here because of the Cyke-lones, did you?"

"The bikers?" I said. "No. Why?"

Crow took his cell out of his jacket pocket and scrolled through photos. When he found what he was looking for, he showed us a pic of a guy—obviously a biker—wearing a sleeveless Cyke-lones vest over a soiled white tank top. Crow used two fingers to expand the image, reorienting it to focus on the man's upper-right biceps. Top and I leaned in to peer at a black-and-white tattoo. It was an "X" sitting in the middle of a circlet of some kind of braided vine. Crow tapped the vine.

"*Euphorbia milii*," he said. "Commonly known as the *corona de Cristo*, which means the 'crown of Christ.'"

"Thorny crown," said Top. He cut Crow a look. "The Cyke-lones are with the Tenth Legion?"

"Most of them are," he said. "Tenth Legion's nothing new to us in Pine Deep. I've been seeing that tattoo and a shit-ton of graffiti lately. Say . . . the last eighteen months, give or take."

"You know of any militia training camps around here?"

"There's two I know of offhand," he said, surprising Top and me. "A small one that's mostly stacks of crates hidden under jungle canopy netting."

"Supply depot," said Top, and I nodded.

"The other one's a lot bigger," said Crow. "Mike's taken some surveillance photos of it because we have a theory they're doing some human trafficking. That's been on our radar since that gig you did with Monk Addison. There's nothing we can prove so far, but enough to make us think we're right about it. Guns, too. With the current gun laws, nothing we're seeing is illegal, especially on private land. They zoned it for a gun range, too. All nice and legal. Can't get in for a closer look without a warrant, which no judge will sign."

"I might be able to help with that," I said. "My boss can make a call and—"

"—and he doesn't know the local judges," Crow cut in. "They're a whole lot more likely to align with those nut bags in the woods. They've been giving open-carry violations and other crimes a soft pass."

"Which means they're in someone's pocket," said Top. "Calling your judges would be like advertising we're here."

"Correct-a-mundo," said Crow. He sipped his Yoo-hoo. "Let me tell you something else. Those Tenth Legion boys are a cut above the average militia types. Mike watched them drill. Most appear to be legit military trained. They train hard, and they're damn good on the firing range. Good solo and group combat tactics."

"Training's one thing," said Top, who had been a drill sergeant once upon a time. "But field experience is another."

"No doubt," agreed Crow. "Just letting you know what's what out at that camp."

"How many men?" I asked.

"At the depot? Maybe twenty. Mike said they look more clerical than combat ready. As for the big camp—has to be an easy hundred. And add to that another hundred Cyke-lones. It's a real army."

"Ouch," said Top.

We sat with that and watched the rain fall.

I rubbed my eyes. "I don't usually believe in coincidences, Crow . . ."

"And yet . . ." he said, then added, "Then again, Pine Deep's always been like that."

"Like what? A haven for white supremacists?"

He shook his head. "That's a side effect, Joe. No, what I meant is that Pine Deep has *earned* its reputation as a weird place. We joke around about it being America's 'Haunted Holidayland,' but that's lemons from lemonade. The truth is that bad things happen here at a higher percentage rate than just about anywhere. It's like there's a magnet here that draws the bad guys to us. Bad people. Bad hearts, twisted minds. And, who knows, maybe there's something in the soil here or the water that amplifies whatever darkness is in your soul." He paused as if listening to his own words, then he laughed. Short and false. "Don't mind me . . . I'm getting old, and the older you get, the darker the nights are."

"Seems pretty dark out here to me, too," I said.

Lightning instantly flashed, and thunder boomed loud enough to rattle the windowpanes behind us. All three of us tried not to take that as some kind of sign.

Then the door opened, and Bunny leaned out. "Guys, you might want to see this. President's about to address the nation."

CHAPTER 120
THE ROSE GARDEN
THE WHITE HOUSE
WASHINGTON, DC

It was broadcast on all networks, with the streaming news services adding text crawls and pop-ups.

The president stood behind a podium wearing a subdued suit and quiet tie. The cameras focused on his face as he prepared himself to deliver the remarks everyone in the country and whole nations around the world were waiting for. Waiting, hoping, dreading. Despite carefully applied stage makeup, hairspray, and a fresh suit, he looked weary. Heartsick and angry, too. He had one of those faces that seldom hid what he was feeling.

"My fellow Americans," he began in a firm voice. "Our nation faces a grave and immediate threat."

He paused and looked out over the sea of faces arrayed in front of him. Reporters, key politicians who were there either in support or for photo ops, Secret Service, members of the White House staff—all tense and expectant.

"There has been a series of incidents over the last several days. In each case, a communicable disease was deliberately introduced in places where innocent people became infected. We have suffered tragic losses, and our prayers go out to the families of the victims. These attacks are unprovoked and the results tragic."

Cameras flashed and flashed.

The president's eyes were sharp as he looked at the audience. "The perpetrators of each attack have not yet been identified or apprehended. However, law enforcement agencies across the country are working closely with Homeland Security and our intelligence agencies, and they *will* be found. And they will be punished to the fullest extent of the law."

Pause.

"They will be punished to the fullest extent of American justice."

It was the first true sound bite, and the words *American justice* would become the catchphrase of the season. The speechwriters knew this when they crafted the speech.

Then the president changed his tone to a more authoritative yet informed one.

"Several radicalized groups have stepped forward to take credit for these atrocities. However, we have yet to determine if those claims are legitimate. And here I ask my fellow Americans to be cautious, to wait for reliable and verifiable information before making judgment or taking action. A number of these claims have already been discredited. It is all too common for ambitious groups to want to borrow power by making such claims even if they are in no way involved. It is also common for political groups to make false claims in the hopes of weakening their rivals and in the hopes that America will strike back. As a nation, we cannot allow ourselves to be fooled; we cannot allow ourselves to be pointed like someone else's gun."

A pause.

"When we respond—and I can promise you that we *will* respond—it will be directed against the true culprits. I know influencers on social media are quick to demand action. They want us to hit back with great force, but that is not the best way. To strike back at a foreign country without irrefutable proof of guilt. Knee-jerk reactions result in needless deaths. Our intelligence networks, in concert with our most trusted allies around the world, are working tirelessly to determine the truth. We have all seen the results of actions taken too quickly and on the basis of questionable information. I will not spend American lives striking out in rage and in doing so cause greater harm."

Pause. His eyes roved over the crowd and looked into the cameras. Wanting and needing to be seen. To be heard and understood.

"We will find the truth," he said. "We will gather that irrefutable evidence. And when we have identified whoever is responsible, believe me when I say they will feel the full weight of our nation's righteous anger. Our allies are ready to stand with us."

He stopped looking at his teleprompter and stared hard into the closest camera.

"I want to speak now to whoever did this, to whoever is behind it," he said. "Hear me. You have attacked us. You have caused the deaths of people who did you no harm. You believe you can act with impunity. You think you will get away with this. See and hear me now and

JONATHAN MABERRY

believe what I say. There is nowhere you can hide. There is no way to escape the consequences of your actions. You will find no safe ground, no hole deep enough, no place far enough to escape the punishment due to you. There is no nation who will protect you. Even now, carrier groups of the United States Navy are moving into position around those areas where some of the threats originated. There is no one who will offer you haven. America is coming for you. Hear that. America is coming for you. And may God have mercy on your souls, for you will find no mercy from me."

Another pause, and he repeated that last line.

"You will find no mercy from me."

The cameras flashed madly, and all around the country and the world, social media exploded.

CHAPTER 121
ACROSS AMERICA

In the wake of the president's fiery speech, all of the major social media platforms were inundated with videos. Many were obvious fakes, but some were so convincing that news networks were scrambling to book experts in deepfake videos and internet propaganda to try to disprove them.

It was an uphill battle, because public reaction was swift and furious, and waves of bot accounts were triggered by keywords to post in support of the videos. Often that support was couched in outraged terms, promising retaliation to any group whose identity was borrowed by the creators of the fakes.

Like many of those kinds of slanted posts, it was damage done. Far more people saw or heard about the messages of the fake videos and accepted them as true than ever saw the rebuttals by cooler heads. And, as soon as the mainstream media sources began decrying the videos *as* propaganda, the pushback and accusations began to fly— with the primary message being that the mainstream media was lying. That they were hiding the truth. That the government was using the media to hide the truth of lack of action, complicity, or weakness.

The national conversation did its best to fracture along party lines, but that process wasn't as severe as it normally was on any given issue. Just as there was in the days following 9/11, the loudest cry was from a unified, frightened, and outraged majority of the American population.

They wanted protection.

They wanted answers.

They wanted payback.

They wanted blood.

CHAPTER 122
THE GUTHRIE FARM
PINE DEEP, PENNSYLVANIA

We were clustered in Crow's den, sitting on overstuffed chairs and cushy couches, watching all of it on the big screen. Somehow we had been slowly and silently invaded by the family's many cats, and everyone seemed to have one on their laps or sprawled atop their shoes. Ghost stayed close to me, feeling outnumbered and threatened.

But our focus was on the news.

"This is nuts," said Bunny.

No one argued.

One video showed a bunch of young Muslims burning an American flag while the crowd chanted, "Death to America." I know for a fact that I'd seen that footage before, and it was old stuff from the war in Afghanistan. I even called Bug about it, and he said he knew and was working on getting the original files to send to the right people in Washington and the media.

Another showed a lab in what looked like a cobwebby basement. Rows of vials of questionable liquids lined a table, and there was all manner of Dr. Frankenstein tubes and beakers and machines. People were speaking in the video, with English translation in subtitles. The conversation went something like this:

Radical guy with a black scarf wrapped around his face was yelling at two scientists in lab coats: "We need more. We want the flesh of the Americans to run like tallow. We want their bodies to bleed. We want God's plagues to waste them away."

It was badly phrased but said with passion, and the scientists made promises that the latest versions of their bioweapons would lay waste to both the people and the crops throughout America's heartland farms. It looked like a bad scene from a cheap movie, and if it was, not even Bug's team could find a source.

"They might be making these clips themselves," Bug told me. "Staged videos or AI deepfakes. Or a combination of both."

"What's Doc say about the lab in that video?"

"She said it's nonsense. The right equipment, but not the right way it should be set up. If they were really working with pathogens, the obvious lack of basic safety precautions would result in contamination of everyone there."

"Can we get that on the news?"

"Sure," said Bug, "but how many will actually see it, and of those, how many will believe it? No one trusts the news anymore."

"Shit."

There were others. Not all of which were purported Muslims. There was a very convincing video of a biological development lab in what looked like a cartel cocaine-processing facility, and everyone in the video was speaking Spanish with either a Mexican or Colombian accent. Whoever made that video went the distance to make sure the containment procedures were obviously in place and that the lab equipment was properly placed.

"That one just came up," said Bug. "My guess is that the people who did the first one realized it looked cheap and then leveled up."

"Is it real or AI?"

"I have Yoda on that. All of the videos have *some* AI, but it's getting harder and harder to tell which. And which parts are computer generated. There are these new *smoothing* programs that futz with the pixels to make it harder to pull them out for a forensic analysis. Like what we're doing with those cobra and bat videos we have. I mean, let's face it, Joe, they *have* to be fake, and Yoda will prove it, but it's tough, slow, nitpicky work. These new videos, though, are at least a couple of generations better. You know how fast computer tech changes. Bottom line, though, is that these people—if it's all one group—have put some real thought and money into this."

"Can your team break this stuff apart? Deconstruct it? Whatever it's called."

"We can and will," Bug assured me. "But in time? And, like I said, Joe, even if we put it all together and explain how fake it is, no one believes the news anymore."

"So, how the hell do we set the record straight before things blow the hell up?" I demanded, even though I already knew the answer.

Bug said it, though. "I don't know if the record will ever be set straight, Joe. I don't even see how it can be."

CHAPTER 123
TENTH LEGION TRAINING CAMP #3
TANNER BAYOU
LIBERTY COUNTY, TEXAS

"Are you somewhere private?" asked Mr. October.

Toombs said, "This about the White House presser?"

"Only in part. We need to talk."

"I just wrapped the last training thing. Got the commandant and a couple of his sergeants here."

"Lose them. Go somewhere else."

Toombs excused himself and walked out from under the big camo netting that was stretched from tree to tree to thwart aerial surveillance. There was a thick stand of trees on the northeast corner, and he went into them. A perimeter guard saw and recognized him and moved off to give him privacy.

"Now what?" asked Toombs.

"You don't sound like a happy person, my friend," said October.

"Yeah, well, I'll scratch my mad place and get happy again once this is all in the rearview mirror. I don't like how this is playing out."

"Are you still mad about the comfort camp?"

"I'm not a fan of it."

"You'll sell weapons of war, and yet you get squeamish if some of the soldiers—our customers, mind you—want some R & R?"

Toombs nearly responded to that with a diatribe he'd been rehearsing in his head, but he took a beat to compose himself. "What did you call about?"

"Joe Ledger and his team are in Pine Deep," said Mr. October.

Toombs said, "*What?* How? Why?"

"From all appearances, they are there to regroup after the hit on their safe house. Ledger is friends with the local police chief."

"He's friends with Malcolm Crow? That's not good."

"It's . . . interesting. I don't know if Crow is in his confidence or not. I tend to doubt it, though."

"You think they're onto us?"

October laughed. "Why? Don't you believe it's a coincidence?"

"Ha ha," said Toombs flatly. "Look, boss, we know they took a couple legionnaires from the trailer park. One of them, Andrew Kemmer, was trained at the camp. We know they were at Norris's trailer, too, and just because Norris is dead doesn't mean he didn't talk. Same with Kemmer and Huberman. We lost touch with the team that hit their safe house. Ledger must have made someone talk. I mean, not everyone is going to crunch down on that suicide tooth, even if they actually think it's just a knockout pill."

"Agreed. Norris knew the most, Kemmer second. Huberman knew nothing of value."

"What's the play here?" asked Toombs. "If Ledger's in Pine Deep, then there's a chance he knows what's what. Give me the word and I'll have all the camps stand down and wait."

"No, no," protested October, "that'll just give Ledger and Church more time. No, we need to step it up."

"Step it up how much?"

"Like maybe launch Firefall for sure tomorrow."

Toombs had to take a longer beat on that. He could feel his blood pressure rising, burning his cheeks and ears. "Is that wise?" he asked with forced patience. "We are nowhere near ready. Okay, some camps are, but not the rest. If we move this up to tomorrow, then we're only going to be able to deploy four Gorgons. Four out of forty. Isn't that going to diminish the overall impact? I thought you wanted 'America under siege.' Four hits will look like just a tiny upgrade to the Typhoid Marys David White was delivering. Sure, bigger body count and all that, but even so. It's not what we've been working toward. No, boss, I think we should go dark and give it six or eight months. Let Ledger chase his dick for a while. Maybe evac the camps here in Pennsylvania and New Jersey. Doesn't take much to set up a new one. We have two dozen plots of land. I can send a cut-and-run signal to everyone. You've seen how fast they can strip it down, pack the trucks, and get into the wind. Hour tops for the big camps, half that for the smaller ones. And shut down the comfort camp thing, because if Ledger gets wind of that, then we'll have Homeland all the way up our ass."

"No," October said firmly. "Not yet, Mr. Toombs."

"But—"

"Shhh," interrupted October. "Listen to me. I'm not convinced Ledger knows all that much. We've kept him running, and there are no reinforcements in the area that we know of. If they knew about Firefall and knew where the camps are, there would be a swarm of FBI, DEA, ATF, and a dozen other agencies converging. Maybe the National Guard, too. And if *any* of that was in motion, our people would know. Senator Harris would know. Key people we have in those agencies would have heard, which means *we* would have heard. No, my friend, I think this is—at worst—Ledger following a lead to the one camp in Black Marsh. It's small anyway—just a supply depot, really. So, sure, send *them* a cut-and-run order, but leave the others in place. That will keep our troops handy if Havoc wants to go in alone."

"And *still* move forward with Firefall tomorrow?" asked Toombs, who did not try to disguise his incredulity.

"Yes," October said firmly. Then he took an audible breath and in a calmer tone said, "Let's do this . . . I'll go to Pine Deep myself. Ledger won't recognize me. He might recognize you, so stay out of town."

"And do what?"

"Fly home and go to the Mansion. Your part in this is done, so you earned some time off. Mary is there. Tell her about this, but say that I want you both to stay there and lie low. Ledger absolutely knows her on sight."

"He thinks she's dead."

"He knows that he shot her. He also knows she was infected with *seif al din*, so we don't know what information RTI has acquired about her status once she was moved to Site 44. Nor do they know if she's active again. Let's not challenge his awareness because that would have definite and dire consequences."

"Okay," said Toombs. "But I'll say it once more, boss. We ought to take a moment here. I've seen what Ledger and his people can do when they're in gear. They could do us a lot of damage."

"Don't sweat it, my friend," said October. "I'll call the commandant and have him send some troops over to guard the Mansion. You and Mary will be safe. And if things go south, there's a back exit through the basement. Mary knows the way."

"Are you going there, too?"

"Eventually. I want to stop at the camp first and make sure that Firefall launches on time and as planned. I'll make that my command post until things are in motion, then I'll join you and Miss Mary at the Mansion for a celebration dinner. I'm sure the cook will come up with something appropriately magnificent."

"Boss . . ."

"That's my decision, Mr. Toombs."

Toombs sighed and said that he'd follow his orders.

When the call was ended, he looked out at the camp of Tenth Legionnaires. "What the hell am I doing?" he asked the trees and the birds and the universe.

CHAPTER 124
THE GUTHRIE FARM
PINE DEEP, PENNSYLVANIA

Before I went up to bed, Crow took me into his private study and showed me his collection of Japanese swords. There were a dozen elegant katanas, ranging from less expensive ones used for solo training to one six-hundred-year-old sword that belonged to an ancestor of Crow's sensei.

"I know you studied jujitsu, too," he said. "Different style from the one I learned, but it's an old samurai family version, too, right?"

"Yeah. It ain't pretty, but it gets the job done," I said.

Several of his cats came in and sat looking at us. Ghost opened his eyes, and for a moment, there was a staring contest, then the boss cat of the Guthrie farm, a one-eyed, scarred gray tabby, walked over, plopped down against Ghost, and promptly fell asleep.

"That's new," said Crow.

Ghost looked at me for answers, but I gave him the "it's okay" finger movement, and he settled down. Soon he was sleeping, too.

We talked for a while about that. He'd gotten into martial arts after growing up with an abusive father who liked knocking him around. Jujitsu was structure and honor and self-control. Crow talked a little about how PTSD from his children pushed him in the direction of alcohol addiction. He went to meetings now.

"You still get on the mat?" I asked.

"With Mike, sometimes. Once in a while with Monk. And I've taught Val and the kids a move or two."

I explained that I'd gotten into martial arts after what happened to Helen and me. I was fracturing, falling into rage and hate, and that same structure, the same behavioral tenets taught in Bushido saved me from a long fall. Maybe saved my life.

Crow took down a sword that was less stylish than the others, though the knuckle guard, the tsuba, had a lovely pattern of crows in a cornfield. He handed the sword to me, and I drew it from the sheath. The scabbard was plain and scuffed, but the sword itself was exceptional. Clean, oiled, and as sharp as any such weapon could be.

"Gorgeous," I said, handing it back with a small ceremonious bow.

Crow did not put the sword back on the rack but instead laid it on his desk.

"In case I need it," he said. "For close work."

"Don't take this the wrong way, man, but are you up to this?"

"Why? Because I'm old?"

"And you weigh less than my right foot."

His eyes twinkled with mischief. "I get by."

CHAPTER 125
THE TOC
OMFORI ISLAND, GREECE

Church, Scott Wilson, and Rudy Sanchez sat together in a quiet corner of a very busy tactical operations center.

The deepfake videos played over and over again on several of the smaller windows inset into the central screen at the front of the big room. Techs and analysts hammered away at computer keyboards. Dozens of specialists were on phone calls, rattling away in a score of languages.

"Tell me, gentlemen," asked a weary Rudy, "is this Mr. October?"

"To be determined," said Wilson.

Church said, "It's my belief that it is."

Wilson began to comment but thought better of it and closed his mouth.

"To what end, though?" Rudy said. "Is his goal a disruption of American politics? Is it to cast further doubt in the reliability of the news services? Is it misdirection so we're focused on all this while he does something else?"

"All of those are likely," said Church. "Individually and collectively."

"Do we know what Firefall is? Or is this it? Some kind of chaos so that resources are so stretched he can get away with something?"

"As I said, Doctor, I'm convinced that October is planning something big and something that will involve guns. The outbreaks, dangerous as they are, have been carefully stage-managed. They created fear, and then the claims of responsibility have turned that fear into anger directed at various groups that have been favorite targets in the past. Muslims, immigrants, and so on."

Rudy frowned. "Do we think that Russia, China, North Korea, or Iran are actually behind any of this?"

"That is currently unknown," said Wilson. "America and her allies have spies and moles inside each of those governments, and there are rumors. Some credible rumors of, if not direct responsibility, a kind of sympathetic complicity. A tacit endorsement, with perhaps some off-board payments to grease the wheels."

"It is highly unlikely any of it comes down through official channels," said Church. "Even in Iran and North Korea. That would be an act of war, and both nations know it's a war they cannot win—militarily or economically."

Wilson nodded. "Which is why China and Russia have been officially appalled by what's happening and have publicly offered full support. Lip service, of course."

Rudy gestured to the front of the TOC. "I saw on one of those screens that those countries are moving their armed forces into oppositional positions. They are getting ready for war."

Wilson shook his head. "They have to do that. Call it a requirement of both saving face and saber-rattling. Optics for the international news. A show of force that nations have always done when *war* becomes part of the political conversation. But we don't think that any of them are willing to engage in that war. For Russia and China in particular, their history is to fight proxy wars—as in the Korean War and Vietnam. They don't want to try to duke it out with the world's greatest military on their home turf."

That mollified Rudy a bit. He changed tack. "I ask again, what is Firefall?"

"We don't know," said Wilson.

"We have assets in play who are working on that," said Church.

"Assets," echoed Rudy sourly. "You mean Joe and his team."

"Havoc, yes. There is an Arklight team in the area as well. They have been working on what we believed was a separate case—"

"—human trafficking," interjected Wilson.

Church nodded. "However, Colonel Ledger has informed us that the traffickers are likely associated with the Tenth Legion."

He related a call he received from Joe Ledger shortly after the president's speech. Then he told Rudy about a call from Violin, who was tracking a comfort camp in the same part of Bucks County.

Rudy's face blanched. "They are setting up a comfort camp for the legionnaires. *Ay, dios mío . . .*"

"Lilith has recommended Violin contact Colonel Ledger to coordinate their response."

"What kind of response? Arklight teams are usually only two or three people, and Joe has four beside himself. There are dozens of legionnaires. Hundreds."

Church gave Rudy one of his very rare smiles. It was not a happy or charming smile, though. "Colonel Ledger is in Pine Deep, and he has friends there. Allies."

"Who? A local cop and his deputy? Against an army? Can't you get Homeland or the National Guard or someone? State police, at the very least."

"There is insufficient evidence useful for bringing in the official police or federal agencies," said Church. "I am, however, reaching out to a few of my friends. Rest assured, Doctor, that Havoc will not be alone if this comes to a fight."

"Can't you tell one of your friends that the Tenth Legion and Mr. October are behind the disease attacks?"

"I have suggested this. But even in such a crisis, the bureaucracy is mired in red tape. And, frankly," said Church, "everyone in the States is focused on the bioweapon attacks and the claims that they are being made by either Muslims or groups in Mexico and Colombia."

"And what do you believe?" demanded Rudy.

"Colonel Ledger and I discussed that as well. We both agree that Mr. October is likely the new Kuga, or someone highly placed in that organization. We know that October runs the Tenth Legion. We're not sure, though, whether the members of the Tenth Legion know of Kuga's involvement. My guess is that they do not."

"Why?"

"Because they are being radicalized; they are forming new militia groups all throughout the United States, under the Tenth Legion banner or by other names. And that results in a significant uptick in gun sales. Arms, big and small, are how Kuga makes its money."

Rudy considered that. "So, all of this—the bioweapons and the rest—it's all about Kuga making money?"

"Very likely," said Wilson. "In America alone? More than you'd think. Back in 2010, there were approximately ten million guns sold in the States, but that number jumped to over twenty-one million by 2020 because of changes in gun ownership laws. As of last year, that number doubled, and estimates are that in the last two weeks, gun sales have quadrupled. Nor is it only in America. In every country where civilians can purchase firearms, there has been an increase."

"Even so, twenty or even forty million . . . is that enough of a reward for Kuga to risk the backlash if exposed?"

"It's not only civilian sales," said Church. "Corporations, PMC groups, private security firms, and others have begun stockpiling weapons."

"He's right," said Wilson. "Bug has been keeping an eye on dark web sales of more dangerous items like RPGs, Stingers, LAW rockets, armed drones, tech based on the Boston Dynamics robot dogs for combat, helicopters, and more. Hundreds of millions in sales, with a jump in sales of about four hundred percent since the first videos of groups taking credit for what happened in Atlanta and elsewhere. At this rate, even with corrections when panic purchases level off, we are talking about sales in the billions. Kuga is the biggest illegal arms dealer out there, Doctor. And they likely have one or more legitimate companies running under layers of removes from the criminal enterprises. Those companies deal in everything from tanks to jets."

Rudy looked like he'd been punched in the stomach.

Wilson put a hand on Rudy's shoulder. "Take heart, Doctor," he said kindly. "We are doing everything we can."

It was a platitude and sounded like it. Rudy nearly snapped at him but forced himself to eerily nod.

Church rose and looked at his watch. "Scott, I'm going to fly to Pennsylvania. I'll take the survivors from Bedlam Team and anyone else I can get. I think it's time we gave Colonel Ledger and the Arklight team some practical backup."

He shook Rudy's hand, nodded to Wilson, and left.

After a moment, Wilson left to oversee the operations at the TOC. Rudy closed his eyes and touched the crucifix he wore beneath his shirt and tie.

"Please," he begged.

CHAPTER 126
HOUSE OF REPRESENTATIVES
THE CAPITOL BUILDING

The Speaker of the House was hesitant to allow a vote on the bill. It was a political hot potato, and possibly a poisonous one. No matter how the vote went, heads would roll and careers would collapse.

And yet . . .

He silenced the chamber and then announced the name and summary of the bill to close all American borders in the continental United States. The only exceptions would be for critical shipping, and in those cases, greatly increased security and inspections would be immediately implemented. No immigrants would be allowed, from any country. It was the total ban the hard-liners on both sides of the aisle wanted and was known as the Harris bill, because Bob Harris had championed it. The nation watched as the gentle dove of a senator hardened into a nationalist and isolationist in real time.

The vote was 402 in favor, 26 against, and 7 voting as "present."

Earlier that morning, several gun control bills were crushed or removed from the docket.

All trading on the stock market was suspended.

Within minutes of the Harris bill vote, death threats began flooding the phone lines, email accounts, and social media message feeds for the congresspeople who voted against the bill. Those who voted present were labeled as cowards, as supporters of terrorism, or as anti-American.

X and TikTok crashed from the avalanche of posts. Instagram nearly collapsed beneath the weight of new videos. Discord, Threads, Mastodon, BitChute, Gab, GETTR, Parler, Rumble, Bluesky, Telegram, and Truth Social had their busiest days since each platform had launched.

The internet caught fire and burned out of control.

CHAPTER 127
ACROSS AMERICA

Two videos launched within hours of each other.

The first video was posted by a social media influencer who had 2.3 million subscribers for his YouTube channel called the Hot Mic. The owner of the channel never showed his face, but was instead an anonymous voice that many people thought was really one of the actors for the Marvel Cinematic Universe. It was not, but the influencer—really a small team working for a company owned by Mr. October—used sound mixing, audio AI, and modulation programs to sell that lie.

The same techniques had been used dozens of times to post hot mic moments. Often for celebrities, building on those producers, screenwriters, directors, and actors known to have loose lips while drunk. Less often, the Hot Mic team would put words in the mouths of politicians, famous corporate billionaires, and others.

The second video posted that evening was accompanied by a clip of the president, downloaded from the "You will find no mercy from me" Rose Garden speech. The voice was easily recognizable as POTUS, and the team had lifted background noise from that press event to layer behind the false accidental sound bite.

The tail end of the press conference after that speech was the lead-in, and then the president said, "Is this off now? Yes? Good. I think that went well. If we spin it right, we'll skate into the second term."

Within minutes, the clip was getting thousands of hits. Within the hour, it was on every social media platform, including those who leaned toward the president's own party. Within three hours, there were voices raised in Congress calling for impeachment.

All night long, the cable news services did little else except dissect that comment, even though the White House issued a strongly worded denial that it was legitimate. The world did not care about legitimate. It fed on controversy, on hate, on bias, on the exigencies of group ideologies.

Mr. October, watching on his laptop, smiled and smiled.

He had Toombs on speakerphone.

"You saw?"

"Shit, boss, aliens on the far side of Mars saw that. Everyone's seen it."

"This president will never shake it off. His wooden tower is collapsing. Can you hear the timbers crack?"

"Since when are you political?"

"Me?" laughed October. "I couldn't care less about politics except as a tool, and this is a sledgehammer we have swung with crushing force."

"Congratulations," said Toombs dryly.

"Now, my friend," October said, "we are absolutely clear to launch Firefall tomorrow."

Toombs merely grunted.

October was too delighted with himself to draw inferences from the tone of that grunt. He settled back in the jet and thought about what he would say to Miss Mary once he got back to the Mansion.

CHAPTER 128
PATRIOT'S PRIDE FIREARMS
WEST FIFTY-FOURTH STREET AND WESTLAKE AVENUE
PARMA, OHIO

Jake Saunders was not what anyone would call a gun nut.

His politics were right but leaning centrist, he did not give much of a damn about who was in the White House, and his store became his on his father's death. But it was his grandfather, a veteran of the Vietnam War, who founded the shop, and he had been a gun nut.

Jake wanted to open a family restaurant and had been shopping for locations, with an eye toward selling the gun store to finance the eatery when everything went crazy. Since Ohio had become an open-carry state, his sales had gone up, and that was great, but he disliked the kinds of conversations that came with it. There was a lot of anger in his clientele—more each year. At first, the sales spikes had been reactionary—people buying guns and wanting to wear guns because they wanted to look tough and hopefully feel tougher. That phase jumped and then slowed.

After that, it was when crime spiked in *other* towns, because the newspeople loved to scare the living shit out of the average home-owner. So, home protection gun sales rose. A year ago, rumors began floating around town about a militia group setting up a camp out-side of town. Nothing too ominous, though—mostly potbellied types who liked dressing up in SWAT team gear and blowing through their paychecks with expensive ammunition. They seemed harmless out-side of their camp, though, so Jake didn't care. Their money spent, and every box of 9mm, .45, .22 long, and shotgun shells was another brick in the restaurant Jake wanted to build. He even had a spread-sheet of ammunition and gun sales profits measured against the po-tential mortgage on the place.

Then the disease things hit the news. People came in to buy gas masks and water purification tablets and first aid kits. He sold out of all of that in a day and paid extra for an overnight restocking delivery. Not that any of that stuff would do anyone a bit of good if they were exposed to anthrax or typhoid fever or, god knows, the Black Plague.

Jake sold what his customers wanted.

When the net and the news announced that radical groups had taken claim for the attacks, that's when the sales went through the roof. It was the first time in his life there had been a line out the door and halfway around the building.

He sold everything.

Every handgun, every rifle, every shotgun. He sold holsters, gun bags, cleaning kits, ammunition, packs of paper targets, and anything else that would make terrified homeowners feel safer and make the militia guys feel empowered.

The money was incredible. Even when he marked up his dwindling stock.

But Jake became increasingly more unsettled as the day wore on.

Several of his customers told him that a war was coming.

For the very first time, Jake Saunders felt that they might be correct.

That evening, he placed orders to restock everything. He had to extend his reach, though, because wholesalers were running low. Each of them promised him that big shipments were on the way.

Jake placed heavy orders.

And every time he made a sale, he felt like his dream of a quiet life as a restaurateur was slipping further and further away.

CHAPTER 129
SPLIT ROCK RESORT
428 MOSEYWOOD ROAD
LAKE HARMONY, PENNSYLVANIA

Miss Mary stepped out of the shower and stood dripping onto the floor.

The pool of water that gathered around her feet was tinged a pale pink. The water in the shower stall was a deeper red. The darkest red still pumped sluggishly from the young man she had brought home from a bar the previous night. He was beyond speech but still alive, and he lay there in a heap, staring with horrid fascination at the small, curled lumps that littered the stall floor. He knew they were his fingers. Had *been* his fingers. But his dimming brain tried to curl them even though they were no longer attached to his hands. The logic of understanding was beyond him now. All he had left was fear and wonder.

Mary took a towel from under the sink and wiped away the blood on her mouth and stomach and thighs. Then she crossed to the big, jetted tub and began to fill it. She poured Epsom salts into the water and leaned her buttocks against the sink to wait.

The man in the shower had been fun for a while, but not for long. In the bar, he had been all flirtation and macho come-on. She had been dressed in goth black with shocking red lipstick and a push-up bra under a lace top. The lace hid her scars.

Once in the hotel room—with its thick adobe walls—she turned on a thrash metal station and cranked up the volume. They'd kissed in the bedroom and then toppled onto the big king bed. He had ten thousand hands and a huge erection pressing outward through his jeans. Mary let him take off her black tights and go down on her, watching his face as he tried not to react to the odd taste of her juices. She knew she tasted strange and acidic. Then he rolled her over, kicked off his jeans, and knee-walked up to encourage her to take him in her mouth.

That was his first mistake.

By the time he saw the autopsy scar that ran the length of her body, he was beyond being shocked or terrified. By then, he had his own underwear stuffed into his mouth and his wrists were broken.

She used him in awful ways before dragging him into the shower. Before she began biting his fingers off.

Mary lost herself in the madness of her hunger. This was her first sexual encounter in two years. The first time since before she had been born as Typhoid Mary. The hungers, the need, the savage ferocity was not what she expected. She *wanted* sex. Mindless fucking . . . something to take her thoughts away from everything. But a black veil seemed to drop in front of her eyes, and there were long stretches of time that night and well into the morning where she lost herself completely. Memories of what happened during those fugues lingered, but as fading fragments.

Now she waited for her tub to fill as the young man bled to death.

She turned and looked into the mirror, which was as wide as the bathroom and went all the way to the ceiling. In it, she saw the red thing in the shower, the jetted tub, the splashes of blood here and there. And her own naked self.

She wanted so badly to be beautiful again. Even if only to her own eyes.

But she was a monster.

Pale, with splotches of gray and yellow on her skin. Scarred by bullets and scalpels and the many, many cuts she had given herself in an attempt to *feel*.

To feel anything at all.

Anything except the hunger.

Anything except the restless need that had no direction.

Anything except the nothingness.

She had lost what little faith she'd ever had. Death, when it first took her, offered no hell or any heaven. She had merely stopped. Now she was back, and that nothingness beyond life loomed like a black tidal wave. What if that was all there was? Nothing.

Her mind. Her intellect. Her accomplishments. Her passions and goals.

Come to nothing.

It filled her with such hatred that it felt as if she would burst apart. How could flesh, especially dead flesh, ever hope to contain such hatred?

She wanted to weep, but lately, even that release was beyond her.

There was only the hate.

And the need to not die alone.

No.

She would not die alone.

Mary was about to step into the tub when her cell rang. She looked at the display. No name, just the icon of a golden autumn leaf. October.

She nearly ignored the call. Her hand wanted to throw the cell phone against a wall or drop it in the tub. Maybe give it to the finger-less naked man in the shower.

Instead, she answered.

"Yes." Flat, no rising inflection.

"Hello, my dear," said October. "Are you home?"

"No," she said. "I went up to the Poconos."

"Why there? We don't have any camps up there."

"I used to come up here a lot," she said. "Before."

"Ah. Feeling nostalgic?"

"Just wanted to be alone."

"I hope you found some comfort in that," said October. "Now look, my dear, I've told Toombs this and hinted to you that I might do it, and . . . well, I'm going to."

"Do what?"

"Launch Firefall tomorrow."

Mary stiffened. "Tomorrow? So soon? Why?"

"I take it you haven't seen the news," October said, mirth and tri-umph in his tone. "Your efforts in Texas and elsewhere have worked even better than we expected. Beautiful work. The president has closed the borders, and demand for our firearms has quadrupled over-night. Don't even get me started on corporate and small-nation sales. Our salespeople are having orgasms."

"Except for that stiff Toombs. I doubt he ever gets hard."

October ignored that and instead said, "The pump is primed for Firefall, and I've moved up the timetable."

"You're really going to launch Firefall?"

"Yes, I am."

"Even though it won't be *all* of it? Only four Gorgons?"

"Yes. As I told Mr. Toombs, we're ready to go. I don't want to let things cool down. Strike while the iron is hot and all that."

"I think we should wait."

"It's only MERS, my sweet. It's quick onset, but not so quick that it'll all burn out. By the time things slack off, we'll be ready with all the other Gorgons. That way, we can steal back the news cycles and dominate the outrage."

"Whatever," she said petulantly.

"Your enthusiasm warms my heart."

"I love you, Daddy," she said. "I just wish you were doing it the way we planned."

October paused. *Daddy?* It was the second time she'd called him that, and he did not much like it.

"Are you okay, Mary?"

"Huh? Oh . . . yeah. Just tired. When I get home, I'll take a nap."

"My dear, once we launch Firefall, there will be chaos. I could not be prouder of you, but you can take a much-deserved rest. Come home for a few days. I'll pull Toombs out of the field, too. I'll be in and out of the Mansion tomorrow, but we can all sit back and watch the fun and games on TV. I'll have the cook make us something special. A feast to celebrate the end of the old world and the birth of the new one."

"I'm not done," she insisted.

"Mary, you *are* done. There is nothing more to be gained from the pathogen part of this operation. One more outbreak or ten and the effort would be wasted. We got the borders closed, and we have the rapid response teams running around like beheaded chickens. All that's left is Firefall to make sure America becomes an armed camp that is convinced it is under siege. We've changed hearts and minds, my sweet girl. It will take at least a generation for America to recover, and by then, the whole world will be nothing but armed camps. And very *well-armed* camps at that."

"What am I supposed to do now?" she asked. "I have more Typhoid Marys picked."

"As I said, come home and relax. Then, when Firefall is over, you can go back to the Poconos or anywhere else you want. Inside the States, of course. At least for now. Plan something fun, go *have fun*, and when you get back home, we can discuss some software mischief that you are eminently suited for. I was thinking of hacking a missile silo. Maybe launch a strike at Mexico. Or maybe send it to some state capital. To be decided based on how things play out." October paused. "Mary, you sound down, and I know I said you could launch more of your little bugs, but really, that phase has so exceeded expectations that anything else would be anticlimactic. And, besides, we want all eyes on Firefall. So . . . come home for now."

"Sure," she said.

And hung up.

The body in the shower had stopped bleeding. Still hearts cannot pump blood.

The tub was full, but she did not turn off the water. Instead, she sat down slowly on the tiled floor and stared at nothing.

At nothing.

CHAPTER 130
INTEGRATED SCIENCES DIVISION
PRODUCTION LAB #3
PHOENIX HOUSE
OMFORI ISLAND, GREECE

Church came into the lab at a brisk walk. He spotted Ronald Coleman and a team of twenty technicians working furiously at a row of large tables. Beside each was a large plastic tub filled to the brim with liquid-filled cellulose capsules.

"Is that the modified Sandman?" asked Church as he came over.

"Yes, sir," Coleman said, handing him one. "These have a fifty-fifty mix of the standard Sandman solution, plus I added succinylcholine as a depolarizing neuromuscular agent. I am pretty sure it would paralyze a walker. As to how long it will keep them down . . . we're working on that."

"We're out of time. I want all of these darts loaded onto my chopper in the next ten minutes. Bring as many Snellig pistols as you can grab from the armory. And if we have the new Snellig LR-06 rifles, bring those as well. Pack a bag, too. Change of clothes and the basics. We're wheels up in twenty."

Coleman blinked at him very slowly. He pushed his thick-lensed glasses up his nose.

"Um . . . much as I appreciate the confidence, sir," he said, "I'm not a field operative. May I ask why I'm coming with you?"

Church smiled and gestured to what was on the tables. "We have ten thousand rounds of modified Sandman, and we probably have thirty or forty Snelligs in storage. Their magazines won't load themselves."

"Oh."

"And you can brief Colonel Ledger and the others once we're on our way."

"Oh."

The technicians had each found something to look at in any part of the room where Church and Coleman were not. It looked like they were trying to be invisible.

Church patted Coleman's shoulder. "Let's go."

CHAPTER 131
TENTH LEGION COMFORT STATION BRAVO
HAMBONE LANE
UPPER BLACK EDDY, PENNSYLVANIA

"Do you really think this is it?" asked Tommy.

She and Violin were once more snugged down beneath their camo screen, rifles loaded and resting on bipods, sniper scopes trained on a cluster of at least a dozen RVs parked in a grove of trees off Hambone Lane. Green-and-brown netting was stretched above them, and sunlight filtered down to dapple the forest floor.

"Yes," said Violin.

"When do we hit it?"

"Soon. But first we need to observe and learn." Violin rose to a kneeling position and looked around. "I'm going to walk the perimeter, count the guards, look for motion sensors. You stay here and keep your eye on those RVs. If you see anything that I don't, tap your mic three times quickly." She demonstrated. "Don't wait for me to reply. Just know I'll be coming."

"What about the kids in there?"

"I'll do my best to check on them. There are few cars here, so my guess is that they are waiting for legionnaires to arrive. That's when we'll make a move—when the men are distracted."

"Isn't that leaving it too late?" asked Tommy.

Violin shook her head. "I won't let anything happen to the children. You be ready to back my play."

She touched Tommy's cheek.

"Keep to the plan, focus on doing this right. If they start shooting, check your targets before pulling a trigger. Cowards like this are not above using children as a shield. I taught you what to do if that happens. Be cold, Tommy. Be precise."

"I will," promised the younger woman.

Violin nodded and moved off, melting into the dark, humid shadows beneath the trees.

CHAPTER 132
INTERSTATE 476
LEIGHTON, PENNSYLVANIA

Miss Mary drove a dead man's car.

No music. No noise except for the faint growl of the engine and the hum of her tires on the road. The night was huge and empty and dark, with few cars on the turnpike.

Mary called David White.

"Hello?" he said, sounding sleepy and surprised. "Miss Mary . . . I didn't expect to hear from you."

"I said I'd call."

"Okay, sure, but Mr. October said that this phase was done and that I should lie low."

"No, no, no," Mary said. "We still have work to do."

A pause. Then White said, "We do?"

"Oh yes. I hope you have the next Typhoid Mary ready to go."

"Um . . . no," he said. "I don't. You know I don't. Word came down that we were done with that. Texas was the last gig."

"Who told you that?"

"I just said . . . the boss called me like an hour ago."

"*I'm* your boss, Mr. White."

"Beg pardon, Miss Mary, but Mr. October called me direct. He said that Texas was a big hit and that we were to stand this part of the operation down."

"I run the bioweapons program," snapped Mary.

"Not arguing with you," White said quickly. "But I was hired by

Mr. October. I've been working for him for a few years now. What he says goes."

Mary opened her eyes and looked up at the cloth on the underside of the roof. A bead of sweat trickled down the side of her cheek.

"David—may I call you David?—David . . . you work for me or you don't work for anyone. Do you understand that? Do I need to be more specific?"

"You want me to go against what Mr. October explicitly said?"

"I want you to understand the benefits to you."

"Are you threatening me, Miss Mary?"

"Do I need to?"

This pause was much longer.

"I am not trying to be difficult here, Miss Mary, but I can't go against Mr. October. Let me call him and get his approval, and then I'll call you right back."

Mary ended the call and kept staring up at the lolling black tongue of the highway.

David White lay in bed in his double-wide trailer, staring at the shadows on the ceiling.

He bounced the cell phone in his palm for several long minutes, replaying the conversation with Miss Mary in his head. He knew what he should do, but he was afraid of having misread things. If he called October and was wrong, what would the reprisal be? Would there *be* reprisal for him double-checking? And what would Miss Mary do to him at some point for having pushed back on her request?

He simply did not know the answers to any of those questions. And so he did nothing.

CHAPTER 133
CRUISER FIVE
DARK HOLLOW ROAD
PINE DEEP, PENNSYLVANIA

The road had no official name. Not anymore.

Back in the 1970s, it was known as Pine Meadow Trail, and it spurred off from Cornflower Lane as it snaked its way through the outer edges of Pine Deep, brushing here and there against the vastness of Pinelands State Forest. The road led to only one place, a house that had been built in the sixties and which burned to the ground in 2006. That road had already been officially abandoned, its name mostly forgotten, and much of the surrounding fields and woods had been burned during the fire that ended the Trouble.

A new road had been made several years back, but it came the long way around through Black Marsh, sharing some stretches with a more official road belonging to the state park. When construction on a new house was completed, that path was also abandoned.

A third road had been dozed and the dirt packed down, and this shared some of the same distance as the no-name road. There was still no street sign on it and only a sign announcing that it was a Private Drive was currently posted.

Gary Maines, a patrolman for the Pine Deep police, was parked in the deep shadows beneath a massive oak still dripping from last night's rain. He was working the midnight-to-eight shift and the nights were long and usually dull. But it was mealtime, and he seldom felt like driving all the way back to town to grab something at the diner. Instead, he'd brought leftovers from last night's grilled chicken dinner at home. Even cold, the sandwich was good, and he settled back to watch the storm.

When a late-model SUV passed him, Maines automatically glanced at the license plate. It took about two seconds for his memory to catch up with the moment, and he snatched his clipboard off the passenger seat and consulted a printout. Then he called into the station.

"This is Six. I'm 10-96 out on Cornflower Lane," he said, giving the ten-code for a meal break.

"Go ahead, Six," said Harry, the dispatcher on the graveyard shift.

"Just spotted an electric-blue Range Rover SUV matching license number on the chief's BOLO."

"Copy that, Six."

"What's the call here?" asked Maines. "Any wants or warrants? Do I stop the guy?"

"That's a negative, Six. Which direction was the SUV heading?"

"To the old Griswold place at the end of Pine Meadow Trail. Didn't they build a new house there a couple years ago?"

"Affirmative, Six. Owned by a trust of some kind," said Harry. "They bought the places for taxes and built a big house. Computer lists it as a single occupant and staff. No warrants, no reason for a car stop or a house check. I'll mark it in the log and text the chief."

That was the end of the call.

CHAPTER 134
TENTH LEGION COMFORT STATION BRAVO
HAMBONE LANE
UPPER BLACK EDDY, PENNSYLVANIA

The sky was darkening prematurely as Tommy pivoted in a kneeling position, swinging her rifle away from the building and along the path she and Violin had taken. She was not immediately sure what had drawn her attention. Probably an animal, but she wanted to be sure.

Violin was off in a different direction doing close recon on the building they suspected was the comfort camp. She was like a ghost and would never have made a noise.

There was another sound. A snap of a twig.

Tommy snugged the rifle stock against her shoulder, but she frowned as she did it. That sound—it was so crisp and clear. As if someone wanted her to hear it.

She went completely still, finger prepared to curl around the trigger.

Then she felt the pistol barrel against the base of her skull.

"Put the gun down," said a male voice. Low, rumbly, gruff. "I'm a friendly."

"A friendly who puts a gun to my head?" said Tommy, trying to sound more confident than she felt.

"A friendly who doesn't want you to fire that gun, sound suppressor or not. And sure as shit not at me," said the man, speaking quietly but not whispering. "Lay the gun down. Be careful not to foul the barrel. Good. Now sit down and cross your legs. Excellent. Okay, I'm going to come around in front of you. Let's don't have any fuss. You don't want it, and neither do I."

She heard him move and then saw a man circle around to stand in front of her. He was a big man with a shaved head, shoulders a mile wide, and arms heavy with muscles. He was not at all a handsome man, and his face looked like it had been punched or kicked by everyone who ever met him—cauliflower left ear, a scar through one eyebrow, and a nose that had been comprehensively knocked askew. He wore jeans and a long-sleeved T-shirt, the sleeves pushed halfway up his bulky forearms. Tommy's eyes widened as she saw the tattoos that covered his wrists and the visible parts of his arms and which peeked above the V-neck of the shirt. They were all black and white, all photo real, and all the faces of girls and women.

He held a Glock in his big fist, the barrel rock steady.

"I'm going to say a word," the man said. "If you're what I think you are, we're going to get along fine."

"What word?" asked Tommy.

"Arklight."

Tommy blinked, then narrowed her eyes. "And what does that mean to you?"

"Like I said, I'm a friendly. An ally."

"One word isn't enough for us to suddenly start making s'mores and singing 'Kumbaya.'"

"Fair enough," he said. "How about this—Violin."

Tommy cocked an eyebrow. "And what's that supposed to mean?"

The man smiled. "It's the name of the woman standing behind me."

Violin stepped out of the shadows between two trees. Her rifle was slung, and she had her matched kukri knives in her hands. She slid them into their thigh sheaths, walked closer, grabbed the man, and gave him a fierce hug. Then she pushed him to arm's length and studied him.

"What the hell are you doing here, Monk?" she asked.

He tilted his chin in the direction of the house. "Same as you two, I expect."

Tommy got up.

"Monk? You're Monk Addison?"

"For better or worse, yeah," said the man.

Tommy held out her hand and introduced herself. They shook.

Violin waved them down, and they crouched in a tight circle.

"*How* are you here?" asked Violin.

"Well," he said, "I do actually live around here. Pine Deep's a stone's throw."

Tommy automatically glanced in that direction.

"We have a lot to talk about," she said.

Monk grinned a gargoyle grin. "Yeah, we do. Then we got to go cut some throats. How's that sound?"

FIREFALL
PART 4

Love, friendship and respect do not unite
    people as much
as a common hatred for something.

—ANTON CHEKHOV

I know not with what weapons World War III
    will be fought,
but World War IV will be fought with sticks and
    stones.

—ALBERT EINSTEIN

CHAPTER 135
THE MORNING REPORT WITH CHUCK O'LEARY
ABC NEWS

"Rioting continues at the US border, with groups for and against the total border closure clashing. Violence broke out around 7:00 p.m. last night during a vigil for Americans who have died from weaponized diseases used on civilians across the country. There have been reports of deaths, though the number is unconfirmed. More than fifty people have been transported to local hospitals for injuries sustained in the conflict. Governor Plemons of Texas has called in the National Guard, and rumors indicate that the governors of Arizona and New Mexico are considering calling up their guard units to secure *state* borders."

CHAPTER 136
THE GUTHRIE FARM
PINE DEEP, PENNSYLVANIA

Ghost heard it first, and he jumped up on the bed, tearing me out of a dream of kissing every single freckle on Junie's shoulders, upper back, and chest. There are a lot of freckles, especially this soon after the end of summer, and I was being diligent in my desire to find every last one. Junie's fingers were tangled in my hair, trying to steer my busy lips to more interesting places.

Then Ghost began slobbering all over the side of my face. That's the kind of emotional left turn that strips the gears and burns out the clutch.

Freaking dog.

I pushed him away and called him a lot of the things you should never say to man's best friend. He responded with a bark and a wag of his bushy tail.

It took a tower crane and several stevedores with pry bars to help me into a sitting position. The last couple of days had done an enthusiastic job of beating the crap out of me. I fisted sleep from my eyes and then glared at Ghost.

"I'm donating all your toys to a cat shelter," I told him.

He just wagged at me.

That's when I heard it. The distant *whup-whup-whup* of helicopter blades.

A half second later, I smelled toast, coffee, and bacon. Then someone banged on the outside of the guest bedroom door.

"Outlaw," growled Top, "friendlies incoming."

I called him some of the same names I called Ghost. His reaction was a deep, gravelly laugh.

Pushing off the bed, I tottered to the window and looked out to see a little bug in the clear air. I kept watching it as I pulled my clothes on, seeing it get bigger and become an old three-engine CH-53E Super Stallion painted for civilian use. No guns. No military markings. One of those birds bought by a private owner when its government days are over. Even so, it looked like it had been given quite an extensive overhaul. And then I saw the logo painted on its door—it was Earth with the initials *FT* stenciled over them. FreeTech. I smiled, even though I knew Junie would not be aboard.

FreeTech was hers, that altruistic company secretly owned by Church but of which he has given Junie full control. They take the nasty toys our field teams take away from the bad guys, repurpose them, reverse engineer the technology, and then use it gratis for people in need all around the world.

It was clear the bird was coming to the farm, and when I craned my neck to look down, I saw Crow and Remy waving it toward a field that had recently been harvested and plowed.

"Come on," I said to Ghost as I ran downstairs.

We stepped out into a humid morning. The storm had ended and everything smelled fresh and almost springlike. There were more storm clouds all around us, but for the moment, the golden sun sparkled down from a blue sky.

Ghost and I reached the edge of the field as the big doors opened. Remy and Crow were already there.

"Wow," said Crow, shouting through the noise, "you brought the supersized whirlybird."

I explained that this kind of chopper was intended to transport troops and equipment, and for a moment, I hoped a couple dozen RTI agents would pour out. If wishes were horses . . .

Instead, Bird Dog came grinning out, his bulky frame stuffed into a flight suit that wasn't suited to his height. I hurried over with my hand outstretched, and we shook and hugged.

"How's Goofy?"

Bird Dog's mouth hardened. "Nearly lost him a couple of times, but the docs Mr. Church called in were champs. They tell me he'll be okay. Gonna be months in the hospital and then rehab, but he'll recover."

"That's great news, brother," I said and shook his hand again. Then I looked past him at the big bird. "What'd you bring us?"

Bird Dog jerked a thumb over his shoulder. "The Big Man said you needed a complete resupply plus."

That was code for comms units, body armor, weapons and ammunition, and a full set of electronics ranging from Anteaters to drones. Remy and I peered inside and whistled.

"Looks like you emptied the warehouse," said Remy.

"I may have erred on the side of kicking some fucking Tenth Legion ass."

"Hooah," I said.

"Hoo-goddamn-ah," said Remy.

Bird Dog gestured to the cargo. "There's about two million dollars of high-tech, cutting-edge technology in here."

Remy held up a hand. "Scout's honor to take good care of it."

Bird Dog gave him a very hard look. "Kid, these ass clowns put one of mine in the ICU, and now they want to start a fucking civil war. I want you to use every goddamn penny of it."

He was so angry spit flew. Remy smiled one of *those* smiles. "Oh, you can count on that. Yes sirree. I'm gon' have me a good time."

The big logistics chief nodded, then he clapped his hands. "You fellas want to help me unload? You ain't my only stop."

CHAPTER 137
THE GUTHRIE FARM
PINE DEEP, PENNSYLVANIA

First thing I did was put on the new comms units—the freckle-sized earbud and mic—and tested them out by calling the TOC. Wilson answered and said that Church was on a fast jet over the Atlantic, heading our way.

"That's great," I said, meaning it. "But we're getting ready to saddle up. There are some things we need to check on."

I explained about the depot, the training center, and the Cyke-lones.

"Copy that, Outlaw."

"And, Grendel, see about getting us more help. Local law is with me, but that's a small shop. We could use some state police, SWAT, maybe the National Guard."

"Do we have actionable evidence yet?"

"Not . . . as such."

He sighed. "I'll do what I can, Outlaw, but without evidence, no official agency can back your play."

"Do your best," I said and rang off.

As I rejoined the others, Top handed me one of the new Snelligs and plenty of magazines of the revised Sandman.

"These rounds will stop someone infected with *seif al din*?" asked Belle.

"That's what they tell me."

I recapped what that disease was for Crow. He looked as deeply disturbed as you might expect.

"You know, Joe, you might want to bring Monk Addison into this."

"I called him," I said. "Went to voicemail, so I left a message. Told him to call you or me, Crow."

"Anyone else we can call?" asked Bunny.

"Not the feds or the Guard," I said and reiterated our need for actionable evidence.

"What about old friends?" asked Top. "Sam Imura, maybe?"

"He's on the wrong side of the country at the moment."

Bunny glanced at Crow. "Any of your other deputies have military background?"

"Hardly." But then he cocked his head and smiled. "Sam Hunter and Antonio Jones will be useful. They were going hunting with Mike this morning anyway."

"We don't need hunters," said Remy. "We need some guys who can kick ass and take names."

Crow laughed out loud. "Oh, I think you'll find Sam and Antonio have some moves."

"Outlaw," said Belle. "You've mentioned Monk Addison several times, but I do not know this man."

"Yeah, why him?" asked Remy.

So, Crow and I took turns telling Monk's story. He had been a shooter with Delta Force. Then he stopped working for Uncle Sam and signed on as a private military contractor. That was fine for a while because Monk was a borderline burnout and was too fried to weigh the value of his actions as long as someone higher up the food chain swore it was for the white hats.

Then something happened and Monk sort of snapped out of it. He looked around and realized that he was so deeply in the gray area that it was starting to look black. So, he just walked off. Left his job, his guns, his uncashed paychecks and wandered. Did kind of a self-discovery vision quest or something like that. He'd apparently always been something of a closet New Ager, and when one of his buddies ran into him in a shrine in Tibet, his friend hung the nickname "Monk" on him. Most people thought the nickname was based on his looks, and he could be a gorilla extra in the next *Planet of the Apes* flick. But it wasn't that.

I guess it's closer to the mark to say he was a shaman. He wandered for years, trying to find answers. Not religious but spiritual in his own way. He learned what he could and went deep inside himself.

It was about there that I paused and glanced at Crow and saw him give me a small shake of the head. So I danced around some of the weirder aspects of Monk's life and wrapped by saying he fell back into the world and became a skip tracer, working for a pair of Philadelphia bail bondsmen whose names are—I swear to God in heaven—J. Heron Scarebaby and Iver Twitch.

Bunny guffawed. "Get the fuck out of here."

Crow pulled out his cell, unlocked the screen, and slid it across the table to Bunny. "Don't believe him . . . look it up."

I leaned back in my chair. Crow opened another bottle of Yoo-hoo. Bunny checked.

"Holy shit," he said and showed the others the page he'd pulled up. Scarebaby was short and fat, Twitch was tall and thin. Neither of them looked like the kind of guys you'd leave alone with either your silverware or your maiden aunt.

Top shook his head. "How much does God have to hate you to let you be born with names like that?"

"And he's local?" asked Remy.

"Lives in town," said Crow. "Couple blocks from my office. He's off the radar, but we left messages. Hope he shows. He's a cross-grained pain in the ass, but he is very useful when things get dicey."

My cell rang, and when I looked at the caller ID, there was an emoji of a musical instrument instead of a name. I smiled, stepped away from the rest of the guys, and hit the button.

"Hello, Violin," I said.

"Hello, Joseph," she said.

"Unless this is important, I have to run," I said. "We're in eastern Pennsylvania and—"

"I know where you are," said Violin. "I'm not too many miles away."

"You are?"

Violin quickly told me about what she and Tommy were doing. I leaned against the field fence, closed my eyes, and tried to will myself to be anywhere else. The far side of the moon, maybe. Six miles under the ocean.

"If you can hold the fort," I said, "we might be able to help you with that later today. We have some pretty big fish to fry first, though."

"Yes. Firefall and the Legion camps."

"How do you know about that?"

"My mother."

"Ah. Did you send her kisses from me?"

Violin laughed. "Oh, of course. And she sends loving hugs and puppies to you." Lilith liked me just a little less than toilet paper stuck to her heel. "But, Joseph, we already have some backup."

"Who?"

"Monk Addison. He says hello."

"Well . . . hell. Tell him to check his voicemail every once in a while."

She covered the phone, but I heard her speaking, then she laughed as she came back. "I won't repeat what he said you can do, but it's unpleasant and would likely hurt."

"Give him a big wet kiss from me," I said. "But, listen, that's just three of you against all of them."

"I know," she said. "Seems unfair to them, doesn't it?"

I laughed and told her to stay safe. She said the same to me and rang off.

CHAPTER 138
THE GUTHRIE FARM
PINE DEEP, PENNSYLVANIA

Mike Sweeney knelt and spread out an aerial map of Pine Deep with key places marked. He pointed to an area right over the city limits.

"That's Black Marsh," he said. "And right there, way off in the woods by what used to be a summer camp, is where we saw the tents with all the crates of supplies. The depot camp."

"Black Marsh?" asked Bunny. "Isn't that where Crow's family is staying?"

"Yes," said Sweeney. "But it's nowhere near that depot."

"Can we get coordinates for that site?" asked Remy.

Mike took a slip of paper from his pocket. "Longitude and latitude."

"Groovy."

The big sergeant touched another spot. "The bigger camp is here in Pine Deep, but tucked into a pretty dense section of forest right against the state park. There's one access road, and Antonio and I saw armed guards walking the perimeter. Coordinates for that are on the other side of that paper."

"Remy," I said, "how long would it take a couple of vulture drones to reach those spots?"

"If we launch from here? Maybe forty minutes for the big camp and an hour-plus for the depot."

"That works," I said. "Get them in the air."

He wheeled away and set to work. Within two minutes, I heard the tiny whir as the drones lifted into the cloudy sky.

"Going to rain like hell," said Crow. "Those things good in high winds?"

"The way we build 'em?" said Remy. "They'll do."

"Okay," I said, "this is the plan. Mike, you take Hunter and Jones with you and go put eyes on that depot. You've been fitted out with comms, so if you see anything at all that looks like something big and bad is about to happen, you make a call. This Firefall thing is going to happen, and my gut tells me sooner than later. Be ready."

"Always ready," said Sam Hunter. He didn't look even slightly tough—nor did Jones—but I knew better. The three of them ran to Mike's cruiser.

"Crow and I are going into town to see if we can get anything useful out of the Cyke-lones," I said. "You say their clubhouse is on Main Street."

"You expect them to tell you anything?" asked Bunny.

"Depends on how nicely we ask," said Crow.

I said, "The rest of you saddle up and head toward that big camp. Pay attention to what the drones show you. If you see anything hinky, let me know and make sure the TOC is on that call."

"Hooah," said Top. "Rules of engagement?"

"This is an intelligence-gathering mission," I said. "Make no contact. Observe and report."

"What do we do if they spot us and want to start a fuss?" asked Remy.

"Retreat if possible," I said. "Nobody pulls a trigger unless fired upon."

"Hooah," they all said, though Belle seemed reluctant to agree.

"Bottom line," I said, "be safe."

They headed off to start loading the SUV with the gear bags. Crow went into the house and came out with his katana, which he put on the back seat of his cruiser. When I looked at him, he smiled.

"Be prepared," he said.

CHAPTER 139
DARK HOLLOW ROAD
PINE DEEP, PENNSYLVANIA

The biker stood watching the men and one woman load gear bags into cars, shake hands, and drive away. He was hidden by shadows and the stalks of unharvested corn, and he had his cell in his hands, having taken photos of everyone.

"Got you, fuckers," he murmured.

Then he turned, already hunching over his phone to send the photos to Mr. October and the commandant. He'd just selected the images for his first email when he almost walked into another man.

The biker gasped, stepped back, nearly dropped his phone, and reached for the Colt .45 tucked into the back of his jeans.

"Who the fuck are you?" he growled.

The man was tall, very old, entirely filthy, wearing many layers of clothes, each sewn with countless pockets. The biker pointed the gun at him.

There was very little movement. Hardly anything.

The gun fell to the muddy ground. So did the cell.

Of the biker there was no sign, then or ever.

The old man walked without hurry to the rail that embowered the cornfield. He leaned his grimy forearms on that rail and watched the last of the cars drive away. Mr. Pockets reached into a pocket and removed a bulb of pale garlic. It was fresh-picked minutes ago, with wormy soil still clinging to it. Large, with a cluster of eighteen fat cloves still wrapped in their paperlike sheathing leaves.

He put the entire bulb into his mouth—leaves, dirt, worms, and all—and ate it slowly. Garlic oil ran from the corners of his mouth. When he swallowed, his throat bulged like a lizard's.

The cars vanished, and the old man turned and walked into the cornfield.

CHAPTER 140
THE GUTHRIE FARM
PINE DEEP, PENNSYLVANIA

While the others loaded the gear, Top Sims walked into the Guthrie house in search of a quiet space.

All through the night and deep into his dreams, the words of the strange old guy out on the road haunted him.

Call your daughter, he'd said. *Tell her you love her.*

It was an odd thing for him to say.

Tell her you love her.

Top settled onto a bench, dug out his cell, and looked at it for a long time. Then he made a call.

"Hello," said a sleepy voice. Then, "Dad . . . ?"

For some reason that he could not identify, the sound of her voice made him want to cry.

"Hey, baby girl," said Top. "Just wanted to see how you're doing."

CHAPTER 141
THE MANSION
UNDISCLOSED LOCATION

Mr. October entered the big house and immediately knew that Mary was not home yet.

The Ecuadorian maid, sleepy but dressed in her uniform, met him at the door to take his raincoat and umbrella.

"Has Miss Mary called?" he asked.

"Not yet, señor."

"Mr. Toombs?"

"No, señor."

"Very well."

October walked into the drawing room, built himself a gin rickey, and took it over to his desk. He sat down at the desk and made a cell call to Commandant Furman.

"Sir," said Furman when he answered, "this is unexpected."

"I told you to stay ready, Commandant."

"And we are ready."

"Scrambler on?"

"Of course, sir."

"Have the warheads been dropped off?"

"Yes, sir. They arrived before dawn."

"All security measures in place?"

"Yes, sir. Your techs oversaw the attachment of the warheads to the rockets. That was done in a sealed tent. No witnesses except for Command Sergeant Ryerson and the field teams."

"Good, good. What's the status of the weapons?"

"The New York team left immediately after the warheads were secured. The driver reported in fifteen minutes ago. Those units are already in place."

"And the Philly team?"

"They left an hour ago. The driver reported that the facilities director will meet them at the delivery gate by 0900. That will give us a full hour to set up before they start letting people in and five hours until Firefall." He paused. "Is today really it?"

"Yes, it is," said October with more force than he intended. It made him sound angry. He took a breath, then spoke in a calmer voice. "Yes, my friend, today is the day we change the course of history. Today we begin the process of saving America from its enemies and itself."

October rolled his eyes as he said it. The dramatics, the posturing, the inflated sense of purpose were all necessary, but tiring. And he was getting very weary. The Firefall project had filled every minute of the last few years, using one project to set the stage for the next. At the same time, this *version* of Firefall had changed radically because of the COVID pandemic. That had not been one of his projects, though he had jumped aboard to have some fun with American political reactions to the outbreak. Casting doubt, using his puppets to engage in the hurling of accusations, destroying careers, keeping a blame game cooking, destabilizing overall faith in both government and modern medicine. Doing all that had been something of a whim, reaching out to be energized by a cultural zeitgeist. The benefits of it all were delicious, but they spawned an idea for using the lingering doubt, mistrust, and simmering hysteria to build a new project.

The Gorgon weapons tech was a surprise and a lovely one. It allowed for an expediency that promised a big punch for less overall effort. Gorgon was the most inarguably sophisticated yet simple delivery system for a pathogen that otherwise struggled for dominance. The fact that MERS was in the same class as COVID-19 was unplanned but strategically perfect.

Priming the pump by stoking the already volatile political climate in America and a few other key nations was easy in theory but difficult and nitpicky in practice. So many people he had to deal with on a regular basis. Playing the bombastic and garrulous CEO of Kuga, affecting the religious fervor of the owner of Tenth Legion, and managing the useful madness of Miss Mary had worn him down to the nub. He was grateful that it was coming to an end. Once he gave the go-code for Firefall, a new era of chaos would dawn across America and then around the world.

He realized that Furman was speaking and tuned in to catch the thread of it.

"—cannot express how proud I am to be a soldier in this army of holy purpose," gushed the legionnaire officer.

"This pleases me, Commandant."

"I do have one question, though," said Furman. "It's about the codes."

"I'll be sending the go-code in just a minute."

"Yes, sir, but with all that's happening around the country, security is getting tight. I know we have things set up in Philly and New York, and if everything goes as planned, then this is truly God's day, but . . . what is our plan if either venue has to cancel because of threats or other problems?"

"Then you'll get a stand-down code," said October. "You already know this."

"Sorry, sir, I am being unclear," said Furman. "I mean, if we have to stand down, what happens if one or both teams is already inside the venue?"

"Ah," said October. "Yes. Well, they have their salvation caps, and if they're taken, I'll have lawyers there before you can say John 11:35."

"What about the weapons, though?"

"If we have to stand down, then I'll be monitoring them. If they

JONATHAN MABERRY

are arrested, they will be separated from the Gorgons. Call it minimum safe distance. Then the warheads will detonate, and the thermite in the rocket and the launchers will detonate. Your men have all been inoculated against MERS. They will be out of range of the thermite explosion—that's only a forty-foot radius. And our lawyers will have them out on bail within hours. A day at most. Once they're free on bond, they'll be taken to a secure facility pending transport to South Africa. New papers and identities. Trust me when I say that we have planned for every contingency."

There was a brief pause, and then Furman said, "Thank you, sir. That is a comfort. I hope I have not been impertinent by asking."

"You care about your men, Commandant. That is admirable. That is what God wants of you. It is what *I* want of you. That faith and fealty will be rewarded."

"It is my honor to serve this cause, sir," proclaimed Furman. October tried not to gag.

He said, "Speaking of rewards, Commandant . . . since the teams are already in motion and we have hours to wait, why don't you take the reward Miss Mary has waiting for you."

"Sir?"

"The camp, Commandant. Pay it a visit now, before the goodies are spoiled. Take your sergeant with you. Ryerson's a good man, too. Have some fun. Relax. Indulge. And know that what you have done—all that will happen today—could not have happened without you doing everything that has been asked and by exceeding even my high expectations."

"That is . . . very generous of you, sir."

"You are a good soldier," lied October. "Now go and take the reward that you earned. The reward that is yours by right."

He hung up and tossed the cell onto his desk.

"If Hitler were as dim as you are, we would never have taken France, let alone Poland."

October drank most of the gin rickey and set the glass down. Then he opened his laptop and pulled up the Firefall command program. He typed in the sixteen-character go-code for Firefall.

do3hm9h#e/lende8

Random numbers, letters, and characters that would automatically be shared with Mary and Toombs. To initiate Firefall, all he had to do was hit Send.

October hesitated, though. He really wished Mary could be here for this. She, much more so than Toombs. The sales manager was in his inner circle, but he was not family. He could be replaced.

Not Mary, though.

As random and crazy and damaged as she was, this whole project was built around her. It was she who rewrote the code for VaultBreaker, possibly surpassing Bug with her innovations. It was sad, even criminal, that she could not publish her work and earn the adoration from those wise enough to understand her genius.

It was she who came up with the idea of the Typhoid Marys. A kind of suicide bomber the world had never seen.

It was she who reverse engineered the science for the Berserkers and the SDs.

It was she who had made herself immortal with generation 16 of *seif al din*.

It was she who October loved. He wanted her to be his true daughter. A fellow immortal with whom he could live out eternity. Father and daughter, bringing chaos to a stale world. Exploring madness and wildness and freedom.

It was she for whom he had devised the Firefall program, coupling Jason Aydelotte's lunatic dreams with Mary's understanding of the terror associated with diseases.

Where was she?

He tried to call her, but there was no answer.

When an hour passed with her still not arriving, he pulled out his cell and opened the tracking app. It found her RFID signal, but it was still in the Poconos, still at Split Rock Resort. But there was something wrong with the telemetry. There was no pulse, no vitals.

The locater chip was still active, but it was not part of her.

"You tore it out, didn't you?" he asked.

The chip signal was steady and uninformative.

October sipped his drink, which was now diluted with melted ice.

"Where are you?" he said. Then something occurred to him. An idea of where she *might* be.

He began to rise, then paused and looked at the go-code on the screen.

"Damn it," he snarled, then hit Send.

CHAPTER 142
TENTH LEGION TRAINING CAMP #18
BLACK MARSH, PENNSYLVANIA

Despite having just spoken with Mr. October, Commandant Furman nearly screamed when he saw what popped up on his screen.

do3hm9h#e/lende8

Ryerson was asleep on the sofa, and Furman got out of bed, hurried over, and kicked his command sergeant's foot.

"What . . . what?" mumbled Ryerson.

Furman showed him the screen display.

The sergeant stood up quickly. "Are you fucking with me?"

"No, I am not."

"Holy shit."

They stood there, wrapped in the dangerous awareness of what that code meant.

Firefall.

After eighteen months of planning, recruiting, training, drilling. After all the secrecy and covert meetings. After the natural doubts each man had that what they were training *for* would ever come to pass.

After all the fears about what Firefall would really mean. Civilian deaths, for sure. Outrage and horror, without doubt. Criminal investigations by every agency in America, absolutely.

They looked at each other.

"Are we really going to do this?" asked Ryerson. He looked diminished by this reality. Even his voice sounded young and scared.

Furman straightened slowly. Making a show of it to his sergeant and also himself. Manning up, as he thought it. Answering the call.

"Yes," he said.

Ryerson licked his lips. "There's only four active Gorgons, though. The others—"

"Forget the others. Let the other camps be content with being footnotes to *our* story. We get to launch two of the Gorgons. Us. Half the job, with Camp #9 doing their part. Two camps. We won't get lost in the crowd when history tells the truth about how America was saved from the niggers and kikes and wetbacks. We'll be heroes, man. When this is all said and done, we'll be on the dollar bill."

There was doubt in Ryerson's eyes that burned every bit as bright as his fear.

"They're going to find us," he said. "They're going to put us in jail. Maybe give us the needle."

"Only if they catch us. Once we launch Firefall, then we fall back to the bunker."

The bunker was a place they had been told about. It was in central Pennsylvania and was a rally point for any teams who launched Gorgons.

They looked at the code again.

"Shit," said Ryerson.

"God bless America," countered Furman. "Let's get dressed and get this *done*."

"Sure," said the sergeant. "God bless America."

CHAPTER 143
CBS MORNING NEWS
WITH ANCHOR WILL KEPLER

"Gunfire and tragedy erupted this morning in the suburbs of Tucson when shots rang out at a playground in a Latino community. Two teenagers are confirmed dead, though we are waiting for additional information. Witnesses described it as a drive-by shooting, saying an SUV with blacked-out windows drove slowly past the Pima Plays recreation park. The windows opened just enough to allow gun barrels to stick out and open fire. We do not currently have any descriptions of the shooters, nor have police arrested anyone. This park is used mainly by the Latino population. Authorities are calling this an active-shooter situation and advise all citizens to remain in their homes with their doors closed and locked. We'll have more as the story develops."

CHAPTER 144
THE MANSION
UNDISCLOSED LOCATION

October had the door open and one foot in his Range Rover when his cell rang. He snatched it out of a pocket, thinking it was going to be Mary.

Instead, it was Furman.

He took a breath and answered, forcing his voice to sound jovial. "Commandant, nice to speak with you again. Is everything ready? Did you get the code?"

"Yes, sir. The code's in hand, and my guys are prepping the Gorgons for the run."

"Excellent."

"But that's not why I'm calling, sir."

"Oh?"

"One of our biker scouts has been watching the farmhouse. There's a bunch of guys there who maybe shouldn't be."

"If you mean Joe Ledger and Havoc Team, then yes, I already know."

"Well, yeah. And a couple other guys. We took pictures and ran facial recognition. Got two interesting hits. One was a private detective from Philadelphia—name of Sam Hunter."

"Name rings a very faint bell," said October, getting into the car and buckling up. "Do you have anything on him?"

"Not a lot. Works doing small-time cases in Philly. Used to be a cop in the Twin Cities but got fired for a couple of cases of excessive force. Hangs out a lot with that big red-haired patrol sergeant, Mike Sweeney."

"And . . . ?"

"That's it on him. The other guy is a dork. Antonio Jones. A skinny black dude who owns a shop that makes Halloween costumes. Won some awards for werewolf makeup and did three seasons back in the early 2010s doing makeup effects on *Bitten*."

"Lot of information that I don't care about, Commandant."

"My biker guy saw the red-haired cop out in a field showing Jones how to put on Kevlar and fire handguns and rifles."

October started his car. "That's a little more interesting. Very small police force for a town with this square mileage, and Halloween's coming up. Their big tourism season. Do we know what the hiring policies are for Pine Deep PD? Do they deputize locals for, say, crowd control?"

"Usually, yeah."

"Did your spy see any of Ledger's people giving him special training?"

"No."

"Then there you go. Ledger knows Crow and Sweeney. He's been in town at least three times that I know of. After what your legionnaires did to those five down in Philly, it's not a stretch to think that Ledger would go to ground among people he knows out in a rural setting."

"They're in our backyard practically," protested Furman. "And with today being Firefall and all . . ."

October considered. "Mmm, I take your point. Okay, do this. Once the Firefall rock teams are on their way, tear down the camp. Go to that piece of property I showed you near Wildwood. No body armor, no visible guns. Be tourists. I don't know, play volleyball or something. No bar fights, no trash talk to people of different races. No touching any girl or woman who isn't at a camp. Is that clear?"

"Yes, sir," said Furman crisply. "But, sir, there's one more thing."

"Make it quick."

"The biker who was sending me reports about the farm . . . he's no longer answering his cell."

October started the car but did not yet put it in gear. "Do you have a couple of good men you can spare?"

"Now? Sure. Except for the Gorgon teams, everyone else is here in camp as ordered."

"Send some to investigate. If Ledger and his team are still there, then let me know. That's best-case scenario, because although he and his boss know some of what's going on—and god knows we've given them some juicy clues—they don't know about Firefall. Once those rockets launch, Ledger and everyone else will have their hands full. By then, all of the camps will be packed and gone."

"And if Ledger's gone?"

"In that case, check the house. If anyone's still there, put them down."

"Chief Crow has a wife and two kids."

"Aww, isn't that a crying shame."

October tossed the phone onto the driver's seat and pulled away from the Mansion.

The bright blue Range Rover came out onto the road and turned northeast.

Miss Mary sat in her car and watched October drive away.

She was alone. David White—what was left of him—was in the back bay wrapped in turn upon turn of black plastic sheeting. He had been too dodgy about helping her infect and release more Typhoid Marys. He also flatly refused her request to help her fetch Gorgons from the basement of the Mansion.

"They're not even ready," he'd said. "They're still full of that Shiva stuff. We don't even have enough of the MERS to fill them anyway. The boss is going with Firefall with just four rockets. Two in Pennsylvania and two in—"

He was pissing her off, and before she realized what she was doing, David's eyes and tongue were gone. Then she had to break his neck because of all the screaming.

"Pussy," she said.

Her fingers were still stained red.

Once October's car was out of sight, she started her engine and turned onto the unnamed lane that whipsawed through the woods all the way to the Mansion.

To home.

CHAPTER 145
CRUISER FIVE
DARK HOLLOW ROAD
PINE DEEP, PENNSYLVANIA

It was the ragged end of a graveyard shift. Still two hours until 8:00 a.m., but Officer Gary Maines felt as if the night were forty hours long. A full thermos of strong coffee kept him awake, but alertness was elusive cruising for hours on empty farm roads. Within a week or so, the Halloween tourists would start coming, and Crow would bring in ten reserve cops and no one would have time to be sleepy.

Maines kept yawning even as he squinted through the early light of a red dawn.

He was about to call in that he was heading back to town to a bathroom break when he saw the electric-blue Range Rover SUV again. It was ahead of him as he climbed Cornflower Lane for a last sweep before heading back to the barn.

Although he had not heard back from Chief Crow when he'd called it in after midnight, he contacted dispatch again and gave them an update. The dispatcher again told him that the call was logged and a text message had been sent to Crow's cell.

Maines saw the car's brake lights come on as it slowed, and then the Range Rover turned down a dirt path. Something about that path triggered an old memory. A story about a very bad man who lived there once long before he was born. But he chased it away. There were lots of spooky old stories in that town. Always had been.

The officer thought no more about it.

CHAPTER 146
VALLEY SQUARE MALL
WARRINGTON, PENNSYLVANIA

Toombs sat in his car, which idled in the parking lot of a Wegmans grocery store. He'd pulled in when the go-code came through.

do3hm9h#e/lende8

"Jesus Christ," he murmured. He put his face in his hands. "You really did it. All this time, I thought it was a bluff. Fuck me if I didn't think it was all a bluff."

He tried to tell himself that a limited MERS outbreak wouldn't be so bad. Besides, they only had four rockets ready.

"Just like the flu," he said. "That's all. Just the flu."

Then he thought about the hit on Gehenna and the stuff they took from there. Ebola, dengue fever, Marburg fever, rabies with a pertussis delivery system. Dozens of others. All weaponized.

October had sworn to him that the biowarfare lab hits were to secure enough of the MERS, along with experimental vaccine supplies for the troops. And Toombs had believed it because it was the lesser of a lot of potential evils.

And yet.

And yet . . .

Toombs had a guy in Mary's lab. Not a scientist—just a tech named Xander. Toombs had recruited him on a bad day when Mary was handing out stinging rebukes for the smallest errors, and even a couple of hard slaps across the face. Toombs had been near the back exit to the Mansion, smoking a joint as he watched the sunset, when the techs came out to basically walk in agitated circles and kick anything kickable.

Toombs had approached Xander, calmed him down, talked, drove him into town for some good drinks and an expensive steak. By the end of that evening, the tech was in Toombs's pocket, with a big bonus promised for keeping tabs on what went on down there.

As a result, Toombs knew something about the SDs, though he had not actually seen one. He knew about the Berserker project and about how far Mary had gone past the intended goal. Almost like she was building her *own* army. Handpicked men, too. And he knew that she had taken some of the most advanced samples of *seif al din* from Gehenna. She had tried to get Rage from Germany, but the blast that was intended to kill Bedlam Team had destroyed the entire facility. Similar to the clumsiness that destroyed the Vault.

Toombs, however, was not personally allowed down into the basement lab. That was for October, Miss Mary, and her team of mad scientists, animal handlers, and Berserkers.

Which made him want to see it.

He was of half a mind to call it a day, leave behind the identity of Mr. Toombs, get on I-95, and see a guy he knew—a Cuban named Cortez—who made the very best new identities in the country. Guy was a wizard.

On the other hand, he wanted to see what was down in the basement. He was okay with MERS because he did not think it was going to be even as bad as COVID-19. Let October and his tin soldiers try to start their civil war. Toombs thought the smart money was on the National Guard and, at need, the regular army, navy, marine corps, and air force. America would take some hits, but she tended to course correct, and since Toombs could not have cared less whose ass was in the big seat at the White House, his interest in the outcome of Firefall was already fading.

The basement lab, though. There could be some tech down there he could sell to some people he knew. Prototypes, maybe. With accompanying computer files. Sell it to a cartel or some other group. Hell, sell it to the same people the Tenth Legion was targeting. Level the playing field a bit. *That* could actually be fun. Once he had new papers and some Brazilian face work—fake pigment, change the shape of his cheekbones and brow—he could watch that kind of limited war in one of those countries with no extradition. He wondered what the weather was like in Bhutan. That was supposed to be a happy place. Or Morocco, Colombia, Indonesia.

With what he had in numbered accounts and what he had in his wall safe in his Mansion suite, he could live like a quiet king for the rest of his life.

That decided it. He turned on the car and headed back to the Mansion.

For one last visit.

CHAPTER 147
THE GUTHRIE FARM
PINE DEEP, PENNSYLVANIA

"You look like you're working your ass right off," said Top as he came outside.

Remy was slouched in an Adirondack chair that was on a wooden pad facing a pond. At least three species of ducks swam there, most in pairs, along with some Canada geese. A raccoon was on the far side of the pond dunking apple slices in a cup of vanilla yogurt. A large stainless-steel thermos of coffee sat next to a coffee cup made to look like a pumpkin. Remy had a piece of sweetgrass between his teeth. Sitting on the arm of the chair was the scuffed and broken windup jack-o'-lantern that the old vagrant had given the young Cajun. The sight of it gave Top a pang.

"Pull up a pew, Top. Show's about to start."

Top did so, and a moment later, Bunny and Belle joined them. Among the toys Bird Dog had brought was a cineplex, which looked like a stack of thin computer screens, each about the thickness of a magazine and attached with magnets at each corner. This allowed the user to pull up and position as many screens as he had drones in the air. Currently, he was tracking four drones—two each of the falcon medium-range machines and two aerial surveillance black vulture drones.

All four birds reported that they were in place and all systems were five by five. Remy engaged their cameras, and all of Havoc leaned in.

"That one's the depot," said Remy. And indeed it did look like a depot, with many stacks of cardboard boxes, wooden crates, and metal equipment boxes, all partially hidden under canopies. Little red dots appeared on the screens.

"You pinging any sensors or alarms?" asked Top.

"No. They have guards walking the perimeter and probably think that's all they need."

"Give me thermals," ordered Top, and Remy hit the right keys. From one of the circling vultures, he got a wide-screen image of the whole camp, and it was littered with glowing red dots. Remy counted.

"Damn, there's closer to thirty of them," he said. "And some of them are weird. Look, there's six of them who are twice as big as the others."

"Berserkers," said Bunny. "Fuck me."

"What about those there?" asked Belle, pointing a long, slender finger to a cluster of six dots that were smaller than the regular men, but milled and moved oddly. "Are they dogs?"

"I don't know," said Remy. "Let me get a falcon over to the side of the camp. Have to be careful to not be spotted. Give me a couple minutes."

They waited, but it was a disappointment. The six dog-sized figures were inside a large metal cage partially covered with a green tarp. All the falcon drone could pick up were snarls, growls, and an odd and inexplicable swishing sound. It was sharp and fast, and sometimes when it came, there was a heavy thud against the crate.

"Sounds like dogs to me," said Remy. "Must have been what that legionnaire was talking about. Give me a second to bring Sweeney and those guys up to speed."

"Now," said Top, "show me the big camp."

CHAPTER 148
TRENTON-MERCER AIRPORT
EWING TOWNSHIP, NEW JERSEY

The Cessna Citation X+ came howling out of the morning sky but landed soft as a whisper on the tarmac. By the time it stopped rolling and the pilot cut the engines, a big white cargo van was right there waiting.

Bird Dog got out of the driver's seat and ran to the stairs as they were deployed. He wore black military trousers and an old Desert Storm camo jacket with lots of pockets.

"Welcome, sir," he said as Mr. Church came quickly down the stairs. Bird Dog was surprised to see that, instead of his usual top-quality suits, Church was dressed all in black, with a gun belt around his waist as well as a shoulder holster. The pistol under his arm was a Glock, but the one slung low was a Snellig dart gun. A vest with many ammunition pouches also supported a fighting knife hung pommel-down and smaller pouches for other items.

It was the very first time Bird Dog had even seen the Big Man dressed for combat, and he found it more than a little disturbing. How bad did things have to be for Church to come into the field dressed for trouble?

Behind Church was the less imposing figure of Dr. Ron Coleman. He, too, was dressed in combat clothes, but they were clearly not tailored for him. The only weapon he had was a Snellig, and he looked incredibly self-conscious.

"The boss and the brain," said Bird Dog. "We run out of field operators?"

"Sadly," said Church, "that's close to the truth. Did you already drop the field kits off to Outlaw?"

"Yes, sir. Gave them the whole shebang from soup to nuts."

"Delighted to hear it." Church turned to indicate the cargo hold of his plane. Two aides who had traveled with him were unloading the crates of Snellig pistols and magazines of the new Sandman Z1 ammunition.

"That what I think it is?" asked the logistics chief.

"It is. I want you to take us and those crates to the Guthrie farm in Pine Deep."

"Just came from there and know a shortcut, boss."

Church and Coleman watched as the crates were loaded into the rear of the van. Coleman climbed into the back, which had fold-down seats. Church went around to the passenger side, but the door opened before he could touch the handle. A woman looked down at him. She looked like she was in her sixties, but that was as much of a lie as how old Church looked. She was elegant, imperious, and beautiful.

"Lilith," said Church, his face lighting up with surprise and pleasure.

"Hello, my love," she said.

CHAPTER 149
THE MANSION
UNDISCLOSED LOCATION

Mr. Toombs drove to the Mansion with an odd mix of trepidation and excitement bubbling in his gut. October had sent him a second and longer text to say that Joe Ledger was in Pine Deep and was possibly gathering allies for a hit. October said that it was not clear which location was the target, but guessed it was going to be the comfort camp.

Even so, the text concluded, *go to the Mansion and ride it out. No one knows about that place but you, Mary, me, the staff, and the science team. I sent word to everyone to hunker down and wait. The Mansion is the only reliably safe place. I'll be in touch.*

Toombs considered calling but decided against it. At a red light, he began composing a reply text and then deleted it.

"Bhutan," he said. "Colombia. Anywhere but here."

He turned on the news and listened to increasingly hysterical reports of new terrorist threats and a veritable tsunami of hate crimes directed at Latinos—even those who had lived in America for generations and were not from Mexico—as well as Muslims. He found that all of the violence was troubling him more than it should.

"Pretty goddamn late to grow a conscience," he told his face in the rearview mirror.

He drove.

A mile later, he yelled, "Hunker down and ride it out, my ass."

He pulled off Cornflower Lane and onto the winding dirt trail that led up to the Mansion. The place was completely impossible to see from any road. He pulled into the shadows beneath a row of beech trees and studied the house with his binoculars. Everything looked calm.

Toombs was about to put the car into gear and drive up to the front door when he spotted another car parked as discreetly as his own. He recognized it as the personal car of one of the group's top agents, David White. He had been Miss Mary's bodyguard and minder during all of the Typhoid Mary events.

"What the hell?" White did not even know the location of the Mansion or that it existed at all. Almost no one did.

Then he saw a figure walking across the lawn close to the house.

It was Mary.

Her dress was splashed with dried blood, and with his binoculars, he could see the crimson on her hands and around her mouth.

"Ohhhhhh shit," he said, fading back into darker concealment.

Toombs did not want to confront her. The woman frankly terrified him. Even though he was armed, he remembered the feral speed and strength she'd demonstrated the first time they met. No thanks—he wanted no rematch with her, gun or no gun.

So he sat down to wait.

An hour later, she emerged from the house wearing the same torn dress, but now it glistened with fresh blood. She was covered in it. Her hair was matted and pasted to her gray-white skin, and there was a look in her eyes that made him nearly cry out. It was the look of someone from whom all sanity had fled. There was a blankness to it that hinted at a total disconnect from anything normal. Anything whole or human.

Toombs got quietly out of the car, drew his pistol, and considered trying his luck with a full magazine. He was a very good shot, but the range was bad. A bit too far for accuracy with a handgun, and besides, the car was in the way.

But Mary walked past the car and headed around to the far side of the Mansion. Toombs edged sideways to a deer path and then jogged through the woods until he could see the rear entrance. The gardener's pickup truck was there, and Mary was loading something onto it.

Toombs knelt and brought the binoculars up again. His heart nearly died in his chest.

Mary was carrying an armful of Gorgon warheads.

He hadn't thought there were any left at the house. They should all have gone out to the camps. No, he corrected himself, they *had* gone to the camps. She had six of them clutched to her chest, but they couldn't be the four loaded with MERS.

What did she want the Gorgons with the Shiva warheads for? Toombs could concoct no scenario that made sense of that. Gooseflesh rippled along his forearms, though.

He watched as she placed them in the bed of the truck, then hurried back inside, returning with six more. On her last trip, she used a cart to bring out several standard RPG launchers, which she also placed in the back of the truck. Then covered all of them with a canvas tarp, which she weighed down with stones that lined the front driveway.

Toombs edged forward until Mary was less than seventy feet away. He took his pistol in two hands, aimed with great care, and pulled the trigger. The bullet caught Mary in the stomach. She staggered and dropped the RPG she had been lifting into the truck.

Toombs fired again, this time his round striking her at the top curve of her left breast. He could hear Mary cough and saw a spray of blood splash the side of the truck. He rose, more confident now, and walked toward her, gun held in both hands as he fired shot after shot into her. She tried to run for the safety of the woods, but he followed, aiming and firing, aiming and firing until his slide locked back.

He paused to drop the magazine and swap in a fresh one.

By then, Mary suddenly broke into a wobbling run and headed straight into the woods. It amazed him that she could still walk, let alone run. He'd hit her with all fifteen rounds from his Glock 19. Was she wearing some kind of body armor under that bloody dress? If so, which kind? It sure as hell wasn't anything from the Kuga catalog. Was it something she had left over from when she worked for Mr. Church?

And yet, he could swear some of his shots were through-and-throughs. That's what it looked like, though of course that was impossible. A woman of her size would have been torn to pieces by that many 9mm rounds.

Doubt slowed him, and he stopped by the edge of the woods.

Listening.

Looking at the blood spatter on the leaves.

Rain was still falling, though not as intensely as last night. It made the blood droplets turn pink and run down the trunks of wild maples and broad leaves of the rhododendron.

"Mary," he called, not sure why. The wind swallowed the name and bore it away into the shadowy forest.

He heard a sound off to his left, and he turned fast. Mary broke from the woods and ran for the gardener's truck. Toombs's mouth went totally dry.

"How . . . ?" he began, but words utterly failed him.

With fifteen 9mm rounds in her slender body, Mary climbed into the truck. The engine started at once, and suddenly, Toombs found himself running toward her, the gun bucking in his hand. His bullets struck the door and shattered the driver's glass and tore meat and blood from Mary's shoulder.

She hit the gas and the truck lurched forward, rear tires spinning in the mud, kicking it up and back into arcing showers that slapped him in the face. He threw an arm over his eyes and fired blind until the slide locked back.

The truck tires found purchase and the vehicle leaped forward, gaining speed, slewing a little in puddles before finding more solid ground. Mary drove away, leaving a stunned and horrified Toombs standing there, covered in mud, the empty pistol in his outstretched hand.

He took two staggering steps before his knees buckled, and he sat down hard on the drying mud.

"What . . ." he said in a phlegmy and choked voice. "What . . . the fuck . . . ?"

CHAPTER 150
CORNFLOWER LANE
PINE DEEP, PENNSYLVANIA

Mary drove ten miles along the road before the pain overwhelmed her.

Her eyes lost focus, and the road seemed to split into four lanes instead of two. Then six, then eight. Each one undulated like a lolling tongue, rippling and twisting unnaturally.

She tried to find the path through all of that strangeness, fighting to keep her head clear.

She blinked.

And blinked again.

During the first blink, she was on the road.

After the second, she lay sideways against the driver's door. The rear wheels were whining, and Mary realized her foot was pressing the gas pedal to the floor but the wheels were in the air.

It took her a hundred years and every ounce of strength she had to lift her foot. The whine slowed and stopped. She fumbled for the key to turn the engine off, but the fob was gone. Then she blindly stabbed the dashboard for the off switch. Her fingers banged off metal with no effect. Then she realized this wasn't her SUV. It was the gardener's truck.

The old pickup truck lay on its side, wheels higher than the hood because she had driven off the road and into a drainage ditch. Mary's hand crawled like a crimson spider to the steering column, and there was the key in the ignition. Old-school. Reliable. She turned it, and the engine sputtered, coughed, and died.

Mary lay there, trapped in the harness of her seat belt. Her vision transformed with unnatural slowness from seeing the late-dawn sun through the trees to seeing a veil of sheer red. Like tulle or gossamer.

She knew it was blood, but it looked so pretty.

She blinked again.

The sun was a little higher.

Am I dead? she wondered.

Some vile part of her mind replied in a malicious whisper.

Yes.

Mary lay there, bleeding. She could feel each of the bullet wounds.

Every.

Single.

One.

CHAPTER 151
THE PAN HEAD BAR AND GRILL
PINE DEEP, PENNSYLVANIA

The bartender's name was King Dong. Pretty sure it was a nickname, but you never know.

King Dong was about my height but maybe four Joe Ledgers wide. Put an ugly head, uglier beard, arms and legs on an Abrams tank and you have a good idea of him. Never saw a spread of shoulders like his. Bird Dog could have landed his cargo chopper on the left one and left plenty of room for a modest three-bed, two-bath town house on his right. The head in between the shoulders seemed to be composed mainly of grizzled black beard, wildly overgrown black eyebrows, old acne scars. Tiny pig eyes and a button nose, with a pouty mouth. Lots of muscle on the arms, though. Too many prison tats to count, and most of them were HH or 88 or the swastika. Pillar of the community, clearly.

He looked me up and down and did not seem impressed. When he looked at Crow, shutters dropped over his eyes.

"Chief," he said in a voice that was just a little rougher than a rock grinder.

"King," said Crow. He looked more or less ordinary in his police uniform. The sword was in the car. Didn't seem to be the right fashion statement for a brief interview.

They gave each other about two seconds of a gunslinger stare.

"Early for you," said the bartender. "We ain't even open 'cept for coffee."

"Then we'll have coffee."

"I'll have a vanilla soy latte with foam," I said. Just to be a dick. And it earned exactly the kind of contemptuous look King Dong gave me.

"Two black coffees," he said and turned away to pour the steaming brew into a pair of mugs that looked like the last time they were cleaned was during the Bush presidency. The first one. He set them on the bar in front of us.

Crow settled onto a seat. I remained standing. We both had nylon windbreakers over our combat gear, but the lumps and bumps of all those ammunition pouches were eloquent, and we saw King checking us out.

"Going hunting?" he asked.

"In a way," said Crow.

"Deer or bear?"

We had rehearsed a story on the way, but Crow must have woken up on the wrong side of the bed and had a full bowl of cranky flakes. He smiled and said, "Lester, you and I have never danced, but you've heard about me. My friend and I are going to ask some tough questions, and if we don't get answers that we believe and that provide material assistance in our current investigation, I'm going to cut your dick off and mount it over my office desk."

King Dong stared at him.

"Say something," I suggested. When he just stood there, I took my knife out of its sheath and stabbed it onto his polished oak bar top. It's a beauty, made for me by Alex Harrison at Night Watch Knives.

"Say, Joe," murmured Crow, "is that the dick-cutting knife?"

"It's the smaller one. Didn't think we'd need medium or large."

"Small will do. Looks sharp."

"Very sharp."

We grinned like a couple of happy fools.

King Dong recovered somewhat. "I make a call and my lawyers will be two miles up your ass by noon."

I tapped Crow's arm. "He thinks we're just joshing with him."

"Joshing? Really?"

"You know what I mean. He thinks we're only talking trash."

"Funning, you mean," said Crow. "He thinks we're funning with him."

"No one uses 'funning' anymore. What are you? Festus from *Gunsmoke*?"

"You're not old enough to know that reference."

"Was my dad's favorite show growing up."

"How is your dad?"

"Well," I said, "funny thing. Some piece of shit killed him and everyone else in my family a couple of Christmases ago."

Crow affected surprise. "Damn, son. That must have made you a bit cranky."

"A tad."

"Cranky enough for breaking procedural laws and cutting a dick off?"

"You know, that might actually make me feel better."

"You assholes think this is funny?" growled King Dong.

"No," said Crow, "not much."

With speed and power you'd never credit in a man of his size, Crow lunged forward, grabbed King Dong by the back of his neck, and slammed him face down onto the bar top. Once, twice, a third time. Then he knotted fingers in his greasy hair and pulled the man's head up as he bent close and spoke in a low, feral voice.

"Listen to me, fuckface," Crow said. "We know you're Tenth Legion. We know about Firefall. And we know about the comfort camps."

King Dong's nose was mashed nearly flat, two of his front teeth were stuck to his lower lip by red blood, and his eyes were filled with pain.

"What . . . the fuck . . . ?" he managed to get out, then half turned and spat blood and those teeth onto the bar. "What do you want?"

"Where is Mr. October?"

"I don't know," he bellowed. But as he did that, I saw him twist a bit as if he were doing something with his foot. Almost immediately, there was noise outside. A door banged open—probably the metal alley door between the bar and the place next to it. Men's voices. And then a low growl and a lot of screaming.

Side note, I love my dog. Just saying.

Crow slammed King Dong's head down a couple more times. By then, I'd walked around the bar. I grabbed the big bartender by the throat and balls, picked him up with a knee to boost him, and slammed him on the bar top. Men, as a rule, do not react well to being picked up. Three-hundred-pound sack-of-shit men even less so. It unnerves them. It fractures their understanding of the world. Lifting him like that was difficult and painful, but I sure as shit did not let it show. Instead, I laughed. Then I grabbed the knife, and with its small, tough, wickedly sharp blade, I cut through belt and denim and boxers and laid him bare from belly to knees. He lived up to his nickname, with a flaccid penis the size of a zucchini.

"Need a bigger knife, Joe?" asked Crow.

"Nah, this one will do," I said, laying the edge of the steel against his balls.

Crow walked over to the door, opened it, then spoke over his shoulder. "Two guys down. Might need some Band-Aids and some Neosporin. Big goofy dog out here wagging his tail. I'm going to call this in."

He was pulling zip-cuffs from a belt pouch as he stepped outside. Ghost came in, happy as a puppy, his muzzle red with blood. Behind the doggy smile, I saw the colder, calmer look of the wolf.

"Ghost," I said, "scout."

He vanished through the curtained partition between bar and jukebox. There were no fresh screams, so I judged Ghost didn't find anyone.

Crow rejoined me. "Two of my cruisers and some EMTs will be here in five. Make this quick."

He bent over King Dong.

"October," I said.

The bleeding man said, "Mansion."

"Where?"

Before he could tell us, there was a big noise outside, but it wasn't sirens. It was the thunder of motorcycles.

"Well, hell," said Crow. Through the open door, we could see heavy machines screaming to a stop outside.

CHAPTER 152
EAST PINELANDS FOREST
BLACK MARSH, PENNSYLVANIA

They moved through the woods like shadows.

Silent, unseen, disturbing nothing in their passage. Every footfall, even while running, was carefully placed. All three of them ran with an easy yet powerful grace.

All three were barefoot.

Mike Sweeney was in the lead. He knew these woods best, and the others—Hunter and Jones—followed. They deferred to him as the leader of their small pack, and Mike led with skill and care and wisdom.

He stopped. No raised fist to signal a halt. The other two froze. Alert and waiting.

Ahead, there was noise. Faint, but there.

The three hunters leaned into it, listening with keen senses.

Men talking. A brief laugh.

Mike raised his head and sniffed the air. The odors of grease and cigarettes and soap and coffee were carried by the faint breeze. Mike began to take a step forward but paused again as a cross breeze brought fresh scents.

Mike frowned, not quite understanding what he smelled. Jones came up beside him and took a long sniff. He frowned, too.

"What is it?" asked Hunter quietly, joining them.

Jones gestured in the direction from which the stranger scents wafted. They all considered the aroma.

"Dog," said Hunter, but Mike shook his head.

"Not just dog."

"Maybe not a dog," suggested Jones. "Smells weird. Smells like the zoo. The big apes' house."

Mike considered. "Maybe what Colonel Ledger told us about. The Berserkers. PMCs with silverback gorilla DNA."

"That sounds weird even to say out loud," said Hunter. "But . . ."

"Yeah," said Jones. "Apes, maybe. But dog, too. And something else."

"Split up," said Mike. "Circle the depot and meet back here in ten."

They glanced at their watches, nodded, and moved off, silent as death.

CHAPTER 153
THE PAN HEAD BAR AND GRILL
PINE DEEP, PENNSYLVANIA

Crow cut me a nervous look. "Out the back or hold the fort until my guys show up?"

"Hold the fort as long as it's not the Alamo."

"Wish I had my damn sword," he said.

"I wish I had Iron Man armor and Captain America's shield. Life sucks like that."

That was all the time we had for conversation. Figures began crowding the doorway. There was the flash of sunlight and bar neon on steel as guns came up. I shoved Crow left and I dove right. Not sure which one of us had a gun out first. I'd like to think it was me because I'm an international troubleshooting gunslinger, but damn if that creaky, skinny old Crow didn't beat me to the draw. His weapon of choice was a Beretta 92F, which was my personal favorite once upon a time.

I wasn't in the mood for a fair fight, though. I shrugged out of my windbreaker, reached behind me, and pulled the Heckler & Koch MP7 machine pistol around. It had a thirty-round detachable box magazine loaded with Action 4.6×30mm Law Enforcement hollowpoint rounds.

I hosed the doorway.

Didn't know if all of these bastards were Tenth Legion or just biker assholes running drugs and little girls, and I frankly didn't care. The bullets chewed them apart, and they toppled sideways and back and down. A couple of their guns went off—one shot the floor, another zipped over the supine King Dong and smashed a bunch of bottles. Crow knelt and fired three shots, taking one man in the belly and another high on the shoulder.

Then I was up and running. I heard Ghost coming up behind me, his nails click-clicking on the floor. We burst out of the bar and saw six men twisting and writhing on the pavement. None of them were dead. None of them were going to get up and cause us more problems.

Two more bikers were in the street, and I pointed my gun at them.

"Hands up," I snapped. "Dismount. Let the bikes fall. Lace your fingers behind your heads. On your knees."

Sirens filled the air, and Crow came outside, holding his badge high and his pistol pointed down. The cruisers screeched to a halt, and Crow signaled to them to cut their sirens. The two officers got out. Name tags said RILEY and MAINES, and they stood gaping at the carnage.

Crow hurried to meet them.

"You two secure this scene. Get their weapons, cuff them. No, I don't care if they're bleeding out. Do it. Call for more ambulances."

He caught my gaze and jerked his head toward the bar. I went back inside and found King Dong trying to climb down from the countertop. His shredded pants slipped down to his ankles, hampering his efforts. I used a finger signal to send Ghost over to smile at him. Those titanium teeth are scary as fuck.

King Dong sank down onto the floor, trying to hide his nakedness with trembling hands. I knelt in front of him and put the hot barrel of the machine pistol against his dick.

"Where is the Mansion?"

He looked at me with fierce eyes that showed less defeat than you might expect, all things considered.

"God will cut you down," he said. "Firefall's coming, and the mud people are going to pay for what they've done to America."

"I keep hearing you dickheads brag about Firefall. What is it?"

"Wouldn't you like to know?"

"I know that it's you fucktards playing with Gorgon rocket launchers."

That jolted him a little. His eyes darted away. "You'll see, cocksucker. You'll all see. You won't live out the day. America is going to take back its own, and the war starts today. God bless America!"

And he crunched down on a back molar.

I squatted there and watched him die. Cursing myself for not assuming that the Cyke-lones had salvation caps, too.

Ghost growled at the corpse.

Crow was still outside and was managing to keep anyone else from coming in. So I took a couple of minutes to go through the place. In the filthy back office, I found a laptop in a ruggedized case, two burner phones, and some flash drives in a locked drawer. I put the small stuff into my pockets and tucked the laptop up under my body armor.

I continued to search the office, but as I pulled out the bottom drawer of a file cabinet, I heard a distinct *click*.

That's never a good sound in situations like this. I looked down into the drawer. There was a chunk of gray clay half the size of a building brick. It had detonators and wires and a little triggering device that winked at me with a furious red.

Ghost began barking, and I yelled at him to run.

We both ran as fast as we could.

Made it all the way to the front door before the C-4 exploded.

CHAPTER 154
CORNFLOWER LANE
PINE DEEP, PENNSYLVANIA

Miss Mary tried to die.

She tried to be dead.

On so many levels, she wanted that.

But the world would not let her die.

She lifted one hand to claw the drying blood from her eyes, revealing by slow degrees the yellow sunlight of an autumn morning. All around her, the trees bent their leafy heads together to gossip about her. Birds in the trees played whisper down the lane, and Mary swore she heard her name over and over again.

Her eyes, though, were clear.

She saw with perfect clarity the spiderweb cracks across the windshield. She felt the constriction of the seat belts, but also their orientation. She pressed the release, but nothing happened. She tried again and again.

Nothing. The locking mechanism was crushed.

Mary had no knife. Her gun was gone. Her nails were short, bitten to the quick over so many months with October. What did that leave her?

The side window against which she lay was cracked. Mary raised her left arm, cocked it back, and struck the glass. Hard. Harder. The pain was exquisite. She hit it again and again and again.

Suddenly, the safety glass exploded into a shower of gummy shards. Mary caught some, sorted through them, found one with a good edge. She used her left hand to pull the waist strap up as high as it would go, and with her right, she began to saw.

Back and forth, back and forth, steady as a metronome.

All the time thinking about the Gorgons in the back of the pickup truck.

"Sometimes you have to burn to shine," she said. Her voice was thick, the words coming out guttural and strange.

And kept on sawing at the strap.

CHAPTER 155
THE PAN HEAD BAR AND GRILL
PINE DEEP, PENNSYLVANIA

The blast picked us both off the floor and hurled us out into the street. We slammed into an EMT and a cop and a parking meter before crashing to the ground. The parking meter goddamn near took my head off.

Windows blew out all along the street. Even the big plate window of Crow's office burst into a thousand slivers of glittering glass. Dozens of car alarms went off. Store burglar alarms, too. Gas and dust belched out of the ragged holes that had been the windows of the bar. A metal box used for distributing free coupon circulars had punched through the windshield of the ambulance.

I lay there, flash-burned, half-deafened, unable to move. I heard Ghost whimpering, and I called out to him. He came crawling on his belly and seemed more scared than hurt. Small mercies. He licked my face, but my head hurt so much that it was like being nuzzled by an orbital sander. I pushed him back and tried to sit up, but immediately collapsed, sick and dizzy and in one hell of a lot of pain.

Crow came crawling to me on hands and knees. One side of his face was coated with ash and blood, and there was a three-inch cut across his upper chest, across the clavicle. An inch higher and it would have cut his throat. He slumped down next to me.

"Ow," he said. Only that.

We lay there looking at the smoking ruin that used to be the Pan Head.

My hearing returned by degrees, and I could hear someone sobbing, someone else coughing, and the sounds of more sirens coming.

My brain was mostly burned toast, with little gaps in my memory. When I touched my scalp, I could feel a lump, and just touching it set fireworks off in my skull. I knew a concussion when I felt one. I've had more than my share.

When I struggled to sit up, my stomach rebelled, and I leaned sideways and puked. Concussion for sure.

"Stay right there, sir," said a voice, and I looked up at a hazy lump of a shape that slowly resolved itself into the face of one of the two police officers who had been first on the scene. What was his name? Mayer? Mears?

No. Maines.

"Help me up," I said.

"No, sir," he insisted. "You need to wait right here for the EMTs."

I almost said something stupid like, *The EMTs are already here*, but then I saw them. Dazed, seared, shaking with pain and trauma.

"Help me up," I repeated and put edge to it. He did not and even tried to gently push me back down onto the ground. I caught his hand and twisted it with a little wristlock. Not to damage but to make a point. He yelped in pain.

"Maines," snapped Crow, "help him up. That's an order."

The cop hesitated, not sure if Crow was in any shape to give orders. But then he nodded, took me in a pair of forearm clasps, and walked backward until I was on my feet. Kind of. I grabbed for the same parking meter that I'd crashed into.

"Help your boss, too," I croaked.

Maines said something under his breath but pulled Crow up, too. Ghost got onto four trembling legs and leaned his shoulder against my thigh.

Yeah, we were all fine. Just peachy.

Every vehicle with a siren and flashing lights arrived. Hoses started spraying the building. EMTs pulled us away and triaged our wounds. They tried to take me to the ER, but I threatened extensive bodily harm. Crow told them to dress our cuts and give us some crack-and-apply cold packs. We sat there with the comforting cold pressed against my head and his jaw. When we looked at each other, we almost laughed.

Didn't, though. Would have hurt too much.

Memories began to slowly reassemble themselves in what was left of my head.

"Firefall," I murmured.

Crow nodded. "He said it was today. But what *actually* is it?"

"Something bad."

A shadow fell across us, and we looked up at Officer Maines. He didn't look a whole lot better than we did.

"Sir," he said to Crow, "do you know if this has anything to do with that car?"

"Car?"

"The one I told Harry about. He said he was going to text you?"

Crow found his cell and looked at it. There were a dozen texts, and he scrolled through to find the ones from Maines. They were there, sandwiched between very saucy texts from Val.

"I have notifications turned off when I'm off shift," said Crow. "Damn."

"What's this about?" I asked, and he explained that he had a weird feeling about a man he saw at a diner down in Willow Grove. He described the man, but he was a stranger to me. "How's this connected?"

"I don't know that it is," said Crow, rubbing his eyes. He looked at some grit on his fingertips and flicked it away. "Just a feeling."

I asked, "Where did you see the Range Rover?"

"Saw him on Cornflower Lane, and he turned off on that old dirt road. You know the one, boss. Where the big fire was during the Trouble. Used to be called Pine Meadow Trail?"

I felt Crow stiffen. Everything about his energy changed in the space of a heartbeat.

"What?" I demanded. "Who is this guy?"

"I don't know who he is, Joe. It's not anything connected with this, but . . ."

"But what?"

"That place. Someone bought the land once owned by Ubel Griswold."

"Wait, that's the guy who was a serial killer like forty years ago?"

"When I was a kid, yes. He was killed by a migrant worker," Crow explained. "A good guy. Oren Morse. A friend. People used to call him the Bone Man because he was so skinny. Then at the beginning of the Trouble, Mike Sweeney's stepdad, a total asshole named Vic Wingate, built a kind of cult around Griswold's memory. Wingate even turned Griswold's old house into a meeting place for his white supremacist asshole friends and then booby-trapped it. Killed a Philly cop with those traps. Nearly killed me. The place burned down, though. Someone else bought it—maybe the guy in that Range Rover—and built a new house there. A big one. Almost a mansion."

"Let me get this straight," I said, "a remote place in Pine Deep that used to be the center of the white supremacist asshole club here in town was bought and a new house built . . . right around the time that *more* white supremacists start setting up militia training camps, comfort camps, and all the rest?"

Crow stared at me, the color draining from his face.

I pulled my cell out, scrolled through my photos until I had a series of surveillance and arrest photos of men we suspected of being in the Tenth Legion. "Crow, Maines, look at these photos. Tell me if any of them look familiar."

They hunched over the screen and went through about sixty photos. Huberman, Norris, Kemmer, and the others from the New Jersey trailer park were there. As was the booking photo for Isaac Tomberland.

Maines reached out and tapped the screen. "I know that guy for sure. Don't know his name, but I've seen him around town. Saw him when Donny and I were out deer hunting, too. He was dressed in camo and said he was hunting, though he didn't have a rifle. When Donny asked him about that, he held up his binoculars and said he was birding."

"You're sure?"

"You kidding? There can't be two guys who look like that."

I tapped my earbud and was relieved that Bug responded. "Bug, was Isaac Tomberland ever apprehended after he escaped from prison?"

"No. He fell off the radar. Hey, what's up? You sound funny."

I ignored that. "Second question: What can you tell me about a property on a disused road in Pine Deep?" I gave him the old name of the trail and the name of the former occupant. It didn't take Bug very long to pull up the information.

"Okay, the property was sold for taxes a couple of years ago. New owner secured a building permit and had a house built. Three stories, really big. Eight thousand square feet."

"Who's the owner?"

"Hmm, that's tricky. It was purchased by a corporation. Gimme a sec. Okay, that corporation is owned by another and another. Bunch of shell corporations, really. They really wanted to keep the owner's name off the books."

"Next question," I said. "How many people in Bucks County own an electric-blue Range Rover?"

I heard fingers tapping.

"Eight."

"How many in or near Pine Deep?"

Bug barked out a laugh. "Yeah, you used to be a cop, that's for sure. One, Outlaw. Registered to John Stankevičius."

I sagged back, stunned and nearly breathless.

"Outlaw . . . ?" queried Bug. "That name mean anything to you?"

"Think back, Bug. The King of Plagues case. The prison doctor at Graterford. Pull up his name."

"Shit. Stankevičius. But he died four years ago. Stroke."

"Can you send me a photo of him?"

"Sure," he said, and he did. I showed the image to Crow.

"Yeah," he gasped. "That's him. How the hell did you make that connection?"

He hadn't heard Bug's side of the conversation. "Tell you later. Crow, are you in any shape to take me out to that farm?"

"Griswold's place?" He looked genuinely frightened.

"Yes."

"When?"

"Right damn now."

Maines protested, saying we were in no shape to go anywhere, and besides, we were the only witnesses to what happened at the bar.

"We'll be back," said Crow.

Together, we limped to the car. Crow climbed behind the wheel. Ghost, more recovered than either of us, bounded into the back. I eased my various achy parts into the shotgun seat. My head hurt really badly, and there was a bit of double vision, but I didn't say anything about it to Crow.

As we pulled away, I could feel Maines and the EMTs staring at us.

Once we were on the road, Crow said, "So you're telling me this October guy can somehow make himself look like other people?"

"I wish that was all he could do," I said, and we drove off.

CHAPTER 156
EAST PINELANDS FOREST
BLACK MARSH, PENNSYLVANIA

The three of them—Sweeney, Hunter, and Jones—met up again after their patrol. They moved two hundred yards back from the depot and hunkered down behind a hillock.

"Well," said Hunter, "that was entertaining."

"What did you see?" asked Jones.

"More of those legionnaires than we thought. I counted twenty-eight."

"That's what I got, too," agreed Sweeney, and Jones nodded.

"Eight of them are frigging huge," Hunter said. "Your size, Mike. A couple even bigger. You reckon those are those ape-soldier freaks? Berserkers?"

Sweeney nodded. "We have to be careful with them. Ledger said that they're above human levels in speed and strength."

Jones grinned. "Well, to be fair, there's a lot of that going around." They all smiled at that.

"And the dogs?" asked Sweeney.

"In cages—and the cages are covered in tarps," said Jones. "I couldn't get close enough to see what kind of dogs. They smell weird, though."

"They do," said Hunter. "Given that those Berserkers were given gene therapy to make them bigger and stronger, I'm wondering what the same scientists might have done to those dogs. I picked up *heavy* scents. Hormones I don't recognize. Very complex blood chemistry."

Sweeney nodded. "I wonder what they'll make of us."

Rain was starting to fall, though lightly. Sweeney looked at the sky and nodded. "Going to hit hard."

"Rain'll mask our scents for the most part," said Jones.

"Theirs, too," warned Hunter.

Jones gave him a steady look as he unzipped his jacket. "Bet we smell them coming anyway."

Sweeney said, "Ledger wanted us to just look and report back."

Jones slipped off his jacket and began to unbutton his shirt. "Dude, these are white supremacists, domestic terrorists, and they're trafficking kids. I didn't come out here to just look."

Hunter removed his jacket. "Kid's got a point, Mike."

Sweeney looked troubled. "If we do this, then we have to do it hard. Go in fast, hit them before anyone can call out. You guys up for this?"

"Like Antonio said, we didn't come out here to look," said Hunter.

"Works for me," said Sweeney.

Jones said, "But . . . we're not going to actually *tell* them about all this, right? Not about those militia assholes, but about us?"

"They seem like nice people," said Hunter with a wicked grin. "Why give them nightmares?"

As the cold rain fell on them, all three of them stripped naked.

CHAPTER 157
THE MANSION
UNDISCLOSED LOCATION

Toombs walked into the house.

He was still smeared with mud. The empty Glock hung limply from one hand. His shoes left prints along the foyer. He stopped walking and seemed to notice that he still held his gun. Toombs absently patted his shoulder rig, not quite realizing that he had used both of the magazines he'd had. Besides that, the gun itself dripped with mud. He opened his hand and let it fall. It made a strangely loud noise.

Toombs stood in the foyer, closed his eyes, and stretched out with his senses. There was no sound, no sense of movement. No life to the place. He could not feel anyone anywhere.

He walked to the foot of the stairs and called for any of the staff.

Nothing.

The whole place had a dead battery sense to it. That was his thought, but then he corrected it. The place itself did not feel dead . . . it felt *of* death.

The door to the drawing room was open, and he went in there, crossing like a sleepwalker to one of the cabinets on the west wall. He had a key for it, but it took him a long time to find it in his pocket and a longer time to fumble it into the lock. Inside were two dozen pistols of various makes and models, including a Snellig dart gun. Without giving it any real thought, he selected another Glock 19, then pulled a drawer open and removed all six of the loaded magazines. Toombs slapped one into the gun, racked the slide, and put the other magazines into his pants pockets. They were a strangely heavy and awkward burden.

Then he went to the wet bar, laid the gun down, and poured four fingers of bourbon into a tumbler. He used one hand to brace himself on the edge of the cabinet as if afraid the world was going to tilt sideways and spill him down.

Down, down, down.

The whiskey burned his throat, but it also chased away the numbness and shock. Not completely, but enough.

Toombs let the glass fall. It bounced on the thick carpet and rolled away. He took a handful of paper cocktail napkins, wet them under the faucet, and washed his face. When he realized that he was making too good and thorough a job of it, he stopped and dropped the napkins. Then he picked up the gun and went looking for the staff.

He found Alejandra, the Ecuadorian maid, first. She was in the kitchen. Most of her anyway. Some of her was in the hall. There was no trace of her internal organs. They were gone. Not cleanly excised by any edged weapon but instead torn out with savage force.

"Jesus Christ," he gasped, then he gagged, spun, and vomited the bourbon onto the floor.

The gardener was on the prep table in the kitchen. His throat was slashed, but he was otherwise untouched. Or so Toombs thought until he peeled back some of the man's clothes. He saw the marks of a savage beating.

The cook was missing, and a long, glistening trail of blood led off to the back door, but he did not follow. There was no point. Even without seeing a body, he knew what he would find, and so he chose not to look.

Toombs searched every room, finding nothing except random instances of pointless damage. A smashed television. Books pulled from shelves, some with pages ripped out and others merely fallen. The sink in the hall bathroom beaten to rubble with a ball-peen hammer, which lay among the porcelain shards.

Mary's bedroom was in ruins, with every piece of clothing slashed to rags, the bed soaked in blood and the mattress torn open. The bathroom mirror was in pieces on the terrazzo, and Toombs stood for a long moment looking down into his own reflection in each shard.

Panic was clawing its way up from the pit of his stomach. The truth was that he had not felt safe since coming to work for October. Hell, he hadn't felt safe since October appeared in the jail with no real possible way for him to be there. That had not made sense, and it left Toombs feeling like the world was on the wrong channel, with all the color values askew.

The cellar door stood between him and the kind of information that, he believed, would let him know if he should stay and see this whole shit show through, or bug out for some place where even October couldn't find him. Maybe the goddamn Brazilian rainforest. Or the fucking Antarctic.

Toombs was not a common criminal, but he had useful skills. Picking locks was one of many skills he'd picked up by association with other kinds of crooks. The door was solid as hell, but the lock was not much better than a high-end dead bolt, and Toombs knew how to bypass it.

Which he did.

It took nearly five minutes of playing with tension wrenches, a half-diamond pick, a hook pick, rake pick, and other tools from a small kit he'd purchased in Milan. When the tumblers clicked open, the door sagged inward a half inch. Immediately, he winced as a mélange of smells smacked him hard in the face.

He winced but pushed the door inward. That itself was unusual because most cellar doors open out. The only ones he ever remembered moving inward were in places where the installer did not want them kicked open. That suggested a threat precaution against something *inside*. He found no comfort in that.

"In for a penny," he muttered to himself, trying and failing to sound offhand. He slid his tools into their zippered leather case and dropped that in his sports coat pocket.

There was a short hallway that had a very heavy collapsible metal security gate. It was secured with slide bolts at top, middle, and bottom. He kept the pistol in his right hand and used his left to slide the bolts back. It was odd that the door was locked, but the security gate had bolts anyone could work.

Toombs pushed the gate into its slot along one wall and passed through until he stood at the top of a set of metal stairs. The stench was fifty times worse, and he fished out his mint ChapStick and rubbed it vigorously across his upper lip and around his nostrils. The mint burned, but it was better than the smell.

There were lights on downstairs, but it wasn't bright. As he crept down the stairs, he could see that the lights only pushed the shadows back a bit but did not eliminate them.

The basement was far larger than he expected. Easily eight times the square footage of the house upstairs. Heavy support columns ran in rows in all directions. The vast room itself was divided into sections, with bulk crates taking up one area and computers another. There were workstations covered with devices Toombs couldn't begin to name. Lab coats and hazmat suits hung from pegs along one wall, and there were several high-pressure showers for decontamination. Three large glass-walled chambers occupied another corner, and from the biohazard symbols on them, he reckoned they were hot rooms for storing the biological warfare weapons Miss Mary had stolen from the various facilities she'd raided.

But farther back, in an area behind steel bars that formed a kind of pen, were dozens of what looked like the kind of cages zoo people used to transport larger animals. They varied in size from ones big enough for a large dog to some that could have accommodated a full-grown rhinoceros.

He went over to the bars and looked inside. The cages were empty. At least, those he could easily see from his side of the bars. There were other cages in small side tunnels at the far end of the holding area. There were sounds coming from back there, and Toombs tried—and failed—to determine what was making the sounds. Growls and grunts, scratching sounds like claws on steel, and an odd whipping noise as if someone were snapping a damp towel.

Toombs looked around and saw a ring of heavy keys on a hook. He licked his lips nervously as he picked up the keys. His heart began hammering as he sorted through them to find one that would open the heavy lock. It clicked, and the barred door yielded to his pull.

With his pistol in a careful two-handed grip, Toombs entered the holding area and began moving slowly toward the darkened far end.

Nothing rushed at him from the shadows, and he hoped that meant whatever was down here was still in locked crates.

They were.

He found a row of twenty crates along the very back, ten on each side of a metal door that he figured was the entrance to the tunnel October had told him about during construction. The light was bad, but his eyes were becoming accustomed to the dark. He saw bulky forms in those twenty cages. All similar.

They were dogs.

They had *been* dogs. Monstrous mastiffs, easily two hundred and fifty pounds each. That was bad enough, scary enough.

But Miss Mary and her team of corrupt scientists had been busy. So very busy.

They had changed the dogs. Transformed them through god only knew what means. Surgery? That much was evident from the barely healed scars. Genetic manipulation? He had to think so, because otherwise it would require actual magic to make what he saw.

These were the SDs that Mary said she was developing. The *D* was for Dog, but before that moment had not known what the *S* stood for. Now he did.

"G-g-god d-damn," he stammered, backing away. But after a few steps, he jerked to a stop. The creatures were terrifying, but they were in stout cages with heavy bars. Toombs licked his lips, which had gone totally dry. Then he raised his pistol and fired.

The first bullet tore screams of pain from the closest animal, but despite that, it hurled its mass against the bars, shrieking with fury.

Toombs shot it again.

And again.

It took three rounds to knock it down and a fourth to kill it.

Then he staggered back, knees turning rubbery. Killing one of them had taken something out of him. Fear and disgust rose up inside him. The pistol fell from slack fingers with a loud clatter. Toombs stood there, looking at the dead monsters. Their cages were littered with bones, and he was damn certain most of them were human bones. He turned and looked back at the lab. Where were the scientists and technicians? Where, in fact, was everyone?

He did not want to look at those bones again.

Toombs bent and scooped up the gun, whirled, and ran. He made it all the way to the top of the stairs before he realized that he'd left the door to the holding pen open. He turned, panting, sweating, nearly crying.

"Fuckfuckfuckfuck," he whispered as he tried to decide what to do.

If he left that door open, then Miss Mary and October would know he'd been down there. What would they do, though? Kill him? Feed him to those monsters? Or . . .

Or what?

They *needed* him.

Or at least they had.

The Firefall event was in motion. He'd done his bit by selling the weapons and providing extensive training. His role was effectively done. There had been no talk at all about what his role would be after Firefall.

That frightened him as much as the things in those cages.

It frightened him because Miss Mary was truly insane. There had been little doubt of it before and none at all now. She was a real-life, no-argument mad scientist and was out of her goddamn mind. October was her enabler and captain of her fan club.

He turned and looked back the way he'd come, recalling Mary putting the Gorgon warheads and RPGs in the truck. Why? What good were a bunch of warheads loaded with MERS? Sure, that was bad, but why do all this damage first? She was second only to October in authority. She could have told the staff to load them for her.

Why didn't she do that?

Why had she, instead, killed everyone?

Why had she released those monster dogs?

What the hell was she doing?

Toombs went back into the lab and looked around. He walked over to the glass door of the hot room. The big cases were open, and there were four empty test tube racks lying on the floor. They were not marked with the blue MERS tags. These had black bands around them and a different set of initials.

SAD.

He knew it wasn't a word. Toombs knew what *SAD* meant, and he staggered back from the glass wall, stumbling, tripping, falling down.

"Oh god," he breathed. "Oh my god."

He ran.

Through the laboratories.

Up the stairs.

Into the kitchen and through the house and out the front door. Then he slowed to a walk and finally stopped. There was no place on earth far enough away to put safe distance between that place and what he now knew.

"God save my soul," he said.

CHAPTER 158
ROUTE A-32
PINE DEEP, PENNSYLVANIA

Crow drove and I made calls.

I used the comms to bring Church, Scott Wilson, Bug, and Havoc in on the same call. I told them about the house in the forest, the connection to white supremacists, the strange vibe Crow got at the diner, and then I told them the name of the person who bought Ubel Griswold's property.

John Stankevičius.

There was a beat, and it was Church who broke that silence. He said what I was thinking. He said what none of us wanted to hear. He said the real name of the man who was pretending to be John Stankevičius.

He said the name of the man who was currently using the nickname Mr. October. Maybe I should have seen it sooner. Maybe we all should have. The Cave 13 case started making a bit more sense. The weird shit that went on during that, and the elusive nature of the case we were on. It all fit a pattern, and with that name spoken aloud, I think all of us understood the full weight and complexity of what we were facing.

The name Church said was one we knew.

"Nicodemus," he said.

CHAPTER 159

TENTH LEGION COMFORT STATION BRAVO
HAMBONE LANE
UPPER BLACK EDDY, PENNSYLVANIA

They waited with slowly eroding patience all through the night and well into the new morning. Violin took first watch, followed by Tommy, then Monk.

At around nine in the morning, they heard the sound of tires crunching on gravel. All three of them flattened out to study the newcomer. Violin and Tommy had their sniper scopes; Monk had his binoculars.

A van came rolling along the path. It was nondescript, with no logos or signs on the sides. White, road-dusty, streaked with some of last night's rain, carrying Jersey plates. A Jeep Wrangler rolled up behind it, and its doors popped open first. Four men dressed in the black-on-black uniforms of the Tenth Legion got out.

Violin touched a finger to her lips and then patted the air. The three of them flattened out, barely breathing. Violin and Tommy had earbuds synced with a pair of mourning dove drones—one perched on a tree branch in the space between the parked vehicles and the main trailer. The other by the small skylight vent atop the trailer.

During the long night, they listened to the nervous whispers and sobs of the children in the RV. There were none of the screams or cries that might have indicated any kind of physical assault, and based on that, Violin had ordered them to wait. Tommy was frustrated because she wanted to go in and free the children now.

"These men are the handlers," Violin had said. "We want them *and* the men who come for the kids. If we hit now, then there may be a contact protocol. If someone does not get a call or text message, then they'll know we're here."

"So?" protested Tommy. "If they come to investigate, we'll take them, too."

"I like this gal," said Monk, grinning. "She's fun."

"She's young," corrected Violin, then gave Tommy a single raised eyebrow that stifled all argument. "The handlers know the logistics, and we'll get that. Whoever shows up to abuse the children are likely troops, and officers always have first pick. That's who we're waiting for—individuals who are higher up the food chain. They know more of what we want to know, and some may even be on the policy level."

"Smart thinking," said Monk. "You remind me of someone else I know."

At that, Violin smiled. "Joseph spoke highly of you, too."

"What happens if nobody comes tomorrow?" asked Tommy.

"Then we'll try it another way," Violin replied. "Sometimes missions change."

"Mission creep," said Monk.

Then they had settled down to rest and prepare.

Now, in the cold light of an October morning, Violin's prediction was playing out. Two of the men from the Jeep had an official bearing. One was slightly short and a little too plump for the tight uniform he wore. The other was taller, rangier, and had the *sergeant* look. It was clear from their body language and close conversation that those two men were friends, but clearly one outranked the other. There was deference that amped up when anyone else addressed them.

Violin pointed to them.

"Officers," she said.

"You sure?" asked Tommy.

"She's sure," said Monk. "Short Round is the boss, that's clear. The other guy's a lieutenant or something lower. Sergeant, maybe. They'll have information maybe no one else in the camp does."

Violin's eyes were fierce. "They are here for first rights."

"We need to take out comms," Monk advised. "No calls, no emails, nothing."

"I'll take care of that," Violin said, laying her rifle down and covering it with a piece of waterproof material. "Wait for my signal."

"What's the signal?" asked Tommy.

Violin gave her a wicked grin and then moved off into the forest.

When they were alone, Monk said, "Never met her before, but Ledger told me some tales." He glanced at her. "Told me about you, too. The airport thing?"

"He told you about me?"

"Yeah. Says you have the makings."

"Of what?"

"Of being one of us," said Monk.

"You mean a killer," she said with more bitterness than she intended.

Monk shook his head. "This is a war, kid. Killing is a side effect, an action that's sometimes necessary. Ugly, but there it is. Even Eden wasn't Utopia. It had talking serpents." He grinned. "What I meant by being one of us don't have anything to do with how well you pull a trigger or how fast you can cut a throat. Nah. It's all about *why*. It's about what you hope to accomplish or prevent. It's about who you can save and who needs to be stopped so they don't do more harm. Think of yourself as a killer and that's what you are. Cold, heartless, ruled by the notches on your gun and the scars on your heart. That's not us. It's sure as hell not Ledger."

"I thought cops and soldiers and all were supposed to never take things personally, never get emotionally involved."

"Whoever said that is a dipshit," said Monk. "I got years of it in the military and twice as much working as a private contractor. It's a coward's statement. You wonder why so many good cops drink? Wonder why so many soldiers come home with PTSD and drop out of society? That damage came from caring."

"That contradicts your point, doesn't it?"

"Does it? Ledger knows what he does is carving away at him. At *him*. He's like a sin eater. You know what that is? It's an old folktale or tradition or whatever where someone—usually poor or desperate—is paid to eat a feast that represents all the sins of whomever hired the guy. He eats the sin so they get clean again. Ledger's *kind of* like that. He takes the hits, sheds the blood, wears the scars so innocent people don't have to. He stands between them and harm. Not for a flag. Sure as shit not for political parties or political agendas. He's an actual good guy. Not saying he's Jesus on the cross, but the idea is the same. Those with power, with skills, have an obligation to do more than whoever pays for their uniform. They do it so that what they do—however awful—keeps the innocent from being taken to the slaughterhouse. Am I making sense?"

"You should write a book on philosophy," said Tommy, though not unkindly. But then she looked at the RVs. "I get it, though. And, I guess you're right. I was one of those kids who was hurt. I know what it feels like."

"And here you are, trained and badass, and you came out here to put yourself in harm's way, but not to be harm's bitch."

"No," she said, "not that. Not to kill. Not for that."

Monk pointed to the van. "For them."

"For them."

"Which is what I meant when I said you're one of us."

CHAPTER 160
THE TOC
PHOENIX HOUSE
OMFORI ISLAND, GREECE

Scott Wilson, Doc Holliday, and Rudy Sanchez stood in a tight row at the top of the stairs in the back of the tactical operations center. Every workstation in the room was occupied, and there was a constant low hum of subdued voices and nervous fingers clicking on keys.

At the front of the room, the big screen was divided into smaller windows, with feeds from drones and body cams. The body cams had an anti-shaking function, but the image still jangled the eyes and nerves. Rudy could feel the vibrations in his chest. He had his hands clasped behind his back in an affectation of casual awareness, but his fists were clenched so hard his knuckles hurt.

"Sir," called one of the techs, "we just lost the feed from the three men who went to the depot. I mean, the cameras are still on, but look . . ."

It was true. The button cams that Sweeney, Hunter, and Jones had each been given were no longer showing anything but fuzz and blurred colors.

"What is that?" asked Rudy.

The tech said, "It looks like clothes."

"They took off their jackets?" asked Wilson.

"Sir," said the tech, pointing, "that's an undershirt. And those, I think, are boxers."

Rudy gaped. "What are you saying? That they took their clothes off? Why would they do that?"

No one had an answer.

CHAPTER 161
ROUTE A-32
PINE DEEP, PENNSYLVANIA

When I finished my call, Crow asked, "Who the hell is Nicodemus?"

Ghost made a low growl at the sound of the name.

How does one answer that question?

I mean, really?

Church knew the man—if *man* was even an accurate word. He knew who and what Nicodemus was. I did not.

"I don't really know," I admitted. "Not for sure."

He cut a look at me. "Your face turned the color of last week's milk, Joe. Don't close me out like that. Who *is* he?"

"I'm not joking when I say that I don't really know," I said. "He's kind of like the Professor Moriarty to my boss's Sherlock Holmes."

"Which makes him what? A master criminal?"

"At the very least. He isn't usually *the* bad guy, but he is behind a lot of the really Big Bads we've gone up against. He enables. He provides all kinds of support. And right now, there's a really good chance that he has accomplished a very hostile takeover of the world's largest illegal arms dealership. Kuga."

"Earlier, you said this Mr. October is Kuga," said Crow. "Did you change your mind, or is Nicodemus one of October's aliases?"

"Other way around. Nicodemus is the name he's been using for a long time. A *very* long time. October is just one name. And, so you get it straight, Harcourt Bolton created and ran Kuga, which is the name he used and also the name of the group. We think Nicodemus killed him and assumed both the identity and leadership of Kuga."

"And he's living in *my* town?"

"I know, who'd have thought a quiet and peaceful place like Pine Deep would attract a creepy slimeball like Nicodemus."

"First," said Crow, "eat shit. Second, we already have enough problems. Not shopping for more."

"Too late," I said.

Crow drove, pushing the pedal down almost to the floor, despite some very unpleasant curves. "And he runs Tenth Legion?"

"Yeah."

"And the Cyke-lones?"

"Yeah."

"And is behind all of this Firefall shit?"

"Yeah."

"And that might involve stolen bioweapons and RPGs with guid-ance packages?"

Ghost uttered a small growl.

"Joe?" said Crow.

"Yeah?"

"I kind of hate you right now."

Ghost barked in apparent agreement.

I said, "Story of my life."

Crow drove for a few minutes. "If we catch up to this Nicodemus October Kuga whatever son of a bitch, do you have any problems with me using my sword to cut him into really tiny pieces?"

"I'm very okay with that."

What I didn't say out loud was, *If he* can *be killed.*

And I really, really, *really* hate having thoughts like that in my head.

CHAPTER 162
TENTH LEGION TRAINING CAMP #18
PINE DEEP, PENNSYLVANIA

Top Sims knelt in the humid green heart of the forest.

The team had taken the long way, avoiding as many public roads as possible and instead driving into Pinelands State Forest, hiding their SUV, and moving through the woods along game trails.

Remy sent a pair of pigeon drones out, each equipped with Ant-eaters. It took the machines nearly forty-five minutes to canvass the entire area around the Legion training camp, but when the data was in, it showed where electronic sensors, trip wires, motion detectors, and other devices were positioned.

"They did a pretty good job of covering their asses," said Bunny. "Got four pairs of guards walking perimeters in overlapping patrol patterns, too."

"And if we were the fucking Boy Scouts, that would be an issue," rumbled Top. He bent closer to Remy's tactical computer. "What I'm not seeing are those dogs. Not a fan of running into a pack of trained combat dogs."

"I'll send some more drones to do thermal scans," said Remy, and he set to work. After a few minutes, he tapped his screen. "Looks like they're still in a pen or something. Clustered together. They're near a cook tent, so that's why the signal is sketchy. Competing heat signatures."

"Okay." Top considered. There was a crack of thunder in the southeast, and the freshening breeze brought the ozone smell of lightning and fresh rain. "It's going to rain soon. That's good for us, but check your comms to make sure they're working. Everyone have backups?"

Because of the EMP weapon used at the safe house, Bird Dog brought extra comms units, each sealed in a small Faraday bag. Everyone nodded.

Then Top began making assignments.

"Mother Mercy, there's a small ridge here. See it? Go scout it. If it's a good sniper post, set up there. If not, find somewhere that gives you protection and a good view of the camp."

"Copy," she said and vanished into the woods.

"Gator Bait," continued Top, "go play with your toys. If we have to get loud and everyone starts running, I want these cocksuckers to find no way out. Feel me?"

"Hooah," said Remy. He slung his gear bag and went into the woods.

"What about me?" asked Bunny.

"You and me are going to circle the camp. Remember, our main job today is surveillance. Make sure your body and helmet cams are functioning. Check feeds when you're behind bushes. We don't need to send pictures of autumn foliage."

"Copy that."

"Let's go."

They were both big men, but they moved with speed and grace and silence.

CHAPTER 163
THE GUTHRIE FARM
PINE DEEP, PENNSYLVANIA

For the second time in one day, a helicopter rotor tore apart the quiet of the morning over the fields surrounding the Guthrie farm.

This time, however, no one came out to watch as the big machine descended to the muddy ground where a week before an abundance of corn had been harvested. Pieces of the stalks were ground into the dirt. The sky above was pregnant with a pending rain. The rotor wash shoved against the trees on the other side of the slat-rail fence and turned every puddle into a rippling pond.

The chopper settled, and three people got out.

One was a very tall, blocky man dressed in a black combat rig. Next was a slender older woman who moved like a young dancer. The third was a stocky, bearded man who clutched a heavy metal briefcase to his chest. Someone on board the chopper handed out equipment bags, which the three picked up. They ran, bent forward beneath the blades, as the helicopter pushed away from the earth and rose into the troubled sky. It turned toward the south and accelerated, racing to beat the storm winds.

Silence fell like a heavy blanket over the farm.

Mr. Church watched the chopper drive out of sight and then turned toward the farmhouse. They hurried to the house and went inside, their footsteps on the foyer floor echoing.

"They're all gone," said Dr. Coleman. "Place is empty."

"Ledger said there were farm trucks in the barn," said Church. "Keys are on a board in the kitchen. Yes, here they are."

Lilith opened the kitchen door and looked across wet grass to a red barn fifty feet away. The big doors were open, and the weak light glimmered on the hoods of three late-model Ford F-350s.

"That will do," she said.

"Okay, so we have wheels," said Coleman, "but the teams are split up. The depot, the big camp, the comfort camp, and this guy October's house. Where *we* go?"

"Let's get on the road first," said Church. "I'll make some calls and then determine where our best destination is."

CHAPTER 164
AMERICAN LIBERTY BANK & TRUST FIELD
STREET ROAD
FEASTERVILLE, PENNSYLVANIA

"It's at the end of this hall, Miss Blair," said the facilities supervisor. "We have a room set aside for you. The fireworks are already in there."

"Thanks," said Karen Blair, the tallest of the four techs. She was a sergeant in the Legion who had worked variously as a bodyguard and PMC. In her twenties, though, she had worked with the family business, Blairs Beauty-Bombs, which had been organizing fireworks for four generations.

The supervisor looked past her. "Are we waiting for the rest of your crew?"

Blair shook her head. "We'll do setup. The others will be here soon. Fourteen crew and one team leader."

"Very good. Right down here."

Blair and the others followed. They all wore coveralls with a patch on the right breast that said LORD ABOVE FIREWORKS. A fake company, but one with a cleverly designed website and social media presence. On the back of each tech was that name, plus the phrase: WE LIGHT THE HEAVENS. The picture was that of a splash of fireworks in the Roman candle pattern.

There were carts set in a row with cardboard signs taped to the handles proclaiming FOR FIREWORKS ONLY. A bored security guard stood watch, and he smiled and nodded to the four techs. They smiled and nodded back.

Everyone at the stadium was smiling.

There were huge banners hung from the balconies with the smiling faces of eight of the preachers from the nation's largest megachurches. Six men and two women, all white, all with great teeth and hair. All with sparkling light in their eyes.

"We can take it from here," said Blair. She tapped her holstered walkie-talkie. "If we need anything, we'll call."

"Thanks," said the supervisor and ran off to deal with the thousand other things he needed to handle.

As soon as he was gone, Blair said, "Let's do it."

The techs immediately set to work. The two biggest men began loading the crates of fireworks onto the carts, while the two women knelt behind the stacks of crates, unzipped their equipment bags, and began assembling the RPGs.

The four Gorgon warheads were removed with great care and placed in matching gray toolboxes, each closed with a thumbprint lock. All four of their prints were logged into each lock.

They worked in silence, having done drills on this countless times at Camp #18.

As they worked, each of them continued the process of acceptance that they were the *only* four who would actively participate in Firefall. The other warheads weren't ready yet. They would be deployed by other teams in other states when the time came.

Today, it was just the four of them on the firing team, and fifty-six others who would focus on launching the actual fireworks displays. The largest team knew that the firing team was there and why they were there, though they did not know what was in the Gorgons. All they knew was that this was what they had trained for—to open the eyes of the country and the world.

Blair and her techs were nervous. Even with multiple escape routes planned and exfil drills done over and over, they sweated badly. They were dedicated Tenth Legionnaires who understood that the duplicitous nature of this attack would cause great harm to people who believed much of the same things in which they believed. It was a sinful act but one for which they—and everyone in the Legion—would be ultimately forgiven.

The Lord, they knew, worked in mysterious ways. Isaac had been willing to sacrifice his own son. Job was tested by having all of his sons and daughters suffer. If it meant that the world would shift to be in truer alignment with God, then so be it. If it meant starting a civil war, then that was what had to happen. America couldn't be allowed to slide further into darkness and further away from what the Founding Fathers had intended.

And so the four of them worked, even as the doors opened and thousands began pouring into the East Coast's largest-ever worship meeting. Fifty-nine thousand people, plus hundreds of presenters, handlers, cameramen, makeup people, ushers, food vendors, souvenir vendors, and arena staff. In total, sixty-one thousand four hundred and two.

Plus the firing team—four elite soldiers of God.

And their four Gorgons.

CHAPTER 165
EAST PINELANDS FOREST
BLACK MARSH, PENNSYLVANIA

The woman who ran the supply depot was a former soldier who was among the first women to earn the Green Beret from Army Special Forces. Her name was Felicia Carby, and she had reached staff sergeant before being dishonorably discharged for selling equipment in collaboration with a friend in the quartermaster group. This friend, Allison Poole, was in the Legion, too, though not at the depot.

Carby strolled through the camp, watching as her team went through the process of packing it up. It wasn't a rush order but a standard camp strike. A third of the tents were already down, and men with hand trucks were moving stacks of crates.

She was content with a noncombat role in the Legion and was very good at her job. She understood what the legionnaires needed and always made sure they got it. Had the other Gorgons been ready in time, there would have been some fun stuff to do, but that hadn't happened and, like all well-trained marines, she adapted and moved on.

She paused by a stack of metal boxes, each of which contained an RPG and accessories. There was a chalked number 1/7 on the top crate, and that made her frown. She looked at her clipboard and saw 1/1–6 and 1/8 ticked off, signifying that they had been loaded onto the first truck.

"Hey, Sims, Gunther," she called out in a strident voice, "why isn't this gear loaded? Sims? *Sims?* Gunther, where the fuck are—?"

Those were the very last words she ever said. The next thing to come out of her mouth was a strangled scream. After that, it was a torrent of blood.

She never saw the hands—if *hands* they could ever be called—that reached out of the shadows beside the truck. She felt her flesh tear, but only for a moment before darkness took her.

When the others started screaming, she was too far down into shadows to hear.

CHAPTER 166
THE MANSION
PINE DEEP, PENNSYLVANIA

Crow took the turn on two wheels. Ghost and I were slammed against the front and rear passenger doors until the car thumped down on the rest of the tires—as God and gravity ordained.

"Getting there alive is a key point," I gasped.

"Sissy," he replied with a maniacal grin, then stamped the pedal all the way to the floor as we shot down a dirt road. I could feel my fillings working their way out as we went over bumps and potholes. I was beginning to understand how he had survived the Trouble. He was crazier and more dangerous than everyone else.

"Just a thought," I said, bracing myself with hands and feet, "maybe try not to hit every single one of these fucking potholes."

He literally took his hands off the wheel. "You want to drive?"

"Jesus H. Polka-Dot Christ," I yelled.

Crow grabbed the wheel in time to avoid a hole that would have snapped an axle. "Big, tough superspy. My name is Ledger. Joe Ledger."

The bumps were teaching my concussion how to scream really loud.

The dirt road wound around big parts of forest. The sunny sky overhead had turned slate gray, and there were flashes of threatening lightning. As we drove, the first fat drops of rain splatted onto the windshield. Crow leaned forward and studied the blossoming storm.

"Oooo, that's going to be a nasty one."

"Look at the fucking road," I begged.

He laughed and then tapped the brakes as we went around another curve. Suddenly, the scene opened up, and there were a couple of big fields cut into the woods, and between them, at the far end of a long turnaround, was a large country house. Not a mansion but close enough.

I swear I could feel the place.

Ghost could, too. He stared through the window and growled. But I saw that his tail was tucked between his legs. There was anger and there was fear. I could relate.

"Slow down and let me out," I said.

Crow stopped by a stand of shrubs. I made sure he was wearing the comms correctly and had it tuned to our shared channel. I'd already gone over the other channels and the basic functions before we left his farm. He nodded.

Ghost and I got out, and I did a quick weapons check.

"Find someplace to park and approach from the north. Keep low and don't enter the house until I give the all clear."

"Um, Joe . . . ?" he said.

"What?"

He pointed through the windshield. "Who's that?"

I turned and brought up my pistol. Ghost came to point and glared at a man who stood on the porch. He was eighty yards away, but I could see that he was tall, very pale, and dressed all in black. He had a pistol in his hand and raised it to show us, then he leaned and set the gun on the porch rail, stepped back from it, turned around, and placed his palms flat against the wall.

"What the hell?" asked Crow.

"Damn," I said. "I think that's Isaac Tomberland."

"Who?"

"Toombs."

"What's he doing?"

"At a guess? Trying not to die."

I gave Ghost a command, and he immediately ran forward, running hard until he stopped at the foot of the porch stairs. He crept up the stairs and then stopped about a foot behind Toombs. Although I could not hear his growl, I knew he was doing it. The command I'd given him was to watch and wait.

He was waiting. He was watching. And I can bet he was hoping Toombs would do something stupid.

I got back in the car, and we drove up and parked in front of the house.

CHAPTER 167
TENTH LEGION TRAINING CAMP #18
PINE DEEP, PENNSYLVANIA

Remy Neddo was a young man—the youngest field agent working for Rogue Team International. He had just turned twenty-five three weeks ago and had already been through several different kinds of hell.

At heart, he was a peaceful man. Born on the bayou, raised among the farmers in the vast green expanse outside of New Orleans. He'd worked on fishing boats, helped rebuild levees after storms, drank beer with his buddies on the school stadium's fifty-yard line, dated pretty girls of all colors, wrecked a couple of junker cars while learning how to drive like a maniac, and saved his money from crap jobs to buy electronics to take apart and play with.

Now he was an operative for the world's most elite private military contractor. A counterterrorism and anti-terrorism gunslinger working for the good guys in a bad and very dirty war.

His mentor had been Andrea Bianchi—combat call sign Jackpot—who had been an Italian former agent of the Gruppo di Intervento Speciale, an elite division of Italy's Carabinieri. Andrea had taught Remy a lot of science, a lot of tactics and strategies, and all the dirty tricks he knew. Andrea's specialty—apart from handling drones and other tech—was to set up a toy box. What the rest of the military call a *kill box*.

The toy box was a problem of mathematics, physics, and psychology. It required getting inside the heads of the bad guys when certain kinds of pressure was applied to them. Start a fire and then decide how they would rush to fight it or flee from it—each direction offering different options for the placing of trip wires, pressure mines, and other devices. Using one kind of trap to drive combatants into specific directions—usually with a bias toward what those soldiers would consider either the path of least resistance when running for cover, where weapons and ammo might be placed, where escape vehicles were parked, and where shelter might be to allow for safety and preparation for a counteroffensive. It had to be thought through,

JONATHAN MABERRY

adjusting decisions based on the type of enemy, the level of their training, the environment, time of day, features of the landscape, the weather, and so on.

It was a puzzle, and Remy loved solving puzzles. He could solve any Rubik's Cube in about twenty moves. He could reassemble a completely disassembled satellite phone in under ninety seconds.

The supplies Bird Dog had delivered were a treasure trove, including some items he'd trained with but had not yet used in application.

It took him a long time, and twice he had to call Bunny up to help him.

Belle was in an old deer stand on a tree thirty yards beyond the camp, and Remy could feel her watching him through her sniper scope. It was a Barrett MK 22, one of the finest such weapons in the world. It was not her preferred gun, but it was the very best Bird Dog could acquire in the available time, and Belle had trained on one very much like it. Despite that scope being mounted on that deadly tool, Remy felt comforted by her presence. And her skill.

"Gator Bait to Pappy," he said very quietly.

"Go for Pappy."

"Toy box is set. Sending map."

"Copy that. Don't activate until I give the word."

The other three synced their tactical computers with the location of all the trips and traps. The Scout glasses they each wore pasted little yellow dots over the forest.

"These fuckers think they're soldiers," said Top. "They want to start a war, then let's show them what war really looks like."

CHAPTER 168
AMERICAN LIBERTY BANK & TRUST FIELD
STREET ROAD
FEASTERVILLE, PENNSYLVANIA

Karen Blair shook hands with each member of the firing team. She hugged them, and they held hands in the now empty storeroom and prayed.

Then Blair personally checked each of the fireworks setups, making sure that the real fireworks were in place. The rest of the team showed up and began the ordinary work of arranging the projectiles, hoses, buckets, mortars, and the rest. Mundane stuff, though they kept catching one another's eyes. Grinning. Winking. Nodding. Acknowledging one another and the moment.

All around them, the seats were filling, and the air of the stadium was becoming electric. A band took the stage, singing rock versions of standard hymns and popular songs of faith.

Blair made sure to touch in with each of them, offering the right words, comforting pats on the back, covert fist bumps.

Soon, she thought, *we are going to save America, starting today.*

It was hard not to weep with joy.

CHAPTER 169
THE MANSION
PINE DEEP, PENNSYLVANIA

Crow stopped near the foot of the stairs, and we got out quickly. There was a slithery rasp as he drew the katana. I drew my pistol.

To Toombs, I said, "Stay right where you are. Move and I'll put you down."

"Definitely not moving," he assured me.

We fanned left and right and looked down the sides of the house.

"Clear," said Crow. "But there's blood on the ground."

"Blood here, too," I said.

Without turning, Toombs said, "It's not mine."

I went up on the porch and put the cold barrel against the base of his spine and clamped my other hand around the back of his neck. His skin was slick with fear sweat.

"Move and I'll blow your spinal column out through your stomach."

"Understood," he said.

I patted him down while Ghost looked on with growing hunger. Crow came up and waited, his gun also pointing at Toombs.

"He's clean," I said, then turned him around and pressed his back against the hardwood siding, holding him there with my hand around his throat, my pistol pressed against his heart. "Isaac Tomberland. Fancy meeting you here."

"Colonel Ledger," he said. "I'm surrendering to you. No tricks."

"In exchange for what?"

His eyes were wide and wet. There was obvious terror there and something approaching despair.

"I'm not here to bargain, Colonel."

"Then why surrender? Big damn forest to get lost in."

"I'm surrendering because I don't want to be part of how the world ends."

Crow and I both said, "What?"

CHAPTER 170
TENTH LEGION COMFORT STATION BRAVO
HAMBONE LANE
UPPER BLACK EDDY, PENNSYLVANIA

Violin spoke to Tommy and Monk via comms.

"I planted a nightbird on setting two," she said, referring to a short-range EMP bomb. Depending on its setting, it could kill everything with a chip in a radius ranging from ten feet to fifty yards. "You should be out of range. Count down from ten on my mark. Monk, come in hot. Tommy, cover him and then pick off sentries. No one else goes into the RV. That's mine. Don't shoot through the walls. All the kids are inside now."

Monk and Tommy readied themselves.

"Mark," said Violin.

Those ten seconds seemed to take forever.

There was no pop or bang, no flash. The lights in the RV went out, and somebody began yelling. Children's voices were instantly raised in fear and panic.

Monk rose and ran through the woods, moving as fast as safety allowed, and pushing the limit hard. A sentry began moving from the perimeter, bringing his rifle up.

He died.

The bullet from Tommy's weapon struck him as he began to turn, punching through his upper biceps and in through the armhole of his Kevlar, through heart and lung and out the other side. His next step was artless, and he collapsed without a cry.

Kid's good, thought Monk.

Another soldier must have seen his comrade go down and turned in his direction. Tommy's next bullet took him in the center of his chest. There are levels of body armor that can stop a rifle round—those with ceramics or polyethylene plates that can absorb the higher-impact energy. The closer the range, the less effective they are, however. And when the sniper is firing tungsten-core bullets, those rounds retain their shape, allowing them to pierce more easily and more deeply. The second sentry puddled down and lay utterly still.

Monk reached the edge of the clearing and circled around behind the parked cars. A third sentry was looking around in confusion. Monk had his sound suppressor screwed onto his gun barrel and shot the man in the chest and head.

He immediately moved away, keeping low, eyes and gun tracking together. He found two more dead guards, but neither had been shot. Their throats were cut with such savage force that their heads were nearly severed. Very efficient and very messy. Monk remembered the things Ledger had told him after the gig they'd done together.

"Violin is the best knife fighter I've ever met," Ledger had said. "She's better than me, and I'm the best knife fighter I know."

Monk had seen Ledger with a knife. If she was better, then she was a demon.

That worked for him.

There were screams coming from inside the RV. Mostly children's screams. It was a sad fact of Monk's life in that he could tell one kind of scream from another. There were the horrified screams of a child about to be abused. There were the heart-ripping screams of terror of someone being assaulted. There were the broken screams of a child or young woman whose innocence had been forcibly torn from them.

There was a sliver of cold comfort that the screams he heard were of simple fear and confusion and not from perverse use. That did not make Monk hate the men inside the RV any less, though. He knew why they were here.

He kept moving through the little camp, looking for targets, following the trail of blood and bodies left by Violin.

He made it almost to the RV door when powerful hands grabbed him and tore him off the ground, spun him, struck him harder than he had ever been hit, and smashed him to the ground. Dazed, filled with agony, bleeding from mouth and nose, Monk looked up into the blazing eyes of a man who was more ape than human. A man with a mouth filled with fangs.

He tried to bring his gun up, but the Berserker snatched it out of his hands, took the pistol by handle and suppressor, and broke the extended silencer off with such force that it bent the gun barrel and buckled the slide.

Then the monster lunged at him with those huge, dripping gorilla fangs.

CHAPTER 171
THE MANSION
PINE DEEP, PENNSYLVANIA

I pointed my gun at Toombs's balls.

"What do you mean by the end of the world? Be very damn specific."

"I . . . I need to show you," he stammered, rising up to his tippy-toes to try to evade the gun. I squeezed the hand around his throat.

"Where's Nicodemus?"

His eyes went blank. "Who?"

"October. The guy you work for, ass-face."

"I don't know where he is. He's gone. Mary's gone. Everyone else is dead. But . . . in the basement. We need to hurry. Maybe there's still time."

"Joe," said Crow, stepping close.

"Yeah, yeah," I said, releasing Toombs and stepping back. He settled down on his feet and exhaled. I used my free hand to slap him and backhand his face back to center position. I did it really hard. Not enough to knock him out but enough to dim the lights on Broadway. "Listen to me, shithead. You surrendered. That's fine. But I didn't come here to take prisoners. If you have something you need to show us, do it. If you blink wrong, fart too loud, or try any fucking tricks, I will shoot parts off of you that you don't want to lose. When you go back to prison, it can be as a quadriplegic or walking under your own power. You pick."

Ghost showed his full set of titanium teeth.

Toombs licked his lips. "I'm not asking for conditions or promises, Ledger. Shit, at this point, if you wanted to pop me afterward, then do it. I can't do this kind of thing anymore. I thought I'd reached that point when Top Sims and that big blond guy arrested me at Aydelotte's pirate lab. That was my chance, and I pissed on it. This is on me."

"Joe," said Crow again. "Ticktock."

He stood with his sword in both hands. In any other scenario, a guy of his age wearing a soot-stained and torn police uniform and carrying a samurai sword would be comical. An *SNL* skit gone sideways. Not now, though.

I pulled Toombs off the wall and shoved him toward the door. "You lead the way. God help you if this is a setup."

"If it were a setup, Ledger, I'd have booby-trapped the porch and been long gone."

He opened the door, and we followed him inside.

We saw the blood and the bodies.

"You do this?" asked Crow.

"Mary did it."

"Mary as in Artemisia Bliss?" I asked.

"That's her. Zombie girl."

Crow shot me a look. I nodded.

"Where is she now?"

"Dead, I hope," he said. "I put an entire magazine into her and she still drove off, but . . . shit. I don't know."

Crow was looking scared, and I wondered what expression was on my face.

The house was big and very masculine, with lots of polished hardwood, stone, and leather. There was a big fireplace in a drawing room, and Toombs pointed to the open weapons safe. There were combat shotguns and automatic rifles that could have turned Crow and me to swiss cheese if he'd fired at us from a second-story window. Grenades, too. I took a couple of those. Standard M111s.

"Kitchen is through here," he said, gesturing. We followed him down a short hall to a spacious kitchen. More blood, more death.

Toombs did his best to step over the pools of blood and unidentifiable lumps of glistening meat. A heavy door led to a short hall, gate, and stairs leading down.

We'd frisked him and knew his pockets were empty. I told him to put his hands deep into his front pockets as he walked down the stairs. He did so without question. At the bottom of the steps, we stopped and stared at the massive laboratory. The floor plan was much bigger than that of the house above.

There was blood and destruction everywhere.

"October built this for Mary," said Toombs. "He hired her some of the best scientists money can buy. I guess you know about what was stolen from places like Site 44, Inferno, and Gehenna. Those bioweapons the Typhoid Marys delivered."

"The who?" asked Crow.

"The women Mary infected and sent to Atlanta and elsewhere. She called them Typhoid Marys after the Irish woman who emigrated to the States in the late nineteenth century. She was an asymptomatic carrier of *Salmonella typhi*. Not the same thing as the typhus one of the Marys delivered, but Miss Mary liked the nickname."

Crow shook his head in wonder and disgust.

"Mary had some other projects, too," said Toombs. "Do you know about the Berserkers?"

"Yes," I said. "How many did she make?"

Toombs shook his head. "Not sure. Thirty, maybe?"

"Christ," gasped Crow.

"Oh, it gets worse," said Toombs. "Wait until you see what her science team was cooking up way back at the far end of this lab. In the tunnels."

"Show us," I ordered.

Toombs nodded and took us back to where there was a wall of bars beyond which were many large animal cages. Big enough for mastiff dogs or even lions. He paused, turning to look at me, using his body to block our view.

"You were with Church when he took down the Jakoby lab on Dogfish Cay, right?"

"I led that team," I said.

"Then you know about the SDs?"

"Not under that name. Show me."

He licked his lips again and stepped to one side so we could see what lay in the cages. They were all dead, but they still scared the hell out of me. Crow made a gagging sound and backed away from them.

"What are they?"

I said nothing, but my mind was filled with memories of Bunny, Top, and me in the tunnels beneath the Dragon Factory, that madhouse of genetic aberration and designer monsters created by Hecate and Paris Jakoby.

"They're dead," is all I said and turned away, pulled by something my peripheral vision had spotted closer to the stairs. I pushed Toombs ahead of me as we went to a worktable on which a number of objects lay. There was a PSRL-1—a Precision Shoulder-Fired Rocket Launcher-1, which is the modified American copy of the Soviet/Russian RPG-7. A shoulder-fired rocket-propelled grenade launcher. That was bad enough. Next to it was an open box filled with straw in which I could see a Gorgon warhead.

"Is that what I think it is?" asked Crow.

"Sadly, yes," I said. "Those plastic canisters are filled with an ergot-based bioweapon called Shiva, which—"

"No," said Toombs. "That's not what's in the warheads. And it's not MERS, either. That was October's original plan—to launch fifty Gorgon payloads filled with Middle Eastern respiratory syndrome. Firing them into crowds at events. MERS rather than COVID because of the Middle East connection."

"To exploit what's going on?" asked Crow.

"No. That's all October. The Typhoid Marys, the groups taking credit, the people in Congress he owns who pushed through all the border bills, and the newspeople parroting the pro-America, anti–everyone else propaganda."

"So Kuga can sell guns," I said.

He gave me an appraising look. "Yes. To sell guns. A lot of guns.

Here and everywhere. That's what October wanted. Chaos and panic equals billions in weapons sales at every level to the homeowner who wants a shotgun in case a fill-in-the-blank foreigner tries to break in to rape and rob, all the way up to small nations buying jets and field artillery. It's all in the Kuga catalog."

"And October is Kuga," I said.

"Yes. He killed Harcourt Bolton and took over."

"What are you, then?" asked Crow.

"Sales manager."

"For the record," Crow said, "fuck you."

Toombs nodded, accepting the scorn.

"So if it isn't Shiva and it's not MERS," I said, "what did Mary put into those warheads?"

Without speaking, Toombs pointed to the hot room. The glass door was closed, but inside, there were scores of vials marked *SAD-1* through *SAD-16*. My heart turned instantly to ice, and via comms, I could hear Doc Holliday actually scream.

Scream.

I would have, too, but there was no air in my lungs and no spit in my mouth.

SAD.

Shorthand for something a lot worse than Shiva. A simple little acronym for the world's deadliest bioweapon.

Seif al din.

CHAPTER 172
THE TOC
OMFORI ISLAND, GREECE

Doc Holliday stood with a palm pressed to her mouth.

The nearby techs were shocked because when things were bad, she was usually jovial, often smiling. Like Church with his impenetrable calm, Doc was a fixed point in the TOC, someone everyone could look to for strength, for reassurance.

Not now.

Beside her, Rudy Sanchez swayed as if the floor were tilting under him. He clutched a handful of his shirtfront, captured and squeezed the crucifix he wore next to his skin.

Wilson wheeled on Doc. "What can we do if one of those warheads is deployed?"

"There's no cure for *seif al din*," she said, her voice sounding as if it came from the end of a very long tunnel.

"There has to be *something*. A vaccine, something . . ."

"It's not a germ. It's not a virus or a bacterium. It's a misfolded protein. It's weaponized *fatal familial insomnia*. It's a rare form of spongiform encephalopathy."

"God damn it, I know what it is. We've had samples for a decade. Are you going to stand there and tell me there's *nothing* we can do?"

Doc looked at him with glassy eyes. "I . . . maybe . . . I mean, we could train up antibodies against the misfolded form of the protein. This could keep the proteins from being able to disrupt the native forms of the proteins and stop the spread. It might not help much once someone was really bad off, but it might help immediately after exposure. If we could mass-produce it. If we were ready with it. It would only be possible because we know that FFI is a misfolding of the product of the *PRNP* gene. It might work. I can't say for sure."

She rambled on like that for a few seconds before her words trailed off and she just stood there, shaking her head.

CHAPTER 173
ACROSS BUCKS COUNTY, PENNSYLVANIA

Top Sims was about to rise from a place of concealment and begin the assault on the camp, but he heard what played over the comms.

Toombs.

Mary.

Mr. October. Nicodemus.

Gorgons.

Berserkers.

And *seif al din*.

Bunny was to his left, and they stared at each other.

"No," said Bunny. "Not after everything we've done to stop it. Not after all those times. The meatpacking plant. Room 12. The Liberty Bell Center. The New York subway. Fucking Dragon Con? Are you shitting me? And now Artemisia motherfucking Bliss put it in rockets?"

Mr. Church was driving and immediately stamped down on the brakes, sending the big Ford pickup into a wet, skidding, sliding, screaming turn. It did a 180, kicking up steaming sprays of rainwater from all four tires. Then he kicked the pedal down, and the car shot back the way they had come.

"*Seif al din?*" croaked Coleman from the back seat. "No, no, no, no."

"St. Germaine," cried Lilith, "where are you going?"

"Havoc Team will have to fend for themselves," he said urgently. "We need to get to October's mansion."

The pickup gathered speed as it climbed a long hill and then flew like a missile down the other side.

Violin had no working comms. Her EMP had blown out all of her electronics.

The comms Tommy had were tuned to an Arklight mission channel dedicated to the two of them. Suddenly, a voice cut in. It was Baba Yaga.

"Break, break, break, all teams," she cried. "This is a level-one emergency. RTI field team in eastern Pennsylvania has identified the nature of the threat. The Gorgon warheads have been filled with *seif al din*. I repeat, they have been filled with *seif al din*. This is Firefall. All other missions are canceled. Coordinate with Grendel at RTI for revised assignments."

Tommy had no idea what *seif al din* was. It hadn't been anything in her current training. She tapped for a direct line to Baba Yaga and asked.

And was told.

She could feel the blood drain from her face.

"I'm with Violin and another asset, Monk Addison," she said. "We're hitting a Tenth Legion comfort station. We think senior officers of that group are in play here. We are attempting to take them prisoner for interrogation. Violin is off comms. Please advise."

Baba Yaga was simple and to the point. "Take them. Make them talk."

Only that, but it was enough.

Tommy got up, leaving her cumbersome sniper rifle where it lay. She pulled an HK416 assault rifle from her gear bag, stuffed magazines into her vest and the waistband of her belt, and ran as if the world were on fire.

Which, in every practical sense, it was.

Remy Neddo was hidden inside a clump of shrubs, his tactical computer alight on his forearm and his head spinning from what he was hearing on the comms.

He had only recently learned about *seif al din*, but what he had learned terrified him. He was frozen with fear. It was the first time in his life he had ever been so frightened that he could not move. Not a hand, not a limb.

Seif al din was the deadliest bioweapon the world had ever known. It was a doomsday weapon, and the only reason it had not killed everyone so far was because Joe Ledger and his team had stopped it, contained it in close quarters, prevented it from spreading. Those fights had happened in factory buildings, in a public museum, on public transit, and at a pop culture convention. The death toll from those was dreadful, yet in each case, the losses were considered light when measured against the lethal potential of the prion disease.

If it ever slipped through containment, then the world would literally consume itself. He had grown up watching too much horror stuff. *Dawn of the Dead*, *Train to Busan*, *World War Z*, *The Walking Dead* . . .

Those were supposed to be fiction. This was the real world.

The fracturing of those lines of distinction was what trapped him in the moment. His heart hammered against his chest like a child trying to escape a burning house. Desperate but helpless.

This is how the world ends, he thought. The line was from a song or a poem or a book. He couldn't remember. Only those six words.

This is how the world ends.

Then he felt something. A movement in his trouser pocket, as if some small animal had crawled in there and was panicking. He heard a whirring, clicking noise and felt something sharp scratch at him through the thin cloth that separated the pocket from the skin of his thigh.

It was such a strange thing that it broke him from his stasis. With nervous, trembling fingers, he slid his hand into the pocket and drew out the object that was making the noise and struggling to get free.

It wasn't an animal at all. No mouse or bug or anything alive.

It was a small, orange, plastic jack-o'-lantern with a green stem and orange feet and a white stem-dial for winding its internal springs. The plastic was scuffed and cracked. It had not worked when the old man gave it to him. It was junk, given as a gift in exchange for an energy bar Remy had offered.

The old tramp had asked if his gift was freely given. Remy had said, *"If you can use it, man. Then, by all means, and God bless."*

Then the man took something from one of the many, many pockets sewn to his clothes. It was the little windup pumpkin, and he had offered it to Remy.

"Better than any alarm clock," he'd told Remy. *"'Specially when you really need to wake up."* He had put emphasis on the word *really*.

Remy had turned the stem to wind it, but the thing remained inert.

The old man had said, *"It ain't time to wake up."*

And now it was.

Remy's head snapped up, and he felt life coming back into his frozen limbs.

In his ear, Top Sims said, "Activate the toy box."

He realized it was not the first time Top had given the order. It was, however, the first time he could do anything about it.

"Time to wake up," he said aloud and pressed the buttons on his tactical computer.

CHAPTER 174
AMERICAN LIBERTY BANK & TRUST FIELD
STREET ROAD
FEASTERVILLE, PENNSYLVANIA

The program down on the floor was rolling along. Each speaker raised the bar with thundering rhetoric about what was happening in the world, what was happening in America, and what needed to happen to bring the nation back to what the Founding Fathers intended.

The sixty thousand people who paid to be there cheered constantly, sometimes drowning out the speakers. They waved banners from their separate churches or groups. They waved crosses inscribed with the names of people who had died in the Typhoid Mary attacks. They had programs signed by their favorite faith leaders.

Blair watched from her perch on the highest balcony. Her team was set and ready for the fireworks display. The exact time was uncertain, though, because a roomful of preachers meant long-winded speeches, improvisational commentary, and the occasional guided prayers.

It would wrap up eventually.

And then she would fulfill her life's mission.

The Gorgons waited with predatory patience for just the right moment.

CHAPTER 175
THE MANSION
PINE DEEP, PENNSYLVANIA

I turned to Toombs, who immediately began backing away from me.

"I didn't know that's what was in it until just before you got here," he protested, hands up in surrender. "I swear it."

"Where are the Gorgons?" I demanded.

His heels hit the bottom step, and he sat down hard enough to make his teeth snap shut. I grabbed him by the shirt and jerked him up and forward until his ghostly face was inches from mine. I wanted to headbutt him. I wanted to bite his goddamn throat out.

"Tell me. Right. Fucking. Now."

"Ledger, listen to me . . . we only got four of them working right. At least that's what I thought. Those four were part of a group of fifty for Firefall. All of them were supposed to be filled with MERS."

"Fuck the MERS. Where are the ones with *seif al din*?"

"The four that were finished went to the training camp here in Pine Deep. Commandant Kurt Furman runs it. He sent them all to one location. To the big megachurch rally that's going on right now at the American Liberty Bank & Trust arena on Street Road in Feasterville. They're going to do a big fireworks thing after the rally, and that's when they'll fire the Gorgons."

"In the rain?"

"It's raining in Pine Deep," said Crow. "Pretty much nowhere else."

"What?" I asked.

"Weird town, weird weather. Rains here a lot. Feasterville? I saw the weather maps on TV. Only Pine Deep and a bit over the line into Black Marsh will get rain. There's nothing to stop those fireworks."

I walked away and tapped my comms.

"Grendel," I said.

"On it, Outlaw. But I need to find someone of authority to—"

"Just get it done."

To Toombs, I said, "What's the timetable? How much time until the fireworks start?"

He looked at his watch. His hands were shaking badly. "Maybe an hour."

"Grendel, call the venue. Tell them there's a bomb threat. Whatever. Just empty the place. Call Homeland and tell them it's a Code Z. They'll know what that is."

"On it."

Toombs shook his head. "Ledger . . . there might be another way."

"Talk."

"You know about the Gorgons from when your team took them from Aydelotte," he said quickly. "You know about Marco Russo's master chip."

"What about it?"

"Mary cracked that chip and uploaded some kind of software patch to each chip."

Bug came on the line. "Outlaw, if that's true, then we can't remote detonate them or cause them to misfire."

I poked Toombs with my gun barrel. Hard. "Tell me something that helps, asshole."

"There's a master code," he said quickly.

"There's a what?"

"Mr. October insisted that he have complete and final control over the Gorgons. He had Mary build in a master control. He had to send out a go-code this morning, and there is a stand-down code. It's not a self-destruct for obvious reasons. It'll just kill all electrical signals to the Gorgon."

"Can't they still fire them with the RPGs?" asked Crow. "They're mechanical, right? Not electronic, I mean."

Toombs was shaking his head. "The guidance package that Russo developed makes *all* of the launchers computer driven. You need either a powerful EMP or the stand-down code."

I put the pistol against his face, right under his left eye.

"The next words out of your mouth had better be that you have that code."

"I don't," he said. "Not on me. Wait, wait, for Christ's sake. It's in October's laptop upstairs."

"Do you have the password?"

He licked his lips again. "No . . . but I bet your MindReader computer can bypass that."

In my ear, Bug said, "Outlaw, we need that laptop. Use an uplink. Let me get inside of his system."

"How long will that take?"

"If there's Wi-Fi? Ten seconds."

I shoved Toombs toward the stairs. "Show me that laptop. Now."

We ran up the stairs. Toombs was so determined to buy back his life, I had to really sprint to catch up with him. We ran through the kitchen, down the hall, and into the drawing room.

The laptop was there. It was open.

And Mr. October stood next to the desk.

Smiling in all the wrong ways.

CHAPTER 176

TENTH LEGION COMFORT STATION BRAVO
HAMBONE LANE
UPPER BLACK EDDY, PENNSYLVANIA

Monk Addison was going to die.

He knew it.

The thing that had him was more than a hundred pounds heavier than he was, and Monk was a big man. The Berserker's chest had to be seventy-two inches around, his biceps at least twenty-four inches. He grabbed Monk and lifted him like he weighed nothing and pulled him toward those simian fangs.

He thrust his forearm under the Berserker's lower jaw and locked his frame to buy himself a second. The brute was so grotesquely powerful that Monk's shoulder immediately began to ache from the effort. With desperate force, Monk began hammering with punches, swinging big, hard overhand rights.

He saw the creature's nose shatter in a spray of blood. He saw one eyebrow crack and the lid begin to swell. He saw the upper lip split.

And it did not matter at all. The Berserker whirled and slammed Monk against the side of the truck. It knocked most of the air from Monk's lungs and darkened the sky. Even so, he kept hitting.

The Berserker threw a punch of his own, and Monk twisted to slip it. The brute's knuckles ripped open his cheek, but the fist hit the truck, knocking a six-inch-deep dent into the metal. Monk braced a foot against the tire for strength and balance, then chop-kicked the Berserker behind the knee. The action required Monk to lift his only standing leg, and then he went utterly slack. The kick bent the Berserker's knee, and the deadweight pulled them both down to the mud.

Monk drew both knees up and kicked out, catching the genetic freak in the hip and crotch. It knocked a yelp of pain from the attacker and pushed those teeth ten inches back. Monk kicked again, twisting to avoid a series of heavy counterpunches. He bent an arm and took one punch on the point of his elbow. That hurt a lot, and the arm went numb, but the Berserker reeled back. Monk saw the big fist and knew that he'd shattered something.

He kicked out again, and the force sent the Berserker backward and Monk halfway under the truck. He instantly squirmed farther under as fast as he could, trying to get out the other side before the thing could get up and run around to stop him. Something hit his lower back, and he reached around to discover his twisted, mud-covered pistol. Then a hand clamped around his ankle, and he was yanked out with savage force.

As soon as Monk's head cleared the truck, the Berserker tried another bite.

Monk slammed the handgun into that gaping mouth with every ounce of his desperation and fear. Fangs snapped and pieces flew. The Berserker howled in agony and reeled back, but Monk followed, swinging the ruined gun into its mouth and eyes and throat, hitting with everything he had.

The Berserker's eyes rolled high and white, and it sagged back, arms flopping to the ground.

Only then did Monk see how pulped and flattened its throat was.

He clawed his way up the side of the truck and looked down at the dying monster.

"Jesus fuck," he gasped.

Then he heard a roar of bestial fury, and he raised his head to see another Berserker racing toward him. Monk pushed away from the truck and raised the bloody gun. The Berserker's head suddenly snapped to one side, and his steps fell into confusion before failing utterly. Most of the top of the creature's head was gone, spilling blood and brains into the mud.

Tommy appeared out of the rain, a rifle in her hands.

"Come on," she yelled and ran past, heading toward the RV.

Monk's knees buckled, and he dropped down.

"I'm coming," he said as he fought his way back to his feet.

CHAPTER 177
THE MANSION
PINE DEEP, PENNSYLVANIA

October stood staring at us.

"Mr. Toombs," he said in a mild, conversational tone, "I see you've made some new friends."

"Do you even know what's happening out there?" Toombs demanded.

"Firefall is what's happening," he said. "It's what we have been working toward."

Ghost took a few steps toward October, who pivoted his head at the big white shepherd. I thought there was a flicker of fear in October's eyes, and I remembered reading somewhere once that certain types of creatures are afraid of white dogs.

Even if that were true, Ghost stopped advancing and held his ground, the fur standing up all along his spine.

I pointed my gun at October. "Step away from the laptop, asshole."

October smiled. "Or what?"

I shot him six times. He staggered and fell back against the wall, his chest pouring blood.

"Or *that*, motherfucker," I said.

Two things happened at once.

Crow yelled, "Joe!"

The french doors in the drawing room exploded inward in a storm of flying shards. I threw myself down, hooking an arm around Crow. Toombs was closer to the window, and the arrows of glass slashed him from forehead to shinbones. He screamed as he fell, and I didn't know if he was dead or not.

I could not care, because figures were swarming into the house from outside. Men. Big ones. Too big. Bigger than Bunny or Sweeney. Dressed in Tenth Legion black but with monster faces.

Berserkers.

Six of them.

They stormed inside, howling with red delight.

CHAPTER 178
EAST PINELANDS FOREST
BLACK MARSH, PENNSYLVANIA

Felicia Carby thought she was dead.

She felt dead. Her body was a block of ice somewhere ten thousand miles from where she lay. When she looked down, she saw blood and torn clothing and . . .

Her mind stopped right there, refusing to catalog the personal damage. It was an unbearable task because of all that it meant.

She was dying. That much was clear.

Carby had been in the military and with Tenth Legion long enough to accept that harm and even death were possible outcomes of her life choices. Even so, she expected it to be from a bullet, or a needle in some prison if Firefall went wrong and the coming war faltered in ways that let the race traitors win.

She had not expected anything like this.

Not even in her nightmares.

And this seemed to *be* a nightmare. Or . . . it should have been one.

Maybe it was, she thought. What she saw wasn't possible. Not in any version of actual reality she believed.

The Berserkers were strange enough. But that was transgenic science. That was gene therapy and drugs and some surgery. That made sense. Even the bestial SDs made sense. Fucked-up sense, but there was science behind them, too. And they should have been the worst thing she ever saw in life. In real life.

But they were not at all the worst thing.

The three things that had come out of the forest were far, far worse. Only one of them was as big as the Berserkers. The other two were smaller, not much bigger than she was. The Berserkers should have overwhelmed them. Torn them apart. The SDs should have ripped them to pieces.

Felicia Carby lay there and watched as the three *things* brought madness and horror to her world. One Berserker sat with his back to a stack of crates, his chest ripped completely open. Another lay bent back over the hood of a Jeep, with everything from mid-chest down simply *gone*.

She watched as the Berserkers and the SDs transformed from a dominant force to things to be hunted and ripped apart.

And consumed.

She watched the slaughter go on and on, and Carby wished so intensely that she could scream. There simply was not enough of her left for that.

All she could do was watch nightmare claim dominion over the real world.

CHAPTER 179
THE MANSION
PINE DEEP, PENNSYLVANIA

One of the Berserkers led the pack, and I swung my gun toward him and opened up.

He wore heavy body armor, and my center-mass shots made him grunt. Only that. He was so fast that before I could snap off a shot at his face, he lunged at me, big hands ready to grab and crush.

Suddenly, those two hands were flying into the air, trailing streamers of red blood. I had an afterimage of a flash of silver, and then Crow was pulling me back, his sword in one hand.

I peeled left away from him, spun, and fired at the Berserker behind the handless one, and my first round took him in his howling mouth. The hollow point blew apart his right cheekbone and sprayed a third Berserker with blood and bone. My slide locked back on that shot, and there was no time to swap magazines, so I stamp-kicked the Berserker I'd shot and knocked him against the others and tore my knife from its drop sheath.

I had recently switched combat knives, and this new one was a beauty. A fixed blade from Night Watch Knives, made specially for my hand size—a drop-point hunter that was only 3.2 ounces, which meant there was zero drag on my hand speed. Less weight overall than the Wilson lock blade I used to carry. It had war-wash chemical etching on the blade that looked pretty, but it was there for abrasion resistance. It was a graceful killer of a weapon, as pure in its way as Crow's katana.

When the next Berserker rushed at me, I moved into him, ducking the swinging arm and licking out with the Night Watch to slash him across the right inner-upper thigh, then checking the swing and counter-cutting the tendon on the inside of his left. He staggered and went down. The Berserker behind him tried to leap over his shrieking colleague, but I shifted toward him, too, using a very hard backward parry with my left elbow that spun him as he jumped, and then drilling into his armpit. A sharp thrust and a vicious quarter turn to make a hole big enough to pull it out. Arterial blood chased the knife as I yanked it free.

I saw Toombs—covered in dozens of bleeding cuts—edging along the wall toward the door, but there was no time to do anything about it. October lay slumped on the floor.

Crow moved past me, and I yielded space for him to cut. He was very good with a sword. Better than I am. He was not at all a fancy fighter but instead used the long reach and sharp pull of the kenjutsu swordplay to slice arms and legs to the bone. The wicked steel did not care about Kevlar limb pads or genetically enhanced muscle fiber.

There was blood and howls of agony and death screams everywhere. There were grunts of effort, the slap of shoe leather on the crimson pools that now covered the floor.

There were six of them and two of us.

Now there were three dead ones and three mortally wounded. Crow and I moved among them, our blades merciless.

Then it was over.

I turned to the laptop.

It was gone.

So was October.

"Find him," I yelled to Ghost, and he vanished. I ran into the foyer after him.

Toombs sat with his back to the wall. He looked up at me with huge, dark, hopeless eyes. His hands were clamped around the handle of an Italian stiletto that was driven to the hilt in the center of his chest. When he tried to speak, all that came out of his mouth was a sloppy pint of dark blood.

Ghost began barking furiously, and then there was a high-pitched yelp of pain.

Absolutely unhindered by compassion for Toombs, I raced past and out onto the big front porch. There was a trail of blood that led to the door of an electric-blue Range Rover. October was behind the wheel, and Ghost lay still and silent on the ground.

All I had on me was my knife, and I needed to bury it in October's black heart. Maybe he was human, maybe not, but I bet that if I cut his heart out, it would end him.

The engine roared to life, and the car lurched forward. But then there was a *crack-crack!* The front and rear tires on the passenger side of the car blew apart, and I turned to see Crow with his Beretta in both hands. He kept firing, shattering windows and hitting October.

The driver's door opened, and October fell out onto the muddy ground.

I reached the car, leaned in through a broken window, and plucked the laptop off the glass-littered seat.

"I got it," I cried, then hurried over and knelt beside Ghost. I pressed fingers into his fur hoping, praying for a pulse.

Found one.

Weak, but there.

I could not see how or where he was hurt, but at least he was alive. For now. I had to get the laptop back into the house, make sure it was connected to the Wi-Fi, and plug in the MindReader uplink. I whirled toward the house.

Crow was staring past me, his eyes and mouth wide in an expression of absolute terror.

I turned and saw why.

There were four huge things running at us. They were dogs, but not dogs. Not anymore. Their bodies were as broad and solid as a bull mastiff's, the hair a midnight black. Each face was a twisted parody of a dog's, but the snout and head were covered with what I first thought was some kind of armor like they used to put on fighting dogs centuries ago. I could have dealt with mastiffs in armor—that was scary, but it wasn't anywhere nearly as terrifying as this.

As the creatures tore across the ground toward me, I could see that the armor ran all the way along the back of each animal, covering their sides and then thinning as it blended with the dog's natural hair. The armor plating gleamed like polished leather. But worst of all was what rose above the dog's back. It wasn't a canine tail at all. Instead, curling over the massive back and shoulders of each dog was a huge, segmented scorpion tail.

I had seen these monsters before. Top and Bunny and I nearly died fighting them in the tunnels beneath the Jakobys' Dragon Factory. They were monsters bred for size and then enhanced with gene therapy and surgery. Like what had been done to the PMCs to make them Berserkers, the Jakobys in their madness had combined mutated scorpion DNA to that of gigantic hounds.

SDs.

Scorpion Dogs.

I bent and scooped up Ghost and ran. He weighed over a hundred pounds, and I could feel something give in my lower back. But I ran anyway. I ran as fast as I could.

The scorpion dogs ran faster.

CHAPTER 180
TENTH LEGION TRAINING CAMP #18
PINE DEEP, PENNSYLVANIA

"Frag out," cried Top Sims as he rose from behind a bushy hydrangea and did an overhand pitch. The grenade soared over the edge of the camouflage canopy, bounced once, and exploded.

The explosion was enormous, with a blast radius of twenty meters and enough high explosives to shred the canopy and set parts of it alight. Seven people were working under that canopy, and the shrapnel shredded them.

Immediately, sirens began blaring, and people screamed as scores of soldiers poured out of tents and RVs and double-wides. Some were dressed in full kit, others were not, but they all grabbed their weapons. Sergeants yelled orders, sending teams up every trail and into the woods.

Into the toy box.

The first trip wire was impossible to see, a slender wire that was buffed to a matte finish rather than a shiny one. The wire was inches from the ground and mostly hidden by withered autumn grass, persistent weeds, and fallen leaves. The two men who tripped that wire were hurled upward and backward, with nothing below their knees but red rags.

Soldiers began firing into the woods, aiming nowhere and everywhere. Thousands of rounds tore through leaves and tree bark and falling rain.

Remy, hidden in a crevice under a blanket covered in leaves, watched with the eyes of his drones and pressed keys on his tactical computer. Cluster bombs he'd strung from tree branches detonated, scything laterally across the compound. A Berserker was standing close to one, and it splashed him forty feet across the ground.

"Over there," bellowed a sergeant, pointing in Top's direction, having caught a flicker of fast movement. "There's a—"

That was all he managed to get out before Belle put a bullet through his chest. He fell sideways, and his corpse tripped another wire. The resulting blast hurled five pounds of jagged fléchettes into the camp at waist height. The tiny, triangular blades hit thighs and groins and stomachs.

"Release the dogs," roared another sergeant. "Release the goddamn dogs."

He died with another of Belle's rounds, but the order was on the wind. Four soldiers ran for a pair of big cages draped in canvas. Bunny rose and fired, killing one and maiming another with his combat shotgun, but the remaining two reached the cages. They tore off the tarps and flipped up the restraining bars before Bunny could cut them down.

The cages banged open, and the SDs burst out.

Eight of them.

"Jesus fucking Christ!" cried Remy.

Belle, high in her post, froze for a moment at the sight of the monsters.

Top's voice smashed through her shock. "Fucking scorpion dogs. Kill them. Mother Mercy, target those fucking things."

Belle was rarely caught off guard. She was rarely even frightened, but the sight of those mutated beasts hit her like a punch to the chest. Her fingers clutched the gun as if it were a lifeline and not a weapon.

Then Bunny stepped out of the woods and leveled his shotgun. He took aim at the scorpion dogs and began firing. Two went down, snarling and hissing, their gigantic tails whipping back and forth. The others scattered, though. In their panic, they attacked anyone close, and Belle saw several of the legionnaires fall screaming. The poisoned stingers struck and struck and struck, and the savage teeth of the mastiffs dripped with fresh blood.

Finally, Belle snapped out of it and aimed her rifle. Her hands were shaking badly, and her next shot missed and thudded into the dirt. She cursed and fired again.

Missed again.

"Get your goddamn head in the game, Mother Mercy," growled Top.

Belle's lips curled as she forced herself to focus. The next bullet took a scorpion dog in the chest.

Several of the Berserkers plunged into the woods, each spraying the rainy shadows with heavy automatic gunfire. One of them walked through a trip wire, and a Claymore exploded sixteen inches from his shins. His companions whirled and ran the other way.

Deeper into the toy box.

As thunder exploded overhead, smaller and more destructive blasts ripped the forest to pieces.

Belle kept firing, and with each new kill, her confidence rebuilt itself. Bunny was running through the camp, making maximum use of cover, dealing destruction with his shotgun. Top lobbed grenade after grenade, and Remy triggered bombs that were not set off by trip wires.

Four of them against a small army.

An army that was shaking off its shock, finding cover, returning fire.

Element of surprise is a great weapon, but numbers also count. There were still dozens of legionnaires, Berserkers, and SDs.

Above them, the storm sobbed and wept as rivers of blood washed through the camp.

CHAPTER 181

TENTH LEGION COMFORT STATION BRAVO
HAMBONE LANE
UPPER BLACK EDDY, PENNSYLVANIA

Tommy reached the RV door and saw that it was not only open but hung by a single twisted hinge. A legionnaire lay with his head and shoulders hanging down over the steps.

There were screams coming from inside, and Tommy grabbed the corpse by the strap on his chest protector and hauled him out, dumping him unceremoniously onto the ground. The rain was coming harder now, and the sound of it on the metal roof and sides of the RV sounded like machine-gun fire.

She stepped up, crouching, rifle slung and a pistol in her hands as she crept up the steps. The RV was very large and had been reconfigured to have four queen-size murphy beds bolted to the sides. A fifth and much larger bed was all the way in the back. Ten children and two young women of about seventeen huddled together back there. All the children had colored dog collars around their necks, and they wore expensive-looking lingerie. Even the littlest ones. The girls' faces were made up with rouge and lipstick and eyeliner. A few had bruises blossoming on their faces. One was unconscious or dead, and her body was held by the others. They were terrified, and they screamed.

The two officers they'd seen enter the RV huddled under the table in the breakfast nook. One held a pistol with the slide locked back, and the other had a long two-prong grilling fork. Their faces were streaked with blood, but they did not look hurt.

In the middle of the vehicle, dominating the space, was a fight involving five people—four big legionnaires in full combat rig. And Violin.

She was bathed in sweat, and she was bleeding.

Everywhere Tommy looked, there were dead people. Men and women, their throats slashed, faces rent to the bone, limbs severed. Tommy could not begin to imagine the choreography of carnage that had unfolded here. Violin had charged into the RV armed only with her kukri knives, going up against soldiers with guns. There were bullet holes in the floor, the walls, and most of the appliances. Guns lay on the floor or still in the hands of people who had believed, in their arrogance, that they were the dominant force here.

One woman had proved how wrong they were.

But the fight wasn't over, and Violin looked like she was flagging. Blood ran down her limbs. Her face was purple with bruises, and there was at least one deep injury on her lower-left side that looked to Tommy like a gunshot wound.

Yet still she fought.

Tommy rose. She kicked the closest legionnaire in the back of the thigh, buckling his leg so that he pitched backward. She caught him with one hand, twisting to redirect his mass, and as he fell, she shot him through the eye.

The blast made another soldier turn, and he brought up a big marine corps Ka-Bar combat knife. The top three inches of the blade were red with blood, and he drove it toward Tommy's stomach.

She snapped off two shots—one taking the knife man in the shoulder of the arm holding the weapon, blowing apart his collarbone and shredding the biceps. Her second shot was aimed deliberately down because the children and Violin were in the direct line ahead. Tommy buried the barrel against the man's belly and fired. The bullet went under the lower edge of the Kevlar vest, tunneled through intestines, and blew apart against his hip assembly. He shrieked as he fell.

Violin slipped in blood and went down to one knee, and the third legionnaire drove a double-edged British-style commando dagger into her back. Violin cried out in pain and collapsed.

Tommy screamed, too.

She screamed as she shot the man in the forehead, the chest, and the groin. Then she snapped out a side kick and shattered the last man's knee with such force that his leg took on an appalling forty-degree backward bend. He fell next to Violin, and Tommy put two more into his face.

The two officers, seeing one attacker down and one with a pistol that was pointing down rather than at them, surged forward. The fat one threw his empty pistol, which Tommy ducked, but the other man stabbed her in the stomach with the grilling fork.

Tommy caved over the fork, raising her gun, but the children were directly behind the attacker. Then both men were on top of her, bearing her to the bloody floor.

CHAPTER 182
THE MANSION
PINE DEEP, PENNSYLVANIA

Crow had his pistol out and was firing, but I was running in such a dead straight line toward the porch I was in his way. One of his rounds passed so close to me I could hear the high-pitched wasp-wing buzz as it flew. Behind me, one of the scorpion dogs yelped in pain.

I ran.

He came down off the porch, swapping out a spent magazine for a fresh one. He ran to meet me, offering covering fire as best he could. I passed him and stumbled onto the porch, tripping, falling, spilling Ghost on the wood planking. He thudded and slid bonelessly. I slid the laptop across the porch floor, too.

I whirled to see the car Crow and I came in go tearing through the mud with a small, bloody, grinning figure at the wheel.

October.

The son of a bitch actually gave us a cheery wave as he fled back to the road. I turned to reach for the laptop, but then Crow screamed.

I whirled to see him go down, his gun spinning off into the rain. A scorpion stinger was buried in the meat of his thigh. He dropped and the creature swarmed atop him, fangs lunging for his throat. But Crow—somehow—got a forearm under those jaws and was beating at the brute.

I came off the porch, my back burning with agony, and slammed into the SD, kicking it with a heel stomp in the ribs. It fell, and I grabbed Crow, tore the sword from its sheath, and hurled him behind me just as the second scorpion dog leaped high to try to bowl me over. I squatted and did a lateral cut, and the thing crashed down, dying.

The others were close behind.

Behind them, walking out of the mist and rain, I saw a woman. She was dressed in bloody clothes, and her hair was rain-soaked rattails.

She was sixty or more yards away, but I knew who it was. Who it had to be.

Miss Mary.

Mother Night.

Artemisia Bliss.

She was smiling at me as she walked without haste behind her pack of monsters.

My heart and my outrage and my desperation wanted to go after her. To kill her for what she was trying to do. For what she had done. So many people were dead because of her. If the Gorgon rockets fired at that arena in Feasterville, then maybe the whole world would die because of her.

There was no way to reach her, though. Even if I did, I had no idea what would kill her. Bullets had only slowed October down. I had already killed Bliss once.

All of this twisted the world into an unrecognizable shape. I fought something that could not be stopped, could not be killed. All my years of training, all my skills, all the good I had done working for Church in the DMS and now with RTI was for nothing. What does it matter if you save the world every time but one?

The laptop lay on the porch, and a MindReader uplink was in my pocket. All I needed was thirty seconds to plug the link in, and then Bug would do the rest. That would, at least, stop *seif al din* from being the last words printed in the book of human history.

But I did not have thirty seconds.

I didn't have five seconds.

I knew that if I turned to run, Bliss's monsters would tear me down. If I stood my ground to fight, I might get one or two, but the rest would rip me apart. Crow was hurt or dying. Ghost was unconscious or dead.

I raised the sword, knowing that there was nothing left for me to do but die trying.

CHAPTER 183
THE TOC
OMFORI ISLAND, GREECE

Scott Wilson was not a particularly well-liked man. He knew that and did little to change the reaction. He was cold, abrasive, demanding, didactic, and intolerant. He knew that many of the staff regarded him as a martinet.

That was fine. He had not signed on to be the chief of operations of Rogue Team International to be liked. His politics and ethics were very much in alignment with Church's. And he was very, very good at his job.

While the battles raged on at the Mansion, the comfort camp, the depot, and the main training center, Wilson was making calls. The video feed from Joe Ledger's body cam and those of Havoc Team had given him the information and—most critically—the *evidence* he needed. One call was to a contact at Homeland. Another was to the governor of Pennsylvania. He called state and local police. He called the FBI, the DEA, ATF, and a dozen other agencies. To the right people, he used those three magic and terrible words. *Seif al din.*

The gears of bureaucracy grind slowly, but every now and then, the gears catch and the lubricant of reliable intelligence makes them turn with increasing efficiency.

What Wilson did not—and could not—know was whether any of the agencies with whom he spoke would get their agents and officers into the right places in time.

He could feel the precious seconds splintering off the board and falling to the floor.

Would there be time?

CHAPTER 184
TENTH LEGION TRAINING CAMP #18
PINE DEEP, PENNSYLVANIA

Top threw his last grenade, then wheeled and ran. Bullets chased him, but he knew how to move through the woods. He cut left, then right, putting tree trunks between his back and the shooters.

"Pappy to Havoc," he yelled as he ran. "Fall back pattern. Repeat, fall back pattern delta."

Even with the air around him burning with bullets, he smiled as he ran.

The legionnaires ran after him. So did the remaining scorpion dogs, and they ranged farther ahead, outdistancing the two-legged soldiers.

Top cut a quick, desperate glance at the display on the tactical computer on his left forearm. The screen was ablaze with colored dots. One was directly ahead of him, and as he reached it, he flung himself forward and up like a broad jumper. He landed hard enough to tear a painful grunt from him but immediately ran up a slope, pivoted, then cut hard left as he headed to a hillock.

The scorpion dogs raced ahead.

And then they reached the spot Top had vaulted.

The blast picked them up, tore them apart, and hurled fur, blood, bone, and chitinous shell in every direction. The legionnaire running out front was impaled by a six-inch spike of bloody femur. He tumbled forward, and his men ran over him.

A Berserker ranged ahead, angling in the direction Top had taken, his long and powerful legs devouring the distance between him and the retreating black man. The Berserker grinned hungrily.

He was grinning when he stepped down on an M16 antipersonnel mine—a Bouncing Betty. Called that because when it is stepped on, there is a one-second delay before it ignites a charge that propels it upward three feet before exploding. The mine blew up between the Berserker and a sergeant who was bringing his rifle up to shoot Top. They fell, maimed and screaming.

Bunny threw three grenades from behind cover, letting the first one sail over the running pack of legionnaires to detonate on the far side. It killed three of them and made the rest of the line swerve to safety to their right.

Except Remy had left no safety. He left other things, and the fleeing men ran right into them.

The last two Berserkers crouched, pivoting on the balls of their feet as they unloaded into the brush with heavy M249 Squad Automatic Weapons. One of them had a thirty-round magazine, but the other had a full two-hundred-round plastic magazine. The heavy-caliber bullets chewed the scenery into green confetti. Bunny dove down into a ravine, but he was pushed faster and harder by a round that struck him between the shoulder blades. His Kevlar-spider-silk vest saved his life, but he could feel ribs break. He landed badly, rolled, and crawled back to the top of the ravine, laying his shotgun over the edge. Bunny fired once, but both Berserkers spun away—one torn by his twelve-gauge slug and the other shot through the chest by a sniper bullet.

Bunny could not see Belle, but he said a quick thanks and crawled away. His back was on fire, and then he realized that blood was running down inside his sleeve. The vest hadn't stopped the round completely after all.

"I'm hit," he said. He sprayed blood when he said it.

"Donnie Darko," called Top. "Can you move?"

"I . . . I think so."

"Head east. There's a bridge over a stream. That'll be our rally point."

"Copy that," said Bunny. He slung his shotgun and began to crawl. He made it exactly forty feet before the cloudy day turned completely black and he collapsed face-first into the mud at the bottom of the ravine.

CHAPTER 185
TENTH LEGION COMFORT STATION BRAVO
HAMBONE LANE
UPPER BLACK EDDY, PENNSYLVANIA

As the two Tenth Legion officers piled on top of her, Tommy wasted no time screaming in pain. The grilling fork was buried in her stomach, and the torment was immeasurable. Bigger than anything she had ever felt.

Violin was out. She lay still and looked dead.

Tommy brought a knee up and caught the taller of the men in the crotch, tearing a howl from him, but the other one punched her in the face. Tommy felt her jaw break, tasted blood in her mouth. She fumbled for a knife, pulled it from its thigh sheath, and began stabbing wildly. Both of the men cried out as the blade chopped, but the tall one grabbed the handle of the fork and gave it a savage clockwise turn.

The knife tumbled from Tommy's hands as agony suddenly defined everything about her.

Even then, she kept fighting. There was no referee, there was no time-out. No one was going to stop this. Either she fought or she simply let them win.

They would kill her.

They *had* killed Violin.

They would take their anger out on the children.

Tommy tried to yell, "No!" but she had no breath. The men were straddling her now, punching her over and over again.

She managed to dig one hand down between her and the tall one with the fork. Tommy clenched her fist around his scrotum and twisted with all the strength she had left. He shrieked and punched her harder. In the face, in the chest.

The light was draining out of the world as quickly as blood poured from her stomach.

And then the tall man seemed to rise into the air as if gravity no longer mattered. His whole body lifted off her, twisted, and went flying into the wall. A heartbeat later, the shorter man was jerked upward by the hair.

Monk Addison, bleeding, looking more than half dead, held the man with one fist knotted in his hair and the other balled up tightly. The tattooed faces on his arm and chest seemed to come alive, to scream in fury as Monk hit the commandant of the Tenth Legion training camp with a blow so powerful, so appallingly devastating, that Kurt Furman's features disintegrated. Monk hit him again and again. Teeth snapped, his nose flattened, one eye vanished, and then all the light went out of the officer's eyes.

Monk dropped him and reached for the tall man. He lifted Command Sergeant Ryerson into the air and then slammed him down on one upraised knee. There was a huge wet *crack*. Monk let the corpse fall.

He staggered over to Tommy.

"V-Violin," she wheezed.

Monk pressed two fingers against Violin's throat.

"She's alive," he said. "Let's . . . get . . . her . . ."

Monk puddled down into a heap, eyes going totally blank.

Tommy, the grilling fork still buried in her stomach, looked at him and at Violin. The children were screaming.

She raised one bloody, trembling hand toward them.

CHAPTER 186
EAST PINELANDS FOREST
BLACK MARSH, PENNSYLVANIA

Felicia Carby's eyes stared at nothing.

The entire depot was utterly still except for lines of blood that ran down the sides of the crates and drip-dripped into the mud. The rain was intensifying, washing the red into the brown mud.

Three figures stood at the edge of the clearing.

They were naked.

Mike Sweeney, Sam Hunter, and Antonio Jones. Sweat and blood ran down their bodies, turning pink in the rain.

They did not say a word to one another. Instead, they turned and began to walk back to where they had left their clothes.

CHAPTER 187
THE MANSION
PINE DEEP, PENNSYLVANIA

The closest scorpion dog ran at me, low and fast, knowing it had me. The sword was in my hand, but I was weak. Whatever I'd done to my back was now a white-hot shrieking agony.

Suddenly, a whistle split the air, and the SDs skidded to a stop, turning inquisitive eyes toward the figure that came walking slowly toward me.

Miss Mary stopped ten feet away from me. Outside of the reach of my sword. Her remaining scorpion dogs clustered around her, wriggling and dancing like excited foxhounds, pressing their muzzles against her for approval.

"Joe," she said. "I can't begin to tell you how much I've been looking forward to this. To meeting you again. I think about you all the time. Every day. Every night."

"Yeah, well, until yesterday, I hadn't given you a moment's thought."

She pretended to look hurt. "Such a meanie. And you're a liar. I *know* that you've thought of me. I mean . . . how could you not?"

"Pretty easy, actually," I said, trying to sound cool and casual and not like a complete train wreck. "You were a nobody who tried to be somebody, and I put you down like the cockroach you are."

I never saw her move. She was that fast.

One second, she was ten feet away, and the next she crouched over me. The sword was gone. She had me by the throat and was lifting me—all two hundred and fifteen pounds of me—off the ground like I weighed nothing. The scorpion dogs danced around, snapping at the air, their tails whipping. Mary pulled my face to within an inch of hers. When she spoke, her cold spit flecked my skin.

"You were always an arrogant piece of shit, Joe," she said. "God, you walked around like you were the hero of the world. Always cracking those stupid jokes. Always acting like no one else mattered but you. Always so goddamn sure that when the chips were down, you would come in and save the day."

She slapped me across the face. It dimmed the world. I sagged down, my jaw aching and my neck blossoming with whiplash. The concussion I'd gotten back at the Pan Head was now escalating into a migraine. There were two Marys, two of every scorpion dog, two of every raindrop that fell.

I fumbled for my knife and got it out.

Mary looked at it.

"A knife? Really? You're going to stab me? Jesus Christ, Joe, don't you get it? I can't be killed."

So I stabbed her anyway. I drove the knife into her black heart with every ounce of strength I had left.

And she laughed at me.

Mary dropped me and straightened. She took a firm grip on the handle and tore the blade from her chest. Then, looking at me and smiling like a demented version of the Cheshire cat, licked her own blood off the steel.

The MindReader uplink in my pocket was there. The laptop was thirty feet away, and an unkillable monster and her mutant hounds stood over me. Laughing.

I forced out a word. Just the one.

"*Why?*"

Mary looked genuinely surprised by the question. "Why *seif al din*? Why Firefall and the Gorgons? Why all of this?"

All I could manage was a nod.

Her face clouded with emotion. Real emotion. Not the false smiles or trash talk or any of that artifice. I saw the mask fall away and the woman behind it.

Mary was lost.

That was it.

She had let herself become corrupted when she worked for Church. Getting caught and sent to jail broke something inside of her mind. That towering genius could not accept defeat. Not by anyone she considered less than she was.

Prison, I think, drove her deeper into psychosis. When she escaped and took on the persona of Mother Night, her madness was evident. The outward façade of her criminality seemed to be about anarchy and terrorism.

That was a lie, though.

She wanted to be famous. She wanted to be the most important person on earth. She knew she could not, though. Her mind was continuing to fracture, her grip on reality disintegrating. Her last act as a person had been to inject herself with one of the advanced strains of *seif al din*. Not to become a mindless monster but to try to achieve a measure of immortality.

Had Echo Team not caught up with her at the pop culture convention in Atlanta, I wonder what the world would have become. We know that she infected her Berserkers back with different strains of the pathogen. She did not want to rule a world of brain-dead creatures. Like Amirah, the creator of the bioweapon, Bliss had wanted to rule over a world of the living dead. Conscious, aware, sentient dead.

But I'd caught her and shot her and killed her.

October brought her back. Maybe he used some kind of science that I don't know about. Fuck it, maybe he used magic. I'm past knowing where one leaves off and the other begins. He brought her back, but what he brought back was infinitely stranger than what fell off that balcony in Atlanta.

I didn't know what strains of *seif al din* were in the four Gorgons. Maybe some were the monster strain and some were the advanced ones. I thought so. She wanted to reduce the world and rule over what was left. That seemed certain.

The uplink was in my pocket, and I could no more use it than I could fly.

Artemisia Bliss had won.

I lay there, battered, concussed, torn, and helpless.

"Maybe I should just bite you," she said. "Bite you and let you come back. If you can. I haven't tried it since I became . . . Mary. Would you come back as undead you or as one of the brainless hunks of walking meat?"

She leaned closer, hunger igniting in her mad eyes.

"Let's find out."

I actually thought she would. But she paused, and I watched a parade of expressions move across her face. There was the madness, sure. There was the monstrosity of her, without a doubt. There was the bottomless hunger for winning, that was crystal clear.

And yet.

I saw her eyes go wet. They clouded with storms of doubt, of confusion. Of sadness.

"I'm a monster," she said, and it came out as a sob. A confession of a kind of personal defeat even in the moment of her victory. I think it was in that moment when she looked into the future and saw nothing. A world that she had killed. No friends, no family, no colleagues, no press, no followers. They were all dead, or they had become monsters, too. Lesser beings. Ruined lives. Soulless and empty in every important way.

"You don't have to be," I said. My words surprised us both. She looked at me and for just a moment saw someone who was broken, too. Someone who, like she had, had looked into the abyss for far too long. She knew my backstory. The five older teens, Helen. My psychic fractures. If October was Nicodemus, then she probably knew about the Darkness that had overwhelmed me and nearly destroyed everything of value that defined me.

"How?" she asked. "How did you . . . come back . . . ? How do you bear it?"

What value was there to lie to her at that point? Really?

I said, "There are worse monsters than me. I . . . I did not want to become the thing I fought."

Mary stared at me, her mouth open as if she wanted to say something, to reply, to ask a deeper question.

But a voice rang out, utterly shattering the fragile moment.

"No!" came the fierce cry. "This ends now."

Mary turned. I turned, even though it hurt so fucking bad to even move my head. We saw three figures standing a dozen yards away. Her hounds had all wheeled around and were snarling at them.

Ronald Coleman, holding a Snellig dart gun in trembling hands.

Lilith.

Church.

Standing in the rain.

Mary screamed. She screamed so loud it shattered that delicate moment of understanding between us. The doubt and fear in her eyes vanished, replaced by rage. By hate.

"Kill them," she shrieked, and the scorpion dogs howled and surged forward, teeth gnashing, tails whipping. Death running as fast as the wind.

Lilith pushed past Church, drawing two long, slender, almost delicate-looking knives. There were runes of some kind traced on the blades. Her queenly face was beautiful but also terrifying in its rage.

The scorpion dogs attacked her.

And each one died. There's no story to tell for that. They were monsters. She was something else. Older, stranger, infinitely more dangerous.

Mr. Church walked up to Miss Mary. He had a gun in his hand. It was not a Snellig. It was a Glock.

"You can't kill me," sneered Mary, touching the many bullet holes that covered her torso. "I can't die."

"No, Church," I croaked. "Don't."

He ignored me and raised his pistol. "Despite everything, Artemisia," he said softly, "I'm sorry for what happened to you. I'm sorry that you lost your way."

He shot her in the head.

And kept shooting as she fell.

Kept shooting as she lay there.

Each bullet punching through that magnificent brain until it—and she—were utterly destroyed.

I bowed my head and wept, though . . . god only knows who for.

CHAPTER 188
DARK HOLLOW ROAD
PINE DEEP, PENNSYLVANIA

The car rolled across the bridge from New Jersey and began climbing the first of the series of steep hills that led out of the town of Pine Deep.

The storm was growing worse, the cold rain falling like desultory tears. The clouds were furious. Lightning burned the sky over and over again; boomed, its tiger growl creeping across the fields and through the forest, finding death and blood wherever it looked. The wind was a chorus of demons.

Mr. October was alone in his car. His body was filled with pain, but with each mile, it was less. Soon there would be no pain at all.

He turned the radio on and cycled to a news station.

The reporters were rattling through the latest developments. A huge evangelical rally in Feasterville was the site of a mass panic as four small explosions blew apart sections of balcony, killing dozens of people. Early speculation was that it was some kind of malfunction of a huge fireworks display intended to close the event.

"Well, shit," he said, and switched off the radio.

All that work, all the planning, and Firefall fell flat, fizzling out. He understood how. Ledger had acquired the laptop. Toombs must have told him about the stand-down order.

It saddened him.

But not entirely.

After all, the entire country was hurtling toward some kind of violence. All those guns. All that hatred. The disruption of the truth and the pollution of the media information sharing.

That reignited his smile.

Kuga was still in operation. There were other wars to wage. And there was this one in America to stoke.

"Not a total waste," he told himself.

He was a bit sad to leave Pine Deep, though. It was a fun place. A sadness magnet. A corruption amplifier. There were very few places like it on earth. For the last few years, the pull to visit the town had been growing in intensity. The flavor of that energy reminded him of other times and places in which he had lingered to play. The blood-soaked beach of Normandy, the darkened chambers of Dachau, the fields where so many died in Gettysburg and Antietam. Every such place its own kind of power. Some sites had a lingering emotional stain that time seemed unable to erase—old battlefields where the losses on either side were so appalling that it cast a pall over any sense of victory; places where witches had been hung by men who were overwhelmed by their fear of women; or where the guillotine blade dropped so often that a blacksmith was on hand to constantly sharpen the bone-dulled steel.

Pine Deep had some of that, but it also had a vitality that seemed immediate and constant. That put it into another category in October's head. Closer to prisons where both the senior inmates and the corrupted guards made the place a living hell.

His car crested a hill and headed down the other side. Then he saw a figure step out of the corn at the bottom of the grade. It was an old man, ragged and filthy, soaked by the rain. The tramp moved with a painful slowness, as if burdened with arthritis, old injuries, and the oppressive burden of age, and October watched him walk onto the road directly in his path.

October tapped the brakes and slowed the stolen car he drove. He stopped a dozen feet from the hobo. There was a sound from deeper in the cornfield—not of thunder but of crows speaking in their ancient, secret language. Not the language of ordinary crows but the far older tongue of the night birds. A language with which October was familiar but one he did not understand. A language he had tried to learn but that eluded him because those special birds guarded their secrets.

Not even October's old enemy, St. Germaine, could understand the language of the night birds.

One of them flapped out of the field and landed on the fence on the north side of the road. It was threadbare and ragged and looked every bit as old as the hobo. It opened its beak and cawed so softly it was almost soundless.

October placed the barest pressure on the gas, edging the car toward the old man. The bumper was six feet from him now.

With no apparent haste, the old man turned toward October as the rain fell in steady gray sheets.

October was amused.

This man was a fool, or he was mad. For fun, October hammered the horn with the heel of his palm. The blare in a flat F-key disturbed neither the tramp nor the crow. Both of them looked through the rain-slick windshield at the driver. The old man's mouth moved as if he were speaking, but there was no sound that could be heard above the thunder and the horn.

October removed his hand from the horn and sat there, frowning. Something was happening here that he did not understand. He rolled down the window and leaned out.

"I'll ask once nicely," he said. "Please move."

The tramp took a step toward the car. Between thunderclaps, he said, "I do not please."

Lightning sizzled across the sky, the brightness picking out every line and crease and scar on the old man's face. It delineated the open and hungry mouth of each pocket in the many garments he wore. The reflection—if reflection it was—of the lightning made the man's eyes blaze for a moment.

Then the man did something inexplicable. He dug into a pocket and removed what appeared to be a plastic-wrapped energy bar. He held it up so October could see it, then he abruptly popped it in his mouth and ate it without unwrapping it. When he swallowed it, his throat bulged like a snake's.

Suddenly, October felt a coldness running through him that he struggled to identify. Was it . . . fear? No. That was too shallow a concept. When the answer came to him, it took the form of a word that in all his long life he had never once felt applied to him. A word he did not think *could* apply to him.

Not to him.

What he felt was *dread*.

A complete and indefinable horror that made his mouth go dry and his hands tremble as they clutched the wheel.

But why?

How?

Dread of that kind was a human emotion. A mortal thing.

So . . . how?

Above him, the storm turned black as midnight and the rain crashed onto the fields and road and the car with terrible force. Storm winds swept out of the east, tearing leaves from the stalks and hurling them at the car. They stuck to October's windshield, obscuring it, momentarily hiding the tramp and the crow.

The thunderclaps shook everything with such force the windshield cracked, the fissures spreading like spiderwebs from side to side. Pieces of safety glass popped out and let needles of rain in to sting October like wasps.

There was one moment of indecision where October debated three options—to drive around the man, to step on the gas and run the old bastard down, or to back up.

He felt something heavy land on his shoulder. A hand. Thin but so very strong. Hot, too. Burning hot. He tried to shrug it off, but could not. He tried to turn, but his head would not move. He strained to look into the rearview mirror, but the interior of the car was suddenly and oppressively dark. Then he felt something brushing against his ear. Lips. As hot as the hand, and rough, as if covered not in human flesh but something rougher. Like scales, like something reptilian.

October sat stock-still, both unable and unwilling to do anything. For the first time in uncountable years, he was terrified. The novelty of the emotion was entirely lost in the awfulness of the moment. He couldn't even speak.

Then the thing in the back seat spoke.

Only one word. Simple, yet eloquent, leaving no room for misunderstanding.

"Mine."

And then it was gone. The winds battered his car. His hands gripped the steering wheel with such force the leather groaned and the plastic beneath it cracked.

But he was free of the stricture that had held him. He instantly threw the car into reverse and stamped the gas pedal all the way down. Then he hit the brakes as he spun the wheel, slewing the car around until it faced the way he'd come. The turn conspired with the wind and rain to tear the corn leaves away from the cracked windshield. The road south was empty. October kicked the gas again, and his car shot down the road as the speedometer climbed past fifty to sixty, seventy, eighty . . .

He was going more than one hundred and ten miles an hour when he crossed the bridge and left Pine Deep.

He did not once look in the rearview mirror.

He did not dare.

On the road, standing like a scarecrow in the savage rain, Mr. Pockets watched the trickster flee.

Then he turned and walked into the cornfield at the corner of the Guthrie farm and vanished entirely. The old crow—the grandfather night bird—lingered a minute longer before flying off toward the town.

EPILOGUE

-1-

So, yeah. We won.

Kind of.

I mean, sure, the big play was ours. I gave Church the Mind-Reader uplink. He put it into the USB port. Bug and MindReader were poised to strike, and they struck hard. They didn't just cancel the Gorgons; they blew them up.

Doc Holliday and Bug agreed that the thermite charges in each Gorgon would incinerate the contents of the canisters. MERS, Shiva, *seif al din*, whatever was in them turned to carbon dust.

Scott Wilson later calculated that we had something like eight whole minutes before the fireworks at the church rally would have gone off. He joked that it wasn't even close.

Scott can kiss my dog's ass.

-2-

Speaking of Ghost . . .

The big fur monster was knocked out. Like his human father, he had a concussion and lots of other bruises, dents, and dings. He got to go to Jessica McNerney's animal hospital.

I went to the ER in Doylestown. Concussion, sprained neck, four broken ribs, cracked cheekbone, broken nose, and some other stuff my head hurts too much to inventory.

I lived.

Junie flew in from Greece and stayed with me until they flew us back home.

-3-

The rest of our little army made it out.

Alive, yes.

Whole? Not so much.

Violin had a collapsed lung and a deep knife wound in her back. The doctors patched her up, and she was doing great until pneumonia set in. That's when Lilith brought in a couple of doctors who work with Arklight. I don't know what they did—some kind of blend of allopathic and homeopathic medicine, but it pulled her back from the edge.

It's strange to think of her being that badly hurt. She is so powerful, so skilled in combat, so bizarrely durable that I've come to think of her as invulnerable. But let's face it, no one is. Church proved that last year.

Violin is in the South of France, recovering.

Lilith, for reasons that make no sense, blames me. I hadn't even *seen* Violin during that whole operation and only talked to her once on the phone. I mean, what the actual hell?

Violin's protégée, Tommy, needed surgery. A lot of it. Some legionnaire son of a bitch stabbed her with a metal fork—the kind you use to turn steaks on a grill. She had facial lacerations, broken ribs, a shattered jaw, and a broken left orbit. She was also in that special hospital in France. Her road to recovery was going to be a long one, but she was tough as nails. She was Arklight tough, and that meant a lot.

As for my guys . . . Bunny was in intensive care. Of everyone, he came the closest to checking out. Aside from his many wounds, he developed a real mother of a staph infection, and it took every specialist Church knew to finally knock it down.

Crow was a close call, too. Here's a fun fact that none of us knew—the intensity of the venom in the scorpion dog's tails was not commensurate with the creature's size. He was sick for weeks, but he survived it. Ron Coleman was on hand to give first aid, and it's fair to say he saved Crow's life.

Crow keeps texting me regular reports. He's hoping the scorpion sting will give him superpowers. I send him Instagram videos of rescue dogs and baby goats in pajamas. That's how we roll.

Monk Addison was the last of the good guys to need medics. But he opted for Pine Deep General Hospital, and his best friend, tattoo artist Patty Cakes, was there every single day.

As for the three guys who took out the depot—Sweeney, Hunter, and Jones—they didn't even get a hangnail.

I know why.

So does Crow.

No one else does, and we can leave it right there.

There was one morning, when I sat on a bench with Junie, looking out at the blue waters off Omfori Island, holding her hand. She said, "So many people."

I knew what she meant.

Of the Tenth Legionnaires, there were ninety-eight casualties and more than eighty wounded.

The final total of deaths from the Gorgon explosions at the church thing was one hundred forty-three.

All the scientists at October's mansion were dead. A total of forty-one civilians died from the Typhoid Mary attacks.

And across America, a spike in hate crimes took thirty-seven lives.

There was death everywhere.

We'd lost Noah Fallon and Felix Howard.

So many people.

-4-

We looked for Mr. October.

Nicodemus. Kuga. Whatever.

No trace of him was found.

Did that mean he was gone?

Please.

I mean, what do you think?

-5-

One afternoon, on my third day back on the job, Rudy and I were sitting in the café at Phoenix House. I was drinking my third cup of Mustapha's gorgeous medium roast. Ghost was on the floor picking apart a cheeseburger, eating each separate component one at a time, the way he likes.

Rudy was drinking one of those concoctions of soy, foam, sprinkles, pumps, shots, and everything else that's not actually coffee. I have become convinced that he drinks that stuff just to piss me off. It's working, too.

We were there for a couple of hours, letting the conversation go where it wanted to go and allowing silences to be as long as they needed to be. When one silence ran particularly long, I glanced over and caught a troubled look on his face.

"What?" I asked.

It took him a long time to answer.

"Five names, Joe," he said.

He knew I knew which names he meant.

I had been thinking a lot about those five names. I just shook my head.

But inside my heart, I could feel the Darkness beginning to stir.

-6-

Church stood in his bathroom and studied his face in the mirror.

Holst's "Saturn, the Bringer of Old Age" was playing. The Slovak Chamber Orchestra version. Moody and dark. Appropriate to his mood.

Lilith was in France with her daughter. The RTI teams were either healing or rebuilding. The fallout from October's plot to destabilize America was considerable. Heads were rolling in Washington, but conspiracy theories were running wild. It would be years, perhaps decades, before it settled down.

In that way, Kuga had won.

Nicodemus had won.

He tried not to let the anger in him turn to hate. That battle had raged for many years.

Church removed his tinted glasses, setting them on the counter. Then he took out his brown contact lenses. His eyes were a pale amber flecked with green and a darker brown.

As he stared at his face, those colors began to swirl very slowly.

BONUS CONTENT
INSIDE ROGUE TEAM INTERNATIONAL

ADMINISTRATION

Mr. Church. . . . . Call sign: Merlin
Scott Wilson . . . . Call sign: Grendel
Rudy Sanchez . . . . Call sign: Chupacraba

INTEGRATED SCIENCES TEAM

Joan "Doc" Holliday . . . . Call sign: Huckleberry
Ronald Coleman . . . . Call sign: Woolly Bear

COMPUTER RESOURCES TEAM

Jerome Wilson . . . . Call sign: Bug
Nikki Bloom . . . . Call sign: Firefly
Yoda . . . . Call sign: Jedi

RTI SUPPORT STAFF

Brian Bird . . . . Call sign: Bird Dog
Mustapha Amar . . . . Call sign: Mr. Bean
Jennifer McNerney . . . . . Call sign: Mama Bear
Noah Fallon . . . . Call sign: Gandalf

HAVOC TEAM

Colonel Joe Ledger . . . . Call sign: Outlaw
Bradley "Top" Sims . . . . Call sign: Pappy
Harvey "Bunny" Rabbit . . . Call sign: Donnie Darko
Aïchetou "Belle" Ahmed . . Call sign: Mother Mercy
Remy Neddo . . . . Call sign: Gator Bait

THE WILD HUNT

Alexander Chismer . . . . . Call sign: Toys
Archie Jones . . . . Call sign: Rugger
Rupert Place . . . . Call sign: Zombie
Colin Hughes . . . . Call sign: Dodger
Martin Hurley . . . . Call sign: Muppet
Dev Sanghera . . . . Call sign: Rent Boy

BEDLAM TEAM

Major Mun Ji-woo . . . . . Call sign: Leopard / Pyobeom
Felix Howard . . . . Call sign: Smoker
Amy Neal . . . . Call sign: Pond
Billy Robinette . . . . . . Call sign: Kingsnake
George Yazzie . . . . Call sign: Mountain Man
Luke Ward . . . . Call sign: Gimli

CHAOS TEAM

Captain Hazi Gifford . . . Call sign: Shrike
Rosemary Wyman . . . . . . Call sign: Fangirl
Anders Strøm . . . . Call sign: Iceman
Corky Majka . . . . Call sign: Sheik
Jeffrey Lui . . . . Call sign: Piglet

ARKLIGHT:

Lilith
Violin
Baba Yaga
Tommy

ACKNOWLEDGMENTS

The Joe Ledger novels could not be undertaken without the help of a lot of talented and generous people. In no particular order, then . . .

Many thanks to Dr. Ronald Coleman, Principal Scientist at International Stem Cell Corporation. Thanks to my friends in the International Thriller Writers, International Association of Media Tie-in Writers, the Mystery Writers of America, and the Horror Writers Association.

Thanks to my literary agent, Sara Crowe of Sara Crowe Literary; my stalwart editor at St. Martin's Griffin, Michael Homler; Robert Allen and the crew at Macmillan Audio; and my film agent, Dana Spector of Creative Artists Agency. And special thanks to my brilliant audiobook reader, Ray Porter. As always, thanks to Dana Fredsti, my superhero of an assistant.

Thanks to the winners of various contests who will have characters named after them. Thanks to Shawn Anderson of Old Town Roasting for launching the two new coffee blends—*A Nice Cup of Whoopass* and *Rudy Sanchez's Brown Sadness Water Decaf.* Thanks to Alex Harrison of Night Watch Knives for Joe's new toy.

Quote by Neil Gaiman used by permission of the author.

Tamileigh "Tommy" Squires used by permission of the character's creator, Marie Whittaker.

ABOUT THE AUTHOR

Sara Jo West

Jonathan Maberry is a *New York Times* bestselling, Inkpot-winning, five-time Bram Stoker Award–winning author of *Relentless, Ink, Patient Zero, Rot & Ruin, Dead of Night*, the Pine Deep Trilogy, *The Wolfman, Zombie CSU*, and *They Bite*, among others. His V-Wars series has been adapted by Netflix, and his work for Marvel Comics includes *The Punisher, Wolverine, Doomwar, Marvel Zombies Return*, and *Black Panther*. He is the editor of *Weird Tales* magazine and also edits anthologies such as *Aliens vs. Predator, Nights of the Living Dead* (with George A. Romero), *Don't Turn Out the Lights*, and others. His Joe Ledger series was optioned for television by Chad Stahelski (*John Wick*).